Mandy Magro lives in Cairns, Far North Queensland, with her husband, Des, their daughter, Chloe Rose, two adorable pooches, Sophie and Sherlock, and the largest personality of the household, Charlie the cockatiel. With pristine aqua-blue coastline in one direction and sweeping rural landscapes in the other, she describes her home as heaven on earth. A passionate woman and a romantic at heart, Mandy loves writing about soul-deep love, the Australian way of life, and the wonderful characters that call the country home.

Also by Mandy Magro

Rosalee Station
Jacaranda
Flame Tree Hill
Driftwood
Country at Heart
The Wildwood Sisters
Bluegrass Bend
Walking the Line
Along Country Roads
Moment of Truth
A Country Mile
Return to Rosalee Station
Secrets of Silvergum
Riverstone Ridge
The Stockman's Secret
Home Sweet Home
Savannah's Secret
Road to Rosalee
Back to the Country
Jillaroo from Jacaranda
Gum Tree Gully
Secrets of Riverside

One More Time

Silverton Shores

MANDY MAGRO

FICTION HQ

Silverton Shores
© 2024 by Mandy Magro
ISBN 9781867264651

First published on Gadigal Country in Australia in 2024
by HQ Fiction
an imprint of HQBooks (ABN 47 001 180 918), a subsidiary of
HarperCollins Publishers Australia Pty Limited (ABN 36 009 913 517)

HarperCollins acknowledges the Traditional Custodians of the lands upon which we live and work, and pays respect to Elders past and present.

The right of Mandy Magro to be identified as the author of this work has been asserted by her in accordance with the *Copyright Amendment (Moral Rights) Act 2000*. This work is copyright. Apart from any use as permitted under the *Copyright Act 1968*, no part may be reproduced, copied, scanned, stored in a retrieval system, recorded, or transmitted, in any form or by any means, without the prior written permission of the publisher. Without limiting the author's and publisher's exclusive rights, any unauthorised use of this publication to train generative artificial intelligence (AI) technologies is expressly prohibited.

This is a work of fiction. Names, characters, places, and incidents are either the product of the author's imagination or are used fictitiously, and any resemblance to actual persons, living or dead, business establishments, events, or locales is entirely coincidental.

A catalogue record for this book is available from the National Library of Australia www.librariesaustralia.nla.gov.au

Printed and bound in Australia by McPherson's Printing Group

*To Helen and Carl Dixon, for the amazing friends that you are!
I'm so happy we've met, and connected,
from opposite sides of the world.
Here's to the many shared adventures awaiting us. xx*

*What do you do when you're met with a dead end?
You go right back to the beginning and start over.*

PROLOGUE

Silverton Shores, way back when ...

Watching through the windscreen of her mum's shiny classic Volkswagen Beetle as she drove past the rolling waves kissing the white-sand shoreline, twenty-one-year-old Annie Sabatini tried to distract her racing thoughts. She'd messed up as a sixteen-year-old, big time, but over the past four years she'd done her best to make up for the mistake that had been the trigger for her family's abrupt move from the hustle and bustle of Sydney to the sleepy Far North Queensland township of Silverton Shores. With a combination of hard work, resilience and genuine belief, she was proof that dreams really could come true. And unlike the shocking day she'd gone and shattered her mum and dad's perfectly manicured world, along with her own, today her parents couldn't be prouder of her achievements. Their prayers had been answered. Their eldest daughter was righting her wrongs. Come tomorrow, it was going to be the beginning of her new life as a nursing student at the University of Sydney. Today was going to mark the end of her exhausting uphill struggle to get there.

Or so she hoped.

As she slowed to match the fifty-kilometre speed limit of the township's main street, a quick glance in the rear-view mirror confirmed seven-year-old Morgan Savage was thoroughly enjoying the toy plane she'd gifted him at the St Augustine's annual church Christmas party two weeks earlier. Morgan didn't live up to his last name – he was the sweetest of the three little boys she regularly babysat for a very fair hourly rate of fifteen dollars. Almost every cent had been tucked away for her move back to the big smoke, because moving out of home and into university dorms was going to be costly. Her parents were helping a bit financially, but she also wanted to prove that she could eventually stand on her own two feet. She hoped Morgan would be happy to wait in the car while she nipped in to see Father Harris. The boy's little ears couldn't hear what she was about to tell the priest in confidence.

Feeling the strong pull of her past, her stomach soured as she recalled the night she'd lost her virginity at a bonfire on Bondi Beach while under the influence of an entire bottle of wine. Barely sixteen, she'd been naive enough to believe she and her nineteen-year-old boyfriend were going to be together forever. Three days later he'd left town to backpack his way around the world, and she'd never seen him again. Word was he'd met and married a Dutch girl. Nobody knew of her deep despair at his sudden departure. Her devout Catholic parents had made sure of that – new town, new start, clean slate, stereotypical picture-on-the-mantelpiece family status intact – so they could bury their daughter's secret nice and deep, down with the worms, so it didn't ruin her father's perfect reputation as a lay pastor. If the Silverton

Shore locals ever discovered the skeleton in her family's closet, their tongues would be wagging like a dog's tail in a butcher shop. In a town as small as this place, gossip spread like wildfire, and she was mindful there were plenty of expert blabbermouths who would be keen to throw the lit match. And it was over her dead body that she, or her well-meaning, sometimes overbearing parents, would become the subjects of gossip among Silverton busybodies. Come hell or high water, she'd promised her mum and dad that she'd take this secret to her grave. As, in turn, would they. And a true Sabatini never made promises lightly. Up until this very moment, she'd made it her mission to remain silent. Her sweet, innocent baby girl deserved that much, as well as way more than she'd ever be able to give her.

She pulled into the empty gravel car park at the side of the quaint seaside church, beneath the cool shade of a blooming jacaranda tree. Ear-ringing silence fell as the rumble of the engine ended. Her insides tipped and tumbled at the very thought of what she was about to do, so she stole a moment to gather herself as best she could. Briefly regarding Morgan, who was clearly in a happy world of his own, and then looking back to the five front steps that would lead her towards what she believed would be her only hope of redemption before embarking on her new adventure, she sucked in a fraught breath, hoping to god she was doing the right thing.

'What are we doing here, Aunt Annie?' Morgan's little voice came from the back seat.

Although she wasn't an aunt through blood, she adored that he saw her this way. 'Oh, I've just got to duck in and see Father Harris for a few minutes.' She offered him a warm smile. 'Will you be okay to wait here?'

'Yes.' He nodded enthusiastically with his tiny thumb held up. 'I'm a big boy, I'll be okay.'

'Thank you, Morgan.' Drawing in a shaky breath, she fumbled with her seatbelt then, grabbing her handbag, she stepped out and into the late-afternoon sunshine before she could change her mind. 'I won't be long.'

'Okey-dokey.' With the broadest of adorable smiles, he waved her off.

Annie's steps quickened as the desperation to finally speak about the secret that had been tormenting her for far too long overwhelmed her. Surely their local priest wouldn't repeat what she was about to disclose, no matter how shocking it might be. Wasn't it his responsibility to keep everything he was told in confession hush-hush? She prayed it was so as she made her way into God's sanctuary where the scent of incense lingered.

Pausing at the doorway, she momentarily felt as if she were somehow caught between her past and her future. Golden sunlight streamed through the stained-glass windows, making the religious depictions glow while sending a kaleidoscope of colours scattering across the wooden floorboards. Her eyes widened as relief struck her. It was a sign, as if God was calling her. She couldn't bail now. She had to do this. Quickly dipping her fingertips in the holy water, she made the sign of the cross. Then, with her quivering bottom lip clamped between her teeth, she looked left to right in search of Father Harris.

He appeared through a doorway, which she knew led to his office. 'Well, hello there, Annie.' Reaching her, the silver-haired priest rested his weight on his walking stick. 'You look concerned, dear. Is everything okay?'

Unable to hold his gaze, she glanced down at her feet. 'Not really, Father.' Fighting off the impulse to make a run for it, she sadly shook her head. 'I was hoping you had time to hear my confession.' Her voice was little more than a whisper.

'Of course I can,' he said, offering a compassionate smile. 'Come now, my dear, follow me.'

'Oh, thank you,' was her quick reply.

She trailed him, her footsteps echoing as she slowly made her way between the pews and towards the ornate confessional box at the far-left corner of the church. With another gentle smile, Father Harris disappeared into his side. Slowly pulling back the red curtain, she stepped into hers and took a seat. She sat up straighter as she waited for him to get settled.

'Okay, Annie, go ahead.' His calming voice carried through the little latticed window.

Glancing down at her wringing hands, she took a breath. 'Bless me, Father, for I have sinned.'

'Tell me, how long has it been since your last confession?' His tone remained soft, kind.

'I'm ashamed to say it's been many years, Father.' Her pounding heart felt as if it were about to burst. 'Too many.'

'I see.' He sighed softly. 'Can you tell me why it has been so long?'

'Yes, I can.' She cleared her throat. 'I was afraid that if I came in here before now, I'd say things that I promised my parents I wouldn't.' Tripping over words as her heart raced, she halted.

'Go on, child,' Father Harris gently encouraged. 'When you're ready.'

Nodding, she sniffed back red, raw emotion. 'No matter how hard I try to keep quiet, I can't keep this in anymore. It's like my secret has grown so big I feel like I could burst if I don't at least tell you, a man of God, what I've done, because hopefully, then, somehow, some way, I can find peace in my heart.' A sob rose, and she choked it back. 'But I'm also frightened that you're going to think badly of me, and my family, when I confess.'

There was a short moment of silence, followed by his outward breath. 'It's clear you have a very heavy heart, Annie, so take your time, and when you're ready, I'm listening to offer my support, and most certainly not to judge.'

The thought that she was about to reveal what her own father referred to as sordid details terrified her even more than she'd thought it would. 'Okay, I just need a moment.'

Her eyes welled with fresh tears and she allowed them to tumble down her cheeks as she finally found the courage to expose her guarded heart. After a deep inhalation, the details she'd kept under lock and key tumbled from her quivering lips in quick succession, until there was nothing left to say.

'Oh, Annie, I understand your worry and heartbreak, you were so young, basically still a child yourself.' Father Harris paused and drew in a slow and steady breath. 'While it was done with the best of intentions, your parents have put you in a very difficult position.'

Nodding in agreement, she sucked in a shuddering breath, keen to hear his advice.

'Aunt Annie, are you in there?' Morgan's little voice carried through the curtain.

'Oh my gosh, Morgan.' Annie shot to her feet and tugged the curtain open. 'I thought I told you to wait in the car.'

How much of her confession had he just heard?

'I know, and I'm sorry.' Morgan screwed his face up. 'I tried to stay there, but I really need the toilet.'

Her hand upon her chest, she fought to slow her galloping heart. 'Okay, come on then.' Planting on a smile that she was far from feeling, she took him by the hand just as Father Harris reappeared. 'I'm sorry, Father, but I have to take him to the little boys' room.'

'Yes, so I hear.' He shone a warm smile in Morgan's direction, but it slipped a little when he glanced back at her. 'God exonerates our sins when we repent, Annie. But someone else has to forgive.' He regarded her with wisdom and kindness. 'When you're ready, and able, you'll have to find a way to forgive yourself, too.'

Annie almost broke then and there. 'I'll do my best, thank you, Father Harris.' Overcome with a dizzying mix of relief, remorse and fear, she was suddenly desperate for fresh air. 'And can you please make sure this stays between us?'

'Yes, of course.' His smile was reassuring. 'This is between me, you and …' he pointed upwards, 'our maker.'

CHAPTER 1

Silverton Shores, 18 years later ...

After hitting the sack at a reasonable hour, and surprisingly achieving a solid eight hours of sleep, Jessica Sabatini had woken at the crack of dawn with a firm belief that even at twenty-two years young, her life couldn't possibly get any better. At least not until she and the love of her life had the two children they'd spoken at length about – a boy and a girl, two boys, two girls, she didn't care, just as long as they were healthy, their dad was Morgan Savage, and they were all calling Savage Acres their home. Then her life would be all she'd ever dreamed of and more, she was sure of it. And as the hours had ticked by, she'd savoured this safe, joyful feeling deep down in her soul. Had tucked it away for the rare days she might need a reminder of just how lucky she was. A realist at heart, she knew life was never all roses. Doing her best to avoid the prickly thorns was all part of the journey.

Now, standing on the balcony of the ritzy penthouse suite at the new Silverton Shores Resort, she smiled as brightly as the mid-morning sunshine caressed her olive skin and the sea breeze stirred her long brunette curls. She looked to the canopy of powdery blue sky stretching cloudlessly to the sun-soaked horizon, then to the turquoise sea sparkling as if studded with diamonds, and her smile spread even wider. She couldn't believe, after imagining it for six years, that the big day for her and Morgan had finally arrived – and by the looks of it, Mother Nature had most certainly come to the party, too. If only her grandparents could have made it across the ocean, but Florence, Italy, was a long way, especially when her nonna's health was deteriorating.

Way too rapidly.

Inside the penthouse, where they were having their hair whipped into elaborate updos by the town's only mobile hairdresser, her two bridesmaids, older sister Annie and best friend Shanti, cackled like a pair of kookaburras. The sound of their laughter sent Jess's already buoyant happiness soaring into the heavens, where she hoped it would meet their recently departed local priest, Father Harris. He'd had a good wicket, making it to one hundred and one, but even so, she was sad he wasn't the one to be marrying her and Morgan. Not wanting to allow her mood to plummet with grief at his passing, she focused on the music playing from the portable speaker inside when Brad Paisley's 'Waitin' on a Woman' was abruptly cut short then Trisha Yearwood's 'She's In Love With The Boy' began.

'Oh my gosh, I love this song!' she called through the open French doors.

'We know you do!' A united response came from Annie and Shanti.

Jess chuckled. 'Oh, do you now?' How could they not, when she'd basically played it to death?

Singing the lyrics with gusto, she jiggled on the spot, once again feeling like the luckiest woman alive to have the hunkiest, kindest, most loving husband-to-be, the greatest of friends, and the most supportive of parents. Very soon she'd officially be calling Morgan's wonderful mum and dad, Carol and Gary Savage, her own, too. Ever since her brother Roberto's best friend, and her secret crush for as long as she could remember, the incredibly desirable Morgan Savage, had leant in and kissed her the night of her sixteenth birthday, her world had been a magical place. And now, in a matter of hours, in front of their family and friends, she'd be hooking her arm into her father's and taking steps down the aisle to legitimately become *the* Mrs Savage. Then, in a matter of days, she and Morgan would be jumping aboard a plane for their chosen honeymoon destination of Florence, Italy, with possible side trips to Venice, the Amalfi Coast and the five seaside villages of Cinque Terre.

Ahhh, la dolce vita … the sweet life.

Her hands going to her swooning heart, she sighed with pleasure. It had been four years since she'd been to what she considered the most romantic city in the world, and she couldn't wait to introduce Morgan to her father's hometown and see her doting grandparents again. An entire month of glorious Italian sunshine, delicious handmade pastas, creamy gelato, juicy Florentine steaks, plenty of lip-smacking vino, and days and nights spent wandering the cobblestone streets hand in hand after making the sweetest of love in their Airbnb – their honeymoon was going to be an absolute dream come true.

Caught up in her Italian heaven, she briefly closed her eyes and exhaled softly. Blessed. Happy. Content. Excited. Optimistic. Head over heels in love. She was all these things, and more. Momentarily transfixed by the jaw-dropping view of her quaint seaside hometown surrounded by lush, green mountains that reached for the skies, she took another tentative sip from her glass of pink bubbly. Raising her hand to shade her eyes, she shifted her gaze from two seagulls sailing overhead to where waves rose, rolled, and then reached for the white-sand shoreline, caressing it with foamy kisses. The ebb and flow of nature's heartbeat was so strong here, and so beautiful to bear witness to.

'Hey, Jessie, it's your turn for hair and make-up.' Her singsong voice carrying, Shanti stuck her roller-clad head out the doorway. 'Would you like a top-up while you're being pampered, my darling bestie?'

'Hmmm.' Jess looked to her almost empty champagne glass, then back to Shanti wrapped up in her pink *BRIDESMAID* robe. 'I want to say yes, but I better not, otherwise I'll be stumbling down the aisle like some drunk-ass beach bum.'

Chuckling, Shanti joined her on the balcony. 'Ha, whatever, you're always class, Miss Jessie.' She poked herself in the chest. 'Whereas I've earned the title of being the ass of our duo, wouldn't you agree?'

'Nooooo, you are not an ass, you loon.' Jess gave her friend a playful shove. 'You're just a free spirit with a wild child that comes out to play when you've been drinking.'

'For reals, I can count the times I've held your hair back on one finger.' Shanti held her pinkie up and wiggled it. 'And as for you holding *my* hair back, I don't have enough digits to make a legitimate show of fingers.'

'True that.' Jess laughed out loud. 'And don't you ever change, because I love you just the way you are, girlfriend.' She grinned wickedly. 'As does my brother.'

'Oh, stop it already, there'll be no shooting of cupid's arrow from your romantic bow, thank you very much.' It was Shanti's turn to give Jess a little shove. 'Roberto likes me as a mate, and that's that.'

'Righto.' Jess pulled an I'm-not-buying-it face. 'Whatever you say.'

Grinning, Shanti gave her the two-finger salute. 'Hey, shouldn't your mum and dad be here by now?' She looked at her watch. 'It's almost eleven.'

'Yeah, they should be.' Jess huffed. 'God only knows what's held them up, literally.' She chuckled. 'Most likely Mum wanting to stop at every roadside produce trailer on the way back from the church Dad was pastoring at.'

Shanti rolled her eyes at the thought – Julie Sabatini was well known for her love of roadside fruit and vegetable stands. 'Maybe give them a call, or I can if you like, while you start getting your hair done?'

'Nah, all good, I'll give them a quick ring.' Grabbing her phone from her *BRIDE* robe pocket, she dialled her mum's number. 'Can you let the hairdresser know I'll just be a sec, please?'

'Sure thing, soon-to-be Mrs Savage.' Shanti beamed then disappeared back inside.

Five rings sounded in Jess's ear, then her mum's recorded voice greeted her. 'Hi, you've reached Julie and Enzo, we're busy right now so please leave your message, and we'll call you back as soon as we can. Ciao.'

'Hey, Mum, it's me, where are you? I hope everything's okay. Call me back as soon as you get this message please.' Hanging up, she gulped a breath of salty air as her heart began to beat faster.

Taking a moment, she tried calling again, but once again it went to message bank. 'Me again, please call me back as soon as poss. I'm starting to get worried.' Turning then stepping inside, she looked to where her big sister was pouting as she had lip-gloss applied. 'Hey, Annie, I just tried calling Mum and Dad, twice, but there was no answer.'

Taking a moment to reply, until the make-up artist was done with her lips, Annie swivelled in her seat to face her. 'They'll be here soon, I'm sure. Dad likely just got caught up trying to leave church.' She rolled her eyes. 'You know how much they all love his sermons and like to tell him so afterwards.'

'Yeah, you're probably right.' Jess offered the hairdresser a smile as she settled into the seat in front of her. 'It's not like them to be late, though, to anything, let alone my wedding day.'

'Annie's right, mate, they'll be here soon.' Reaching out, Shanti gave her arm a reassuring squeeze. 'Your mum's most likely knocked the silent button again, and she just can't hear your calls coming in.'

'Yeah, you're both probably right, but you know me, I'm a worry wart sometimes.' Trying to ignore the snowballing sick feeling in her belly, Jess looked Annie up and down. 'Wowsers, sis, you look bloody amazing.'

'Ha, yeah, take my scrubs off and I can scrub up like the best of them, my sweet Jessie.' Hugging her fluffy pink *BRIDESMAID* robe to her, Annie turned left to right, posing as if she were Marilyn Monroe. 'You just wait until I pop my bridesmaid dress on, then I'll be turning heads quicker than you can say bombshell.'

'Truth, Annie, I'm so used to seeing you in your nurse's uniform, I forgot there's a whole lotta woman underneath all that starched blue.' Chuckling at her much older and, in her opinion, much prettier sister as she struck a few more poses, Jess tried her best to ignore the growing sense that something was wrong.

* * *

Ribbons of gold sunlight filtered through the paperbark trees, and the chatter of crickets, lowing of cattle and whinnies of horses carried across the rolling thousand acres that was the renowned Savage Acres Angus Stud. Standing on the wide back verandah of his parents' sprawling two-storey Queenslander homestead, a cold mid-strength beer in hand, with Chris Stapleton's honky-tonk voice carrying from the speakers, Morgan Savage enjoyed the sensation of the early-afternoon sunshine warming his back while the laughter of his groomsmen kicking back on the outdoor settee set the tone for what he was sure was going to be a gloriously happy day.

Leaning on the railing, he smiled to himself. *You're one lucky SOB, Savage…*

Soon he'd get out of his singlet and boardies, and slip into his tailored navy suit, snakeskin boots and brand-spanking new black Akubra. He'd been counting down the years, months, weeks, then days, then hours, until this very day, and he couldn't be any happier that it was finally here. Just picturing his stunning bride-to-be walking down the aisle, towards him, to be with him forever, his heart picked up the pace from a happy canter to a saddleless gallop. Jess Sabatini had a way of making him feel so alive, so happy, so loved. After six and a half years together, their connection had only strengthened, deepened, intensified as each day had passed. He found it hard to believe that he could love her any more than he already did, but with a bond like theirs, it was inevitable he would one day die a very happy man after spending his life with her by his side. And once they added their longed-for children into the mix and made the two of them a family of four, he could only imagine just how wonderful their life was going to be. He was a very lucky man to be loved by a woman as magnificent as his precious Jess.

With his phone chiming from his back pocket, he plucked it out and looked at the caller ID. Why would Jess be calling him now? She should be sliding her beautiful self into her beautiful gown – heck, she'd look good in a hessian bag – then into the back of the classic candy-apple red 1968 HK Holden Monaro he'd had restored as a surprise matrimonial car for them.

'Hey, my sexy bride-to-be.' He couldn't wipe the smile from his face.

'Morgan, it's me, Annie.' She was sobbing so hard she was barely comprehensible.

'Annie, is everything okay?' The wild gallop of his heart was no longer pleasant.

'No, it's not.' Annie's voice shuddered. 'It's Mum and Dad, they've been in a terrible accident.'

'Jesus.' The world suddenly swayed, and he grabbed hold of the railing with a vicelike grip. 'Are they okay?'

'We don't know.' Racking sobs echoed as the phone muffled.

Momentarily lost for words, and worried sick about how Jess would be handling this, he dragged his gaze from the recently renovated cottage up the rise – the one he and his new bride were about to call home – and instead looked to where Jess's brother, Roberto, was clinking beers with another of his groomsmen. How in the hell was he supposed to pass this horrendous information on to his best mate?

'Hey, Morgan.' Shanti's trembling voice came down the line. 'All we know is that they've been involved in a head-on with a drunk driver.' She sniffled. 'Mum's on the phone now, trying to find out more, so when we hear anything, anything at all, I'll be sure to let you know, okay.'

'Okay.' A supportive hand came down on Morgan's shoulder, and he turned to catch eyes with his father – the grief in his dad's gaze let him know he'd just taken a similar call. 'How's Jess doing?'

'Oh, Morgan, she's not good at all.' Sobs sounded in the background and Shanti cleared her throat. 'I better go and comfort her and Annie, talk soon, mate.'

Morgan wasn't about to sit around at home while his sweetheart was suffering such devastating heartbreak. 'Please let Jess know I'm on my way there.' He would carry whatever pain he could for her, no matter how crushing it was.

Please God, let Enzo and Julie be okay.

'Why don't you wait until we know more?' Shanti's tone was way too hopeful. 'I mean, it might not be as bad as we think.'

'No way, I can't leave her to handle this without me.' It was then he watched Roberto take a phone call that brought his solid-as-a-rock best mate falling to his knees. 'I'll bring Roberto with me.' The clench in his heart stung, really damn bad.

Julie and Enzo Sabatini were nowhere near okay.

'Of course, good idea, I'll let Jessie know you're both on your way over.' Shanti sniffled again. 'Let's hope and pray for the best, see you soon.'

'Yup, we'll be there before you know it.'

Morgan ended the call and slumped against his father. And for all of thirty seconds, he allowed himself to be consoled by his rock, his confidant, his hero, then he straightened, took a breath, readied his shoulders to carry his loved one's tears and anguish, and took determined strides across the verandah, where he took a crumbling Roberto into his arms and did what only a best mate could do at a time like this; he offered him solace before the storm that his instincts told him was about to change all of their lives forever.

* * *

It had been seven devastating days since the drunk driver had killed himself and cruelly taken her parents with him, and day by day, as Jess had come to accept this was a nightmare she'd never wake up from, her heartbreak had only intensified and become all-consuming, to the point where she could no longer feel anything else. Not even love for Morgan. Feeling oddly numb considering her nerves were on edge, she stared blankly out the window of the car. In the back seat, Shanti comforted Annie, although her older sister's sobs weren't subsiding. If anything, they were getting louder, shriller, more excruciating to hear. Jess wanted to cover her ears, squeeze her eyes shut, block it all out, but that would be childish. She needed to cope. She needed to handle this.

No!

She needed to get the hell out of Silverton Shores for a while.

Everything here felt way too surreal, as if she were watching a horrific movie from the inside out. She didn't even notice they'd pulled to a stop at the cemetery until Roberto placed his hand on her bouncing leg, steadying it, but not steadying her.

She doubted she'd ever feel stable again.

The God her parents had taught her about didn't exist.

How could he when he'd gone and done this?

Before stepping from the passenger side of her brother's Holden Commodore, she made sure nobody was watching as she pressed another Valium from the foil packaging and quickly popped it into her mouth. Taking a glug from her water bottle, she swallowed down hard, wishing she was anywhere but here, about to say her final goodbye to the two people in the world who had mattered the most. Overhead, the bright blue sky she'd watched appear that morning was now darkening at an alarming pace as the shadows of the raging, ominous clouds chased the daylight away. Bearing witness to Mother Nature's broodiness, she swore her broken heart was darker still. It had to be. What other explanation did she have, to have fallen out of love with the love of her life?

Raising her umbrella, Shanti stepped in beside Jess, Annie and Roberto, the four of them silently acknowledging one another's heartbreak as they briefly locked tear-stained gazes.

When the church proceedings were over, Jess, Shanti and Annie followed the other mourners through the tall, wrought-iron gates of the Silverton Shores cemetery, then weaved their way along a narrow path shaded by weeping willows, towards what would be Julie and Enzo Sabatini's final resting places. Her parents would be side by side forever. Jess watched as Roberto went in the opposite direction, towards the hearse parked up the rise, to fulfil his role as a pallbearer. Her broken heart split deeper, further, as she watched Morgan give her brother a supportive hug.

If only she could feel something, anything, for the wonderful man who'd won her over. But in a single heartbeat, from one second to the next, everything, and everyone, had changed.

As she reached the cover provided by the outstretched branches of an old gum tree, she saw people paying their respects, congregating as they waited for the final part of the service to begin. Jess took her place at the front of the gathering, sandwiched between Annie and Shanti. Somewhere in the surrounding scrubland, a flock of screeching cockatoos momentarily concealed the sound of her raspy breath. And up the rise, the pallbearers took slow steady steps as they carried the two mahogany caskets towards the gaping, black holes. A week to the day after she'd heard the news, now dressed head to toe in black polyester instead of ivory silk and lace, all Jess could do in this heart-wrenching moment was imagine herself in another life, another time, far away from Silverton Shores, far away from the heartbreak and crushing grief, far away from those who loved her most. Somewhere she could pretend to be whole, happy, hopeful. To lose a parent was one thing, but to lose both was unthinkable, a child's worst nightmare. And yet, here she was, with her reality a living nightmare.

The caskets arrived. She turned her cheek, unable to look directly at the boxes that held her lifeless parents. Time flickered between slow and steady and rapidly fast, all the while with her careening between the two. She watched the new young priest's mouth moving, but she couldn't hear what he was saying. The caskets were lowered. Sobs sounded. Then it was time to drop the two roses she wasn't aware she'd been holding, and so very tightly the sharp thorns were digging into her flesh. As she placed one foot in front of the other, Shanti hooked her arm into hers and helped her to the first grave. Unclenching her fingers, she watched the velvety petals tumble then hit the top of her father's coffin. Annie broke down beside her. Roberto came to her aid. Jess sucked in a shuddering breath. She couldn't cry, because she was afraid she'd never stop. Taking a step to the left, her gaze met with her mother's dirt tomb. Holding the rose out, she let go and watched it drop in slow motion, twisting and turning, until it hit the casket headfirst. Bouncing, it toppled and wedged down the side of it. The irrational part of her brain wanted her to climb down and straighten it, because her mother would have hated the untidiness. The rational part of her, her father's deeply imbedded characteristic, told her to stand her ground, remain steady, be strong.

Turn to God, Enzo Sabatini would have said.

Like hell she'd be doing that.

Because the God she'd believed in wouldn't take such wonderful people so soon.

Blinking through the rolling emotions, she stepped aside as people began to step forward, saying their final goodbyes then offering their condolences. As if on autopilot, she nodded and accepted their sympathy, as did Annie and Roberto. Finally moving to the edge of the crowd, she spotted Morgan, standing with his hands in his pockets and his head hung low. He looked so alone, so broken, so dejected. And she knew, without a doubt, that she'd done that to him. It was all her fault he was heartbroken. As much as she wished she could go to him, to both offer comfort and seek it, she couldn't face the aftermath of her actions. So, she turned away, and step by step, put an agonising, irreparable distance between them.

CHAPTER 2

Florence, Italy, nine years after the funeral

For the entirety of her close-to-perfect childhood, Jess Sabatini couldn't wait to grow up, but now she was a fully fledged thirty-one-year-old adult, she was experienced enough to acknowledge that adulting could really suck sometimes. Bad days. Good days. And then there were all the mediocre days in between. Groundhog Day had nothing on her life. With the awful state it was in, each day seemed to roll into one big continual uphill struggle. Her darling nine-year-old daughter, Chiara, was her only saving grace, the shining light in her sometimes-dark life. But the newest dilemma was tipping her over the edge and making her question her sanity.

How could she have lost something so crucial?

Was she losing her mind?

It certainly felt like it.

With her hands going to her hips, she groaned as she surveyed the chaos of her apartment. Every drawer had been pulled open, and every single bit of paperwork had been dragged from the filing cabinet. She'd crawled beneath both beds, searched beneath the cushions of the couch, even stood on a chair and scanned the top of her fridge out of utter desperation. But other than discovering where dust went to rest in peace, she'd come up empty-handed, just like she had a month earlier, and ever since, each and every time she tore the place apart. She was almost certain she'd popped Chiara's passport into the filing cabinet with her other important documents. Her own was still there. It was very odd. How in the heck had she gone and lost Chiara's? She knew she'd tucked it away for safekeeping, could still remember holding it in her hands six months earlier, when it had arrived in the post, but for the life of her she had no idea how it had crawled out of the filing-cabinet drawer and seemingly vanished into thin air. Surely Chiara was telling the truth, and hadn't touched it? And why would she want to? Her darling girl had been so excited about her very first trip to Australia. Her ex-husband, Salvatore, on the other hand, had been none too happy about the idea. He may have turned out to be a crappy husband, and a half-arsed father, but surely he wouldn't have stooped so low as to have broken in there and taken it.

The idea was ludicrous.

So she shook off the gnawing sensation.

Mostly.

With her past still nipping at her heels, Jess wasn't sure what she'd expected when she'd hightailed it all the way over to the other side of the world, nor when she'd signed a prenup and married a man on a whim, but it certainly hadn't been this. She'd made her vows and kept them, but as for her cheating ex, Salvatore hadn't followed through. Not that it was all bad. She and Chiara had a roof over their heads, the unconditional love and support of her nonno, and a job she loved at a local museum. She also appreciated the extra hours at Nonno's beloved restaurant, now managed by her cousin. For Chiara's sake, she hoped and prayed she could somehow turn things around and find her way as a recently divorced single mother, but she knew that inevitably, in the long run, that meant telling the cold, hard truth. First, she needed a conclusive answer. Once she had it, the very thought of revealing her secret terrified her. She hadn't told a living soul back in Australia. Not even Shanti. Her nonno was the only person alive who knew. Her nonna had taken it to her grave eight years earlier. What would everyone – especially Morgan – think of her once they found out she'd lied to them all this time?

Stepping out and onto her little balcony for a much-needed breath of fresh air, she briefly closed her eyes and inhaled the delicious scents of lemon, truffle and sweet pomodoro sauce wafting up from the line of trattorias below. Noisy chatter accompanied the mouth-watering aromas. She'd left the five-bedroom house she'd shared with her wandering-eyed husband a week after she'd found out he'd been having not one affair, but two, and home these days was a small two-bedroom flat in an apartment block overlooking the animated Piazza Santo Spirito. The square was a gathering place for tourists, bohemians and students alike, and was considered the artisan quarter of the Oltrarno district. It was also one of the cheaper areas to rent in, given it was in more of a local area, rather than one of the tourist hotspots in the historic centre. Hopefully, if she continued to save half her pay cheque each week, she'd have just enough to put a deposit down on a place of her own. Maybe somewhere in the Chianti hills, twenty minutes out of town. A little chalet in the Tuscan countryside, with winemakers and olive groves all around her; now that would be perfection.

Her mind changed scenes and her belly flip-flopped as she imagined arriving in the diverse landscape of Far North Queensland. As much as she loved Florence and the Chianti hills, she did miss the contrasting sides of Silverton Shores. With lush green towering mountains on one side, the far-reaching Pacific Ocean on the other, and rolling rustic countryside stretching towards the centre of Australia, the sleepy little township was like heaven on earth in its own unique ways. In fewer than seventy-two hours, she'd be breathing in very different scents to the ones below her – floral lychee and mango blossoms, sweet sugarcane, horses and cattle, and sun-baked Aussie earth. It had been a long time coming. Almost a decade. It broke her heart that Chiara wouldn't be able to join her – there'd be no getting out of Italy without a passport. But as much as she didn't want to leave Chiara behind, she had to go. Thank goodness for Nonno offering to look after her; there was no way she'd be leaving her darling girl with Salvatore for an entire fortnight. Half of her couldn't wait to arrive on her brother's doorstep, and the other half wanted to run and hide.

The ringing of her phone had her almost jumping out of her skin. Racing back inside to grab it from the coffee table, she took the international call just before it went to message bank. 'Shanti!'

'Jessie!' Shanti's joyful voice carried down the line, wrapping her up in a far-reaching hug. 'How are you, my soon-to-be-official sister-in-law?'

Jess's heart warmed. 'I'm floating along, how about you, hon, how's the wedding planning going?'

Shanti groaned then laughed. 'Boy oh boy, I've almost throttled your darling brother a million times, but all in all, everything is finally coming together.'

'Ha ha, I can only imagine Roberto and his lack of wedding planning skills.' She rolled her eyes. 'He'd be an absolute nightmare.'

'Tell me about it.' Shanti giggled. 'He's lucky I love him so much.'

'Yes, he sure is.' Jess thought back to Shanti and Roberto's most recent trip to Florence, where she'd witnessed the loved-up pair for a month solid. 'I'm so sorry I haven't been able to get there sooner, so I can help you more.'

'No, don't you dare apologise. I totally understand how tough you've been having it lately.' Shanti's tone was full of compassion. 'I wish I could be there with *you*, helping you out of the mess Salvatore left you and Chiara in, the cheating lowlife bastard.'

'Thanks, Shanti, but I'm okay.' She wasn't, but the truth wasn't going to do anyone any good. 'So, tell me, what theme did you end up deciding on for the reception hall?' Anywhere other than her messy life was a good direction for the conversation to go in.

'Oh, have I got a surprise for you,' Shanti squealed excitedly. 'We, or should I say I, ended up deciding on a real shindig of a hoedown kind of wedding.'

'Yay you!' Shindig and hoedown didn't ring right for her fine-dining-loving brother, but she knew he'd do anything to make his bride happy. 'And what does this theme entail, exactly?'

'Well, if I have my way, the seats are going to be hay bales and the food is going to be a spit-roast buffet with all the trimmings.'

She sighed. 'And I've agreed to meet Roberto halfway, so we can have posh stuff too, like fairy lights and classy table decorations.'

Jess sank onto the couch and smiled into the phone. 'It sounds perfect, Shanti.' She'd been a bride in another lifetime, so she totally understood her best friend's excitement. And she was excited for them. She just wasn't thrilled about going back to Silverton Shores, especially without Chiara. 'I can't wait to see you in your wedding dress.'

'It's having the final alterations tomorrow, and then I have to basically starve myself until the big day, so I don't put any weight on.' Shanti chuckled.

'Yeah, right.' Jess chuckled too. 'Final last words from the queen of fast food and sugar highs.'

'I know, right, I'm a sucker for burger and fries, or doughnuts, and don't even get me started on my newest addiction of salted caramel popcorn, oh my god, I have to stop, I'm making myself hungry.' There was a short pause as Jess laughed, and then Shanti sighed. 'Are you sure you're okay with leaving Chiara with your nonno, Jessie?' Concern rang in her usually calm voice. 'I'd understand if you had to change your mind about coming all this way without her.'

'I do wish I could bring her with me, but her passport is nowhere to be found, and there's no way I'm going to miss your and Roberto's magical day.' Her heart tripped but she caught it before it stole her breath. 'Anyways, stop worrying about me and get back to organising the final details of your wedding to my very loveable, yet sometimes very exasperating, brother.'

'Will do, and I'm counting down the sleeps until you get here.'

'Me too,' Jess replied.

'Toodle-oo, bestie, see you real soon!'

'Yes, you will, toodles, love you, hon.'

'Love you, too, Jessie, big time.'

Ending the call, Jess cursed the decision she'd made all those years ago, and the secret she now had to keep because of it. It had given Salvatore way too much power over her. One day she'd make it right. She had to. At least for Chiara's sake. Maybe she should send the paperwork off before she left Italy, to get the ball on a roll. At least, then, once she arrived back here, she'd know for sure. And then she could plan her next steps.

Wandering back out to the balcony, she felt the combination of sleep deprivation and worry twist nauseatingly in her stomach. Leaning against the green railings, she looked to the plastered facade of the Santo Spirito church. The Renaissance-era basilica was the perfect example of not judging a book by its cover. So very plain on the outside, so unassuming to the naked eye, but take a step through the arched doorway and the visitor was met with priceless treasures, including a wooden crucifix crafted by none other than Michelangelo when he was only seventeen years old. Florence was a melting pot of history and beauty, that was for sure. With a resigned sigh, Jess looked to her watch. It was time to head to her part-time gig at her family's trattoria.

Jess shoved the crumpled paperwork into her oversized handbag, just in case she felt driven to post it, along with her favourite pair of low heels, then hopped from one foot to the other as she slipped her bare feet into her memory foam sneakers before closing her apartment door behind her. Having to descend eighty-two steps was one thing, but a twenty-five-minute walk to the renowned Sabatini Trattoria was another – heels weren't made for the cobblestone streets. The women who tried to walk in them usually ended up with a sprained ankle, or worse. She'd helped her fair share of embarrassed heel-wielding tourists up from the pavement over the years.

Heading downstairs and out the ancient front doors, all around her the air shimmered with heat and lingered with endless possibilities. Florence was a magical city, one that encouraged romance at every corner. And every which way she looked, couples were holding hands, kissing, loving on one another. But she didn't feel that way. She honestly didn't know if she'd ever allow herself to feel the butterflies of falling in love ever again. Because it never lasted, and when it didn't, it hurt way too much. Her fragile heart couldn't take any more of a thrashing. All the loss she'd endured in her short life was way too much for a whole lifetime.

First, her parents.

And then, Morgan.

Her stomach backflipped at the memory of him.

With each of her hurried footsteps resounding upon the narrow cobblestone street that led past the Pitti Palace and towards the medieval mouth of the Ponte Vecchio Bridge, lined with overpriced jewellers and wide-eyed tourists, she considered the soul-crushing decision she'd made all those years ago. Here, she had been able to hide from it. Now she had to face it, literally. It had been a good idea in theory, finally returning to her hometown after so many years spent avoiding it, but now the wedding was only around the corner, the reality was hitting her mighty hard. She was exhilarated that her brother and best friend had finally found the time to tie the knot, but she was also terrified of going back to Silverton Shores. Home was where the heart lived, apparently. Returning to the place that had once been a respite from the rest of the world was going to be tough, but add in seeing the only man who'd ever given her his whole heart – well, it was going to make it even tougher. Especially with the life-altering possible truth she was keeping from him.

Not one for social media, she wondered what Morgan looked like now. Had he aged well? Had he let himself go? Would she even recognise him after all these years? Would he recognise her? Respecting her wishes, Shanti never spoke of him. Although, more recently, and understandably, she'd had to hear his name several times as he was Roberto's best man, which meant she'd have to be around him, converse with him and, lord help her, perhaps dance with him on the wedding night. With him at the forefront of her mind, she couldn't help but think about what might have been, if she'd been in her right mind and chosen differently. A mixture of regret and longing swirled as she desperately tried to get rid of the anxiety gripping her stomach. La dolce vita, the sweet life, that's what she craved. But no matter which way she turned, no matter how many years she put between herself and the past, that sweetness eluded her. And likely would until she discovered the truth and, if it was what she thought it to be, made things right.

The row of matchbox shops jutting out and over the Arno river drew her towards the beating heart of the Renaissance city. Weaving her way through the hordes of tourists, her freshly washed and blow-dried hair fell freely about her bare shoulders. Having chosen her favourite ankle-length dress, she liked the way the silky material fluttered sensually against her legs. It was a typical Florentine summer evening now that the dark clouds had dissipated, taking the threat of rain with them, although the heat and humidity of the day hadn't fully subsided. Drawing in a deep breath, she looked to the south, up at the hilltop villas surrounded by towering cypress trees and gnarled olive groves almost as ancient as the stone walls of the buildings surrounding her. Even after nine years of calling Florence home, she was still wowed by the medieval buildings and the grandeur of the Duomo.

As she approached the alleyway that was a short cut to the trattoria, a black Fiat 500 zoomed around the corner, slowed and then pulled to a stop beside her. Her gut tightened, and she steeled herself. The window wound down, and she was greeted with her daughter's cheerful face, and her ex's seemingly ingrained scowl.

'Hi, sweetheart.' Leaning in the window, she met her daughter's kiss. 'How was school today?' She was so glad her baby girl had been attending an international school, giving her an advantage with her English curricula.

'Oh, you know,' Chiara huffed as her shoulders lifted. 'It was a bit boring.'

'Yes, it can be sometimes, but other times it can be lots of fun, too.' She crouched down a little further. 'Salvatore.' Her tone was clipped.

'Jessica.' Salvatore raked his fingers through his impossibly thick, jet-black hair. 'Don't worry, I'll have her home by nine-thirty, like the court order states.' He'd snappily answered what was going to be her next question before she'd even had time to ask it.

Why did he always have to mention the court order in front of Chiara?

Gritting her teeth, she forced a smile. 'Great, thank you.' He was almost always late, or worse still, now that he had a new girlfriend, quite often forgot his designated night during the week and every second weekend with Chiara. 'You have a nice time and I'll see you at home then, love, okay?'

Chiara beamed her a bright smile. 'Okay, Mum, I love you.'

'Love you too, sweetheart, lots and lots.' She stepped back a little. 'Bye for now.'

'Hang on, Jessica.' Salvatore's imposing voice pulled her back down to his eye level. 'Are you really sure you want to go all the way to the ends of the earth for some wedding, and leave Chiara with your grandfather for two whole weeks?'

'Yes, of course I am, she'll love her time with her great-nonno.' She hated how Salvatore played her as the bad guy in front of Chiara. 'And for the record, it's not just *some wedding*.'

'I wish I could see Uncle Roberto and Aunty Shanti, too.' Chiara pouted. 'I *really* wanted to come with you, Mum.'

'I know you did, sweetheart.' Jess's heart squeezed as tightly as she was gripping the windowsill. Damn Salvatore and his maliciousness. 'But I haven't been able to find your passport.'

Chiara's high ponytail swished, as her freckle-dusted face crinkled. 'I know that you've tried to.'

'Yes, well, if it were me, I wouldn't be going,' Salvatore cruelly added.

Without slinging mud back in Salvatore's face, Jess didn't know what to say, and she wasn't going to be *that* kind of parent, one who pushed the other under the bus to save face.

Salvatore blew a weighty sigh. 'Oh well, Chiara, your mother has made her mind up, and when she does that, trust me, it's useless trying to change it.' His steely gaze cold as ice, he offered Jess his practised smile. 'You have yourself a good night, won't you?'

Before Jess had a moment to catch her angry breath, he hit the accelerator and was zooming away from her. 'You piece of crap,' she muttered beneath her breath while waving Chiara off. 'One day, you'll get your comeuppance,' she grumbled as she strode in the opposite direction.

Minutes later, she stepped through the wood-framed glass doors of her nonno's life's work, Sabatini Trattoria, where a family-style atmosphere reigned, and laughter and chatter could always be heard around the communal tables. Here, locals enjoyed home-style specialities to be proud of, and tourists got to try unknown dishes that quite often became their favourites. With many friendships forged here, love stories born, and problems given thoughtful solutions, the walls of the open-beamed, terracotta-floored, wine bottle–filled room would be able to write the juiciest of novels. Every day there was a different menu, depending on what produce was locally available. Her nonno, and now her cousin, were sticklers for supporting local producers and using what was in season. And the open kitchen gave customers a bird's-eye view into the goings-on of an authentic Italian cucina.

The scent of basil and fresh tomatoes permeated the air as she strode into the kitchen. 'Ciao, Nonno.' She paused to peck both his cheeks – even though he was retired, he couldn't stay away.

'Buongiorno, bella.' Turning from where he was stirring a massive pot of sauce, he regarded her intently, his bushy dark brows scrunched together.

She didn't realise a tear had slipped until his arms came around her. 'What has he done to you this time?'

'Just the usual, painting me as the baddie in front of Chiara.' She sniffled and shook her head. 'I hate how he plays such hurtful games.'

'Chiara isn't silly, she knows you love her very much, and everything you do is with thought for her.'

His kind words and baritone voice soothed her. 'Thank you, Nonno.' She offered him a sad smile. 'I honestly don't know what I'd do without you.'

'That's what family are for, si?' His warm smile reached deep within her broken heart. 'We're meant to care for and protect one another, always.'

Her smile filled with the warmth of his. 'Si, family is everything.' She kissed his cheek again. 'I better get to it, before we're bombarded with hungry customers.' After hanging her bag on a hook, she changed her flats to her heels, put on her work face, then popped a CD in the stereo, making sure to turn it up.

Listening to the famous Louis Prima – one of her favourite musicians – she, her nonno and her cousin Alessandro sang along to their hearts' content to the tune 'Che La Luna'. The song always put her in a happy place – how could it not, with its catchy, upbeat tempo and fun lyrics. Grabbing a pile of freshly laundered red-and-white checked tablecloths and linen napkins, she headed back out into the dining room to begin setting the tables while wiggling her hips in time to the melody. In the middle of each table, she placed a vase with a fresh red rose, along with a bottle of balsamic vinegar and fruity olive oil. Next up, her foot tapped rhythmically to the sassy song 'Buona Sera' as she sliced the fresh bread that they offered for free, so the customers could la scarpetta – mop up all the juices – as it was sacrilege to leave them behind. And as she followed her usual routine, to the music that filled her soul to the brim, she couldn't help but feel better as the minutes ticked on. At least when she was here, she could be herself, warts and all. And no matter what, Alessandro, Nonno and their loyal staff of eight, who were all related in one way or another, loved her unconditionally. There was a lot to be said for the way Italians put the love of family before anything else. It was one of the main things she loved about being in Florence – the feeling that she belonged here.

CHAPTER 3

Silverton Shores, Far North Queensland

Morgan Savage had been born into this world an adrenaline junkie, which explained his chosen career as a Royal Flying Doctor Service pilot. He'd started his quest to seek anything that spiked his pulse almost as soon as he could walk. Everything from climbing on unbroken horses, skydiving, hang-gliding, bull riding, scuba diving with sharks, rally-car driving, motorbike riding, chopper mustering, and the list went on. Throughout his thirty-four years he'd defied death way too many times to count. His poor mother had endured many scares and hospital visits. His poor father had been the one to have to soothe her concerns as well as give his son a firm reminder of his mortality when needed. Which had been often. He was their only child – they'd poured all their blood, sweat and tears into the family property, and into him. And the fruits of their labour had paid off when his father had been recognised as a leader in cattle production and scored his dream job of travelling the world to teach others the ways of animal husbandry. His parents had grabbed the opportunity with both hands, sectioned off the property with Morgan's encouragement, sold off most of it, then gifted some of the profit and one hundred acres with the homestead and cottage to their cherished son.

And very soon, Jessica Sabatini was going to be back in Silverton Shores. The very place she had been meant to spend a lifetime with him as her husband, raising their two envisaged children. But, as per usual when it came to his life, not everything had gone to plan.

He'd just learnt to roll with the punches.

A phone call from Roberto the day before had stirred deep emotions, not that he was going to let on to his best mate at a time like this. Morgan thought back to Roberto's words as he kept his gaze on the glowing horizon from his seat in the cockpit. One busted main water pipe, he'd said, and Jess's arranged accommodation had been rendered uninhabitable. Morgan felt for Roberto and Shanti, having to shack up at Shanti's mother's tiny two-bedroom place until their house was liveable again, which could be a couple of months – but damn fate and its meddling hands leaving himself as the only viable option for accommodation for Jess. Everything else in the township had been booked by interstate wedding guests, and Annie's tiny studio-style unit wasn't an option either, given there was barely enough room to swing her Persian cat. Just how Jess was going to take the news he hadn't a clue; he'd find out soon enough when he collected her from the airport the next morning. Another task given to him as Roberto and Shanti dealt with the aftermath of a flooded home, and Annie found herself unable to skip a shift at the already understaffed Silverton Shores hospital.

Not that he believed Annie should have Jess stay with her anyway. There was pressing unresolved business there that he wanted laid out on the table before Jess went back to Florence. Not that Annie was coming to that particular table without a fight. Even though he understood and was compassionate about her reasons for wanting to remain tight-lipped, he wasn't letting her off the hook. He couldn't carry the overwhelming weight of her secret any longer, and he'd told her as much.

With a heavy-hearted sigh, he thought back to when Jess had left town, and him. A broken man, he'd deliberately headed for trouble, but with some tough love from his father and Roberto along with the kind-hearted support of his mum and Shanti, he'd eventually pulled himself back together. Not that he could ever forget Jess, as much as he sometimes wanted to. As if branded there, she was burned into his heart. She was a sweet memory. An enigma from his past. And the leading part in the secret he'd so innocently discovered as a seven-year-old boy.

A secret that had been kept because of a promise made.

A promise that could possibly have an end-by date.

He turned his full attention to the here and now as a familiar cluster of buildings came into view. Dropping from the twilight-hued sky, he expertly landed the twin engine plane on the runway and taxied to a stop. A minute later, its propellers slowed then came to a standstill. The two nurses and doctor bustled in the back, tending to the patient that was due to have her baby any day. With the unborn child in breach position, she was going to need a caesarean, not something that could be done at an outback cattle station. Following protocol, he made sure all his ducks were in a row before he slipped his headset off, along with his seatbelt, and rose from his helm in the cockpit. Just shy of six-foot four, he couldn't wait to step onto the tarmac, so he could straighten out the kinks in his back. And having an entire month of annual leave ahead of him was adding a spring to his step.

Raised by a third-generation true-blue cattleman, and with a love for horses running in his country veins, he hadn't set out to be a pilot for the RFDS. He'd never lain awake at night, dreaming of the day he'd fly a team of medical professionals into the yonder to birth babies and save lives. But true to form, fate had other plans. One of his best mates had died in his arms after a fishing trip up the tip of Australia went horribly wrong, and he'd made a promise to the powers that be to devote his life to doing what he could to save others.

And here he was, doing just that.

It was amazing what the human body could withstand and heal from. Accidental shootings, snakebites; being trampled by a bull or gored by wild pigs; unsuspecting kids catapulted from trees and trampolines; and the list of ailments and accidents went on – far-flung cattle stations could be extremely dangerous places. Morgan knew that all too well after serving eight and a half years in the cockpit, with his crew of doctors and nurses catering to a landscape the size of Western Europe. The things he'd seen, the people he'd helped save and the ones they'd sadly lost, had all left their mark on his guarded heart. Now it felt good to know he had four weeks of leave before getting back to the grindstone of dusty airstrips dotted with livestock and roos the size of small cars.

The good lord knew he needed it.

Alighting from the plane, he met with his colleagues just as the ambulance they'd organised for the pregnant woman drove away. 'I'll catch you lot on the flip side.'

'Sure thing.' Doctor Jacob gave him a friendly slap on the back. 'You enjoy that well-earned break, won't you, mate.'

'Cheers, Jacob, I'll give it my best shot.'

'Catch you, Morgan,' the pretty new nurse said with a flutter of her extra-long lashes.

As uninterested in her as he was in almost every other woman who had made her attraction to him clear, Morgan flashed her a smile. 'Thanks, Shelly.'

'You take care, and don't forget about us while you're enjoying your break, Morgan.' The head nurse pulled him into a tight, motherly hug. 'Because we need you back, so don't go thinking about retiring just yet, you hear me.' She waggled a finger at him.

Morgan chuckled and shook his head. 'I'm not going to retire just yet, Mavis.'

'Glad to hear it.' She shooed him off. 'Now go, get, and put those boots of yours up.'

'Right you are.' He offered a wave over his shoulder as he headed towards the car park of the rural airport.

He climbed behind the wheel of his trusty LandCruiser GXL Troopcarrier, revved it to life and allowed it to idle for a few moments while he pondered the fact that there were two sides to him. On one hand, he loved his office window from the cockpit, where the horizon seemed to stretch into infinity, but on the other, give him a good horse and well-worn saddle and he was one hell of a happy man. All in all, he only really wanted for one thing, and one thing alone, but she was long gone. Hell, he'd tried to move on, had enjoyed a few flings and one serious relationship since losing the love of his life, but every single time he hadn't been able to feel the love he craved, the kind of buoyant, soul-deep love that he had shared with Jess. It sucked, but it was his reality. One that he'd grown accustomed to living day in, day out, one lonely night after another. One of these days, if pigs flew, he might be lucky enough to meet another special lady, one who made his heart race like the clappers and his soul ache for a connection to hers, but until then he'd rather be on his own than feel like an incomplete companion to a woman who deserved to be loved wholeheartedly.

After taking a swig from his water bottle, he wiped his lips with the back of his hand then veered out of the car park, in the opposite direction to where the ambulance had headed, and onto the long dirt track that would lead him home. With the waning crescent of the moon providing little light, dense darkness clung to the untainted landscape and up ahead the horizon had all but disappeared. After navigating the corrugated dirt road for almost half an hour, the tyres of his four-wheel drive finally gripped bitumen. Sighing with relief, he threw his Troopy into top gear, turned the country music up and, pedal to the metal, he chased the white lines of the winding coastal road while singing along to Waylon Jennings' 'Only Daddy That'll Walk the Line'.

If he had a baby girl, he'd be walking the line for his daughter, that was for sure.

* * *

The following morning, before the sun had hinted at its arrival, Morgan had donned his favourite timeworn cowboy boots and dusty Akubra, saddled up and ridden into the low light of dawn. An hour later, sitting astride his buckskin horse, Cash, with his weather-beaten wide-brimmed hat angled low, he gazed into the dawn sunshine. Soon, the baking summer heat would have him sweating heavily, but for now the briskness of a cool spring night still lingered, and he was using it to his advantage as he kept his eyes peeled for newborn calves. With almost one hundred acres to tend to, there was a lot of land to cover before he headed down the range, to the Cairns airport and the woman who had inadvertently shattered his heart. If only she could have leant on him, sought his comfort, allowed him to help her heal, instead of cutting herself off from him, from this place, from the life she'd known with Julie and Enzo Sabatini.

Remember to roll with the punches, Savage ...

Spread out before him, his fertile land stretched away and down the hill. As he cleared the rise then neared the bottom paddock, a wholehearted smile spread. He brought Cash to a stop at the railings, where deep brown eyes stared back at him as the newborn calf took wobbly steps towards its mother. The moo-ma, a name he fondly called his mother cows, began to lick her calf clean. This was a sign that she wouldn't reject her baby, and that made his smile spread further still. This, right here, was what he lived for, to see such innocent life be born into what could sometimes be a big, bad, heartbreaking world. The scene before him gave him the hope he needed, the drive he required, to get out of bed and devote his whole heart to this majestic place. Thanks to his wonderful parents, he'd grown up with a deep-set love and reverence for the land, and the country-hearted people who shaped it and called it home. Bearing witness to the magic of it made him, in his firm opinion, a very blessed man indeed.

Two hours later, turning Cash towards home, he gave his horsey mate the cue to open his stride and gallop for gold. Cash didn't need any more of an invitation. Careering at breakneck speed, Morgan relished the sound of the wind whipping past and the thunder of powerful hoofs striking the earth. Wrapped up within the fleeting moment he felt free, alive, at peace. Beginning to ease off the pace as they neared the stables, Cash came to a sliding stop as Morgan drew the reins. Alighting after giving the horse a hearty neck rub in appreciation, he unsaddled, gave a very sweat-lathered Cash a hose-down, then led him back into his paddock where he gave him a treat of molasses.

'Catch you tomorrow, buddy,' he said as he wandered away.

He passed the chook pen, and as he crossed the driveway his other four-legged mate appeared from his usual shady spot beneath the verandah and rocketed towards him, all fur and slobber and gangly legs.

'Whoa, there, Teeny.' Steeling himself for the incoming pile-up, he chuckled when his Great Dane cross wolfhound slid to a stop on top of his boots, with his tongue lolling out to the side and his tail whacking the ground. 'You're a nincompoop, you know that right.' He ruffled Teeny's big ears lovingly. 'One of these days, I reckon you're going to plough right through me.'

Teeny fell into step beside him, and man and dog headed through the picket gate, up the pathway, around the corner and towards the back steps. Off to the side of the homestead, the windmill creaked as it spun lazily in the gentle breeze, pumping water from below. After kicking his boots off at the back door, Morgan headed inside with Teeny hot on his socked heels. He whipped himself up some breakfast, then carried his extra-strong coffee and two pieces of Vegemite on toast to the swing chair, where he enjoyed the raucous chorus of the kookaburras perched on his clothesline. Teeny settled himself at the top of the stairs, as if guarding his master. Morgan loved the big goofball with all his heart, and then some. He pondered whether Teeny would take to Jess, and her to him. From memory, she loved dogs, and they had always loved her, but that was nine years ago. Unlike then, now he didn't know her, and likewise, she didn't know him. They were essentially strangers. So much had changed him, shaped him into who he was today, and he supposed the same could be said for her. If he was on social media, he would have likely looked her up over the years, but he wasn't, and didn't ever want to be. Surfing the web was a waste of his precious time. Besides, he didn't want the world knowing his business. He was a private person, with a private life, and he liked to keep it that way.

Rising then wandering to the edge of the verandah, he rested his forearms on the railings. Staring out and into the brightness of the day, he felt buried memories rise and wash over him. Their first kiss. Their first official date at the local drive-in. Their first night out dancing at the local nightclub. The rainy days they'd spent cuddled up on the couch, watching movies. The sunny days they'd spent gallivanting in the great outdoors, by foot, riding motorbikes or on horseback. The night he'd gotten down on one knee and asked her to be his forever. The excitement written all over her pretty face when she'd said yes. Then, that one passionate night they'd let their passions take hold of them, and made the deepest, sweetest love, just three days before they were meant to get married. If Julie and Enzo had found out, they would've throttled them both.

Sex before marriage had been a sin in their deeply religious eyes.

Closing his eyes against the bittersweet memories, he sighed. Only a couple of hours, and Jess would be here, in the cottage across the drive, mere metres instead of thousands of miles from him. He couldn't believe the irony of her finally residing within the walls of what had once been the home where they were going to start their married life. After she left him, he'd never thought he'd see the day. How living near each other for the next two weeks was going to pan out, he hadn't a damn clue, but he was going to give developing a renewed friendship his best shot. Why not? They were both adults who should have moved on and past it all. Hopefully she felt the same way. They'd shared so much love, so much life, just … so much. But then she'd vanished, as if she'd never existed in the first place. And he'd never heard from her again. For the first year, her profound silence had torn his world apart, but then piece by piece, he began putting it back together. He may have forgiven her, but he'd never forgotten the pain of the heartbreak. So no matter how much he might still secretly feel for her deep down in his soul, somewhere nice and dark, there was no way he'd allow such heartbreak to tear his life to shreds again.

CHAPTER 4

'Ladies and gentlemen, we're about to begin our descent into the Cairns airport where the local time is two-fifteen in the afternoon and the temperature is a balmy thirty-two degrees.' The practised voice of the chirpy attendant echoed through the plane's speakers. 'Please make sure your seat is in the upright position, your tray table is stowed, your window shade is up, and your seatbelt is securely fastened.'

Feeling a little airsick after twenty-five hours of travel, Jess wondered how the woman could sound so upbeat after a long-haul flight. Groaning, she rested her head back and prayed that she wouldn't need to use the brown paper bag clutched in her hands to catch the unpleasant food she'd eaten two hours ago. Or was it her emotions sending her stomach into turmoil? Possibly a bit of both. After all the hours spent in the air, along with a four-and-a-half-hour stopover in Singapore, with not much to do but remember her past, and the terrible, hasty mistakes that she'd made, her heart had turned upside down and inside out. There were pieces of her life's jigsaw missing. She knew exactly what they were, and she also knew she had the power to somehow put them back together, but she was terrified of the ramifications.

In the end, it could go either way.

Holding her breath as the man on her left coughed for what felt like the umpteenth time, she counted to twelve before daring to take another inhalation. A second bout of Covid was the last thing she wanted or needed. Utterly exhausted, her senses were heightened, and everything was annoying her now – the cold air blowing from the vent above, the fact that she felt crammed in between the people beside her and the kid kicking the back of her seat. She'd already asked him three times to please refrain from doing so, and it was taking every single bit of her resolve not to turn around and give him what for. With her busy life back in Florence, she was so used to being able to divert her contemplations, but strapped into her seat, beside an armrest-hogging stranger, without an inch of wriggle room, there was nowhere to hide, nothing to do to distract her thoughts. Try as she might, she couldn't ignore the dread that now sat like lead in the pit of her stomach. Arriving back in the place that was riddled with ghosts and haunted with memories was going to be tougher than she'd envisioned.

Her stomach dropped as the plane quickly descended through the blanket of clouds. The clunk of the wheels swiftly sounded and soon enough, after a quick flash of sparkling water and tropical green, the plane bounced then gripped the tarmac. That was the very moment the secret she'd been harbouring deep down in her soul scratched and clawed like a banshee trying to break free. And her very next thought was of Morgan Savage. Although she'd done her best to move on, her first and only true love had never truly left her mind, or her heart. And rightfully so. He still unwittingly played a massive part in her life. Maybe. Possibly.

Oh, who in the hell am I trying to kid?

If her timings were right, almost definitely.

After a long taxi, the plane pulled to a stop, and before the seatbelt light had flickered off, almost half the plane's occupants were already on their feet. The nice air hostess's voice became dictatorial as she commanded everyone stay seated. Only half the people listened. Jess rolled her eyes at their urgency. Nobody would be getting off in a hurry. Staying put, she grabbed her phone and tried to turn it on. Realising it had gone flat, she cursed beneath her breath and shoved it into her handbag, hoping to god she wasn't going to need it to reach out to Shanti and Roberto. She waited edgily until the aisle beside her was free before rising, then grabbed her carry-on bag from the overhead locker and joined the long queue. Like cattle being led to the slaughter, the long line of travel-weary passengers made their way out of the aircraft, up the airbridge, through passport control, then to the baggage collection area. Unceremoniously lugging her heavy case from the carousel, Jess popped a mint in her mouth then made her way through customs and towards the security doors.

Although nervous, and bedraggled after her long flight, she was also excited to see her loved ones. A warm glow filled her at the thought of wrapping her arms around both her brother and her best friend. Stepping through the sliding doors, she planted a wide smile as she rose on her tippy toes and looked left to right. A sea of faces met her, but none were familiar. She took a few more steps, then did the same again. Where in the heck were they? Her name echoed across the arrivals lounge and every nerve end fired to panicked life. With her pounding heart leaping into her throat, she dared not look in the direction of the deep, gravelly voice. She didn't need to see the mouth her name had just tumbled from. She'd kissed it enough times to know the owner of the arousing voice. Clamping her trembling lips together, while holding back some four-lettered words, she did her best to fight the panic building in her chest as she forced herself to turn around.

Pull yourself together, Jess, right now!

And as she spun, guilt washed over her in an engulfing tide. No longer a memory, but instead all tattooed, sun-kissed flesh and broad shoulders, not the lanky twenty-five-year-old she'd left behind but a solid tower of virile man now striding towards her, and essentially back into her life, Morgan Savage had aged mighty well. As he neared her, she could see the shaggy hair she used to run her fingers through curling from beneath his Akubra. And once he was close enough for her to reach out and touch him – which she was hesitant to do, so she didn't – her eyes collided with the brilliant blue of his, and in that fleeting instant, she was right back to being a twenty-two-year-old bride-to-be, and the impact of the memory-punch made the ground feel as if it had given way.

If only she could fall through it.

'Hey, Morgan.' With a conscious effort, she willed herself to breathe. In. Out. Repeat.

'G'day, Jess.' His voice was deep, dreamy and quintessentially Australian. 'Long time no see.' His tone was overtly playful, but there was a sheer drop of cobalt depth in his eyes. 'How was your flight?'

'It was long, but okay, I suppose, as flights go, you know.' Tripping over her words, she flashed him a brilliant smile. 'I wasn't expecting you to be here, to pick me up, I mean.'

Stop blabbering, Jess!

'Yeah, about that, it's a bit of a long story.' Grimacing good-humouredly, he extended a strong hand. 'First things first, though, it's really good to see you.'

Oddly formal, given the fact they'd almost married each other, but she accepted his gesture. 'It's really nice to see you, too.' She sucked in a breath, shocked by how familiar his touch was and how it still made her feel instantly safe. 'So why aren't Roberto and Shanti here, is everything okay?'

'Not really.' He sucked air through his teeth. 'They woke up to a very flooded house.'

Eyes widening, she gasped. 'Holy crap.'

'Literally, seeing it was the sewage line that burst.' He grimaced again. 'Sooo, now they are at Shanti's mum's, likely until at least after their honeymoon, and as for you, the plan is you're staying with me, well, not with me, but at my place.' He rubbed a hand over his stubbled jaw. 'Sweet Jesus, get your words right, Savage.' He shook his head and chuckled. 'Not *at* my place, but in your own place at my place, in the cottage.'

'Oh, right.' She wanted to refuse his proposal. But beggars and choosers, and all of that …

Then it struck her. 'You mean, our, *the*, cottage.'

'Yes, the one and only.' Warmth lingered in his baritone voice.

'Uh-huh.' Somehow taller, stronger and more handsome than she remembered, he was a feast for her weary eyes. So much so, she wanted to tear his Wranglers right off him like some lustful hussy – her need to do so ran way deeper than just being aroused by how he looked. And that terrified her. 'Well, I suppose I should say, thank you for coming to my rescue.'

'No worries.' He waved a hand through the air. 'Shanti was so upset that she couldn't be here to welcome you home, I mean back, but she and Roberto are tied up trying to sort out the mess.' He cleared his throat and took a breath. 'She said she left you a voice message and sent a text as well.'

'Oh, my mobile's flat. And of course, yes, I could only imagine the state their place is in, poor things.' His familiar scent settled into her soul, jarring loose a long-lost memory from where she'd tucked it away, and as she remembered the way his hand used to rest in the crook of her back whenever he kissed her, a warmth crept up her neck and to her cheeks. 'Well, then, should we make a move and hit the road?'

'Yeah, yup, for sure.' His chiselled features stretched into a charming smile as he thumbed over his shoulder. 'The Troopy's this way.' He reached for her heavy suitcase. 'Here, let me.' Taking the handle, he wheeled it in beside him and eyed the bulging zipper. 'Far out, did you bring the kitchen sink with you, too?'

'That's enough of that, Savage.' She felt the load on her heart and shoulders lighten with his spirited teasing. 'I'm a woman, and we need lots of stuff.'

'Righto.' He chuckled. 'I'll take your word for it.'

Side by side they wandered out of the airport, where she felt a slap of tropical heat to the face, then after debating over who was going to pay for the parking – Morgan won – they headed to his four-wheel drive decked out with all the country bells and whistles. Making it to the passenger door first, he opened it and gestured for her to hop on in.

'Still the gentleman, I see.' She clambered up and got settled. 'Thank you,' she added as she tugged her seatbelt on, and with an acknowledging smile he closed the door.

A few awkward minutes later, and they were heading down Sheridan Street, towards Port Douglas, where they would then head a little further north to Silverton Shores. In what she suspected was an effort to dull the silence, Morgan reached out and turned the stereo up, but only enough that they could still talk. Waylon Jennings' unmistakable voice filled the void nicely with his song 'Good Ol' Boys' from one of her all-time favourite TV shows.

'Oh, my goodness, I haven't heard this song in years.' She noted her foot was tapping in time to the catchy tune.

'I'm guessing you don't listen to much country music in Florence?'

She shook her head. 'No, not really.'

'If my memory serves me correct, I recall you used to love *The Dukes of Hazzard*.' He offered a lingering sideways glance. 'Have you watched any re-runs since you've been overseas?'

'I actually haven't, but I should show my little girl, because I reckon that she'd love it.' She'd blurted it out before she stopped to consider that she'd asked Roberto and Shanti not to mention Chiara to anyone here, other than Shanti's mum.

'You have a daughter?' His words came out in a woosh.

'Mm-hmm.' She didn't know where to look, so she kept her gaze out the windscreen.

His long pause stretched, and lingered. 'How didn't I know that?' He shook his head as though baffled. 'Roberto and Shanti haven't said a word.' He half shrugged. 'Mind you, we don't make it a habit, talking about you.'

'That's understandable, I'm not much of an interesting subject.' She tried to make light of his comment, but knew exactly what he meant, because she and her brother and Shanti had made the same pact. It used to hurt way too much, hearing about Morgan, so they'd stopped talking about him altogether. Many years ago. She knew his parents had left Silverton Shores, and that he was a RFDS pilot, but that was it.

Silence stretched then lingered again, before he asked, 'How old is she?'

Shit!

An image of her twenty-two-year-old self effortlessly slipped into her mind, and her stomach somersaulted with the recollection of what could have been his baby, their baby, cradled within her womb. 'She's nine.' This was way too close for comfort.

'Wow, okay, I suppose now I understand why you married Salvatore so quickly.'

His surmising made her anger flare, but she bit it back. 'Mm-hmm.' She reminded herself that if he only knew the truth of the dilemma she'd found herself in, and the uncertainty she'd chosen to ignore at the time, the angry shoe would be on the other foot.

'What's her name?' His fingers were drumming the steering wheel now.

Shit shit shit!

'Chiara.' It was the one they'd picked, together, for when they had a little girl.

'You used our name?' His voice was laced with hurt.

'It was a name I really liked, so yes, I did.' She drew in a breath and sighed it away. 'Can you please keep Chiara to yourself, Morgan, I don't really want the whole town knowing my business.' Being a topic of gossip, and scrutiny and judgement, was not on her agenda, especially when it came to her darling girl.

'Yeah, sure, of course I will.'

Silence fell again, but this time she settled into it. She hadn't lied. But she hadn't told him the whole truth, either. Hell, how could she when she didn't know for sure, either way. And she didn't want to risk stepping into blatantly deceitful territory, so, while he navigated the curving road, she rested back into her seat and enjoyed the picturesque tropical landscape flashing past her window. She must have drifted off, because a little nudge from Morgan had her sitting up straight just in time to catch the township's welcome sign out the window.

Silverton Shores, population 5322

Her heart squeezed as she wondered whether they changed the sign each year, adding the births and subtracting the deaths. *Her* parents' deaths, particularly. 'Sorry for crashing like that, I'm a little jet-lagged, I think.' She rubbed her eyes and tugged her hair into a messy bun.

'All good.' His warm, genuine smile had returned. 'Some things don't change, huh, you were always a snoozing shotgunner.'

'I can't help that your driving always puts me to sleep.' Their banter was familiar, comfortingly so.

'Oi, fair play, I drive to the conditions, especially when I have precious cargo.'

'Well, thank you for driving carefully.' She liked to think he still considered her *precious cargo*.

'Does it still look the same?' He glanced at her then back to the ocean-kissed horizon owning the entirety of the view out the windscreen.

'It does, but somehow it's even more beautiful than I remember.' She relished the sight of the ocean crashing against the ragged rocks below, almost as much as she was relishing being in this man's company again.

'Well, here we are.' Slowing as he reached the edge of town, he dropped from fifth gear to fourth. 'Home sweet home.'

Like a free diver rising from the ocean's depths to take a life-giving breath, she inhaled her first glimpse of the sleepy seaside township she used to call home. Silverton Shores was very much a throwback to yesteryear, familiar, comforting, welcoming. She recognised most of the shopfronts with their sun-faded awnings, and even the people walking down the street still had that Far North Queensland easy-as-it-goes swagger.

'Gee whizz, not much has changed,' she said dreamily.

'Ha, yeah, people like things to stay as they are around here.' His broad shoulders lifted ever so slightly. 'And I have to say I'm in total agreement with them.'

And there it was, that slow, dangerous grin that had swept her off her centre axis all those years ago. 'That's a nice way to look at it.' A sudden longing to be drawn into his big strong arms, so she could rest her head against his chest, made her a little breathless.

'Actually, there are some fancy new cafés behind some of those old shopfronts, and crowds of tourists on the weekends these days.'

'Hmm, modernisation I suppose,' she replied, totally distracted by him and his charisma.

Ten minutes later they were pulling through the gates of Savage Acres. 'This all looks the same as I remember, too, except for the fence line – it seems, closer, maybe.' Pulling her eyes from the glorious rolling hills dotted with horses and cattle, she turned to him.

'Yeah, Mum and Dad sold off most of the land when Dad took the new job and left me with just enough to run my own herd.'

She nodded, taking it all in. 'So, you're living in the homestead now?'

'Sure am, have been for seven years, or thereabouts.'

'On your own?' She had to ask, seeing as she'd be calling this place home for now.

'Uh-huh, all on my own.'

She didn't like the fact that learning he wasn't shacked up with some lucky woman made her heart skip an excited beat, but hey, she used to love this man with all her heart, so it would've been hard to meet his newer, better half, if there had been one. They followed the meandering gravel drive lined with bush lemon trees, then pulled to a stop, and her vision momentarily blurred as she took in the glorious two-storey building on one side, and the quaint chocolate-box cottage over on the other. Painful could-have-beens pummelled her heart, but she sucked in a sharp breath and shook the sensation off as she stepped out of the passenger-side door. Morgan hightailed it from his side and barricaded her, as if protecting her. Before she had a chance to process any more emotions, or assess if there was indeed impending danger, a mountain of fur came out of nowhere, bounding straight for her.

'No, buddy, manners maketh man, remember.' Hooking his finger into the fuzzy Great Dane's collar, Morgan successfully stopped the incoming missile in its tracks. 'You cannot lick every one of our guests to death.' He ruffled the top of the dog's head. 'Even though I know you really want to.'

Jess stepped forward but kept a little distance. 'So, who do we have here?'

'This here is Teeny-weeny.' He grinned. 'Or, Teeny for short.'

'Teeny, hey?' With the woolly mammoth staring back at her, she couldn't help her explosion of laughter. 'Have you seen the size of him?'

Chuckling, Morgan nodded. 'You should see the amount of food he eats, and don't even get me started on the size of what comes out his back end.'

'Way too much information.' Laughing, she waved a hand through the air. 'So, tell me, is he as scary as he looks?'

'No way, he's a big teddy bear, aren't you, Teeny?'

Sitting on his haunches, with his tongue drooping out to one side, Teeny tipped his head a little and whined.

Her heart turning to mush, Jess bent, took the paw he cutely offered her, and shook it. 'Hey, buddy, it's really nice to meet you.' Having been given what he clearly felt was an open invitation, Teeny proceeded to plonk himself onto her feet as she straightened. 'Are you right there, mister?' She smiled down at him.

'Come on, buddy, I'm sure Jess doesn't want you playing the part of a foot warmer.' Morgan clicked his fingers, and Teeny faithfully raced back to his master's side.

'Come on, I'll show you to the cottage, then I'll grab your luggage for you while you settle in.' He took steps towards the cottage, with Teeny hot on his heels.

Jess followed, adoring the way the two seemed the best of mates. Morgan had always had a special way with animals. It was one of the many things she'd adored about him. Climbing the three front steps, she admired how the scuffed timber floorboards of the verandah anchored the white weatherboard cottage to its surroundings. And the lush blooming gardens, popping with so many colours, were to die for.

Without needing a key, Morgan opened the timber door and waved her inside. 'Ladies first.' He glanced down at Teeny. 'You stay here, bud.'

After kicking her shoes off, she stepped in, and Morgan followed her. The slap of the flyscreen sounded as she turned left to right, surveying the recognisable, yet updated lounge room. Gone were the old louvred windows, replaced with sliding glass doors and bay windows that drew the majesty of the outside in. Wandering to the middle of the room, she stopped on the cowskin rug and turned in a circle, her mind's eye recalling how it used to look all those years ago. Memories bombarded her, and the weight was overwhelming. Feeling tears building, she stepped out of Morgan's line of sight, desperate to pull her emotions into check. Padding over to the bay windows, she peered outside, drinking in the endless views of untainted beauty.

'It's absolutely perfect.' Turning away from the familiar view, she smiled. 'Thank you, Morgan, for letting me stay here.'

'No need to thank me.' Reaching out, Morgan briefly touched her arm. 'You get comfortable, while I'll go and grab your luggage.'

'Okay, thanks.' The brush of his hand left a seductive kind of warmth that spread through her like an ache.

'There's some essentials in the fridge, and tea, coffee and a couple of other things in the cupboard, including a couple of bottles of local red,' he said, taking steps towards the front door. 'I remember you used to love wine.'

Jess sucked in another shaky breath as emotion welled at his kind-heartedness. 'You didn't have to go and do that, Morgan.' She blinked faster. 'But thank you, so very much.'

'I know I didn't, but I wanted to.' He paused in the doorway. 'I'll have a cuppa as a thank you, if you're making yourself one.'

'Ha.' She instantly relaxed. 'Bossy, much?'

'Always.' Chuckling, he grinned playfully.

'I'll get to it then, still two sugars?'

'Yup, a man can never have enough sweetness.' His laughter wrapped around her like a familiar hug.

* * *

Nightfall had arrived at Savage Acres, and the crickets and frogs were in chorus with one another after a fleeting sunshower had carried the eventful day to an end. The encroaching night air had an edge to it, unsettling Morgan's already frazzled nerves. He was closer to his past than he'd ever been, and it felt surreal, daunting, confusing, and at the same time, it carried the promise of a new start, a clean slate where hopefully a nice friendship could form with Jess.

Against all odds, it had really happened.

Jess Sabatini was back.

Here.

With Roberto and Shanti over at the cottage with Jess, even though he'd been invited to join them for a takeaway dinner of pizza, he'd decided to stay home. Not only because he wanted to give the three of them time to catch up, but he needed time to catch up with his own churning emotions – as well as give himself a stern talking-to. There was no going back to what he and Jess used to be. There was way too much turbulent water beneath that bridge. Trying to get back what they had once had would be perilous. He wouldn't make it. Having her here had seemed like a doable notion at the time. But realistically the ex-love of his life was way more than he bargained for.

When he'd first caught sight of her amid the sea of faces, the intensity of feeling as if *he* was the one arriving home had shaken him to his core. And her eyes, with all the years that had passed them by, he'd gone and forgotten just how magnetic the green windows to her soul were. Hopefully, he'd hidden the poignant sensation coursing through him well enough. Because he didn't want her knowing he still felt anything other than friendly towards her. The crushing pain of their break-up was seared into him. Forever. Once bitten, twice shy. There'd be no getting back up on that horse – it had long ago bolted. He was every broken-hearted analogy and every sad country song. And he loathed the fact. Wished he could find a way to move past it. Wished he could move on with one of the local women who had made their fancy for him known, and made a life, had a family. But he just couldn't bring himself to. He couldn't find the key that opened his heart up again. And no woman deserved to be loved lukewarmly.

Even so, he did hold the belief that with the amount of time that had passed them by, giving them both the space to grow and heal, they could move past their past. But then again, his gut was telling him that he had no control over the outcome of this situation, or what would come of her being here. And not having control of the reins scared him. What he did know without a shadow of doubt was that since Jess had left, and he'd put all the broken parts of himself back together, he'd made damn sure that he was always in control of his life, and he liked it that way. Making himself unavailable, impenetrable, somewhat stand-offish, had saved him a whole world of drama, headaches and heartbreak. It had also cost him – his unfulfilled dream of becoming a father was a deep regret. At thirty-four there was still time, but the reality of it never coming to fruition was closing in on him.

Releasing his deathlike grip on the top railing, he straightened. He didn't want to go down that same old road of self-pity again. He'd travelled its potholes and bumps way too many times, and he knew all too well it only led to devastating dead ends. Flexing his fingers back to life, he briefly squeezed his eyes closed and took a breath as an explosion of riotous laughter carried on the night air. It was coming from the cottage and straight over to him. Although he didn't feel comfortable within himself to join in, he couldn't help but be happy for the reunion of loved ones. If only he could have included himself in the equation, but he was no longer part of the Sabatini *family*, in the true sense of the word.

Wandering over to where Teeny had curled up on the day bed, he sunk down beside his doggy pal. With his head resting on his paws, Teeny acknowledged him with a kind-eyed, brow-scrunched stare, one that spoke of just how much he understood how Jess being here was affecting his human. His unwavering compassion meant one hell of a lot.

'I know, bud, I know.' Morgan gave his mate a tender pat. 'Only a couple of weeks, and I'll be back to myself in no time, I promise.'

Yeah right, who are you trying to kid, Savage, Teeny or yourself?

Morgan shook his head. Sweet, sassy, Jessica Sabatini. He'd always been able to read her heart and soul like a book, although now, with her substantial walls up, not so much. But a person rarely changed *that* radically. Leopards, spots, and all of that. In the book of her life his referential bookmark was between the pages of way back when. He knew that. And in nine years, he was certain there'd been a hell of a lot of new threads, plot twists, black moments and unexpected turns added to her story. Nevertheless, just one look at her, with that cute smile and scattering of freckles over her elfin nose – well, hot damn, their story had all came flooding back. The heartache. The hurt. The happiness. The powerful love that they'd shared. It was all still there, faded and hazy in parts, but definitely there.

In a flicker of a moment, between his quickened breaths, he was right back there, early in the morning of their wedding day, experiencing all the feelings that came with imagining her as his wife. He wanted to get a firm grip on the images, and hold each still, so he could reminisce, but with one forced deep inhalation came the painful memory of Enzo and Julie's fatal accident, and just like a mirage, the happy memories rippled then hovered, before he forcibly grabbed hold of the bittersweet sensation and shoved it back to where he'd hidden it for all these years. He didn't need to go over stale emotions.

No effing way!

What he did need was to get a grip on now, today, reality, and face up to it. They'd had their chance, and they'd missed it. End of story. There was none of this happily-ever-after nonsense on the cards for them. He'd become habituated to his heartbreak, had learnt to live with the echoing emptiness she'd left within his heart. So it should be a cinch to do it for a couple of weeks when he'd been able to endure the hurt for almost a decade. There'd be no chance of a sequel to their tragic love story. Neither of them was crazy enough to pen that. And even if she was, he sure as hell wasn't.

CHAPTER
5

The new day dawned mighty bright through the open curtains, much to Jess's exasperation. Not that she could point the finger at Mother Nature. It was all on her, being woken up so early. If she hadn't played a big part in guzzling three bottles of red wine with Shanti and Roberto, she might have closed the blackout blind before faceplanting into the plush mattress sometime after midnight. Hazy memories of them dancing around the lounge room to Dolly Parton's 'Jolene' made her chuckle, then wince when her head pounded in a snappy retort. Rolling onto her side, she eyed an empty pizza box alongside her strewn clothes as she tried to encourage her body and mind to life. There was a lot to be done over the coming week in preparation for the wedding. Just thinking about the list Shanti had shown her made her instantly weary. Florist, dressmaker, baker, good lord she might as well add in the candlestick maker too, because somewhere on the list of to-dos was the decor shop to finalise the table decorations.

Drawing in a deep breath, she wiggled her fingers and toes, then stretched her arms above her head. She could hear the distant chick-chick-woosh of sprinklers along with the whinny-chatter of horses. Both enjoyable sounds, and ones she hadn't heard in many years. She hadn't had the pleasure of a colossal backyard since living in Florence, and horses were only ever seen hauling carriages of people along the cobblestone streets around the Duomo.

After a few deep breaths and her eyelids finally becoming lighter, she glanced at the bedside clock and adrenaline fired like bullets through her vino-clogged veins. So much for it being bright and early, as she'd wrongly assumed. Holy moly, it was almost ten. Kicking the covers off then heaving herself out of bed, she wandered over to the bay windows and shoved both open. The day smacked her in the face, nice and bright. Blinking faster, she rubbed her eyes. The cloudless sky was a brilliant blue, and the fresh scent of untainted earth promised a beautiful spring day. Just the sight of Morgan's extensive property made her hangover a little less hungover, although the aftermath of her drinking wasn't going anywhere fast. A strong coffee and something to soak up the alcohol remnants, that's what she needed to help kick it in the butt.

So, deciding to nourish herself before having a steaming hot shower, she shuffled down the hallway of the cottage while tugging her knotty hair up and into a messy bun. A quick glance into the lounge room confirmed they'd mostly cleaned up the night before, and she was relieved she didn't have to contend with a mess now. Passing the black-and-white aerial shot of Savage Acres in its heyday, the very one that used to hang on the wall in the homestead, she paused to admire the family treasure. It reminded her of the days when she, Roberto, Shanti and Morgan used to spend every waking hour outside, exploring the countryside with tousled hair, mud-splattered clothes and the widest of smiles. If only they could turn back time. What she'd give to be able to feel the freedom of that again. And to have Chiara experience growing up like that – well, that would be magical.

Sighing, she straightened her skew-whiff pyjamas as she headed towards the kitchen for a much-needed hit of caffeine. Jet lag really did suck. As did the adverse result of a long-overdue catch-up with her brother and best friend. Too many hours of being crammed into two consecutive planes, as well as dealing with the time difference, was bound to take a toll. Factor in way too many glasses of wine and overly salty nutrient-deficient food, and it was no wonder she felt like death warmed up. With no concrete plans for the day given that Roberto and Shanti were still dealing with their flooded house, she supposed she should just go with the flow of it, and see where it took her, or didn't. Either way, she wasn't fussed. A rest day was probably a good idea. Tomorrow she'd be hitting the ground running as the wedding planning resumed.

Ten minutes later, taking her coffee and peanut butter on toast out to the balcony, she was greeted by a very eager Teeny. Catapulting across the driveway, all legs and paws, he headed down the garden pathway and skidded to a stop at the bottom of the steps, his big brown eyes wide and his tongue lolling out to one side as he panted like billy-o.

'Hey there, buddy.' She tapped her leg, welcoming him up the stairs. 'Come on, come and say hi then.'

He did so with enthusiasm, and after she raised her hand to stop him from bowling her over, Teeny sat politely on his rump at her side, with his leaf-laden tail swishing back and forth over her bare feet.

'You look like you've been up to no good, mister.' She ruffled his ears, cackling at the state of his dirty schnozzle. 'Whatever have you been sticking that nose of yours into, huh?' A whiff of something rotten was her swift reply. Swishing the intrusive air away, she screwed her face up. 'My goodness, Teeny, you reek to high heaven.' She pinched her nose. 'How about we go for a wander, and let you air out a bit.'

Leaving her cuppa on the railing, she took her toast with her and munched away as she and Teeny strolled around the outskirts of the cottage. It made her heart ache to know this would have been her and Chiara's home, but she couldn't dwell on the sensation, for it would have her crumbling to the ground in tears. Looking left to right, the sheer scope of the horse-dotted paddocks along with a mob of moseying cattle up the rise left her speechless. It had been far too long since she'd immersed herself in the Australian countryside, and she wished with all her heart that she could be sharing the experience with Chiara. Her little girl would adore it here, she was certain of it. The sun-kissed landscape that Morgan called home was like the pot of gold at the end of the rainbow. It was also the destination the two of them had never reached together. The very thought of what they could have had stabbed at her heart again. They would have been so happy together. That was a given with the love they'd shared.

Hindsight was a royal pain in the butt.

Reaching the fence line at the side of the cottage, she turned and looked back. Dappled sunlight danced across the manicured lawn and the gentle breeze played the wind chimes dangling from the corner of the balcony. Turning to her right, she looked towards the two-storey homestead with its enveloping verandahs shaded by wide wraparound awnings. The blooming gardens had evidently had quite a bit of love poured into them. Just as his mum had been when she'd called the house her home, it was nice to see how house-proud Morgan was. And that pride most certainly extended to his land, too. Every nook and cranny she could see was preened to perfection, and all the buildings were glowing with tender loving care. How he found the time between here and his job with the RFDS, she hadn't a clue. But she commended him, tenfold, for achieving such a mammoth feat.

Lost in thought until the rumble of a four-wheeler motorbike caught her attention, she spun to see Morgan heading in her direction, looking bright and handsome as ever. Oh god, she could only imagine the state she looked. Abandoning her bun, she ruffled her hair into what she hoped was an artful tumble of silky locks. If only she could have caught her reflection, she would have been mortified, she was sure of it.

'Hi.' She offered a quick wave.

'Hey, Jess.' Morgan pulled to a stop at the other side of the fence and Teeny met him there. 'Bit of a rough night?' The engine silenced when he turned the key.

She feigned ignorance. 'No, why?' Desperate to smooth out her crumpled linen pyjamas, she instead stuffed her hands into the pockets.

He stepped off the bike, then leant in, a cheeky grin on his lips as he plucked a leaf from her hair. 'Looks to me like you've been rolling around in the garden.'

'Oh, ha ha, I'm not sure where that came from.' Oh no, she was Teeny's doppelganger. 'Oh, hang on.' She suddenly recalled Roberto waltzing her down the path when their lift back home arrived in the form of the township's one and only taxi. 'Ahhh, that's right, my two left feet caught me off guard when Roberto decided it was time to teach me some tango moves so I could wow the dance floor at their wedding.'

'Right.' Morgan grinned then chuckled. 'I would've liked to have seen that, but then again, I might get a repeat performance at the wedding.'

'Ha, yeah, last night's tango wouldn't be one of my finest moments.' She was alarmed at how comfortable she was in this dazzling man's company, even when she was bedraggled and under the weather. 'And no, there'll be no drunken dancing on their special day.' She gave him a cheesy grin, one she mentally slapped herself for. 'Come to think of it, why didn't you join us last night, Morgan?' She tipped her head a little, waiting for his delayed response.

'Oh,' he said, shifting from boot to boot. 'I wanted to give you three time to yourselves.'

'Okay, that was nice of you.' The muscles of his jaw were the only giveaway that he was grappling with some strong emotions. Even so, she didn't want him to feel excluded from the group that used to be inseparable, so she hastily added, 'Next time, though, you have to join us.'

'I don't *have* to do anything, Jess.' He looked instantly apologetic for his snappy response. 'Sorry, I didn't mean it to come out so …' he floundered, and he sucked in a breath.

'Crotchety.' She finished his sentence. 'Grumpy, grouchy.' Planting a smile on her face, she made sure to say it playfully, hoping it would entice some healthy banter.

Remaining silent, he briefly turned his downtrodden gaze to her, instantly searing through the protective wall she'd built and right into her soul. And in between her shortened breaths, she could feel his heartbreak, and she knew instinctively that most of it was due to her. And she hated herself for it.

'Grouchy sums it up.' He half smirked.

'I'm sorry, I didn't mean to come across harsh.' Talk about royally putting her foot in it. 'I was just playing around.'

'You've never been one to beat around the bush, Jess, and I am being a bit of a grump.' He shook his head and sighed. 'I'm the one that's sorry. It's no excuse, but I didn't sleep well, and I've just spotted a gaping hole in the new fence, thanks to my cantankerous new-to-the-crew stud bull, so now my day is going to be spent doing things I didn't plan for, instead of focusing on the mountain of things I should be getting done.' He rolled his eyes. 'So much for having a month off, hey.'

'All good, Morgan, there's no need to apologise.' Noting the black rings beneath his eyes, and the slump in his shoulders, she realised he did look exhausted, and she felt for him. 'Would you like me to come and give you a hand to fix it?'

'Oh, nah, but thanks for the offer.' His downtrodden expression faded. 'You shouldn't have to work on your holiday, Jess.'

'I don't mind getting my hands dirty one little bit.' She shrugged at his look of scepticism. 'Honestly, it'll give me something constructive to do, instead of sitting around twiddling my thumbs, and besides, two sets of hands are better than one, right?'

He took a breath, regarding her. 'Yeah, seeing as you seem keen, a helping hand would be great, thanks.' His charming smile broke and spread. 'And while we're both being honest, I'd welcome a human sidekick for a bit, rather than this scallywag who does nothing but get up to mischief.' He looked to Teeny, now leaning up against his leg with his doggy eyes glued to him. 'You're all about fun and adventures, aren't you, bud?'

Teeny responded with a hearty woof.

Jess smiled at their exchange. 'Do I have time to grab a quick shower?'

'Of course. I'll go and chuck the tools we need into the Troopy, and make us some lunch to take, and then I'll be back to grab you in about half-a, does that work for you?'

'Yes, groovy as, I'll be ready and waiting.'

And true to her word, she was, five minutes earlier than promised. As for Morgan, he was right on time, as always. Meeting him, she climbed into the passenger seat, and went to tug her seatbelt on.

'We're only going half a k or so up yonder, so no need for that, Jess.' He chuckled. 'Unless you don't trust my driving, that is.'

'No, it's nothing like that.' She'd never sat in a car without a seatbelt since her parents' deaths, nor would she ever, no matter where she was, or how safe someone's driving was. 'But if you don't mind, I'd rather wear it.'

'Fair enough, you do you.' He pulled a casual 'whatever' face then turned the Troopy around. 'I suppose you're used to having to belt up in Italy, hey; driving city streets would turn anyone into a bit of a city slicker.'

'I do belt up over there, yes, but it's not because I've become citified, Morgan.' Feeling annoyingly misunderstood, she took a cautious step into uncomfortable territory. 'It's because of my parents' deaths that I wear it.' She said it far too bluntly to come across as casual as he had, and she instantly felt bad for doing so.

'Oh, crap, yeah, sorry.' He shook his head as though mad at himself. 'I didn't even think of that being the reason why.'

'It's all good.' She flashed him a smile. 'It's easy to let slip after so many years.'

'Not in the slightest, Jess, I promise you that.' Heading up a steep rise, he changed gears. 'I think of Enzo and Julie quite often.'

Jess found it odd he called both her parents by their first names, when he'd always called them her mum and dad, but she shrugged the thought off. 'I still miss them both so much.' She sighed forlornly. 'If only we had more than one set of parents, maybe I wouldn't have felt like I'd lost my entire world when they died.'

He remained silent, but the look in his eyes when he briefly turned in her direction let her know just how deeply he understood her, and how compassionate he was about her loss. She returned his gesture with a sad smile, stopping herself before she said any more on the topic of her mum and dad's deaths. Sucking in a breath, she clasped her hands in her lap. Why was she suddenly so eager to pour her heart out, when she'd kept her pain holed up for all these years? She hadn't even wanted to open up like this to Salvatore in all the years they were together. Was it being in Morgan's presence that commanded her to speak the truth of her heart? She hoped not, because he might be shocked to discover what she hid there.

And that would be really bad, when she wasn't certain of the truth herself, yet.

Rising panic about him uncovering her secret before she was ready to dig it up herself fuelled her into action. Maybe she should say something off topic, talk about something light, like small-talkers liked to do. But bearing witness to his rigid profile, the clenching of his jaw, and the way he was gripping the steering wheel so tightly his knuckles were white, she decided the best course of action right now was to say nothing. So, apart from Teeny panting in the back seat, silence rode with them. It was obvious to her that Morgan, just like her, was keeping something buried deep down inside his soul, too, something that might have a hell of a lot to do with her. Was it residual heartache from their long-ago break-up, or was it something from the present?

Whatever it was, she couldn't let her curiosity get the better of her.

Because soon enough, whether she liked it or not, she may need him to understand her choice of silence. And if that was to be the case, she prayed he was going to forgive her for it.

* * *

Late that afternoon, with his foot flat to the floor, and the sun appearing to be resting atop the mountain ranges, Morgan manoeuvred the winding road as he thought back to the few hours Jess had spent with him, fixing the fence and munching down on corned beef and pickle sandwiches. Unlike the first few minutes in the Troopy, on their way across the paddocks, when he'd silently battled his guilt at keeping such a secret from her, they'd managed to keep the conversation light, fun, easy. As she'd done as promised and gotten her hands dirty, he'd enjoyed her company, a little too much for his liking. Nine years clearly hadn't proved long enough to prepare him for laying his eyes on her again, let alone being around her so much. But even though the attraction was still there, for him at least, he'd rather walk through a blazing fire than risk heartbreak a second time round.

What in the hell had he been thinking, agreeing to her staying in the cottage?

He hadn't been in his right mind, obviously, because this unanswerable question kept circling as he momentarily glanced up from the white lines he'd been chasing in his classic candy-apple red 1968 HK Holden Monaro, to see an eagle seeking the same sort of freedom he was right now in the cloudless azure sky. In theory, he'd made himself believe he could pull this off. Roberto and Shanti had always been there for him, and he wanted to be there for his mates. What was two weeks in the grand scheme of things? But in reality, keeping such a life-altering secret from her was killing him from the inside out. Annie needed to seriously rethink her decision to remain tight-lipped because he was sick and tired of suffering beneath the weight of her cloak-and-dagger attitude towards the past. What she expected of him was morally wrong. Enzo and Julie were gone. And although he partially understood her vow of silence to them, the situation seemed to be evolving. Annie Sabatini needed to do the same. If she didn't, she'd leave him no other option other than to do it for her. And he was sure as hell that wasn't going to end well, especially for him. Not that he cared about himself; this was all about Jess knowing what she rightfully should. That's what he needed to keep reminding himself.

Hugging the edge of the sheer drop into the Pacific Ocean beneath, he accelerated out of the corner and headed towards home. He'd been right in deciding he needed this drive, and another night in, over joining Jess and Annie at the cottage for dinner. Driving his classic car always gave him a clearer head, a sense of calm. He needed to hang on tight to the sensation. Just knowing of the elephant that would be sitting in the dining room of the cottage tonight made his moral compass spin backwards. He'd already been way too lenient. Way too understanding of one side of the story. It was high time the truth came out. He contemplated this as the V8 engine ate up the home stretch.

An hour later, he straightened from the sun-dappled day bed when he spotted fine dust rising up from the end of the driveway. Annie was incoming, and he needed to get to her before Jess did. Just knowing what he was about to say, if he hopefully got the fleeting chance, a sick feeling washed over him. Annie had clearly stated on more than one occasion that she wasn't about to budge on her decision, but he wasn't giving up. Especially not now Jess was so close he could reach out and touch her, if he chose to. Somehow, some way, he'd get Annie to see sense. He had to. So, taking steps towards where she'd just pulled up beneath the big old gum tree, he clenched and unclenched his hands as he pushed his growing anxiety aside.

Spotting him as she stepped from the driver's side, Annie offered him a warm, wide smile. 'Oh, hey, Morgan.'

'Hey.' He met her in the shade. 'You got a minute?'

'Of course.' Shutting the door, she slung her handbag over her shoulder. 'What's up?'

'I can't do this.' He spat the words out.

She eyed him cautiously. 'Do what, exactly?'

Morgan cleared his throat. 'Not tell her.'

'Morgan, please stop, we've already spoken about this, over and over again.' Her gaze pierced through him. 'And like I have told you every time, you have to try and find a way to keep your mouth well and truly shut, for all our sakes.'

'No, Annie, I do not need to keep my mouth well and truly shut.' He'd begrudgingly agreed to stay mute before, many years ago, on the understanding that Annie would eventually tell Jess, and Roberto and Shanti, after Enzo and Julie's deaths, when she went and visited Jess in Italy, twice. But every single time, Annie had found excuses, reneged, backed out. This time around, he was going to stand his ground.

'Yes, Morgan Savage.' With her warm smile well and truly gone, Annie's resolute gaze narrowed. 'You damn well do.'

Well aware he was poking a mama bear with a stick, he resigned himself to the fact that he had to follow his gut, or risk nobody ever knowing the facts, other than him and Annie. And he simply couldn't live with that, or take such information to his grave like Enzo and Julie had. Because he knew deep down in his heart, in the long run, that Jess would benefit from knowing the truth. In fact, something told him it would make her life a whole lot better, and might even lure her back here, to Silverton Shores, where she and her daughter belonged.

'Well, Morgan, say something?' Annie's tone was icy cold.

But Morgan refused to appease her. So their muted stand-off lasted a few more seconds before her sharp-eyed gaze pierced through his cool calm persona. 'Please, I beg you, don't go down that road, because it's not going to end well, for any of us.'

'I beg to differ, Annie, for everyone's sakes, you have to tell the truth and make this right.'

She tipped her head, as if trying to understand him. 'Okay, you tell me how this is going to change anything?'

Morgan couldn't believe her ignorance. 'Oh my god, Annie, it'll change everything.'

'Pfft, yeah, for the worse.' She rolled her eyes. 'Jessie will hate me, and I wouldn't blame her in the slightest.'

'Yes, she'll be upset at first.' He raised a hand and rested it on Annie's arm. 'But I know, in time, she'll forgive you.'

Annie faltered, but only briefly. 'How can you be so sure about that, huh?'

'We both know she's a kind-hearted person.' And Jess was, to her own detriment at times.

'You're right, Jessie does have that, but even the tender-hearted have a breaking point, wouldn't you agree?'

He knew she was referring to his rebellious ways after Jess had skipped town, but he wasn't about to rise to the bait. 'Can you just think about it a bit more, Annie, please?'

'I have thought about it, Morgan, and I'm not going to change my mind, so just drop it, please, because this conversation is getting mighty old.'

'Annie, hey, sis.' Jess's voice carried along with her racing footfalls. 'You're here!'

'Jessie!' Annie circled around him and met Jess with open arms. 'It's so good to see you!'

Morgan watched the pair embrace tightly, his heart squeezing tighter still as Jess wiped tears from her eyes. If only she knew …

Jess threw a glance in his direction. 'Are you sure you don't want to join us for my famous ragu tonight, Morgan?'

'No, but thanks.' He forced a beaming smile. 'You two enjoy your catch-up.'

'Oh, we most certainly will.' Wrapping her arm over Jess's shoulder, Annie all but dragged her away before he could say any more or change his mind about the offer of dinner.

All he could do was offer a wave as he watched them walk away. Annie wasn't out of the woods yet, because he wasn't giving up. One way or another, Jess was going to learn the truth.

CHAPTER 6

Bending, Jess popped her teaspoon into the dishwasher as she enthusiastically listened to Chiara's sweet voice.

'Nonno let me do his make-up, and he looks really funny, Mum. I wish you could see him.' Chiara's cackling laughter carried through the phone, as did her nonno's echoing chuckles, and both softly landed in Jess's heart.

'I wish I could, too, love, sorry the video on my phone doesn't seem to be working.' She wandered into the lounge room with her warm cup of Milo, and carefully sank down on the couch. 'Make sure you take a photo of him and send it to me, won't you.'

'I will as soon as we hang up,' Chiara said with unbridled enthusiasm. 'I told him he could wash it off when I was finished, but he said I did such a great job he didn't want to.'

'He's a funny one, our Nonno.' Pressing the phone to her ear, Jess had to use every bit of strength not to burst into inconsolable tears. 'I miss you both heaps, sweetie.'

'We miss you, too, Mum, soooo much.'

Jess could picture Chiara, arms and eyes wide as she proclaimed just how much she was missed. 'Only twelve sleeps, and I'll be back home with you.'

'Yay!' Chiara's squeal echoed. 'Then we can make my chocolate birthday cake!'

Smiling into the phone, Jess nodded as she imagined Chiara turning double digits. 'Yes, we sure can, and then we'll eat it for breakfast, lunch and dinner.'

'Oh my gosh, really?' Chiara sucked in a breath. 'Do you really promise?'

'Yes, it's your tenth birthday, so I *really* promise.' And she meant it. 'I should let you go so you can go and have your dinner before it gets cold, sweetie.'

'Okay, please give Uncle Roberto and Aunty Shanti a big hug from me.'

'I will.' Jess gritted her teeth against a sob. 'And make sure you do the same from me to Nonno and get him to give you a hug back from me.'

'But who's going to hug you from me, Mum?'

'Oh, my sweet girl.' The insistent tears were now coming thick and fast, and she was helpless to stop them. 'You always say the most beautiful things.' She sniffed. 'I'll make sure Aunty Shanti and Uncle Roberto give me a group cuddle from you.'

'That's a great idea.' Chiara sighed a little sadly. 'I love you to the moon and back.'

'I love you to the moon and back, too, my darling.' She had to get off the phone, now, before she broke completely. 'We will speak again tomorrow, if you're not too busy having lots of fun with Nonno, that is.'

'I'm never, ever, having too much fun to stop and talk to you, silly.'

'You're so beautiful, my darling Ciara, I love you.'

'Ciao, Mum, I love you sooooo much.'

With the call ending, Jess took the time to sob her heart out. Ten minutes later, she stood, dropped her empty mug into the dishwasher, went to the bathroom and stepped into the shower. In a little bit, Roberto was picking her up and she was spending the day with him while Shanti did some of the wedding errands with her mum. It would be a nice distraction from her pressing homesickness for Chiara, and she was also looking forward to spending some one-on-one time with her brother.

* * *

'Here you go, sis.' Roberto plonked her overdue lunch in front of her. 'And you better enjoy it because I've been slaving over the stove for hours to make that.'

'Ha, yeah, whatever.' Jess chuckled and rolled her eyes. 'It looks delicious, thanks, bro.' Starving, she wolfed down her ham, cheese, tomato and onion toasted sandwich while Roberto did the same across the bench. 'The simple food is always the best, hey.' She dabbed her lips with a piece of paper towel, then took a swig from her glass of creaming soda.

His mouth full, Roberto nodded. 'It sure is,' he garbled.

Silence fell as they both inhaled their food.

Taking their plates over to the sink, Roberto rinsed them then popped each one into the dishwasher. 'Right, little sis, I have a bit of a surprise for you.'

Stifling a soft-drink burp, she spoke through her hand. 'You do?'

'Uh-huh, so come on, follow me.' Wandering past her, he motioned her with a swing of his hand.

Shooting to her feet, Jess scurried after him, through the cosy lounge room and out the front door. 'What is it?' She was both excited and nervous.

Turning to her, he tapped his nose, then placed a finger against his lips.

'Oh, come on, you know how much I hate surprises.' *Like when I arrived at the airport to Morgan ...*

'Yes, I know, but trust me, you're going to love this one.' He stopped short of the door to Shanti's mum's backyard garage. 'Ready?'

'I don't know.' She jiggled on the spot as she watched him shove the sliding door upwards, then tug a sheet from the top of what she suspected was a car of some sort.

'Tada!' Roberto cried out as his hands went wide.

Her mum's old 1972 Volkswagen Beetle gleamed back at her, its fresh coat of Marina Blue paint making it look like it had just been driven out of the showroom. 'Oh my gosh, Roberto, when, how?' She blinked through her tears.

'She's pretty damn sexy, hey.' Lightly running his fingers down the bonnet, he glanced up and flashed her an almighty grin. 'The only vintage car restorer in town has been working on her for almost two years now, and only finished the restoration last week, just in time for the wedding.'

'I can't believe it. He's done such an amazing job.' Taking slow steps around to the back end, she shook her head. 'It looks brand new.' She blinked back tears. 'Mum would have loved it.'

'I wouldn't have let anyone other than old Johnno work on it, because knowing Mum and Dad like he did, through the church, he knows how precious it is, to all of us.' Roberto's smile faded a little, as if he was regrouping spilt emotions. 'Mum always said she wanted you to have it one day, so …' He handed her the keys. 'She's all yours while you're home, except for the wedding day, when you, Annie and Shanti get to be chauffeur-driven to the ceremony in it.'

'Really?' Eyes wide, and with a hand on her racing heart, she stared at him.

'Yes, really.'

Her breath caught on an exhale as sweet memories of them heading out as a family, squished up in her mum's beloved car, to the catchy tunes of the Beatles, sank in bone-achingly deep. Heavy tears gathered and tumbled. 'Oh my gosh, I'm such a sook.' She fanned her face, smiling through her tears of joy and hurt – it was a bittersweet moment, poignant in its intensity.

'Just make sure you take it nice and easy around the bends, sis, because she doesn't handle like our new cars do.'

'I most certainly will, thank you, Roberto.' Wrapping her arms around him, she squeezed him nice and tight. 'You're the bestest brother ever.'

'Ha, and don't you forget it.' After a few more cherished seconds, he untangled from her. 'Now come on, in you get.' He opened the driver's door for her. 'I want to see what you look like behind the wheel.'

'Okay, here goes.' Gliding onto the shiny seat, she wrapped her fingers around the slender steering wheel, recalling all the nights she and Morgan had held hands and kissed in the front seats while parked up at the drive-in cinema.

Roberto leant on the windowsill. 'It suits you, Jessie.'

'It does?'

'Yes.' Tapping the sill, he straightened. 'Now be gone with you, so I can go and suffer in silence while Shanti and her mum make me pick what colour napkins we need.'

'Ha, good luck with that.'

'Thanks.' His brows rose and he grinned. 'Don't you worry, she'll have you suffering in silence soon enough.'

Jess tipped her head, grinning at her brother's overly serious expression. 'I think it's fun, planning a wedding.'

'You would, you're a girl.' He threw his hands up in the air in defeat.

'Deep breaths, bro, you got this.' She grinned as she revved the grumbling engine to life. 'I'll catch you tomorrow.'

'You will, bye, sis.'

'Toodle-oo.' Waving goodbye, she carefully made her way down the short driveway.

Her warm smile slipped as soon as she turned onto the highway and she found herself having to juggle between changing gears while being at the helm of a classic car. On high alert, she turned the stereo down so she could think straight. The last thing she wanted was to put a scratch on the paintwork, or worse, so she kept her keen focus on the road. Drawing in a breath, she counted to five, then released it. Then repeated. Several times. Minutes later, she drove through town, and in two shakes of a lamb's tail was out the other side and heading towards Morgan's place.

Her safe haven.

Her home.

For now.

If only things had been different, and it had been hers forever.

You really need to stop thinking like this, Jess!

So, instead, she tried to think about her night ahead with Shanti and Annie. If someone asked her, right now, to choose between a drop-dead gorgeous man like Morgan Savage, and spending a night on the couch with a tub of ice-cream and a line-up of chick flicks with her nearest and dearest gal pals, she would choose the latter.

Three hours and forty-five minutes later, she was cosied up beside Shanti on the couch, doing just that when the front door swung open. Coming off back-to-back shifts at the hospital, Annie traipsed into the cottage, dropped her bag with a weary sigh, and after pecking Jess and Shanti on the cheek, gratefully accepted a towel and headed straight for the shower. Wanting to take care of her big sister, Jess busied herself making a hot chocolate that was thick enough to stand a spoon up in, then she added lashings of Baileys Irish Cream, Annie's favourite.

'Something's smelling mighty nice in here.' As she padded into the kitchen, Shanti's effervescent energy filled the room.

Stirring the pot of ragu she had meant to make the previous night, before she and Annie decided on Chinese takeaway instead, Jess glanced over her shoulder. 'I hope it tastes as yummy as it smells.'

'I bet it tastes even better than that.' Springing on her tippy toes, Shanti plonked herself onto the kitchen bench. 'Thank goodness all the flood repairs are almost sorted now, so I can turn my full attention back to the wedding.' She reached for the suncatcher dangling in front of the window above the sink, her engagement ring catching the last of the daylight pouring through.

'My goodness, woman.' Jess pretended to shield her eyes. 'Stop waving that thing around, or you're going to blind someone.'

Staring at the rock on her finger, Shanti smiled from the heart. 'He's a keeper, your brother, that's for sure.'

'Uh-huh, he sure is.' Taking Shanti's hand, Jess took a long, admiring look at the detail of the princess cut diamond. 'I tried to tell you back in the day that he liked you, didn't I?'

'Yes, I know you did.' Shanti's smile was a little coy. 'I kind of knew he had a crush on me, I just wasn't ready to admit it then.' Her soft gaze filled with perception. 'Kind of like you and Morgan nowadays, wouldn't you agree, Miss Sabatini?'

'No, I would not.' Jess dropped Shanti's hand like a hot cake and spun away so her best friend couldn't see the truth in her statement. 'Morgan and I just have a connection from way back, that's all.'

Shanti prodded Jess's hip with her big toe. 'Here, grab hold of this.'

Jess smirked in her direction. 'What do I want to grab your foot for?'

'Then you can pull my leg while you keep telling yourself such nonsense.' When Jess refused a response, Shanti tipped her head, eyeing her kindly. 'Come on, Jess, he's never stopped loving you, and you've never stopped loving him.' She sighed and smiled a little sadly. 'If you can't admit it to yourself, at least admit it to me.'

'I honestly don't know how I feel about him.' Jess shrugged. 'Or how he feels about me.'

'Well, let me tell you that from where I'm sitting, I can see, and feel, the love you two shared even to this day.'

'I don't know about that, Shanti.'

It was Shanti's turn to shrug. 'I'll agree to disagree.' She hopped off the bench. 'Anyhoos, I'm going to nip to the loo, I'll be back in a sec to help with the rest of dinner.' And off she padded, leaving her sandalwood perfume oil lingering.

Plonking the sautéed carrots, onion and celery back into the pressure cooker, along with the seared oxtail, two bottles of thick sweet passata, and a decent chunk of butter, Jess locked the lid and set it to cook for forty-five minutes. Next, she busied herself setting the table as she thought about how nice it was to be back in Morgan's company. He'd certainly changed over the years, as had she, and that made things a little awkward at times, as did the lingering sense of the heartbreak she'd caused him all those years ago. She was sure it'd get easier day by day, but for now the shame she felt about having left him so broken plagued her. And while she was being honest with herself, so did the fact that she hadn't gone to her parents' resting places since the day they'd been placed into the earth. The very thought of doing so made her catch her breath. But it was something she needed to face. Pausing in the middle of the kitchen, she took a moment to steady herself as she made the decision to visit the cemetery while she was back here.

Able to move her feet again, she headed over to the cutting board and roughly chopped the handful of basil she'd plucked from Morgan's herb patch – with his blessing, of course. It would go in the ragu right before serving. Just like following a recipe that led to the perfect meal, one step at a time, bit by bit, she needed to take steps in the right direction, so she could get her life back on track. Starting from now, she needed to stop making excuses. Instead, she needed to take action, and she prided herself on the fact that once she'd made her mind up about something, she would do everything she could to follow through. No matter how tough it would be. Tomorrow was a chance for a fresh start, turning over a new leaf. Tomorrow she was going to face her fears. But for now, she was going to draw courage and comfort from her sister and best friend. She was going to encourage joy into her heart by living in the present and not in the past.

* * *

In the early hours of the morning, Jess found herself lying in the darkness, with the new day yet to hint at its arrival beneath the hem of the blackout curtains. She'd enjoyed her time with Shanti and Annie – they'd eaten dinner and dessert to bursting point and sensibly drank just one bottle of vino between them – but once they'd bid their goodnights around eleven, and she'd been left to her circling thoughts once again, sleep had basically eluded her. Tomorrow had arrived at today, and she'd made a promise to herself to turn the page, start anew, take steps in the right direction.

As weary as she was, as soon as she caught a glimpse of sunrise peeking into the room, she allowed it to lure her from the comfort of the doona cocooned around her. Anything to get away from her relentless contemplations. An hour later she was nursing a cup of Earl Grey tea on the day bed on the little back verandah of the cottage. The encouraging glimpse of blue sky at first light had now all but vanished, and the listless clouds had speedily turned dark and moody. But before she gave in to the broody weather and tucked herself inside the cottage all day long, it was time for her to get things on a roll.

Somehow, she managed to coax herself to her feet, into the shower, into some clothes and into her mum's Volkswagen. Before she knew it, she was easing off the accelerator, not because she needed to slow her speed, but because she needed to slow her racing heart. Having driven on autopilot, she was surprised to be pulling up out the front of the cemetery in what felt like the blink of an eye. Before she could change her mind, she slipped out of the driver's seat, shut the door, locked it, and turned to face her fears. As she caught sight of the headstones, her legs refused to go another step. Slowing her breath, she looked to the lush, green grass, manicured to within an inch of its life, sweeping out and over the landscape like a comfortable blanket.

I can do this.

I have to do this.

If not for me, then for Chiara, so I can be strong, resilient, healed.

Thinking it might make her a better mum if she could lighten her heavy heart was all the coaxing she needed. With one foot in front of the other, she wandered past the weeping willows. She dared not stop until she reached her destination. All the way she couldn't hear the sweet song of birds, or the mower off in the distance – instead all she could hear was the pounding of blood in her ears. Reaching the towering old gum tree that the mourning guests had long ago congregated beneath, everything came back into sharp clarity for her, including the scent of jasmine and the sounds of life. Standing between the final resting places of her mother and father, she reached out and ran her fingertips over the cold marble of the two headstones. Bright sunflowers were in the vases, blooms she was sure her brother and Annie had left on their fortnightly visit. And to think this was only her second time here. Tears stung as she felt pulled back to the horrible day that had changed her life forever. But as strong as the temptation was to tumble into the emotions of it all, she wouldn't allow the skeletons of her past to get a firm-fingered grip on her. She would remain firmly footed here. In the now. A different person. A hardened woman. A determined mother. A loving daughter.

Brushing her tears away, she stepped closer. 'I love you two, so much, and miss you more than ever.' Her words were whispered as she sank down and onto the grass, content to just sit here, for a little while, and maybe fill them both in on all they had missed while she was there.

After a few moments, with a heavy-hearted sigh, she said, 'How about I start at the beginning.'

She took a deep breath and began to speak. She told her parents about her struggles with motherhood, her disastrous marriage to Salvatore, and how broken she was when she found out he'd been sleeping around. She spoke of her fears of being a failure, her worries about not being able to provide for Chiara, and the test she'd sent in to finally find out who the father of her little girl was. She recounted the sleepless nights, the endless crying, the feeling of isolation and loneliness that sometimes overwhelmed her. She talked about her job, her nonno, and the beauty of Italy. She spoke about all the things she'd learnt since their passing, all the things she wished she'd told them before they were gone. And as she spoke and cried and laughed through her tears, the weight on her chest began to lift, and she felt a sense of peace settling in. Then as the shadows of the day lengthened, and began reaching for her outstretched legs, she realised she'd been carrying this burden alone for far too long, that she'd been trying to be strong for everyone else, without allowing herself to be vulnerable. But here, with her parents, she could be honest, she could be herself, she could be loved. And that, in itself, was one of the biggest steps, one of the biggest realisations, she'd ever had.

CHAPTER
7

Morgan's day had started at a sparrow's fart, before the sun had peeked over the mountains. Dreams of Jess having her way with him had replayed all night long. It exasperated him that even in sleep, she tempted him. Pent-up and frustrated after a lengthy sex drought, he'd hit his home gym and taken some frustration out on his punching bag. At noon he'd found himself helping to birth the newest addition to his herd of cattle, before allowing its moo-ma to bond with her new baby. It was now close to sundown, and he hadn't stopped for a breather all day long. Hadn't trusted himself to, for fear of collapsing into the couch and accidentally falling asleep. Now, feeling overloaded, and overworked, he laughed cynically at the fact that he was officially on annual leave as he eyed his glowing computer screen. So much for being able to kick back, catch up on sleep and rest his weary soul. Teetering on the edge of burnout wasn't on his agenda. He had to find a way to slow down, rest up and enjoy his rare days off. Maybe some time with Jess would be just what the doctor ordered.

Or would it?

Closing his laptop, he tried to rub the weariness from his eyes. He wasn't cut out for accounting, but it had to be done. He wasn't about to pay someone else to do it for him. Add in trying to wrestle images of Jess from his mind as he wrestled with spreadsheets and numbers, and he was fighting a losing battle. He'd gone out on a limb, and pushed himself out of his comfort zone, by having her stay here, and he just hoped and prayed he'd made the right decision.

Groaning, he gave in to his exhaustion. The office chair creaked beneath his weight as he rested back, laced his hands behind his head and sighed. No matter how hard he tried to ignore the attraction, Jess's heart-shaped face and bright green eyes got him every single time. She was a heady combination of drop-dead gorgeous and fiercely independent, yet also extremely fragile. A perfect package of woman that he innately wanted to love and protect. But he didn't have the right to, nor did he want to risk having his heart shattered again.

Closing his eyes, he tried to quell the burning ache for her. The day he'd gotten down on one knee and asked her to marry him, and she'd shrieked *yes yes yes*, he would've never believed he'd be here, very single, very broken, and very alone. And now the one true love of his life, the woman of his dreams, was back here, at his property, within his reach yet again, yet so very far away in the deepest sense. If only she'd open up. If only *he* could open up. Would things be different? *Could* they be different? Words had the capacity to really hurt, but silence – now that could send a man crazy. And it was doing exactly that. Every time he was around her, he sensed she was keeping something from him. And he wished she could tell him what it was, so she could allow him to help her through it. But then, who was he to talk when he was keeping something so shocking from her?

Huffing, he shook his head at his turbulent thoughts. He couldn't sit around, pining over what could have been or fantasising about what could be. He had errands to run in town before closing time. And as the saying went, time waited for no man. He needed to get a shift on. Straightening, he made his way out of the office, down the hallway, and outside. Striding towards his Troopy, he caught a glimpse of Jess through the cottage window. She was sitting at the dining table, hunched over a mug of coffee, staring out into the distance. He paused for a moment, watching her, feeling the familiar tug of desire in his chest. But then he squared his shoulders and reminded himself that his heart couldn't take a second beating.

He climbed into the driver's seat, turned the key, revved the engine to life, and headed down the driveway. Every place he passed on his way to the hardware store reminded him of her, of *them*. So many memories. So many happy times. Sometimes it was just the two of them, other times it was with their group of friends. The old movie theatre, where they'd sat in the back row, sharing popcorn, kisses and hand-holding. The Silverton Shores showgrounds, where they'd gone to watch visiting bands and devotedly attended the annual fair – she'd always end the night with a fluffy prize from the sideshow alley thanks to his shooting skills. Their high school where they'd had their graduation night – how proud he'd been to escort her. St Augustine's, where they were meant to become husband and wife. The cemetery, where they buried Enzo and Julie. His grip on the steering wheel tightened along with his heartstrings. She'd been his girlfriend, his best friend, his partner in crime, his confidante, his fiancée – and then he'd become her nothing. She had disappeared in a puff of smoke. Untouchable. Unreachable. As if she'd never existed.

Until now.

He should be over it, over her. But he wasn't. And if he were being absolutely honest with himself, he never would be. He loved her, goddamnit, and always would. It was a shame the same couldn't be said for her. She'd gotten over him. She'd moved on with her life. He had to build a bridge and get over it, over her. And he needed to spend more time with her to do that, while he had the chance to. Avoiding her when he could clearly wasn't working, so maybe he needed to try a different tactic. Decision made. He was going to ask her over for dinner, and hopefully she would accept.

An hour later, cursing beneath his breath, he stared at the rolling digits of the fuel bowser, willing it to speed up. Jess had texted him back with a *yes, that sounds lovely, thank you*. Even though it wasn't anywhere near being a date, he still wanted to make a lasting impression, and let her see what she'd missed out on. He didn't have the time to make a roast, but the next best thing was his juicy lamb chops. And just on sundown, the meaty scent of his local butcher's finest wafted from the oven as he turned the tray of rosemary potatoes and slices of butternut pumpkin on the shelf above.

'Helloooo.' Jess's voice carried from the front door.

'Coming,' he called back. 'Hey.' Loose auburn hair blew around her face, giving her a just-out-of-bed-after-being-ravished-all-night-long look. If only that were the case. 'You're right on time.' He pushed the flyscreen door open and she passed him a bottle of red wine. 'Thanks, but you didn't have to bring anything.'

'In Italy, it's a sin to arrive to someone's place for dinner without a gift, so …' She half shrugged, stepped in beside him and sniffed. 'Wow, something smells delicious.'

'Thanks.' She was blushing ever so slightly, and he liked to think it was because of him. 'I whipped us up an Aussie classic.'

'Mmm, I can smell that.' Her smile became warmer. 'Lamb is my absolute favourite.'

Gazing at her glossy lips, he wondered if her lip-gloss was flavoured. 'Me too.' Needing a distraction from her kissable mouth, he turned and took steps down the hallway with her padding beside him. 'Would you like to make use of the cool night and eat out on the back verandah?'

'That would be lovely.' Pausing at the oven, she peeked in. 'Oh my gosh, Morgan, I can't wait to tuck into this gorgeous food.'

'Good, it'll be ready in two shakes of a lamb's tail.' He grinned as he busied himself opening the wine bottle. 'See what I did there?'

'Uh-huh, so cheesy but also so funny.' She chuckled, shaking her head a little. 'Can I do anything to help?'

'You can grab two red wine glasses out of the cupboard over there, if you like.' He gestured in the general direction with a tip of his head.

'On it.' She sashayed over, reached up, grabbed two long-stemmed glasses, and returned. 'Here you go.'

'Thanks.' He poured two glasses, passed her one, then held his up for a toast. 'To happy days ahead.'

'Yes, to that.' She clinked her glass to his.

Taking a sip, he groaned in pleasure as the rich, velvety wine filled his mouth. He swallowed and closed his eyes, enjoying the warmth that spread through his body. When he opened them again, he saw her watching him with a coy smile on her glossy lips.

'What?' he asked, feeling a blush sneaking onto his cheeks.

'Nothing,' she said before taking another sip of wine. 'It's just, it looks like you're having a very intimate moment with that glass of wine.'

'Ha, not likely.' He chuckled and shook his head. 'It's just a very nice glass of red.'

'I can tell,' she replied, smiling over the top of her glass. 'I'm glad you like it so much.'

I like you even more ...

'Right, time to get this food plated up, so we can eat, hey,' he said hurriedly – anything to get away from those come-hither eyes of hers.

Minutes later, with plates and wine glasses in hand, they headed outside to the back deck with a jaw-dropping view of the surrounding bushland. Sitting at the table, they ate and chatted in comfortable companionship.

With her plate basically licked clean, Jess groaned and rested back. 'Now that, Morgan Savage, was one of the most delicious meals I've eaten in a long time.'

'You're just saying that.' He playfully waved her compliment off. 'I'm sure the food in Florence is top notch.'

'True, it is, but I miss wholesome Aussie food like you wouldn't believe.' She offered him a grateful kind of smile. 'And you cook it magnificently.'

'Well, thank you.' She'd so effortlessly caught his attention and wasn't letting go. He raised his second glass of wine to hers. 'And thank you for this amazing wine.'

'My pleasure, it's the very least I could do.' She leant in to gather the empty plates. 'As is the clearing up.'

'No, please, leave it. I'll do it later.' Standing, he flicked the overhead light off, allowing light from the twinkling stars to reach in further. 'For now, let's move to the comfier chairs and enjoy this incredible view, hey.'

'Sounds good to me.' She rose and followed him over to the swing chair, positioned nearer the railings, and sat. After a few moments, she sighed softly then said, 'I swear the stars burn so much brighter here than anywhere else in the world.'

'I have to agree, but then again, I'm biased.'

'Of course, you would be, and I can't blame you.' She cleared her throat. 'This place, the way you've put such love into it, is like paradise.'

'Thanks, Jess, it means a lot that you think so.'

She offered a small, sideways smile. 'You're very welcome.'

He caught the flash of heartbreak in her eyes before she dropped her gaze and veiled it with her lashes. There was a lot of water beneath the bridge, but by god he still cared, he still wanted to help her, he still l—

Don't go there, Savage …

'Is everything okay, Jess?'

Damn it, you just can't help yourself when it comes to her!

'Yes, and no.' She laced her fingers around her drawn-in knees, her bangles jingling as she hugged her legs to her chest. 'But isn't it like that for everyone?' His shoulders lifted in a tiny shrug. 'I mean, nobody's life is perfect, hey.'

'Yes, and no.' What else was he meant to say? 'Just so you know, I'm here, anytime, if you want to talk about anything.'

It seemed like she almost did, but then her lips pressed together, like she was clamping down on the secrets he was dying to coax from her, even though he knew he shouldn't.

'Sorry, I shouldn't be prying.' He had a sense he should leave her be, as most men likely would, but he couldn't leave her alone to deal with whatever was weighing on her beautiful heart.

'Don't apologise.' The shadows beneath her eyes seemed to darken, and he saw secrets hidden within her forest-green eyes. 'There's just some things I'd rather not talk about.'

'Yeah, I get that.' His heart was beating so damn hard, he swore she'd be able to hear it. 'I really do.' Suspended in time, old feelings rose up as they stared at each other for a long, breathless moment.

* * *

Caught up in all that made Morgan the wonderful man he was, Jess was experiencing all the feels. Fear, longing, uncertainty, closeness, security, vulnerability, and god forbid, love. With her eyes seized by his, and with everything around her stilled, hushed, she briefly considered what would happen if they gave in to whatever this was still between them, and kissed. And with the contemplation her cheeks heated, as did her heart. Then reality hit her smack bang in the chest. What was she doing? She wasn't some loved-up young woman anymore. First and foremost, she was a mum. She didn't have the liberty to throw caution to the wind. And she most certainly didn't have the right to live dangerously. But damn, the pull between them was palpable. The air felt charged, electric, and she couldn't deny the way her heart raced as he looked at her with those piercing blue eyes. She knew she should stop this before it went too far, before she lost herself in him all over again. But she couldn't bring herself to move, couldn't pull her gaze away from his.

He shifted ever so slightly, and their legs brushed together. It was then that she felt his warmth seep into her. Electricity buzzed around them like flittering fireflies. Her heart raced in her chest. She knew she should look away, but she couldn't. She wanted to kiss him, to feel his lips on hers again. It only felt like yesterday that they'd thrown all caution to the wind, only days before their wedding day, and made the most beautiful of love. And she missed the way his hands felt on her body and the way his voice sent shivers down her spine. She missed the way he made her feel so effortlessly loved, in every single way. But no matter how much she wanted this, wanted him, she couldn't give in. So she looked away, far, far away, so he couldn't read her mind, or feel her racing heart.

Swallowing the lump of emotion from her throat, she mentally slapped herself. She, they, didn't need to complicate things. She wasn't going to let whatever this was she was feeling ruin what had developed into a wonderful night. Essentially, besides the fact that they'd almost married, they were childhood friends, and she wanted to try and rekindle that side of their relationship. Morgan was a good man, a decent man, a man she would have loved to have ended up with. But she'd royally stuffed that chance up. And she wasn't about to try a second time. She didn't deserve him. And he most certainly didn't deserve her shortcomings. She couldn't let herself fall for him. She knew it would spell disaster, and heartbreak, for both of them. She didn't want that for herself, and she most certainly didn't want to put him through any more than she already had. And without him knowing the truth, well, that would just be plain selfish of her.

'Jess, are you okay?' The brush of his hand sent a tingle up her arm and zapped towards her heart, but then the rush sidetracked and made a beeline for her brain.

'Yes, all good.' She forced a wide smile.

'You sure?'

'Uh-huh.' She wasn't sure if it was the two large glasses of wine that she'd drunk, or the fact that Morgan was kickstarting her heart, but either way, she felt dizzy and breathless.

He offered her a gentle smile. 'Maybe we should both think about hitting the sack?'

No! I want to stay here, with you, like this, forever!

'Yeah, I reckon you're right,' she said softly.

He stood and so did she, on very shaky legs. 'Thanks for a lovely evening, and a yummy dinner, Morgan.'

'You're welcome, Jess.' He walked her past where Teeny had crashed hours earlier on his rug, and over to the steps. 'If I don't see you in the morning, I'll catch you at the pre-wedding barbecue here tomorrow night, yeah?'

In the heat of everything, she'd almost forgotten all about it. 'Yes, of course, I'll be here with bells on.'

'Good, great.' He leant in and pecked her cheek. 'Night.'

The heat that rushed through her from the brush of his lips was close to engulfing. 'Night,' she squeaked, before hurrying down the steps and into the embracing darkness. 'Catch you tomorrow,' she hollered.

'With bells on,' he hollered back.

His husky chuckle followed her to the cottage, accompanied her inside, and he effortlessly slipped deeper into her heart as she slipped into bed.

CHAPTER
8

With the wedding planning having shifted into a higher gear, the following night rolled around as if on fast forward, and Jess abruptly found herself in the same spot she'd imagined kissing Morgan, stealing glances at him with the same roiling emotions that had overcome her when they'd locked eyes twenty-two hours earlier. But this time they weren't alone, which was a godsend, because it meant there was no chance of another heart-to-heart moment. They hadn't really even spoken since they'd bid each other goodnight the night before. It was almost if they were avoiding each other. Or at least she was doing her best to avoid him. Her attraction to him, and the feelings he aroused in her, terrified her. The best she could do to evade such sensations was to try and steer clear of him, at least for now, until she pulled her emotions into line. But that didn't mean she couldn't appreciate his masculine attributes from afar.

Or did it?

Either way, she couldn't help herself. Twilight had lit the landscape in a rosy hue, and from her viewpoint she could secretly watch him manning the billowing barbecue, flipping burgers, turning sausages, timing the steak to be rare, medium or well done – the last was a terrible shame in her opinion – and the concentration on his face was adorable. Beside him, Roberto and another of his mates stood with beers in hand, supervising as if their lives depended on it. Even though she was trying to be stealthy, she knew her quick glances were turning into prolonged stares. She needed to stop it, now, before someone picked up on it.

'Are you liking what you see, my darling friend?'

Too late. Shanti had busted her.

Jess pulled a 'whatever' face. 'I don't know what you're on about.'

'If you say so.' Shanti grinned and took the last sip from her champagne flute. 'I'm going to go and grab us another bottle of bubbly, back in a sec.'

'Okies,' Jess replied as she tried to rid the caught-with-her-hand-in-the-biscuit-tin flush from her cheeks.

As much as she wanted to look in Morgan's direction again, she forced her focus onto the gabbing group of women she was sitting with. Shanti's mum, Jaye, was stealing the limelight with stories of her youth, sending the younger ones into cackling laughter, and the older ones into playful denial while under scrutiny from their wide-eyed daughters. It was merry company to be in, but she couldn't fully be present knowing Morgan was only a glance away. And right before she went to sneak another peek at him, she could feel him behind her the second before she turned her cheek in his direction.

His breath tickled her neck as he leant in closer to whisper in her ear. 'Are you having a nice night, Jess?' he asked, his voice low and velvety.

She turned to face him, feeling her cheeks flush with embarrassment. 'Yes, I am,' she said with a smile, hoping he wouldn't notice the way her eyes lingered on his chest above his almost buttoned-up shirt. 'You?'

He chuckled, the sound making her heart flutter. 'Sure am.' He gestured to the spare seat beside her. 'Mind if I sit for a bit?'

'Of course not.' She wriggled over a little.

They chatted casually about the food, the guests and the nice weather, the easiness of his company feeling like a balm to her soul. It was nice to feel like they were just two old friends hanging out, without any of the complicated feelings that had been simmering beneath the surface the night before. But even as they laughed and joked, Jess couldn't help but feel a sense of unease. She knew that the longer she stayed in Silverton Shores, and especially at Savage Acres, the harder it would be to resist the pull between them.

Nine sleeps and I'll be gone ... I can do this.

But then he gazed at her with a familiar fondness and she couldn't bring herself to look away. They'd always been connected beyond any tangible explanation. Twin flames. First loves. True loves. Soulmates. In between her next inhalation and exhalation, she wished with every part of her heart that she could tell him everything, so she could give him something tangible to possibly heal the wound created by her. But the words were lodged in her throat, and she couldn't bring herself to speak them. Instead, she smiled weakly, hoping to convey the words she couldn't say. He smiled back, a look of understanding in his eyes. Her heart was suddenly thumping, and her mind was suddenly racing. How was she meant to spend time with him without always ending up feeling like this? For another beat, he just sat there, looking at her, as if she'd arrested his gaze.

But then he blinked, smiled, and tipped the brim of his hat. 'I'll let you get back to the girls, while I go and get the last of the food sorted.' He stood, and before she'd found her voice again he was sauntering away.

Jess remained in a weird daze all through the lively dinner and the chaos of the clearing up, and then carried it to a quiet, shadowed place around the front of the homestead, where she hoped to try and make sense of it, and somehow shake it off. But then the sound of approaching footsteps came, and Morgan had taken the corner and walked straight into her reclusive bubble, unwittingly popping it.

'Oh, hey.' He halted, beer in hand, then followed her gaze to the star-studded sky. 'It's a ripper of a night, huh?'

Oh, sweet baby Jesus, that smile …

'It sure is.' She glued her gaze to the brightest star.

One breath, two breaths, three breaths, four …

'Roberto and Shanti seem to be enjoying themselves.'

She nodded. 'Yup, they sure do.'

Another scratchy silence ensued.

'So, did you go for the steak, the rissoles or the sausages?' Morgan's voice didn't carry his usual casualness.

'I actually went for all three.' She rubbed her stomach. 'And because of having eyes bigger than my belly, I'm royally stuffed to the brim.'

'Ha, yeah, me too.' His voice trailed off as he took another swig of beer, although his gaze remained locked to her this time, instead of the sky.

Jess didn't know what to do, or what to say, so she stood there like a stunned mullet. Their small talk had waned, leaving them nowhere to go, with nothing to hide behind. She shifted from sandaled foot to foot, finding this rare uncomfortableness between them quite unsettling.

Morgan eventually sighed. 'Come on, Jess, spill.'

Caught off guard, she shook her head and blinked – she wasn't ready to spill anything. 'What do you want me to spill?'

'Righto, I'll take the lead.' He paused, inhaled, seemed to stand taller before tipping his head a little as he regarded her. 'Why do you stay in Florence when you're not happy there?'

She almost gasped but held it back. 'Who said I'm not happy?'

He lifted his shoulders. 'I just did.'

'Uh-huh.' Jess feigned indifference as she nodded ever so slowly. 'And what makes you think you're right?'

'Your eyes.' Two simple words said with utmost conviction.

And that threw her. 'My eyes, huh.' She managed a half-smile. 'Interesting.'

'People aren't lying when they say they're the windows to the soul, Jess.'

'Mmm, interesting,' she repeated.

Breathe, Jess, breathe!

Morgan took a step closer, so she was facing him. 'Am I right, are you unhappy over there in Italy?' His face was a picture of concern and compassion.

And this softened her reply. 'Sometimes, yes, but not all the time.'

'And do you feel happier here?'

'Sometimes, yes, but again, not all the time.'

He grimaced, then nodded. 'I see.'

She was about to ask *what do you see, Morgan? Do you see how much I care for you still? Do you see that I regret what I did to you, to us?*

But just like he was doing now, she clamped her lips shut.

Don't go there, she told herself, with a shake of her head. She had enough roiling emotions to deal with; she didn't need to add how she felt, or didn't feel, about Morgan. Soon enough, she'd be heading back to Italy to get on with her life, far enough away from him to avoid the flood of guilt she felt just by being near him.

He stepped a little closer. 'Jess, please, talk to me.' His face was etched with concern.

Even if she wanted to speak, the emotional lump in her throat was making it impossible. So she did all she could do, and wrapped her arms around herself to stop from falling apart.

As if sensing her inner turmoil, Morgan reached out to take her hand. 'Whatever it is, just know that I'm here for you, okay?' he said tenderly, his eyes meeting hers.

Jess felt the last little bit of her resolve crumble, and she leant into him, feeling his arms wrap around her in a comforting embrace. Burying her head in his chest, she breathed in his familiar scent, feeling safe, cared for, protected. They stayed like this for one joined heartbeat after another. He gently stroked her hair, trying to soothe her. If only she didn't ever have to leave the safety of him. If only they could go back in time and do things over. But this was reality, and she couldn't do this. She couldn't stay here, wrapped up in him. So she untangled, and took steps back, making a safe distance between them. Morgan watched her, his eyes questioning. Jess could see the hurt in his gaze, and she knew that she was somehow breaking his heart all over again.

She couldn't let herself fall for him, not when she knew they could never be together. Not when she had a secret that could destroy everything.

'I'm sorry,' she whispered, her voice barely audible. 'I can't do this tonight. I have to go.'

Morgan nodded and his jaw set in determination. 'I understand,' he said, his voice filled with regret. 'But know that I'll always be here for you, no matter what. You can always count on me.'

Jess forced a smile, even though her heart was breaking. 'Thank you,' she said. 'I'll never forget that.'

'Good.' It was his only response.

'I'm going to head back to the cottage,' she said, her voice barely above a whisper. 'Can you say goodbye to Roberto and Shanti for me, and just tell them I had a headache, please?' She smiled sadly. 'I don't like lying, but I don't want them to worry about me.'

He nodded. 'Sure, will do.'

'Thank you.' She turned to walk away. 'Night, Morgan.'

'Night, Jess.'

* * *

Slamming into reality from the depths of sound sleep, Jess sat bolt upright, her breath held and her hearing honed as she tried to figure out what had startled her awake. A few seconds passed and nothing but the quiet of night met her. She glanced at her bedside clock: 3.23 am. It must have just been the wind. She needed to chill out. Chastising herself for being so paranoid, she settled back into her pillow and tugged her doona up to her shoulders. As she closed her eyes, the smack of something against the side of the house had her heart slamming again. Grabbing her phone, she hit the torch button and, shooting from the comfort of her bed, she tiptoed towards the window. Peeling the curtains back with one finger, she peeked through the crack as she reminded herself to breathe. The glowing, beady eyes of a possum stared back at her. Her hand going to her thrashing heart, she burst into laughter. She really needed to stop being so, for lack of a better word, *uncountrified*.

Five hours later, she stirred to sleepy life with the realisation that she needed to get a grip, stop crushing on Morgan and find her centre again, or risk falling off the edge and into volatility. Shanti needed her. Roberto needed her. Chiara needed her. Her nonno needed her. She didn't have the luxury of going off the rails. Before the rug of her existence had been ripped out from beneath her feet, the day her parents had died, her life had been so put together. Heck, she'd been born with all her ducks in a row. But after losing her mum and dad, which wasn't her fault, then losing Morgan, which was all her fault, then marrying a son of a bitch, more fool her, her life had become disorganised chaos at best, a raging tornado at worst. But there was no feeling sorry for herself. She needed to get up. Face the day head-on. No matter what. Even though overwhelming exhaustion was wrapping itself around her like a heavy cloak, she was hell-bent on welcoming the new day in with a smile. Fake it till you make it, and all of that. She had this. She could do this.

Blah blah blah!

With her speech to herself over with, she threw her legs over the side of the bed, stood and took determined steps towards the kitchen, where she would slap her senses to life with a strong cup of coffee. But first, she needed some water. Yanking the fridge open, she reached inside and grabbed a bottle. Halfway to grabbing an apple, she thought better of it. Why did she have to be so goody-two-shoes with her food choices all the time? To hell with it, she was on holidays, and she was going to eat whatever she felt like. Heading over to the walk-in pantry, she grinned at the packet of salt and vinegar chips. It had been yonks since she'd sunk her teeth into such deliciousness. But she hadn't forgotten how the taste could cure almost anything, especially once she got to the bottom of the bag, turned it inside out, and licked the remnants of the flavouring. That always made her eyes twitch.

Next up, she was going to call her beautiful little girl.

Twenty minutes into the conversation, tears filled her eyes, but she quickly blinked them away. 'You make sure you keep being a good girl for Nonno, won't you, Chiara.' If she allowed as much as a tiny sob to escape her, she'd be a goner.

'I promise I will.'

'I miss you, my sweet girl.'

'I miss you, too, Mum, sooooo much.'

'I'll call you again tomorrow, okay, and you can tell me all about your school party.'

'Okay, Mum, I'm sure there'll be lots to tell you.' Chiara squealed and giggled. 'I love you, nighty night.'

From her seat at the dining table, Jess stared through the kitchen window into the bright morning sunshine. 'Nighty night, sweetie.'

Ending the phone call, she felt her frayed heart squeeze excruciatingly tight as her breath caught in a painful knot somewhere deep within her chest. A soul ache. That's what she had. And resistance was futile. She needed to let it out. And the best way to do that was to head outdoors. So she quickly cleaned her teeth, washed her face, stripped off her pyjamas, slipped on her favourite bikini, whipped herself up another coffee and sculled it while jigging on the spot because it was too hot. Then she grabbed her straw hat, sunglasses and half-eaten packet of chips, along with her bottle of water, some mind-numbing reading material, her AirPods and her phone, and made her way to the back door.

Stepping out of the coolness of the cottage, she almost retreated back inside, then thought *stuff sitting around, cooped up all day long*. But holy moly, it was hot. Actually, it was hotter than hot. Too hot to think straight. Not that she cared, because she was done with overthinking everything anyway. Running on her tippy toes, she balanced her armful of belongings as she raced along the scorching floorboards, sighing with relief when she reached the coolness of the back lawn. Spreading her towel on the old sunlounger, she adjusted her bikini, popped her hat on, and then got herself settled with her magazine and a playlist of her favourite seventies music.

Halfway through reading about the latest Hollywood break-ups, a sixth sense washed over her, and she turned just in time to see Morgan striding towards her, but he didn't appear to have seen her, his gaze instead glued to the back door. She quickly plucked her AirPods out as heat flooded her, the thudding of her heart drowning out any other noise.

He came to a sudden stop, a few metres from her. 'Wow, hey there.' He didn't seem to know where to look.

'Hey, Morgan.' She pushed her sunglasses to the top of her head. 'What's up?' Like it or not, her attention was caught and captured. Hook, line and sinker.

And going by the sparkle in his eyes as he lifted his sunnies, so was his.

'Nothing's up, just thought I'd stop by and see how you were doing.' He lifted his hat and ran a hand through his wind-tousled hair.

The gesture triggered the soft spot she still held for him, and him alone, in her heart. 'Other than melting in this heat, I'm good, thanks.'

'Yeah, it's a bit of a scorcher today.' He looked towards the sun, squinting as if to underline the fact, before looking back at her.

A too-long, too-silent pause made her heart pound faster, harder. He wasn't in a rush to fill the silence. And she didn't have any decipherable words to blurt out. So she sat up, grabbed her water bottle, twisted the lid off and took a decent glug. The time it took for her to do so helped to slow her galloping pulse.

'Right, well, I'll let you get back to it, and I'll get back to it too.' He flashed her a brazen smile, then turned on his boot, and strode away.

'Catch you a bit later, then,' she called after him.

'Yup, will do,' he said with a wave over his shoulder, without looking back.

Feeling a little, no, *a lot*, chuffed that the sight of her in her bikini had left him a little tongue-tied, she eased back down and closed her eyes against the glare of the sun. The lingering warmth of him, and the heat of the day, had her drifting off to floaty places. Sighing with the peaceful feeling, she sunk deeper into it. It was nice to feel so relaxed.

But that all changed when big fat raindrops fell, stinging her skin as they struck. Sitting bolt upright, she grabbed her towel and made a run for it. She sprinted up the stairs, but she was dripping wet by the time she reached the back door. Giggling to herself, she looked at her watch, surprised to see the time – she'd been asleep for almost two hours. It was amazing what could happen when she chose to pick up the dragging reins of her life and get a firm grip.

If only she could continue to do just that.

* * *

Morgan heaved a sigh as he kicked off his boots and stopped to smell the proverbial roses. For the first time that day, Teeny left his side and wandered over to his rug, slumped down and was asleep in seconds. Meandering over to the railings, he leant against the banister. If wishes were horses, his property would be full of them. One day, when he was able to survive wholly and solely off his blood, sweat and tears, he would give up his job as a pilot. For now, though, it was a work in progress. Looking over to the cottage, he thought back to his chance encounter with Jess that morning. The sudden appearance of her in that shiny jet-black bikini had stopped him dead in his tracks, and at the same time rendered him speechless. He just thanked the powers that be that he'd had a few seconds to catch his breath, and find his voice, before her eyes had met with his. She really was one hell of a sexy woman.

Straightening, he thrust his hands deep into his pockets. What to do? Stay here, and think about her all night long, like he had been lately, or head on over there and spend an hour or two in her company so he could get his fill of her? The latter sounded much more appealing. And why not, they were friends, weren't they? Sinking down on the day bed, he rested back. He'd give himself ten more minutes of chillax time, then hit the shower and head on over to the cottage.

What felt like hours later, showered and clutching a bottle of wine from his collection, he watched the cottage door swing open and Jess's pretty face met him.

Judging by her wide-eyed stare and the way she was gathering her robe in tight, she wasn't expecting a visitor, especially him. 'Hey, Morgan.' Candlelight flickered behind her.

'Hey yourself, sorry if I've interrupted you, but ...' He held the bottle of wine up. 'I've been saving this little beauty for a special occasion and given the fact it's all the way from Chianti, I thought you might like a glass.'

She paused for the briefest of moments, then smiled. 'It's Friday night, so why the heck not?' She pushed the screen door open and stepped aside to let him in. 'Come on in, you know your way around.' She gestured towards the hallway with a tip of her head. 'I'll just go and make myself decent while you pour us each a glass of vino.'

'Sounds like a plan.' Norah Jones's voice filled the cottage. 'And nice choice of music.'

'Yes.' She stopped mid-step and looked to the stereo. 'Her voice always relaxes me.'

'Me too.' He raked a hand through his damp hair.

Turning to face him again, she lifted her gaze, meeting his, seemingly oblivious to the effect she was having on him.

Or was she?

He couldn't quite tell, but the way she bit her bottom lip, the way her eyes lingered on his, made him think that maybe she *was* aware of the chemistry between them.

Clearing his throat, he tried to shake off the feeling, and gestured towards the kitchen. 'I'll be in yonder, sorting this out.' He held the bottle up. 'See you there.'

'Groovy, back in a sec.' And off she sashayed, her hips gorgeously swaying and her hair hanging freely down her back.

He couldn't stop staring at her as she walked away, admiring how her body moved so effortlessly. He felt a sudden urge to grab her and kiss her, but he knew he had to control himself. A rush of heat filled him with just the thought of acting wild and reckless. If he were allowed to get his hands on her beautiful skin right now, they'd be in a world of uninhibited, unadulterated, euphoric pleasure. Instead, he walked to the kitchen, struggling to calm his racing heart and growing desire as he poured the wine into two glasses. Her soft footfalls approached minutes later and as she entered the kitchen, he handed her the glass. They clinked them together before taking a sip, then stood there for a moment, just enjoying each other's company and the hypnotic music filling the air.

Clothed in a slinky ankle-length dress, Jess leant against the counter, crossing her ankles and taking another sip of her wine. He couldn't help but notice how the soft silk clung to her curves, accentuating her body in all the right places. He took a deep breath, trying to push the thoughts of how he wanted to feel those curves against his body out of his mind. But when he caught her looking at him from beneath her lashes, he knew it was impossible. She knew exactly what she was doing to him, and he couldn't help but feel grateful for it. Unable to hold back any longer, he set his glass down, taking a step towards her.

'You know …' he said, his voice low and husky. 'You look absolutely stunning tonight.'

She smiled, a coy look in her eyes as she took another sip. 'Why, thank you. You're not looking so bad yourself, Savage.'

He chuckled, his hand reaching out to brush a strand of hair from her face. 'I've been thinking about you all day,' he confessed, his voice barely above a whisper.

Her hand reached up, gripping his shirt as she pulled him closer. 'Well, don't stop now,' she murmured, her lips parting slightly.

There was no more of an invitation needed.

He leant in, his lips hovering over hers as he savoured the moment before finally closing the gap between them. Their kiss was electric, filled with raw passion and years of pent-up desire. His hands found their way to her hips, pulling her closer as she melted into his embrace. Then they broke apart, both gasping for air, their eyes locked onto each other's.

'I want you,' he whispered, his voice laced with urgency.

'I want you too,' she replied, her fingers fumbling with the buttons on his shirt.

They stumbled towards the bedroom, their hands exploring each other's bodies as if it were the first time. Clothes were discarded, and the soft glow of the candles cast shadows over their entwined bodies. He revelled in the feel of her skin against his, the way she moaned his name as he kissed her neck. Their lovemaking was hungry and uninhibited, each touch igniting an inferno between them. And as they climbed to the peak of ecstasy, they clung to each other, trembling and moaning as they reached the erotic heights of bliss. Sated, spent, satisfied beyond belief, he tried to fight the exhaustion that was creeping up on him, not wanting to lose contact with her, but the pull of sleep was too strong, and he succumbed.

And that's when he woke, in the dark, on the day bed, at his homestead, hungrier for Jessica Sabatini than he'd ever been. Damn him for falling asleep. And damn his dreams for taking control over him. No matter what he did, no matter how much he fought it, she lived in his heart. He had to find a way to get over this insatiable need for her. Sooner rather than later.

Or he was going to find himself in a world of trouble.

CHAPTER
9

The following day the scorching temperatures had dropped a few notches by mid-afternoon, and with an encroaching storm imminent, the wind had also grown fierce. But the raging inferno of longing inside Morgan hadn't subsided, and unlike the weather, there was no means to cool down. If anything, after spending the afternoon with Jess and Roberto – he and his best mate had tried on their suits for the final fitting while Jess gave them her honest opinion, which was a broad smile and a big thumbs up – the ache of longing to be able to play out what his mind had been tantalising him with, awake and asleep, was incredibly overwhelming.

But he was never going to get the chance to live out his imaginings, he knew that.

It wasn't just the intensity of the physical attraction, although Morgan couldn't deny he found everything about Jess incredibly sexy. It was something deeper, something more primal, as if he and Jess had been born to be with one another. He wanted to possess her, body and soul – not in a greedy kind of ownership, but with the knowledge that she was giving her body and soul freely to him, and him alone. Forever. He wanted to live with her, love with her, have children with her, grow old with her. He wanted to pass into the next life knowing she'd be joining him so they could write their love story all over again. For he would have to die first or die of a broken heart close behind her. Because he wouldn't be able to stand a day without her near, if he'd been blessed enough to love her for a lifetime.

Only one thing was certain now: his love for her was eternal.

Glancing across the lively table as he took a swig from his schooner of mid-strength beer, he caught eyes with Jess, and she offered him a cute smile. He flashed her a charming one back. For the briefest of moments, it felt as if it were only him and her in the pub's packed dining room. But just as suddenly as this feeling had risen, it disappeared as cackling laughter carried from the end of the table, drawing her attention away from him. Shanti's mum was at it again, filling Roberto and Shanti's friends with her light and laughter. He'd always adored that about Jaye, and he loved how she'd passed this quality on to her daughter. Even so, all the organised get-togethers before the wedding were daunting. Usually happy in his own company outside of work hours, he found the constant socialising exhausting. But he couldn't deny that he was going to miss Jess once the wedding was over. She was the only reason he wanted time to slow down, so he could relish every second he got to spend with her before she headed back to Florence.

At his side, Roberto nudged him with his elbow. 'Mate, you look a million miles away. Is everything all right?'

Morgan forced a smile. 'Yeah, just a bit tired, I guess,' he said, trying to brush off the intensity of his feelings towards Jess. 'I haven't been sleeping that great.'

'Sorry, bud.' Concern wrapped around Roberto's dark features. 'Anything I can help you with?'

'Nah, all good.' Morgan spun the beer coaster he'd been fidgeting with in his fingertips. 'It's just a case of my mind not shutting off, that's all.'

Roberto looked at him sceptically but didn't push the matter any further. That was the difference with guys, they usually knew when to apply the brakes and give their mate time to come to them, if and when they chose to. Women were more innately nurturing and needed to get to the bottom of things way faster. Maybe he, and the rest of his menfolk, needed to follow their lead, but not tonight. Tonight, he was too tired to talk about just how much he still loved Roberto's beautiful sister.

Turning his attention back to Jess, he relished watching her having fun with Annie and Shanti. The way her head tipped, the curve of her lips, the sound of her laughter; bearing witness to her little traits made him crave her all the more. He knew the longing he felt was impossible to gratify, but he couldn't help himself. Try as he might, his thoughts were clouded with images of her naked body writhing beneath him, her moans ringing out in ecstasy as she clung to him, and her grasp softening as they fell asleep afterward in each other's arms with her head resting upon his chest.

Dammit, he wanted her more than anything he'd ever wanted before.

Unable to withstand much more, he shook his head, hoping it would somehow dispel the vivid fantasies. It did, just enough to calm his breath, but the desire he felt for her remained, and probably always would. A sigh escaped him as he took a swig of his beer, while wishing like hell that he could turn the workings of his heart off. Why was it so difficult to just be her friend, and let her move on with her life without him? The more he tried, the more the thought of her being with someone else, of her making a life with another man, made his insides turn. It wasn't fair of him to think like this, he knew that. He also knew there wasn't anything he could do to change how he felt, but that didn't mean he had to let her know just how badly he wanted her. He owed her the respect of remaining only friends. He could only hope that eventually, his heart would agree.

As the night wore on, the group began to disperse, saying their goodbyes and promising to see each other tomorrow. Watching as Jess began to gather her belongings, he could tell she'd drunk more than a few glasses of wine, but she was still in control and he was impressed. Rising then meeting Jess, he kissed Shanti's cheek goodbye, gave Roberto a friendly handshake, bent to hug Shanti's mum, then side by side, he and Jess headed towards the exit. Her gaze on the front doors, she held her own with poised strides. Not many women he knew would be able to walk through a crowded pub in the skyscraper heels she was wearing, with a number of wines under her glittery belt, without stumbling at least once. Then again, there were a lot of things Jess could do that other women couldn't, or wouldn't, even try. That's what made her special. That, and so many other things. But then, as soon as they reached the door and stepped through it, Jess stumbled.

Grabbing her elbow, he kept her upright. 'Easy, tiger,' he joked.

Jess grimaced as she laughed. 'Oops. Sorry.'

He grinned at her playful expression. 'Nothing to apologise for.' Hooking her arm into his, just to be on the safe side, he led her through the car park, towards where he'd parked the Troopy.

'You're a really nice guy, Morgan.' She threw him a sideways glance. 'Has anyone ever told you that?'

'Nope, never.' He couldn't help the grin that spread.

'Well, you are. So, there, now someone has.' Her nod was exaggerated.

Morgan chuckled as they reached his Troopy. 'Okay. Whatever you say, Jess.' With his free hand, he beeped the locks open.

'And you're cute, too.' Her smile was a little lopsided.

'I'll take that,' he said, helping her up and into the passenger seat.

'And, hot.' She waggled a finger at him. 'I can't forget how hot you are.'

He took it with a grain of salt. 'Righto.' This sozzled side of her was quite funny. 'You've had a bit to drink tonight, haven't you?'

'Nuh-uh.' She wobbled her head from side to side. 'Just enough to feel really good.'

Morgan sighed as he rested a boot tip on the sidestep. 'I'm going to miss you once the wedding is over,' he admitted before he had a chance to think better of it and stop himself.

She smiled and took his hand in hers, squeezing it gently. 'I'll miss you too, but on the plus side, we'll always have the memories of this precious time all together, hey?' she said, her eyes glistening with unshed tears.

Sniffing his emotions back, he looked down at their entwined fingers and swallowed. Connecting with her like this made the already painful thought of saying goodbye to her in a little over a week that much harder. But she was right, this time was precious, and he was going to appreciate it, and enjoy it.

'Morgan?' Her sweet voice broke through his thoughts. 'You okay?'

'Yeah, all good.' Taking a deep breath, he pushed away his fears and met her eyes, smiling as best he could. 'I'll never forget our time together, Jess. Never.'

'Good.' She returned his smile and nodded. 'And neither will I.'

With a stoic sigh, Morgan squeezed her hand, then released her, shut the door and walked around to the driver's side, where he jumped behind the steering wheel and revved the four-wheel drive to life. Needing a long moment before looking at her again, he backed out of the car park, stopped at the T-junction, indicated, and turned towards home.

Rubbing his five o'clock shadow, he relished the darkness of night surrounding them as he thought about what he was going to say next. He was overcome by the need to let Jess know how he felt about her and to somehow explain that he didn't need her to do anything with the knowledge other than be aware of his feelings. What did he have to lose by being honest, at least about this? Maybe it might help lighten the load on his shoulders, and his heart.

He hesitated for a moment before finally speaking up. 'Jess, there's something I need to tell you,' he said, his heart racing with anticipation.

Ear-ringing silence was his only reply.

Fleetingly glancing sideways at his precious cargo, he saw she'd curled up against the door and fallen asleep, with her head resting on his rolled-up Driza-Bone. He quickly made sure the central locking was on before taking another appreciative glance at her. How she could look so beautiful every second of every day, even in sleep, with her mouth hanging open and little snores now echoing, was beyond him. A faint smile formed. He was one lucky SOB to have made love to her that one mesmerising time, even though it was all those years ago, when he'd been a clumsy, inexperienced virgin.

Looking ahead again, he was quietly relieved fate had stopped him from blurting everything out, because once he started the honesty ball rolling, after he'd revealed how much he still loved her, he might have gone on to tell her about Annie, and what she was keeping from her. And that, right now, would have been a very bad idea. Something that life-altering wasn't a topic of conversation when alcohol had been enjoyed a little too much.

Get a grip on yourself, Savage, before you do something stupid …

Shaking his head, he continued the drive home, determined not to disturb the beautiful woman beside him. At least not until they pulled up at the cottage. For now, he was going to enjoy the silence, and her nearness, and try not to think about how he was going to deal with the inevitable goodbyes in a week's time. He knew without a shadow of doubt that she'd forever remain the woman he'd never be able to get out of his mind, or heart, no matter how hard he tried. She was his greatest grief, and his greatest love, all rolled into one gorgeous package. It was the most heartbreakingly tragic thing he'd ever experienced, having loved her, then lost her. But he'd never want to have lost out on the experience, the chance, to have loved her so deeply.

And he still did.

A flash of lightning lit up the sky and landscape as if it were daytime, and a booming crack of thunder echoed in the distance.

Moments later, the sky cracked open and hard droplets of rain pelted the Troopy. Jess didn't move a muscle. Armageddon wouldn't even be able to wake her. Turning off the highway and down the long road that would eventually lead them to Savage Acres, he turned his undivided attention to Mother Nature's sudden deluge. He flicked the windscreen wipers on to top speed, and soon realised they were no match for the torrential downpour. Slowing, he cautiously leant forward. He was having a tough time seeing the white lines, let alone the sides of the road. The last thing he wanted was to lose traction or, worse still, hit stray livestock.

Slow and steady, he'd get them home safely.

Flicking the demister on, he smelt the raw, invigorating perfume of renewal and promise floating through the air vents, reminding him there was always a glimmer of hope for a fresh start. It was good to remember that things could always turn around for the better. Just how that was so, given his situation with Jess, he hadn't a damn clue, but he was going to cling to the concept, as it gave him some kind of peace. Settling into this feeling, he drove cautiously through the storm, his mind still consumed with thoughts of his stunning passenger. He couldn't believe how lucky he was to have her back in his life. Even as a friend. It meant the world. One day he hoped to meet her daughter. If only Chiara was his, now wouldn't that have been magical. He would've been so proud to be the father of Jess's child. Just the thought of the three of them, living as a family, made him long for such a miracle. But at least, beside him for now, Jess's soft breathing soothed his anxious heart. He knew he'd do anything to protect her, to keep her safe from harm, and that protection extended to her child, too.

By the time he drove through the front gates of Savage Acres, the rain had subsided to a light drizzle. He breathed a sigh of relief as he pulled up in front of the cottage and turned off the engine. Gazing over at Jess, he gently touched her arm and watched as she stirred.

Blinking her eyes open, she sat up, her hair now in disarray. 'Oh, hey, we're home.' She rubbed her face. 'Sorry I feel asleep.'

'Nah.' His heart swelled with warmth at the sight of her smile. 'All good.' He got out of the car and ran around to the passenger side, opening the door for her.

She kicked her heels off, gathered them and her handbag together and stepped out. 'Thanks, Morgan.' Her hand clasped his tightly as they made their way towards the cottage, both of them dodging puddles of water. 'Did it rain heaps on the way home?'

'Did it ever.' He chuckled. 'I don't know how you slept through it.'

'I reckon it might have been a wine-induced coma.' She giggled and shook her head as they climbed the four front steps.

'Thank you, Morgan,' she whispered, letting go of his hand. 'For being so kind and letting me be a part of your life after everything that's happened.' She sniffled and blinked faster. 'It means a lot, and I hope you know that.'

Hating seeing her upset, Morgan struggled to hold his composure. 'You're welcome, Jess,' he said, his voice cracking.

A tear rolled down her cheek, and she quickly brushed it away.

'Oh, please don't cry.' He pulled her into a hug, and she softened into him, her arms going around his back.

Then they just stood there, clinging to each other.

'I'll always be here for you,' he said tenderly.

'I know you will be,' she murmured into his chest. 'And I'll always be here for you, too, if you ever need me. No matter that I live thousands of miles away.'

Her last sentence hit home, mighty hard. Morgan didn't answer. He couldn't. The lump in his throat had grown so thick that he couldn't have uttered a single word if he'd wanted to. All he could do was hold her close and pray that the moment would never end.

After a little while, she pulled back and smiled at him, her eyes bright with more unshed tears. 'We'll always be connected, you and me.'

Morgan's heart swelled with emotion as he looked into her eyes. 'We sure will be, no matter what.' He wanted to hold her, kiss her and take her back to his place.

'I better hit the sack.' Jess smiled up at him, her eyes shining like stars in the silvery moonlight. 'Nighty night, and again, thank you for everything.' She rose up on her tippy toes and pressed a soft kiss to his cheek before turning and disappearing into the cottage.

'Night, sweet Jess,' Morgan uttered after her.

He stood there for a long moment, feeling the ghost of her lips on his cheek, his heart heavy with longing and his mind swirling. He knew he couldn't keep denying his feelings for her. She was everything to him, and he wanted nothing more than to hold her close and never let her go.

* * *

Sometime in the middle of the night, a loud rapping at his front door woke Morgan with a start. He jumped from the bed, rushing down the staircase and towards his visitor with his heart pounding like a boxer's fists.

'Oh, hey, Jess.' He rubbed his face in a bid to wake fully. 'Are you okay?'

Wide-eyed, she shook her head. 'No, nope, not at all.'

And that's when he caught sight of the cricket bat dangling from her left hand. Fuelled by a shot of adrenaline, he grabbed her wrist and dragged her into the safety of the homestead, looking left to right as he did for whoever, or whatever, had unsettled her. 'What's happened?' he asked, turning to her.

She was trembling like a leaf. 'There's a massive snake in my bedroom.'

'Ah, I see.' He breathed a sigh of relief. 'I gather that's why you're holding a bat?'

'Uh-huh.' She raised the weapon as if she was about to hit a six. 'And I'm damn well going to use it if I have to.'

'Let me lay it out straight for you.' He placed both his hands on her shoulders and looked her square in the eye. 'Right now, you have two choices.'

'Okay.' She brought the bat end back to the floor and eyed him seriously. 'What are they?'

'I can go over there now, and try and find it, or you can crash here, and I can sort it out in the morning.' He dropped his hands to his sides and shoved them into his boxer pockets.

'Oh no, I'll stay here, if that's okay.' She seemed to let this sink in while shaking her head a little. 'Besides, I don't want you traipsing around in the dark.' She frowned. 'Because what if you get bitten?'

'Well …' Trying to keep from chuckling at her stunned expression, Morgan drew in an overexaggerated breath. 'I'll either die a slow painful death, or very quickly in your arms.'

Her seriousness gave way to a sassy grin. 'Stop it,' she said, backing her statement up with a playful slap to his arm.

'Ouch.' He pretended it hurt.

'Whatever.' She rolled her eyes, laughing.

Now he felt safe to laugh at her, and with her. He couldn't help but feel relieved that Jess was only there because of a snake and not some other emergency.

'Come on, follow me.' Crisis averted, he did his best to ignore the way her pyjamas clung to her curves. 'You can crash in the spare room, and we'll sort everything out in the morning.'

'Thank you, Morgan, you're my hero.' She grinned playfully. 'No, seriously, thank you, because there was no way in hell that I would've slept another wink if I had to go back to the cottage.'

'Don't worry, I got you.' He tossed a heroic arm over her shoulder, his expression a picture of mirth. 'You're safe here with me.'

CHAPTER
10

Jess awoke with a start, knowing she'd been dreaming, but other than feeling heartsick, she had no idea what it had been about. Blinking sleep-heavy eyes into the golden glow of sunshine pouring in between the parted curtains, she glanced around the unfamiliar room, realising she wasn't in her bedroom at the cottage but in one of the spare rooms at the homestead. Then she recalled the terrifying encounter with a coiled snake at the foot of her bed, somehow becoming the proprietor of a cricket bat, and hang on – mentally reversing, *beep beep beep*, reversing a little more – oh yes, the ride home in the Troopy with Morgan after a boozy dinner at the pub, rewinding still, oh lord help her, what had she said to him in her Dutch-courage state? With the resurfacing emotions that she'd been hiding from him, and everyone else for that matter, including herself, she could only imagine.

Oh crap, Jess, what have you done?

Trying to sit up but with shooting pain making her think better of it, she rolled over to her side, away from the bright sunlight, and hugged a pillow. Her eyes felt as though they had sand in them, and her mouth was a sticky, disgusting mess. Oh god, her hangover was one from the depths of hell. Not wanting to move a muscle for fear of the headache it might trigger, she took an extraordinarily long time to land somewhat steadily in the present moment. And talk about dehydration – she'd almost kill for some water. Knowing it was going to hurt even more when she stood up, she chose to lie there a little longer, groggy and aching. The oppressive feeling was like being trapped in a cocoon, and even the slightest twitch or breath sent waves of agony through her head and down her neck and shoulders. Every muscle and joint felt as if it were on fire, and the pounding in her skull felt as if her brain was trying to force its way out. Considering the way she'd been thinking of late, she couldn't blame her mind for wanting to escape her. But she refused to feel sorry for herself. This was self-inflicted. Consequently, she'd just have to put her big girl knickers on and find a way to deal with it.

But as soon as she rose to her feet, the impending headache pounded triumphantly behind her eyes. Squeezing them shut, she pinched the bridge of her nose, flopped backwards and relaxed into the plush mattress. Right now, there was nothing at all she wanted to do other than go back to sleep and return to the peace and serenity of dreamy oblivion.

If only she could have Chiara here with her. With just a simple cuddle, her little girl would make everything better. She always did. Damn her own stupidity, for somehow losing her passport. And then the thought that Salvatore had something to do with its disappearance struck her again. And this time, the sense grew, bigger and bigger, until she totally believed it to be true. How else would it have just vanished into thin air? He'd never wanted Chiara to go to Australia, so this would be the perfect way to stop her without seeming like the bad guy. Instead, he'd painted her as the one who'd ruined Chiara's chances of being there. Salvatore was totally capable of such malice. So why was she ignoring the possibility?

If he *had* taken it ... how dare he?

And how dare she keep allowing him to walk all over her?

A sudden rush of red-hot fury gave her the oomph to sit up through the wave of dizziness. Lying around was going to achieve nothing constructive. She knew what she had to do to rectify the situation. She had to get her big girl knickers by the corners and reef them up nice and tight, because once she returned to Italy and opened the results of the paternity test, she was going to need all the girl-power she had, and then some, to face the truth and make things right. Because deep down, she was kidding herself if she believed there was a possibility that Salvatore was Chiara's father. Even though there could be, Chiara was nothing like him, physically or emotionally.

Swinging her feet over the side of the bed, Jess hovered for a moment, trying to somehow work out how the room was rotating. Clutching the side of the bed while shaking her head, she tried to clear the hangover haze before slowly rising. Grabbing her phone from the dresser, she tried to bring it to life, but it was dead as a doornail. A quick glance at her reflection in the mirror gave her a moment of pause. Her hair was a wild mess and her mascara had smudged underneath her eyes. She looked like a hot mess, but she didn't have time to worry about her appearance. She should find her rescuer and thank him for being so accommodating.

Totally unaware of what time it was, she quietly tiptoed from the room, grimacing when the door squeaked as she opened it. In a few quiet strides, she was standing in the upstairs hallway, looking down the corridor towards Morgan's bedroom. His door was shut. All was quiet. From what she could tell of the golden rays streaming through the skylight above her, the sun was well on its way to owning the day. Surely he'd be at work by now. As she made her way towards the staircase, she tried to push away thoughts of lying in his bed, cuddled up against his strapping chest after a night of toe-curling intimacy. She tutted. Far out, she had it really bad for him. She needed to slap some common sense into herself, real quick.

Tiptoeing along the hall, she wondered if she should check if he *was* still in bed, so she could thank him for letting her stay the night, before absconding. It would be the right thing to do. So, stopping short of his door, her heart pounded in her chest as she raised her hand and gently knocked. She held her breath. There was no response. She knocked again, a little firmer this time, and the door creaked open. She peeked in, noting the neatly made king-size bed and open windows. His room was so manly. She liked it a lot. She couldn't help but smile as a long-ago memory found wings and fluttered up from the depths of her heart. They'd only made love the once, but Morgan had proved that passionate night that he was everything she'd ever wanted and more. He'd been gentle yet voracious, tender yet possessive. Knowing it was her first time, just as it was his, he'd taken his time, exploring every inch of her body, making her feel like she was the only woman in the world. Making her feel loved, cherished, adored, safe.

She shook her head, trying to disperse the poignant thoughts that were threatening to consume her. Morgan had been the best thing that had ever happened to her up until that very pivotal point in her life. And then along came Chiara. Now her daughter was the centre of her world. The very reason she lived. The best thing that had ever happened to her. One day, she hoped, Morgan would feel the same, because becoming a parent was the best feeling in the world. One day, if the paternity test confirmed what she felt in her heart, she hoped he would love Chiara just as much as she did.

Feeling like an intruder, she turned away from his private space just as the scent of bacon smacked her appetite into overdrive. Following the delicious aroma, she made her way down the stairs and along the hallway. Then she watched, unnoticed, from the doorway as Morgan moved around the kitchen like a well-oiled machine. Her heart melted a little more at the sight of him in another of his elements. The strong realisation that this handsome man, after all she'd put him through, had still taken her under his wing, had been prepared to be her friend again, and had looked after her so caringly since arriving here – well, he was a saint. She, on the other hand ... She had no idea what she'd done to deserve his warm hospitality and his kindness, but she was eternally grateful for it.

Thoroughly enjoying the view, she stood watching him for a few more moments, taking in every detail of the wonderful man she'd lost. She needed to drink all of him in before making her presence known. He looked so moreishly rugged, in a sleep-tousled kind of way, and wore only a pair of boxer shorts. Her gaze swept over his broad shoulders, wide enough to carry the weight of the world, and his strong arms worthy of holding some lucky woman real close. Tattoos wound around him, in all the right places, adding to the bad-boy edge he now possessed in spades. He was muscular but not overly so, just enough to give him that naturally masculine, rugged look. His hair was slightly messy, likely from sleep, and her fingers itched to comb through the thick strands as she pressed up to kiss him good morning. Back in the day, that would've been exactly what she would've done, when she'd had the right to.

Now, she didn't dare.

She felt that familiar pang of guilt in her chest. She had no right to stand here, watching him. But she couldn't help it. She missed him, missed the way he used to hold her, the way he used to whisper in her ear, the way he always made her feel so safe, so loved.

As if sensing her eyes on him, he turned, unwittingly bursting her bubble as he flashed her his charismatic smile. 'Hey, morning, Jess.'

Her stomach performed a little backflip as she took a deep breath, trying to steady her racing heart, and stepped into the kitchen. 'Good morning,' she said, her voice a little husky.

'I thought I'd whip us up some fodder, before heading out to start my day.' He turned to her with a warm smile, his eyes crinkling at the corners.

'I can see that.' She effortlessly returned a smile as wide as his as she walked towards him, feeling a little flustered under his intense gaze. 'And it smells absolutely delicious.'

'Cool, well let's hope it tastes as good as it smells then, hey.' He turned back to the stove and flipped the bacon over.

Pulling up just short of being able to reach him – she couldn't trust her self-control right now – she watched as he expertly scrambled some eggs and poured them into a buttery pan. His movements were smooth and effortless as he folded the eggs from side to side then sprinkled grated cheese over the fluffy mound.

'Pull up a seat, Jess,' he said, gesturing towards the stools. 'It'll all be ready in a sec.'

She felt bad sitting while he was doing everything. 'You sure I can't do anything to help?'

'Nope, I got all of it covered, but thanks.'

She nodded and took a seat at the kitchen bench, her eyes never leaving him.

'How did you sleep?' she asked, resting her chin on her clasped hands.

'Like a log.' He turned to face her again. 'How about you?' His voice was a little husky.

'Same, although I woke up with a doozy of a hangover.' She squinted against her headache.

'Yeah, I thought you might've, and I have just the trick to get rid of it for you.' He paced over to her, and reaching into his pocket, drew out a blister packet of tablets. 'Take two of these.' He took off towards the sink, and grabbed a glass of water, returning swiftly. 'Pop them in, wait until they're dissolved, throw it back, and you'll be feeling a hundred percent in no time.'

'What are they?' She turned the foil packet over, reading the name.

'A mixture of vitamins, taurine and zinc, and they work a treat, trust me.'

Trust him? She most certainly would, with her life. 'Great, thanks, Morgan.'

She tossed two effervescent tablets into the water and waited, while watching Morgan once again. The muscles in his arms flexed as he gathered plates and cutlery while also whipping up two cups of coffee. He was certainly a man who knew his way around the kitchen. Her heart ached to bear witness to this each and every day, or better still, to be joining him on his culinary adventures, and she was forced to look away before she crumbled into a sobbing mess. Grabbing her glass of purple fizzy remedy, she tossed it back then jiggled in her seat. It tasted horrible. But hopefully, as he'd said, it would work a treat. As Morgan plated their breakfast beside her, the air around her felt as if it crackled with electricity, and her skin prickled with goosebumps. She wondered if it was only her, or if he felt it, too. He was close enough now that she could smell his intoxicating scent, a mixture of soap and something else, something distinctly Morgan, and she had to fight the urge to lean in and inhale deeply.

'Voila, Miss Sabatini, breakfast is now served.' He set a plate in front of her, loaded with crispy bacon, scrambled eggs, half of a grilled beef tomato, mushrooms and a hash brown.

'Holy moly, thanks, Morgan, it looks amazing.' Her stomach growled, and she blushed a little, thankful for the food to focus on so she could try and ignore the animal attraction she was feeling towards him.

'Sounds like someone's really hungry.' Morgan chuckled as he pulled up a seat beside her. 'Dig in while it's nice and hot.'

They ate in silence, between sips of delectably strong, sweet coffee. She stole glances at him whenever she could, and she could've sworn she caught him doing the same. The few times their eyes locked, her skin tingled and she felt insane heat creeping up her neck and cheeks. So much so that by the time she'd finished her breakfast, her heart was racing, her palms were sweaty, and she was fighting off the urge to grab him so she could kiss him while tearing his boxers off. Her thoughts then veered to him ravishing her on the breakfast bench, her moans of ecstasy echoing through the homestead. She took a deep breath, trying to shake off the erotic thoughts, but they only intensified. She really needed a cold shower.

Seemingly not aware of her inferno of longing, or hiding it extremely well if he was, Morgan stood and cleared their plates. Like a prowling panther, her eyes followed him around the room as he moved about, gathering their cups and plates and setting them in the sink.

'You've gone to so much effort.' Pushing her stool back, she plonked her feet to the floor. 'At least let me help with the cleaning up.'

'No way, you stay right where you are.' Turning from the sink, he leant back against the counter, his eyes locked on hers. 'All I want you to do is relax.'

Doing as she was told to, Jess swallowed, her stomach fluttering. He was looking at her in a way that made her body temperature spike higher still.

'After I get dressed, I'll head on over to the cottage, and try and find that troublesome snake.' He smiled a slow, sexy grin. 'But if I can't,' he stepped closer and leant on the bench, 'what are we going to do about your sleeping arrangements?'

'Ummm.' She could feel the heat radiating from his body and her heart was beating so fast she was sure he could hear it. 'I actually don't know what I'll do if you can't find it, because I know I won't be able to sleep a wink, worrying that it's still in there, somewhere, waiting to get me.'

'Hmm.' Leaning closer into her space, his eyes burned into hers.

Unable to utter a word, Jess felt like she was drowning in their blue depths.

'I have an idea.' His voice had dropped an octave. 'You're very welcome to stay here, with me – in the spare room, I mean.'

Jess's heart skipped a beat. Stay in the same house as him? In a room just down the hall from him? As tempting as it was to know she'd be safe and sound, far away from what could be a venomous snake, she instinctively knew it could turn out to be a very bad idea. Her breath caught in her throat as she held his gaze, feeling the tension grow between them. It was as if there was an invisible forcefield that pulled them closer, making it impossible to resist each other's magnetism. She knew she shouldn't let things go too far, but her body was betraying her – it craved his touch, his kiss, his everything. She bit her lip as she tried to keep her composure, but it was a losing battle.

'Jess?' His voice wavered into her warping reality.

'I don't know, Morgan,' she said, her voice barely above a whisper. 'I don't want to risk complicating things between us.'

'Hmm,' he said again as he slid a little closer, until he was so near that if she leant forward, he would've been able to kiss her.

Oh – was he about to?

But he didn't. Instead, he brushed a strand of hair behind her ear and gazed into her eyes with a tenderness that made her heart swell. 'I understand your concerns,' he said softly. 'But we're both adults, Jess. We can handle it. And besides, it's just for a few nights until we find that snake and you feel safe again.'

His words were like honey, drizzling into her senses and making her feel warm and tingly all over. She bit her lip and looked away, trying to fight her lust-fuelled urges. But deep down, she knew she wanted to be with him, even if it was just for a little while.

He tapped the bench and straightened. 'You make yourself at home while I'm gone, and I'll be back as soon as I can to let you know how I went, okay.'

She nodded briskly. 'Yup, okay.'

With one last smile he turned and headed out of the kitchen, leaving her alone with her whirling thoughts and her body still tingling from his closeness. And that's right when her heart sank. What had she been expecting? A kiss? A declaration of love? She shook her head at her insane foolishness. Of course he hadn't been about to kiss her. He was her friend, nothing more.

And she wanted nothing less.

So, therefore, she needed to stop gushing like some lovesick fool over him.

However, remaining tight-lipped, guarded even, was proving exhausting. So many times, she'd considered coming back here. To apologise to Morgan for breaking his heart. To tell him her deepest secret. To make things right. Good intentions, if not acted upon, didn't change a damn thing. If only she hadn't been so damn scared. The fear had stopped her from returning sooner. Fear of finding out he was Chiara's father. Fear of what he might say or do when she told him what was weighing so heavily on her heart and soul. Fear that he'd never be able to forgive her.

Fight or flight.

And she'd taken the easy path when she should have fought, for him, for them.

Now she regretted it, immensely.

CHAPTER
11

The following day, Jess woke in the spare room of the homestead before the birds had begun to sing. The snake had been nowhere to be found, and there was no way on this earth she was going to share lodgings with such a skin-crawling creature. Morgan had gone to the cottage with her, keeping guard while she'd packed her things. God love him. In the evening they'd watched a few episodes of *Peaky Blinders*, a show Morgan loved, and she now did, too, while devouring toasted sandwiches for dinner and half a tub of cookies and cream ice-cream for dessert, before hitting the sack nice and early, in separate rooms of course. Today she would unpack and make this her home until she headed back to Florence. She was acutely aware she was now staying in the same house as the man she'd been in love with for years – she'd finally admitted it to herself, but over her dead body would she admit it out loud – so she knew she had to tread carefully, or risk ruining the fragile friendship they'd established. Because there was no way she wanted to lose him out of her life yet again, by her own doing. Little did he know that he might be meant to be in hers for a lifetime. She'd deal with that soon enough, if it were the case. But for now, she wanted to focus on the wedding. Excuse, or not, it felt like the right thing to do.

As she stretched her limbs to life, she looked around the room and smiled. It was cosy, with a wooden bedframe, matching bedside tables and dressing table, and a fluffy duck-feather doona that made her feel sleepy as soon as she climbed beneath it. And there were bay windows that looked out over the paddocks dotted with his beautiful horses and healthy Angus cattle. The four-bedroom, three-bathroom, two-storey sprawling Queenslander home was a far cry from her small apartment back in Florence, but in a way it felt like home. And she liked the sensation. She was going to savour it with all her heart, if only for this little while. What a dream it would be, to move back here with Chiara, so she could raise her darling girl in the same way she had been, with the mesmeric Australian countryside surrounding her.

If wishes were horses ... beggars would ride.

Closing her eyes, she inhaled a big, appreciative breath, and then sighed it away. It was not quite dawn, and through the open curtains the sky was a moving kaleidoscope of lavender, scarlet and sapphire. On the flitter of breeze, she could smell the mango and lychee blossoms on the air, could sense the gentle waking of Mother Nature as the warmth of the rising sun stirred her great beauty to life. It was the gift of a brand-new day, to start afresh, to start over, to take steps to make things right. When the time was right, that was. Until then, Roberto and Shanti had her full attention, as did finding her passion back in the kitchen – cooking had always been her favourite pastime. Drawing in another deep breath, she forced her thoughts in the right direction, for all their sakes. She was here for their wedding. And that was it. There were no stones to be overturned right now, no new chapters to be written. Silverton Shores was her past. Florence was her inevitable future. She'd do well to remember that. Humouring the thought of ever moving back here with Chiara was ridiculous. She could never leave Nonno behind. Not ever. But then, once she learnt the truth of Chiara's parentage, maybe it was going to be the only option? Because she'd want Morgan in his little girl's life. Would it be a case of her having to choose between Chiara's best interests and her nonno?

Damn her tempestuous thoughts. She needed to get up and do something constructive.

An hour later, showered, with a cup of tea and two pieces of Vegemite on toast in her belly, and eager to spend the day cooking up a storm, she strapped on an apron and got to work. First up was a batch of chocolate chip biscuits, then an orange and almond cake made with the oranges she'd just picked from Morgan's tree out the front and the eggs she'd collected from the chook pen, then whatever else took her fancy for their dinner. Thankful for their new-found connection, she was going to make sure Morgan arrived home from his day working the property to a kitchen filled with home-cooked goodness, filled with her love. And as she hummed to herself, carefully measuring ingredients into a bowl, she couldn't help but think about what a wonderful man he still was, even more than she remembered. The way they'd been so comfortable beside each other on the couch the night before, the way his laugh had filled the room, the way his fingers had twitched as he tried to resist another spoonful of ice-cream, the way she'd found it almost impossible not to love him all the more for how his company made her feel so at peace, and so happy. It was wonderful how life could be, if they were by each other's side.

But it was a fleeting reality that would soon become a memory.

She shook her head, trying to clear how much she wanted to be with Morgan from her thoughts. She had no business thinking like this. He was her friend, and that was all. No matter what came, they couldn't go back to what they were. They could only move forward, at the very least for Chiara's sake. She couldn't risk ruining the bond they'd once again formed by giving in to her desires. She needed to be on speaking terms with him if they were going to survive the possible bomb that she might eventually detonate in his seemingly peaceful world.

But as she rolled out the biscuit dough and cut perfect circles, she couldn't shake the thought that maybe, just maybe, Morgan felt the same way about her. Could he still love her, just as much as he had the day they were meant to marry? No, that was ridiculous. Too much time had passed. Too much water had flowed beneath their bridge. Knowing the upfront, forthright man he was, he would've said something by now, surely. She shook her head again, trying to force the thoughts away, but they refused to budge. Damn it, couldn't she get through one day without torturing herself with what they could have been, or fantasising about what they could be, if given half a chance.

Stop being ridiculous, Jess!

Taking it upon herself to snap the hell out of her Morgan Savage trance, she spent the next couple of hours lost in her cooking and the music playing from the radio. Having decided on a slow-cooked chicken, bacon and mushroom dinner, coupled with cheesy mashed potato and steamed greens, she made sure she'd tidied the kitchen before settling herself at the dining table and opening her laptop. She couldn't wait to see Chiara's face, or hear her singsong voice as she relayed everything that had happened since they'd spoken two days earlier. Logging in to Skype, she eagerly waited for her daughter to answer.

As soon as the call connected, Chiara's face appeared on the screen, her big blue eyes lighting up at the sight of her mother. 'Hi, Mum!' she said, waving excitedly.

Jess's heart swelled with love and warmth. 'Hi, my love. How are you doing?'

'I'm good,' Chiara said, grinning. 'I miss you, though. When are you coming back?'

'Only six more sleeps, sweetie, and I'll be home.'

'Yay!' She turned and Nonno's smiling face came into focus. 'Hi, my sweet bella, how is everything going?'

'Good, Nonno, really good.'

Slipping into her Italian lingo like a second skin, Jess went on to explain all the good stuff, and how she was really enjoying staying with Morgan, other than having a slithering late-night intruder. As usual, all three of them talked excitedly over one another, and laughed wholeheartedly. With the ache in her chest intensifying, she wanted to crawl through the computer and right back to her daughter and Nonno. She reminded herself that she'd made the tough decision to come to Silverton Shores for Roberto and Shanti's wedding, without Chiara, and she couldn't let the longing to be back with her loved ones overshadow the little time she had left here. She had to be strong for Chiara, for herself, and for her future. She also wanted to relish every second of her brother and best friend's wedding – it had been a long time coming.

Wiping happy tears from the corner of her eyes, she sighed. 'I suppose best let you both go, so you can get to sleep.' She screwed her face up. 'I miss you both, so much.'

'We miss you too.' Chiara opened her arms wide. 'This much.'

'Aw, sweetheart.' Blinking faster, Jess kissed the screen. 'Talk again soon, okay.'

'Okay, I love you.' Chiara kissed the screen back. 'Bye, Mum.'

'Love you both, with all my heart.' She waved. 'Bye for now.'

Both waved back and Jess pressed the end button before she broke. This time, before she gave in to her emotions, she opened up the wedding planner app on her laptop and began going through the checklist for the next few days' tasks. She didn't want Shanti to be a ball of stress on her big day, so she wanted to make sure she had everything well and truly covered. The flowers needed to be picked up from the florist, the cake needed to be delivered to the reception venue, the bales of hay had been vetoed and they now had seats, after a little persuading on Roberto's behalf, and the photographer needed to be confirmed for the day. As she checked off each item on her list, she couldn't help but feel a sense of satisfaction wash over her. She was making progress. She was doing something productive. She was distracting herself from her own thoughts and feelings, even if just for a little while.

An hour later she was back in the kitchen, tending to the last of the dinner prep, when the sound of a diesel engine snapped her out of her reverie. Putting the creamy mash to the side, she wiped her hands on a tea towel and headed to the window over the sink. The Troopy was bouncing up the driveway, kicking up dust in its wake. It pulled up in the usual spot and Morgan got out, looking tired but happy to be home. Teeny leapt out beside him and lumbered towards the back door. She couldn't help the smile that spread across her face as she watched him walk towards the house, his broad shoulders and confident stride as attractive as ever. For a fleeting moment, she imagined them as husband and wife, and how wonderful it would feel experiencing this scenario every day, for the rest of her life. Briefly dropping her gaze, she quickly checked herself. He was just a friend, nothing more. She took a deep breath and went to greet him, opening the door with a smile.

'Hey there, welcome home,' she said cheerfully, trying to push away any thoughts of longing.

'Hey, Jess.' Kicking off his boots, Morgan grinned and stepped inside, giving her a quick hug before directing Teeny to his corner of the room. 'It smells amazing in here; what have you been up to?'

For a moment, she felt all of twenty again. 'A spot of baking, and now I'm just getting dinner ready.' There was a flicker of excitement in her belly as he surveyed the line of delicacies, like a string of fairy lights had just glimmered to life.

'Wow, this all looks amazing.' He turned back to her with his grin as wide as it had ever been. 'It's awesome to come home to a house smelling of yummy food,' he said, his eyes lighting up. 'You didn't have to go to so much trouble, though.'

'It was no bother.' There was a day's worth of dark stubble over his jaw and she ached to reach out and touch it. 'It gave me something to do.'

He met her, and bringing his hand to her cheek, he brushed a lock of hair behind her ear, then trailed his fingertips to her dangly earring. 'You've had these little beauties forever.'

'Oh yes, I have.' Her hand came to the opposite earring. 'I can't believe you remember them.'

'Of course I do.' He chuckled, shrugged. 'I remember a lot of weird things.'

They chatted as they set the table and served up dinner, enjoying each other's company as they caught up on the day's events. Jess couldn't help but feel comfortable and safe around Morgan, despite the underlying tension of her secret. Transported back in time as they ate, she recalled the cool-headed, strong-willed, kindest, most loving man she'd ever met. Even though his laugh lines had deepened, and his eyes now wore the strains of adult life, he was still all the man she remembered, and more. Just being near him tugged at the feelings she'd tucked away. What had she gone and done, leaving him high and dry? After spending the past week with him, she could easily picture their lives, together, happy and content. Her heart ached more than ever. Losing him, wrecking them, it was all her fault. And even after a lovely night, spent rehashing old times and chatting about the new, she carried this heaviness in her heart, to bed, and into her dreams. Tumbling into slumber, she was helpless to stop the workings of her unconscious mind. It was as if the ground had opened up, and she'd jumped in feet first.

Eyelids flickering, she felt herself climbing the steps of the homestead, and then she strode to the front door as a woman way more confident than she was in reality. 'Hey, Morgan, are you home?' Her voice carried through the flyscreen and down the hallway.

Silence met her but the scent of burnt toast and freshly made coffee lingered. Refusing to move until he answered the door, she nudged her sunglasses up to the top of her head as fat raindrops began to fall, pounding the tin roof with deafening intensity.

'Morgan, please, at least let me explain.' She yelled this time, and her echoing voice felt as if it were bouncing around her mind.

Suddenly, as if in a magical click of her fingers, he was there, inches from her. He shot her a look full of storm clouds. Shocked at his forlorn expression, she felt his silence stretch, linger and then settle heavily. Her mind raced, but she couldn't find anything worthwhile to say. She managed a tight smile as she stood frozen to the spot, her heart pounding in her chest. Desperate to clear the air, to have him at least offer her a smile, she fought to find her voice. It pained her, seeing him with so much hatred and hurt in his eyes. She opened her mouth to speak, but no words came out. He could see she was struggling, but unlike every other time, he wasn't coming to her rescue, and the silence stretched on for what felt like an eternity.

Finally, Morgan spoke. 'What are you doing here?'

'I—I came to apologise,' she stammered, feeling small and vulnerable in front of him.

Morgan's face wavered then came back into angry focus. 'For what? Breaking my heart? Leaving without a word? Keeping my daughter from me? Which one is it, Jessica?'

Sobbing now, Jess winced at the truth in his words. 'Yes, for all of that.' She wiped her cheeks, but the tears kept on coming. 'I was young and stupid, and I should have turned to you when Mum and Dad died, instead of running away.' She slowly shook her head. 'I'm so deeply sorry.' She tried to reach for him. 'I should have told you about Chiara, long before this.'

Stepping away from her, Morgan crossed his arms over his chest, his jaw clenching. 'You think an apology is going to fix everything? That you can just waltz back into my life after all these years and make everything right?'

'Yes, I think we can make everything right.' The ground beneath her was unsteady now.

'Well think again, Jessica Sabatini, because I never want to see you again.'

Then the ground opened up and swallowed her whole.

CHAPTER
12

Morgan gave a weary sigh. Daylight was beginning to fade, as was his energy. But he just needed another ten minutes to finish what he'd started. Steadying himself on the top rung of the ladder, he dipped his brush into the light blue paint then glided it along the tattered weatherboard. It was going to look like new once he was done. He'd been working on the old shed for the better part of the day, and his muscles groaned in protest as he stretched them out. But it was a good kind of ache, the kind that came from a hard day's work. And it was satisfying to see the progress he had made.

Turning to survey his handiwork, his gaze was drawn to the homestead, and the figure of Jess silhouetted in the kitchen window. He felt a familiar tug in his chest, and he couldn't help but smile at the sight of her. She'd been a constant presence in his thoughts ever since she arrived back in Silverton Shores. It was as if the last nine years had melted away, leaving only the memories of the woman he had once loved so deeply. And now that she was here, it was hard to ignore the feelings that still stirred within him. He'd tried to keep a safe distance, to be respectful of her boundaries, and his own need to safeguard his heart, but it wasn't easy when all he wanted was to pull her into his arms and never let her go. But he knew that wasn't an option.

Not anymore.

Not ever again.

Their past was too complicated, too painful, to be easily forgotten or forgiven. And yet, he couldn't help but wonder if there was still a sliver of a chance for them. If he could convince her that they could make it work, that they could build a future together, with her beautiful Chiara by their side. But surely Salvatore would never allow his daughter to move over to the other side of the world? He wouldn't, if Chiara was his own. That was for certain. He shook his head, knowing that it was a foolish thought. Jess had made it clear that their relationship was strictly platonic, and he had to respect that. He had to be content with the fact that she was here, as his friend, and that was all that mattered.

Turning back to his work, he dipped his brush into the paint once more, and continued where he'd left off. He had a lot of projects to finish before he went back to flying, and he didn't want to waste any more time thinking about what could have been. He'd loved Jess with his whole being, and yet she'd left him without a look back. Many long years had passed them by, and yet he was still healing from the hurt she'd caused him. They could never rekindle what they'd had. And yet the very thought of her finding someone else, someone who deserved her love, made his heart clench in pain. He couldn't imagine anyone else making her happy, not when they had so much history between them. But one day, even though it hadn't worked between her and Salvatore, it was inevitable she would meet someone else who would love her for who she was. He just hoped he could say the same for himself. He longed for the one, the woman to start a family with, and time was ticking.

Way too fast.

He descended the ladder, popped the lid of the paint back on, and carried it over to the shed. With everything packed away in its rightful place, he switched the overhead light off and called it a day. As he walked towards the house, he saw the door open and Jess stepped out. She was wearing a simple sundress, her hair pulled back in a messy bun. She looked stunning in the golden light of the setting sun, and he felt his heart skip a beat. He couldn't help but notice the way her dress clung to her curves, accentuating her every move, or the way her lips curved up into a sweet smile as she saw him, and he certainly couldn't ignore the way her eyes sparkled with a hint of something he couldn't quite place. And as he climbed the steps and kicked off his boots, now up nice and close, her natural beauty pinned him to the spot. It usually took quite a lot to impress him, he'd made it that way so he didn't fall easily, but when it came to Jess, she didn't need to do anything but be her raw, authentic, real self.

'Been hard at work, by the looks.' Her gaze swept towards the shed and then over him.

Taking off his hat, he nodded, trying to keep his voice casual. 'Yeah, just trying to get some things done before I head back to work in a couple of weeks.' He couldn't help but notice the way her eyes lingered on him, and he felt a rush of heat spread through his body as they both stepped through the back door and into the kitchen. 'What about you? How's the wedding planning going?' he asked, hoping to steer the conversation away from the intense emotions he was feeling.

'It's all coming together nicely.' She stretched her arms high and leant side to side. 'We still have a bit to do before the big day, but we'll get there.' She paused, and he could see the sadness in her eyes. 'I just wish Chiara could be here with me.' Elbows on the centre bench, and hands clasped, she rested her chin on them. 'She so wanted to come with me.'

'Oh, Jess, I'm sorry you couldn't find her passport; it must have been really hard, deciding to come without her.' Morgan's heart ached for her, knowing how much she missed her daughter. They'd talked about Chiara quite a lot, and he loved learning about her little girl. 'I'm sure she's having a great time with your nonno, though,' he said, trying to offer her some comfort. 'And you'll be back with her before you know it.'

'Yes, time flies.' She smiled but it was a little wobbly. 'It'll be good to get back into the sweet Italian life, too, I do miss it.'

While grabbing a glass of water from the tap, Morgan bit his tongue. It was as if she was acting, pretending to be content with her life back in Italy. But she wasn't fooling him. Not in the slightest. He innately knew she'd be happier back here, with Chiara, surrounded by family and friends like him, Roberto and Shanti. And she was hiding something. He could feel it deep down in his bones. Not that he was going to try and pry it out of her. Essentially, it was none of his business, and besides, he was hiding something too. But not for much longer. Annie was on the clock.

Turning back to her, he cleared his throat, trying to shake off the thoughts that plagued him. 'I'm going to run through the dip, then I'll be back to make us that dinner I promised.' He gave her a small smile before making his way towards the door. 'And don't you do a thing, because it's my turn to cook.' He pointed towards the lounge room. 'In fact, how about you go and pick a record, or pop some tunes on the stereo.'

'I reckon that sounds like a good idea.' Her voice was warm, and her eyes held a hint of sadness that he couldn't quite place. 'Enjoy your shower.'

'Thanks, will do,' he called over his shoulder, at the same time thinking, *I'd enjoy it a lot more if you were showering with me.*

By the time he got back downstairs, Jess was nowhere to be seen and the weather had taken a turn. Gusts of wind lashed the trees down one side of the house. Humming to the Garth Brooks tune playing – he liked Jess's choice of music – he looked up to the ceiling as the lights flickered when the electricity surged. Pan and tongs in hand, he held his breath. He'd decided against candles, just in case Jess thought he was trying to be romantic, but now he probably needed to light some in case there was a power cut. And just as he sparked the lighter and lit the last one of the six that he'd dotted around the kitchen and lounge room, there was a crack of lightning and the homestead fell into flickering dimness.

Thank goodness he had a gas stove. He flicked it on, and a whoosh sounded as the flame caught. He turned it down a little, not wanting to burn the two pieces of prime scotch fillet to a crisp. Next up he'd boil some sweet potatoes for a nice buttery mash and steam some green beans. Hopefully he had mushrooms in the fridge so he could make his favourite steak sauce. As he worked in the kitchen, the smell of the sizzling meat filled the room, and he couldn't help but feel a sense of contentment.

Cooking was his passion, and he loved nothing more than sharing it with the people he cared about. When he heard Jess's footsteps on the stairs, he glanced over his shoulder, watching as she walked into the room, wrapped in a cosy blanket with the torch on her mobile phone lighting the way.

'Is the power still out?' she asked, her voice soft.

'Yeah, looks like it.' Morgan nodded, turning the steak over in the pan. 'It's okay though, we've got candles and a gas stove. We'll make do.'

Meeting him at the stove she smiled, her eyes glittering in the candlelight. 'You always know how to make the best of a situation, Mr Savage.'

He grinned back at her, feeling that familiar pull in his chest. 'It's just one of my many talents.'

As they got ready to sit down and eat, the conversation flowed easily between them. He'd always loved her laugh. Sweet, melodic, infectious, it was music to his soul. They talked about everything and nothing while they set the table, enjoying the simple pleasure of each other's company. Pulling up a seat opposite her, he couldn't help but feel a sense of happiness wash over him as he watched her take her first bite of the steak. Her eyes closed momentarily, savouring the flavour, and he knew he had nailed it.

'This is amazing.' She set down her fork. 'And this mushroom sauce, oh my goodness, you really are a fantastic cook.'

He felt his cheeks heat up at her compliment. 'Thanks, I'm glad you like it.'

They ate in comfortable silence for a few moments, until Jess spoke up again. 'You know, Morgan, I've been thinking a lot lately.'

Stabbing a piece of medium-rare steak, he fell short of bringing it to his mouth. 'About what?'

Jess took a deep breath, her gaze steady on his. 'About what we mean to each other and what that means moving forward with our newly formed friendship.'

Morgan's heart rate quickened, and he felt a sense of anticipation building inside him. 'I don't understand what you're getting at,' he said, trying to keep his cool.

'I suppose that I hope you'll come over to Italy sometime, and stay with me and Chiara, so we can spend more time together.' She cleared her throat. 'As friends, I mean.'

Morgan felt a pang of disappointment wash over him. He'd been hoping for something more, but he knew he couldn't force her into feeling anything she didn't want to. 'That sounds great,' he said, trying to keep his voice light. 'I'd love to visit you and Chiara, and get to see all of Florence with you two as my tour guides, for sure.'

Jess smiled at him, and he couldn't help but feel a sense of relief that she still wanted him in her life, even if it was just as a friend. 'Good,' she said. 'I think it would be great for Chiara to have another positive male influence in her life, other than my nonno.'

'I'd be honoured to be that for her,' he said, meaning every word. He loved kids, and he had a feeling that he would really like Chiara if he ever got the chance to meet her. He chose his next words carefully. 'You don't talk about Salvatore much. Does Chiara have a good relationship with her father, even though you've separated?'

Jess sighed, her gaze dropping to her plate. 'Salvatore and I ended things on a bad note, and unfortunately, Chiara has been caught in the middle of it all this past eighteen months. He seems to be more interested in chasing women than spending time with her, and sadly, he's made that quite clear.' She shrugged. 'He tries to make up for it by buying her gifts and taking her out occasionally, but it's not the same as being present in her life on a daily basis.' She finally looked up at him, her eyes filled with sadness. 'It's hard, you know. Trying to be both a mother and a father to her. And I quite often feel as if I'm failing at both.'

Morgan felt his chest tighten with anger. How could anyone just abandon their child like that? He reached across the table and took Jess's hand, giving it a gentle squeeze. 'I'm sure you're doing the best you can. And from what you've told me, and how you talk about her, you're doing an amazing job.'

Jess gave him a watery smile, and he could see the gratitude in her eyes. 'Thank you, Morgan. That means a lot.'

He felt a sudden urge to take her into his arms and hold her close, to comfort her in any way he could. He knew that they were just friends, but the way he felt about her was more than that. It was an ache that he couldn't ignore. 'Jess, you're an incredible woman, and Chiara is lucky to have you as her mother.' Leaning across the table, he gently brushed a strand of hair away from her face. 'You're doing an amazing job, and you should be proud of yourself.'

Jess looked at him, her eyes shining with tears. 'Thank you, so very much,' she said softly. 'You always know how to make me feel better.'

Their eyes locked onto one another's, and he felt an all-consuming, heart-wrenching emotion. It was love. And it both buoyed and hurt him in equal measures. All he could do in that poignant moment was smile softly, while his heart ached with a deep tenderness that he couldn't express. He wished things were different between them, that they could be more than just friends. But they weren't meant to be anything but.

With their plates empty, he stood to clear everything away. Jess helped him to pack the dishwasher, with her rinsing and him stacking. They worked like a well-oiled machine and he treasured how the conversation flowed so freely. All concern had now left her gaze, which was now lit with the flicker of candlelight. As he leant on the kitchen bench beside her, the intimacy of her gaze had the power to undo him, but he wasn't about to let all his years of hard work in building a wall around his heart crumble. Being attracted to her was one thing, wanting her with every inch of his heart was another. And he couldn't deny the magnetism he felt towards her, nor could he ignore the feelings that were bubbling up inside him. It was like a wildfire that he had to fight to control, one that threatened to consume him whole if he didn't.

He needed to move, now, before he did something reckless. 'I reckon we should retire to the lounge room.'

'Sounds like a plan, Savage.' As she disappeared down the hallway, he followed her.

They sat down on the couch, and he took a deep breath. He couldn't help but feel a sense of comfort and contentment sitting here with her, relaxing the night away while listening to music, even if it was just as friends. Eventually, as the night wore on, Jess snuggled up to him and rested her head on his shoulder. He could feel her breaths coming slow and steady, and not long after he knew that she'd fallen asleep. He draped an arm around her, pulling her closer to him, feeling at peace for the first time in a long time. He wouldn't trade this moment for anything in the world.

* * *

Jess had woken in the middle of the night, wrapped in Morgan's arms, as he stirred to the brightness of the lights that had just come back on with the power. A little uncomfortable with their intimate closeness, she'd quickly untangled, and he'd done the same, sliding a little down the couch, giving her a few inches of space. Then they'd bid each other goodnight, stood, and wandered up the stairs, each going in their opposite directions. But as she'd slid into bed, she'd felt lost and alone without him to go back to sleep with. It was a sensation that she still carried with her hours later, one that made her feel heavy-hearted in knowing their time had been and gone, that they could never again be as one. Add in the longing to hold her daughter in her arms, and she could've almost just broken down and wept herself into tomorrow.

But she couldn't crumble, not when today was all about joy.

Mentally slapping herself back to the present moment, she offered Shanti a smile as they stepped out of her car. The sleepy little town she'd grown up in had boomed. Cafés rubbed shoulders with clothing shops. A busload of tourists was alighting. A group of mothers pushing strollers and dressed in activewear rushed past her. Mornings seemed to be when everyone came out of their hiding places. As had she. Without breakfast. It was almost nine-thirty now, and her stomach growled in protest. She could almost hear the bacon sizzling and the thought of hot buttery sourdough toast with fried eggs and grilled tomato had her mouth salivating. As did the idea of a coffee fix.

Stepping into Shanti's favourite foodie haunt, she glanced around the boho-themed space. With golden sunlight streaming through the floor-to-ceiling windows, colourful paintings on the walls, and a vase of bright flowers on each mosaic table, the little café was delightful. Freshly baked goodies lined the shelves of the display fridge, and the scent of hot food wafted from the kitchen. Even though she'd been dreaming of a savoury breakfast since leaving the florist, her gaze was drawn like a magnet to the pretty fairy cupcakes, the fresh cream topping each one sprinkled with just the right number of hundreds and thousands.

Shanti followed Jess's gaze and chuckled. 'Go on, my darling friend, you know you want to.'

'Oh yes I do.' Jess grinned. 'Bugger the bacon and eggs.'

As Shanti ordered a cupcake for Jess, and one of the same for herself, along with two mochas, Jess's mind wandered back to the previous night. She couldn't shake off the sensation of being held in Morgan's arms. She hadn't experienced feeling so safe, and so loved, especially by a man she was interested in, in a very long time. Probably since she was loved-up with him, all those years ago. And boy oh boy, had she missed it. Missed him.

Her hands full of treats, Shanti nudged her. 'Come on, Jess, pick a table.'

She pointed. 'That one looks perfect.'

They each took a seat and the cosy atmosphere snuck up and enveloped her. The way the sweet delight was decorated made her feel like it was okay to let go, live in the moment and indulge her senses. And as she bit into the cupcake, she closed her eyes and savoured the taste. It was so delicious that she couldn't help but moan in pleasure. Shanti chuckled and she blushed at the sound of her wantonness. Still smiling, she wrapped her hands around the mug of mocha and grinned at the mound of whipped cream.

As she took a sip, the sweet warmth offered her solace. Shanti did the same, offering her a creamy-moustached grin. Jess followed suit, and together they giggled as if they were teenagers again, getting high as kites on sugar.

With everything demolished, Shanti looked at her watch. 'Well, my darling friend, it's now time for us to go and get pampered.' She stood and hooked her arm into Jess's. 'Pedicures and manicures, here we come.'

Twenty minutes later, seated in a vibrating chair, with both her feet dangling in the warm water, Jess did her very best to offer Shanti a peachy-perfect, I'm-all-good smile, when all the while, enduring a sugar plummet, all she could think of was how much she missed Morgan.

'So, tell me,' Shanti said, regarding her shrewdly. 'How are things going with your flatmate?'

'Morgan?' Jess felt her cheeks heat up at the mere mention of his name. 'We're just friends,' she said, rolling her eyes at Shanti's face while trying to sound casual. 'And it's never going to be any more than that.'

'Are you sure about that?' Shanti raised an eyebrow. 'Because from where I'm sitting, I beg to differ.'

Jess's heart jolted. Was it that blatantly obvious, how she felt about him? Shifting in her seat, she tried to keep her composure, but Shanti's knowing gaze was making it difficult. 'I have no idea what you're on about,' she stated, feigning ignorance.

Shanti leant in closer, her voice low and confidential. 'Jessica Sabatini, it's written all over your pretty face. The way you talk about him, the way you look at him, the way you light up whenever he's around. It's very clear to me that you're still very much in love with him.'

Jess's heart felt like it was about to burst out of her chest. She'd tried so hard to deny her feelings for him, to push them aside and pretend that they weren't there. But hearing Shanti say it out loud made it all too real.

'I am not still in love with him.' She pronounced each word carefully, hoping it sounded convincing.

Shanti offered an I'm-not-buying-it face. 'You might live thousands of miles away from me, but I still know you inside out, so when are you going to admit you still have the feels for him, Jess?'

Jess slid her friend a don't-go-there look. 'Never, because I don't.'

Shanti laughed. 'Oh yes you do!'

Despite her best efforts, Jess's heart gave a little relieved sigh. 'Okay, all right.' Groaning, she took a breath, and huffed it away. 'If you really need to know, I do still care very much for him.'

Shanti's smile filled with tender warmth. 'Love him, you mean to say.'

As the vice around her heart tightened, Jess nodded and sniffled as she swiped the sudden tears away. 'I'm such a sook.'

'No, you're not a sook.' Shanti's hand instantly came to hers. 'You're an empath, Jess, like me, with a big beautiful heart.'

'I'll take that.' Jess nodded again and smiled through her anguish. 'And on another, much lighter note …' She gazed down at her legs, grimacing. 'I really need to shave this Amazon jungle.'

'Yes, you most certainly do, my friend.' Shanti giggled. 'And if the state of your legs is anything to go by, you may need to introduce a razor to your private bits while you're at it.'

'Shhh.' Gobsmacked, and amused, Jess gave Shanti's arm a playful shove. 'Stop it.'

Shanti flashed her a mischievous glance. 'I might, if you're lucky.'

Feeling a little lighter with the banter, Jess rested her head back as she watched the lovely nail technician working wonders with her tired feet. And once again, when she wasn't distracting herself, her thoughts wandered to her unexpected housemate. Morgan Savage was proving time and time again to be a true gentleman at heart. No matter how much she'd hurt him, he'd chosen to remain her friend. And that meant the absolute world to her. *He* meant the absolute world to her.

A few hours later, with matching coral-coloured fingernails and toes, Jess followed Shanti into the haberdashery store, where they were going to buy a few metres of silky material to zhoosh up the tables by running it down the middle, beneath the candelabras Shanti had chosen. As they made their way up and down the aisles, Jess couldn't help but feel a sense of excitement at the prospect of what their end result would look like. Trailing her fingers down the various fabrics, she admired the way the light shimmered across some of them.

'What do you think of this one?' Down the end of the aisle, Shanti held up a copper-coloured fabric to the light.

Jess walked over to her, and felt the silky material between her fingers. 'It's beautiful,' she said, nodding in approval. 'It will definitely add some warmth to the room.'

'Perfect,' Shanti said, grinning. 'And it will match the candleholders perfectly.'

Jess took the roll of fabric from Shanti's hands. 'This is my shout,' she said, and before Shanti could argue, she added, 'and I don't want to hear another word about it.'

She headed up to the counter and plonked the roll down. The young girl on the other side studied her mobile phone as though her life depended upon it, her fingertips skating across the lit screen. Growing impatient, Jess drummed the countertop. Then, when she still wasn't greeted, she did it a little louder.

The girl finally lifted her gaze. 'Oh, hey, sorry, I didn't see you there.'

'I gathered,' Jess said with a tiny smile.

It was so different to the lifestyle she'd become accustomed to in Florence, where people were too enthralled in their surroundings to be staring at their screens.

'Hey, Jess.' Shanti's voice carried over her shoulder. 'What is Morgan doing in a haberdashery store?'

She turned to follow Shanti's gaze and her breath caught. Man, he looked mighty fine as he took long, easy strides down the aisle, seemingly lost in his thoughts. His country swagger screamed testosterone and fortitude. And with that smile on his handsome face, as he paused to ask an assistant something, he should come with a warning label – *high voltage*. If she hadn't reined her libido in, she'd be gushing like a few of the other local women, ogling him as they strolled past where he stood. What she really liked, though, was that he didn't seem to notice the attention one little bit.

'Hey, Shanti.' His deep voice resounded. 'Jess.'

Jess felt her heart racing as his eyes met hers. 'Hey, Morgan.' She tried to ignore the way her body responded to him, and the way her skin tingled when he was near. 'What are you doing in here?' she asked, hoping to sound casual.

'Oh, I needed some fabric for a project,' he said, holding up a roll of deep green material. 'What about you two?' His gaze lingered over her like a heated caress, igniting places she didn't want roused.

'We're sprucing up the tables for the wedding with this,' Shanti explained, gesturing to the folded fabric in Jess's hands.

'I reckon that's going to look beautiful,' he replied, his eyes lingering on Jess for a moment longer than necessary.

'Hopefully,' Shanti added, looking from him to Jess.

As time froze, Jess felt a flutter in her stomach. The heat between them was palpable. His sharp blue eyes pierced hers, evoking feelings she wasn't prepared for, feelings she didn't want reminding of. Helpless, she tumbled into his eyes. For a few brief seconds. Before she firmly reprimanded herself for being so lovestruck. The air shifted as he moved closer to let a lady past. He smelt so good. Edible. Extremely aware of how close he was to her, she took a little sidestep in Shanti's direction before she could forget herself, grab him and bury her face into his chest. She fanned her face as he paid for his fabric – it was suddenly stifling hot in here.

'You all good?' Shanti whispered in her ear.

'Uh-huh.' Drawing in a deep breath, Jess gathered her scattered emotions. 'I'm fine and dandy.'

Bill paid, Morgan turned and flashed them both a smile. 'I'll catch you two later.'

Jess nodded. 'Yup, see you at home.'

See you at home, she repeated silently. *Now that sounded nice.*

'Catch you, buddy.' Shanti offered a wave.

Watching him disappear outside, Jess finally remembered to breathe. She gasped in a lungful of air, then looked to Shanti, who was watching her with amusement written all over her face.

'What?' she asked, her cheeks feeling hotter than hot.

'You know what.' Shanti took her hand. 'Come on, let's go meet your big sister, so we three can have those massages we've been looking forward to.'

They arrived at the day spa ten minutes later, along with Annie, and as soon as they stepped inside, Jess felt a wave of relaxation wash over her. The air was thick with the scent of lavender and lemongrass, and the soft sound of relaxation music filled the air. The masseuse greeted them warmly, and they were led into a dimly lit room, where they were left to change into plush robes. As they all picked a table to lie down on and the masseuses began to work their magic on their tense muscles, Jess tried to focus on the feeling of the warm oil flowing over her skin. She took a few deep breaths, letting the tension slowly melt away with each passing minute. With skilled hands moving to her shoulders, she felt herself drifting into a state of utter relaxation. She could feel the knots in her muscles slowly dissolving, and a sense of deep calm washing over her. It was a welcome reprieve from all the chaos and stress that had been consuming her lately. Closing her eyes, she drifted off with the gentle rhythm of the music, letting the warm oil and trained hands take her to a place of pure bliss.

CHAPTER 13

With his joggers on his antsy feet and AirPods snugly in to drown out the world's noise, Morgan stepped out of the coolness of the homestead and into the first light of day. Deciding on the longer track, he headed west, away from the main buildings and up the ridge. As his feet rhythmically hit the ground, one after the other, a light sheen of sweat covered his body. As tough as the incline was, he increased his speed, pounding his legs harder and harder as he went upwards. He felt the blood pump through his veins, and with that his mind emptied. By the time he'd reached the top, sunshine poured over the landscape below, igniting the distant ocean in glistening splendour. Admiring his view, he turned right, following the track that hugged the hill and overlooked the sea. It was here, where he could run and see the vast, empty expanse before him, that he felt truly at peace. Keeping his breathing in check, he could just make out the bobbing boats, moored in the harbour, along with the glint of the hall where Roberto and Shanti were holding their reception.

Running was his escape from reality, a momentary reprieve from the stresses of life. Here, he only needed to focus on the rhythm of his breathing, the pounding of his feet on the ground, and the direction he was heading, and it felt invigorating. Anything to keep his mind off Jess was a good thing. But try as he might, his thoughts kept drifting back to her. It was hard not to think about her when she was only a stone's throw away. But he had to. To save his sanity. Stretching his legs in a bid to widen his gait that little bit more, he relished the thumping of his feet upon the earth he called home. Pushing his limits helped him ignore the pestering thoughts of Jess being way out of his reach. Glancing at his smartwatch while maintaining his pace, he checked his heart rate then, happy it was in the fat-burning range, kept pounding the dirt track that would lead him back down the hill, and back to Jess. He could have chosen to go the other way, the easier way, but that was no fun. No fun at all. He liked to test his limits, make it that little bit tougher, because it all added to his gain.

As he descended, to his frustration, Jess's face kept popping into his head. He'd been trying his hardest to ignore the feelings he had for her, but they were becoming increasingly impossible to deny. The way she looked at him, the way she smiled at him, the way she made him feel so high on her when she was around him, it all made his heart race. But he had to be careful. He didn't want to ruin their friendship or make things awkward between them. He'd already seen the way she'd reacted to him at the haberdashery store, and he didn't want to push his luck.

Slowing, he turned the corner of the machinery shed and there she was, out on the front verandah, her feet resting up on the railings as she sipped from her ritual morning coffee. And right beside her sat Teeny. The morning sun illuminated her features, highlighting the softness of her skin and the curve of her lips, making her hair and eyes sparkle. He couldn't help but feel drawn to her like a bee to honey as he approached. She looked up and their eyes met, and a jolt of electricity shot through him. Their connection was almost too much for him to handle.

Slowing as he went through the front gate, he pulled to a complete stop at the bottom of the steps. 'Morning, Jess.'

'Hey, Morgan.' Her voice was softly sweet. 'You're keen.'

'Yeah, running helps clear my head.' Leaning over, he untied his laces.

'I'm doing the same thing just by sitting here,' she said, taking another sip of her coffee. 'It's nice to have the time to enjoy the peace and quiet before the chaos of the day starts.'

Morgan nodded, taking a swig from the water bottle he'd left on the bottom step. 'It's beautiful out here, huh.' He took in the sweeping views. 'Mind if I sit with you while I cool down?'

'Of course not.' She jostled over and patted the seat. 'Come, join in the serenity with me and Teeny.'

Taking the steps two at a time, he sank down beside her. Wearing white shorts and a navy T-shirt, she had damp hair, like she hadn't long stepped from the shower, and her skin looked silky smooth. As his eyes wandered covertly over her, he noticed her bare feet, and her toenails painted a pretty coral pink. And boy oh boy, she smelt so good. They sat in a companionable silence, the only sound the gentle rustle of the leaves in the breeze. It felt so good, so right, just being with her, doing the simplest of things. An ache clawed at his chest as his heart skipped. He wanted to tell her how much he loved having her here. And how her presence lightened the dark world he sometimes found himself within. He also wanted to tell her just how badly she'd hurt him. But he locked his lips shut, thinking better of it. What good would come of such revelations? Lightning never struck the same place twice. He couldn't afford to let her know just how much he still felt for her, nor did he want to see the pity in her eyes if she learnt how his heart was still so broken from her. No. He needed to stay firmly planted on his side of the line. And she on hers. Safely out of his reach. Humouring any thoughts of rekindling their old flame was dangerous. He didn't want to dwell on their relationship of the past. He wanted to relish their friendship in the present. But as he watched her take another sip of coffee, he couldn't help but feel the temptation growing stronger. In a perfect world, he'd cross that line, he'd reach out and touch her, feeling the softness of her skin beneath his fingertips. The unspoken words that lingered between the breath she'd just stolen and his next one was palpable. He needed to apply the brakes to his yearnings. Immediately. They'd been down this road once before, and they'd hit a dead end. He wasn't about to try it all over again. It would end up in the same place. With her gone. And him broken.

With his heart desperately reaching for hers, he knew he had to do something before he lost control. So he jumped to his socked feet, and said, 'Catch you on the flip side.'

Tipping her head in his direction, she looked at him oddly, a smirk on her lips. 'That's pretty hip lingo, Morgan.'

'Oh yeah, oops.' He shrugged his awkwardness off. 'I should've said, I hope you have a good day.'

'Okaaay, I hope you have a good day, too.' She sounded as confused as he felt right now.

He shook his head as he strode away, trying to clear the jumbled mess, but when he glanced back, she was still there, staring at him like he'd lost his marbles. He slowed as he approached the door, then disappeared inside. Talk about acting like a loon. He really needed to get his head straight before he faced the day. A dunk under a freezing cold shower should hopefully do the trick. First things first, though, he thought as he headed to the kitchen to make himself an extra-strong cup of coffee. The caffeine might help to jolt some common sense into him. As he waited for the water to boil, he gazed out the window, slowing his breath, and his thoughts, while taking in the beauty of the morning out the window.

Suddenly, there were footsteps behind him, and he jumped, startled. He spun around and flashed Jess a smile. 'Hey.'

'Hey, I've been thinking, and I really need to talk to you,' she said, her eyes full of emotion. 'You got a minute?'

Morgan hesitated before nodding. 'Yeah, of course, what is it?'

'Can we sit?' She placed her empty cup down. 'I promise it won't take long.'

'Sure.' He led her to the lounge room and sat down across from her on the one-seater couch.

They sat in silence for a few brief moments before she cleared her throat and spoke up.

'I know I hurt you when I left here, Morgan.' She paused, and sniffed, as though reining in tears. 'And I'm so sorry for that.'

Morgan's heart clenched with the apology he'd longed for, for years, as memories of their past flooded his mind. 'It's okay,' he said, trying to be nonchalant. 'It's been a long time.'

Jess shook her head. 'No, it's not okay. I was wrong to leave you like that. I never should've walked away, no matter how broken I was.'

Although grateful for her apology, he wanted to let her know he was compassionate about what she was going through at the time of her sudden departure. 'I understand you left me because you needed time to figure things out, I just wish you'd come back to me after you did.'

'Thank you for understanding.' She looked down at her wringing hands, and then back at him, blinking fast. 'I should've talked to you, explained what was going on in my head. I just … I was scared I'd never be able to put myself back together after losing Mum and Dad like that.' Her voice trailed off as she looked at him with sadness in her eyes.

He felt a rush of sympathy for her. He knew what it was like to be scared, to be unsure of what to do next. 'Honestly, it's okay, Jess. We all make mistakes.'

Her eyes glimmered with unshed tears. 'I never stopped thinking about what I did to you.'

Morgan's heart skipped a beat. Could it be possible that she still had feelings for him? Was she about to tell him that?

Please, please, please …

'I want you to know that I'll do everything in my power to maintain the wonderful friendship we've formed.'

His heart sank. 'I appreciate that, and your apology, I truly do.'

'Thank you for being such a wonderful man.' She stood and came to his side. 'Can we hug it out?'

He stood, took her into his arms and held her tight. Feeling her warmth pressed against him, he couldn't help but be transported back to the times when they were together. The way she fitted perfectly into him, the way her body moulded against his. It was like they were made for each other. And as they pulled apart, he couldn't deny the pang of desire that amplified inside of him.

The way her eyes fluttered open, the way her lips parted, it was like she was inviting him into her. But he knew better. He knew he couldn't allow himself to get caught up in the moment. Not when they'd just rekindled their friendship. Yes, he was still in love with her, but she was just a friend now, and he couldn't deny the relief he felt that they'd cleared the air between them.

Hours later, with his gaze lost out the kitchen window, he was contemplating just how easily Jess had slipped back into his heart, and his life. Her heartfelt apology had meant the absolute world and, if anything, it made him love her deeper, harder. Watching the setting sun paint golden hues across the sky, his thoughts drifted back to the days they'd openly loved one another. The way she used to look at him, with so much love, so much hope, so many promises. He missed being the man she wanted to be with for the rest of her life and couldn't help but wonder what their children would've looked like, what they would've grown up to become. Just how she had a way of bringing out the very best in him, she would've also brought out the best in their kids. And the loss of that future made his heart squeeze painfully tight. But he couldn't allow himself to drown in the sorrow of it. Those days were gone. He had to move forward.

*　*　*

The soft swish of her dress had him turning to find himself completely lost for words. With her hair twisted into an elaborate bun at the nape of her slender neck, a few loose curls around her face, and fine dangly earrings complementing her toenails and elegant dress, she looked like royalty. He couldn't help but feel his heart skip a beat at the sight of her. It was like seeing her for the first time all over again and a pang of desire coursed through him as he admired all that was her.

She smiled at his obvious loss for words, a hint of shyness in her gaze. 'So, Mr Savage, how do I look?'

'You, Miss Sabatini,' and relieved he'd found his voice amid the breath she'd just stolen from him, his smile morphed into a full-throttle beam, 'look absolutely stunning.' Her sweet, musky perfume reminded him of nutmeg, honey and wildflowers.

Returning from turning in a full circle, she had a blush on her cheeks. 'Why, thank you.' Playfully curtseying, her hands went to her hips as she looked him up and down. 'And I have to say, you've scrubbed up pretty dapper yourself.'

Her compliment made his swooning heart race even faster. 'It's amazing what a bit of hair gel and a suit can do, hey.' He struck a heroic pose. 'Just call me Bond, James Bond.'

She laughed, the sound like music to his ears. 'Well, Bond, James Bond,' she joked, 'which of your snazzy cars are you taking me to the ball in tonight?'

'That's for me to know, and you to find out.' Her banter was damn sexy. 'I can tell you, though, it's not going to be in some dingy taxi.'

'Aw, I'm intrigued.' She stepped a little closer, curiosity prowling in the green of her eyes.

As if on cue, the crunch of tyres on gravel drew his gaze out the window. 'Come, my queen.' He offered her the crook of his arm. 'Your chariot awaits.'

She accepted his gesture, and together they headed outside to the stretch limo he'd ordered from the neighbouring township. It had cost him a pretty penny, but from the astonished look on her face, it was worth every cent. He watched with amusement as she stared at the car in disbelief.

'Wow, you really went all out,' she said, turning to him with a wide smile. 'You always did know how to make an impression.'

'I thought you'd like it,' he replied, opening the door for her.

As they settled into the plush seats, Jess couldn't stop admiring the luxurious interior. 'This is amazing.' She ran her hand over the suede upholstery. 'I feel like a celebrity.'

'Good.' Morgan chuckled. 'Because you deserve to feel special.'

'Thanks, Morgan. That means a lot to me.' Their eyes locked in a breathless moment, then she looked away, her cheeks flushing.

He regarded her as she gazed out the window, his heart pounding in his chest. The way the golden light of the setting sun danced across her delicate features made her look all the more beautiful. If that were even possible. As the driver pulled away and headed out of the front gates of Savage Acres and towards town, he found himself stealing more glances, unable to shake the feeling that this was a moment he'd remember for the rest of his life.

Way too soon, they were pulling up in front of the RSL. Arm in arm, they walked through the doors of the private dining room. Jess's eyes widened as she breathed in the elaborately decorated space. Red velvet drapes hung from ceiling to floor, and lit candles flickered down the centre of the table.

Jess looked to him and shook her head in awe. 'Wow, this place looks like it's right out of a fairy tale.'

'Doesn't it ever. Shanti's mum has gone to a lot of trouble, by the looks.' At the thought of spending a few hours here, alongside Jess, warmth poured through him. 'It'll be nice to let the world fade away for a little while.'

She nodded as if agreeing wholeheartedly.

Finding their nameplates, then pulling out her chair, he waited for Jess to sit before taking his next to her. Shanti and Roberto clearly weren't giving up on the notion of getting them back together. He had to give them credit where credit was due – not that their efforts were going to come to anything. His life was here. Jess's was a million miles away. Or at least that's what it felt like. A waiter arrived at their side in seconds and poured them both a glass of bubbly, and the night officially began.

Jess took a delicate sip. 'This champagne is yummy.'

Morgan did the same, grimacing. 'I'll have to disagree, I'm afraid.'

'Ha, yes, you're more of a prosecco and red wine man, aren't you?'

'Hell yeah, and beer, I like beer.'

She giggled, nodding. 'Yes, you do.'

The rest of the night flowed along without a hitch. The food was delicious, the company was excellent, and the conversation was easy and enjoyable. And as the night wore on, he found himself growing more and more relaxed in her company and he could feel the weight of the past slowly lifting from his shoulders.

Before he knew it, it was his turn to stand and raise a toast. 'To Roberto and Shanti.' Holding the stem of the champagne flute, he raised it. 'May they continue to make all of us envious of the amazing love they share.'

Glasses were raised as cheers erupted.

He took a swig and tried not to grimace again. Give him beer over this dry, expensive muck any day. At least he could get a firm grip on a beer bottle. After a few more toasts, the night slowly began to wind down. The guests started to leave, and he once again found himself alone with Jess. As they made their way through the packed club, he couldn't help but feel a sense of sadness. He'd truly enjoyed her company more than ever, and he didn't want the night to end. Stepping into the cool night air, he sensed everything around him stilling as a wave of nostalgia hit him hard, along with something else he couldn't quite put his finger on. It was strange, because for the first time in a long time, he felt the emptiness of being childless and very single. Would he ever find the one, who'd outshine the glow that this beautiful woman beside him had left in his heart? If he didn't, he'd die a very lonely, regretful man. He wanted a wife, he wanted a family, he wanted to share every day with his better half. He just wished it was Jess, because the love they'd shared could happen again in a heartbeat. He was sure of it.

She swayed a little in her heels as they walked towards the waiting limo, and he placed a steadying arm around her. As much as he longed to make love to her, he was going to see her home like a gentleman should. Make sure she was tucked up in bed before he hit the sack himself, alone, like he had for years. The ride home was quiet, but comfortably so, as she rested her head on his shoulder, and they watched the stars out the open roof. When they arrived home, way too fast for his liking, he headed up the front stairs and into the homestead.

Slipping off her heels, Jess tilted her head and glanced up at him. 'Can you sit with me, just for a little bit, so I can wind down before bed?'

'Yeah, of course I can. Would you like a hot chocolate with all the trimmings?'

She smiled softly. 'That sounds perfect, thanks, Morgan.'

'You get yourself comfortable wherever you like, and I'll be back before you know it.'

'Okey-dokey, I think I'll go out to the back verandah.'

He liked her thinking. It was a perfect night for it. 'See you out there soon.'

Ten minutes later, with two mugs of hot chocolate topped with lashings of canned whipped cream and dusted with cocoa, he carefully made his way out to her. Teeny had made himself comfortable at the foot of the swing chair and Jess had her legs curled up beneath her. The moon was high in the sky, casting a soft light over everything around them. He handed her a mug, and she smiled gratefully. Then they sat in another comfortable silence, sipping their hot chocolates and looking out and over the property.

Finally, Jess spoke up. 'Thank you for tonight. I had a great time.'

Morgan smiled. 'Me too. It was nice to spend time with you again.'

The easy conversation continued, and they chatted about their memories of growing up in Silverton Shores. Both were in agreement about how wonderful it had been. Reliving their happier times made him feel as happy as she looked, and it felt good to be the reason she was smiling. But then, in what felt like a blink of an eye, she brought her fingertips to her cheek, to wipe a few stray tears away.

Backpedalling in his mind, he tried to think of what he'd done, or said, to upset her. 'Oh, Jess, sorry if I put my foot in my mouth.'

'No, it's not you.' Her hand momentarily rested on his arm. 'It's just, being back here makes me miss my mum and dad so much.' She sucked in a breath. 'I just wish I could have one more day with them, you know, so I could tell them how much I appreciated and loved them.'

'I'm sure you made them know that every single day they were here.' He placed his hand over hers, gently squeezing her fingers, at the same time wishing to god he could tell her what he knew. 'I suppose, in a way, coming back here is like peeling back a band-aid.' There was still so much grief in her eyes, and it killed him to see it.

'That's a perfect analogy.' Her tear-ravaged eyes met his, and almost broke him in two. 'It's been so long, and I didn't think it would hit me so hard.'

A sudden surge of protectiveness overcame him, and he wished he could erase the pain from her eyes and make everything better in an instant. But for now, there was only one thing he could do. Hold her close. So he pulled her into his arms, feeling the warmth of her body against his. She rested her head on his chest, and he could feel the softness of her hair tickling his chin. It was an intimate moment, and he couldn't help but feel a familiar stirring in his chest. For a long moment, followed by another, they stayed like that, wrapped up in each other's arms, taking comfort in each other's presence. He could feel the rise and fall of Jess's breaths, and he knew that she was starting to settle. He stroked her hair gently and whispered words of comfort, promising that everything was going to be all right. She nodded, then met his gaze. And in that fleeting moment, it actually felt like it could be.

CHAPTER
14

Morgan couldn't wipe the smile from his face. And it felt damn good to be so happy, content, at ease. Because some days, no matter what he did, things just didn't seem to go right. But thankfully, today wasn't one of those days. In fact, today was the exact opposite. It was one of those days where everything seemed to fall perfectly into place, like the universe was conspiring in his favour. He'd woken up with the smile on his face, feeling rejuvenated after a peaceful night's sleep. He'd gotten dressed and headed downstairs to the kitchen, where he brewed himself a strong cup of coffee and actually sat down to enjoy it. And as he made his way outside to start his daily tasks, he couldn't help but feel a sense of gratitude. The sun was shining brightly in the sky, and the air was cool and crisp. It was the perfect day to get some work done on his treasured property and soak up the fresh air. Everything seemed brighter and more beautiful today. Even the kookaburras sounded happier than normal, their laughter filling the air with a cheerful melody.

Without a doubt in his mind, he put it all down to the gorgeous woman he was so lucky to have loved so deeply, and the connection they'd renewed over the past ten days. If only it could be more, if only he could get down on one knee again and ask her to be his wife – but he didn't want to focus on what they couldn't have, he wanted to focus on the close friendship they did have. Because that, he knew in his heart of hearts, was priceless. His thoughts drifted back to the night before. The way Jess had looked up at him with those tear-stained eyes, and the way he'd held her close as she cried, it had all felt so natural, so right. She really was the most amazing soul he'd ever met and, he guessed, ever would.

With Jess consuming his thoughts the hours flew by and before Morgan knew it the sun was slowly slipping from the sky, setting it on blazing fire – twilight would be hinting at arrival real soon – he did the math. There was about thirty minutes of sunshine left. After sweating through three clean shirts, it was almost time to be calling it a day. He took off his wide-brimmed hat and wiped his brow with the back of his arm as he surveyed the new railings of the round yard with quiet pride. His day of hard yakka had paid off, and it was looking pretty schmick. Tomorrow he'd start spending a bit of time with his newest horsey recruit. And he couldn't wait to make friends with the striking blonde palomino, aptly named Malibu.

He glanced over to where the rescued horse was grazing in one of the top paddocks. She'd been there for a few weeks, relaxing in her new home. He'd wanted her to have some quiet time, after her past few years of being owned by a man with no heart for horses.

The bastard. If only he could take an iron rod to him, as the cruel SOB had done to Malibu, but hopefully karma would have her way with such a despicable person in time. He looked forward to the challenge of showing Malibu that some humans could be kind, could be trusted. The key was to work her on the ground, on a long lunging rope, give her enough space but also keep her in check while changing directions often to keep her guessing, so she didn't become too sure of herself, but instead placed her trust in him. It would require persistence, patience and skill, because rushing her would result in her losing more of her spirit, and he didn't want that. He wanted her spirit to resurface and shine bright. He had high hopes for her, and sensed she'd be a keeper.

If only he could say the same about Jess. He would have kept her safe and happy for all of their days together. But it wasn't to be. On the up side, he was beginning to understand the workings of their new-found friendship, and respected the boundaries of it, but he'd be a fool to try and tell himself that the intense feelings he had for her didn't have the power to overcome him, if he let his willpower slip. He sucked in a sharp breath at just the thought of doing so. With her long flowing hair, and eyes green enough to pierce through snow, one lengthy glance from her and he was almost a goner. Every. Single. Time. He knew there was no chance for them, no chance at all. She had a life far away from here. And his life was a far cry from what she'd grown accustomed to. Even so, she'd always remain the absolute love of his life. And he was going to have to find a way to be okay with that so that he could meet another wonderful woman, to marry and settle down with. Because damn, he wanted a family, and a life with a loving woman by his side.

But would anyone else ever live up to Jessica Sabatini?

It would be a tough gig, that was for sure.

He sighed at his suddenly disheartening train of thought. He knew he should be happy, at peace even, with what he'd already accomplished in his life, but he just couldn't seem to get rid of a deep restlessness that made him feel like he had *almost* everything, and yet nothing. They'd been so in love, so happy, so hopeful for their future together. Or so he'd thought. Even though she'd lost so much, gone through so much heartbreak with the deaths of Enzo and Julie, deep down he still couldn't understand why she hadn't turned to him for the support she'd needed, instead of running for the hills of Tuscany. Hell, he'd even believed she'd eventually return to him. But she never had. Instead, she'd gone and married another man within a year of leaving him. And it was this part that stung him the most. Finding out she was another man's wife had been one of the hardest days of his life, the pain of it on par with the day she'd left Silverton Shores, and him, behind. Knowing she and Salvatore hadn't worked out was bittersweet. He felt sorry for her, and her daughter – broken families were never nice – but it also gave him a tiny bit of hope that maybe, by some miracle, by some stroke of luck, or fate, or destiny, whatever it was that made this world spin round, this time she might come back to him, if given enough time and space, if shown that love and trust had been there all along. The emotional merry-go-round he was on when it came to her was both invigorating and dizzying, and at some point he knew he was going to have to get off.

Familiar footfalls had him spinning to meet her gaze, and he quickly swallowed down the mixed emotions his contemplations had evoked. 'Oh, hey, Jess.'

Jess smiled, tucking a strand of her hair behind her ear. 'Hey, Morgan. The spruced-up training yard looks awesome.' She looked left to right as she walked up to him. 'You've done a great job.'

'Thanks.' His heart skipped a beat at the sight of her, and it took everything in him to not reach out and pull her into his arms. 'I was just thinking about working with Malibu tomorrow,' he said, trying to keep his voice steady. 'It's time, I think, for her to get to know me.'

Jess nodded, her eyes sparkling with interest. 'I'd love to watch, if that's okay. I've always been fascinated by the way you work with horses.'

'Sure thing.' His heart leapt at the thought of spending more time with her. 'It's not going to be anything too exciting, though, just some groundwork to start off with.'

'No worries, I can't wait to see you two bonding.'

He couldn't help but feel a sense of warmth spread through his chest with her enthusiasm. 'How was your day with Shanti and Annie?'

'Long. But productive.' A look of exhaustion crossed her face. 'Thankfully we're almost there with all the wedding prep.'

'Glad to hear it.' He ducked through the railings of the yard. 'It sounds like we could both do with an icy cold beer, you keen?'

Jess pulled an are-you-kidding face. 'Damn straight I am.'

'Great, let's head back home and grab ourselves one.'

Side by side, they wandered back towards the homestead with Teeny hot on their heels. Taking the steps two at a time, Morgan flew past Jess and opened the little bar fridge at the corner of the verandah, grabbing two cold beers. He handed one to her, then they headed over to the swing chair and got comfortable. The silence between them was companionable, so much so that he didn't feel any need to fill it as they sat and watched the sunset. And as the sun eventually dipped below the radiant horizon, a sense of peace settled over him. It was the way things always were when they were together, just the two of them, as if the world slowed down. They'd been through so much pain and heartache, but they'd managed to find a way back to each other, even if it was just as friends. Appreciating this, he swigged his beer and let out a contented sigh. It was times like these that he cherished the most, sharing the simple pleasures of life with the people he loved reminded him what was truly important.

Sighing in the same appreciative way, Jess shifted beside him. As she crossed her legs beneath her, her thigh brushed against his, and his heart skipped a beat. Her presence swiftly surrounded him, and he was suddenly, intensely, aware of her. It was so easy to forget they were just friends, and so hard to accept there was nothing more between them. He knew their old flame would be so easy to rekindle and catch fire, but he wasn't going to risk being left with nothing but a pile of ashes. So, tearing his gaze away from her, he focused back on the darkening sky. The first star was starting to twinkle, and with it he felt a sense of wonder at the enormity of the universe. There was something humbling about realising just how small and insignificant he was, and yet, at the same time, how he felt incredibly connected to everything around him, and this included Jess.

Her hand gently brushed against his, and he turned to her, noting her eyes were brimming with emotion. 'Is everything okay?' he asked, his voice soft.

She took a deep breath as her gaze remained locked on his. 'I was just thinking,' she said slowly, 'about how much I've missed being with you, in our own little world. It's like nothing has changed, even though everything has.'

A lump of raw emotion formed in his throat, but he forced it down. 'Yeah,' he said, keeping his voice steady. 'I know what you mean.' He tipped his head and shrugged. 'It's strange how life can suddenly take us in such different directions. But I'm grateful that we can still be here together, like this.'

Jess nodded with her eyes still trained on his. 'Me too,' she whispered, and before he knew it, she was leaning in, her lips so dangerously close to his.

And he was about to succumb to her, to them, but his willpower stormed to the forefront and kicked some sense into him. He, they, couldn't do this. He yanked himself back, against the side of the chair, well out of her reach, unable to speak. Her eyes widened and a flush rose on her cheeks before she turned away from him and focused intensely on Teeny at her feet. In the long awkward silence, he heard the lowing of cattle, and the pounding of his racing heart. He inwardly winced. He needed to put a stop to this, before they undid all their hard work at keeping this connection platonic.

But Jess was the first to speak. 'I'm sorry, Morgan. I didn't mean to make things awkward.'

'It's fine,' he replied, trying to keep his voice even. 'You just caught me off guard, that's all.'

'Of course, it would have.' She took a long sip of her beer. 'Hell, it caught me off guard, too.' She sighed sadly, shaking her head slowly. 'It's tough, not giving in to what we both know could still be there, if we let it.' She shrugged a little while picking at her beer label, then looked back at him. 'I promise I won't do anything like that again.'

If you only knew just how much I wish we could …

He quickly drew in a breath, trying to clear such thoughts from his mind. 'I feel the same way, Jess, I really do. It's weird, just being friends, but it's the only way forward.'

She nodded. 'Yes, it is.'

'I'm sorry, Jess, it's just …' He paused, shook his head. 'I've done a whole lot of missing you, and a whole lot of self-searching to try and get over what we lost.' He finally met her eyes again. 'I never truly got over you, and I can't go back there, to that heartbroken place, when you go back to Italy.'

'Oh, Morgan, I'm so sorry.' Her eyes softened. 'I totally understand the way you feel.' She reached out and took his hand, her fingers intertwining with his. 'And I don't ever want to hurt you like that again.'

'I don't want either of us to hurt again,' he said, gently.

She let his hand go and clasped both of hers around her beer bottle. 'Do you ever wish you could give up flying and make a living off your land?'

'Hell yeah, it's my goal to do just that.'

She smiled from her heart. 'That's great, and with your hard work ethic, I reckon you'll get there quick smart.'

'Let's hope, hey.' He took a swig from his beer. 'This place is all I've got, so it's easy to put my whole heart and soul into it, wherever I get the chance.'

'What do you mean?' She frowned. 'You've got so much more than that.'

He turned to look at her, his heart racing. 'Do I, Jess?'

Her eyes met his, and for a moment he saw a flicker of pain and regret. 'I know I messed things up between us, and you know I'm deeply sorry for that, but that doesn't mean you don't have anything else in your life.'

He sighed heavily. 'I know that logically, but it doesn't always feel that way.' He took another swig of his beer, trying to calm himself down. 'I just wish things had turned out differently between us. I wish we could have made it work.'

'I know, and believe me, so do I.' She reached over and placed her hand on his arm. 'But we can't change the past. All we can do is try to make now, and the future, better.'

'Exactly.' She'd hit the nail on the head, and he was going to continue doing exactly that.

* * *

Jess spent the next two days chastising herself over the fact that she'd almost lost all self-control and kissed Morgan. What had she been thinking, acting so reckless? She could've gone and ruined everything. And for what? It wasn't like they were getting back together. Ever. Morgan wasn't interested in anything more than a friendship. He'd made that very clear when he'd recoiled from her momentary lapse of reason like she was some poisonous creature. She just thanked the powers that be that he understood her moment of bad judgement. Even so, she'd done her best to steer as clear from him as possible while living beneath the same roof, more because she was embarrassed than because of him. And she wasn't going to tell another living soul about it either, not even Shanti. This was something she had to find a way over, or through, hopefully sooner rather than later.

The distinctive thud of a horse's hoofs striking the earth caught her attention. Placing her magazine down, she rose and padded over to the railings of the verandah. There, kicking up a cloud of dust, was a mesmerising man and his magnificent horse.

With the sun in her eyes, she squinted as she honed in on the horizon. Galloping at breakneck speed, Morgan was silhouetted by the late-afternoon sunshine on his back. Wanting to appear completely casual, she sat back down, grabbed her magazine and pretended to be engrossed in it, instead of him. Waiting, she wondered how her hair looked, then mentally slapped herself for caring. As he neared the homestead, her insides quivered with anticipation as his wide-smiled stare pinned her to the spot.

Dismounting from Cash like a gymnast, he stretched to his full height, his tight-fitting blue T-shirt, snug well-worn jeans and five o'clock shadow enhancing his muscular physique. 'Howdy, Jess.'

'Hey, Morgan.'

'Would you like to head down to the beach with me, to catch the sunset?' His deep, masculine voice carried to her as he made his way down the pathway, towards the homestead.

Not having found the time to spend at the beach yet, she almost leapt to her feet with excitement. 'Would I ever!'

'Great.' He stopped at the foot of the steps. 'I'll go and put Cash away in his paddock and be back to grab you soon.'

She watched from the verandah as he led Cash towards the paddocks, her eyes tracing the lines of his back muscles as he sauntered away. She couldn't believe she was feeling this way about him after all these years, even after everything that had happened between them. But it was impossible to ignore the way her body reacted to him, the way her heart leapt in her chest whenever he was near. Shaking her head to clear her thoughts, she rose and went inside to change into something more comfortable for the beach. She opted for a bikini and a loose sundress. Morgan was back before she knew it, and they were on their way. Cattle, sugarcane fields and fruit orchards zipped past as she stared out the open passenger window. Johnny Cash serenaded from the speakers and Morgan sang along, hitting the baritone perfectly.

'That's mighty impressive, Savage. Maybe you should give up your day job.'

He grinned charismatically. 'I've thought about it, but I don't reckon I could handle the spotlight.'

'Oh, come on, you're far from shy.'

'I like remaining mysterious.' He waggled his brows.

She couldn't help but laugh at his playfulness. 'Ha ha, yes indeed you do.'

Reaching the glimmering ocean, they parked and stepped out. A warm, salty breeze drifted, stirring the palm fronds lining the beachfront. With her thongs dangling from her fingertips, she enjoyed the feeling of the water lapping over her bare feet as she and Morgan strolled the shoreline. His slightly guarded gaze met hers and like a deer caught in headlights she couldn't drag her eyes from his blue depths as the wall she'd built around her heart splintered that little bit more. It was just a hairline crack, but she thought it might be enough for him to catch a glimpse into her heart. Eventually they reached the pier, and after wandering the weather-worn timber planks, they reached the end and sat, side-by-side, their feet dangling over the edge.

'This is really nice,' she said with a contented sigh. 'It's lovely to slow down and take a real deep breath, hey.'

Morgan studied her for a beat before looking back at the sunset. 'I may have lived life full throttle when I was younger, but yeah, life in the slow lane suits me now.'

Acknowledging him, she smiled warmly. 'Yeah, it really does.'

After the sun had well and truly set, they made their way back to the homestead where both of them ducked into their respective bathrooms for a shower. And both of them exited at the exact same time, too, literally walking into one another.

'Oops, crap, didn't see you there.' Jess clutched her towel to her chest.

'Sorry, just on my way to the laundry to grab my basket of clean clothes.' His lingering smile spread.

'Ah, yup, I'll get out of your way.' Jess stepped to the left, letting him pass her.

She couldn't help but watch him saunter away. His towel was slung deliciously low on his hips. One flick of her finger, and it would be on the floor.

Argh, a girl can dream!

An hour later, with her belly full of leftover ravioli, and her video call with Chiara ended, Jess settled herself on the chair swing and took a careful sip from her hot chocolate. Morgan had gone to bed early, leaving her some much-needed time to herself. Looking to where the tiny lights strung along the eaves of the back verandah twinkled against the darkness, she sighed as the sounds of night enveloped her. Her conversations with Chiara were leaving her feeling like a fraud. It was different when she was all the way over the other side of the world, where she could ignore the inevitable, but being here, so near Morgan, was making everything so crystal clear. She hoped the test results were going to confirm her intuition, because Chiara deserved to have a dad like him in her life. As for Salvatore, she'd been so lost, so heartbroken, so desperate to fill the gaping hole left in her heart by her mum and dad's deaths, she'd grabbed hold of him without really getting to know him. Handsome, and attentive at first, he'd seemed like the answer to her prayers in her time of need, until he'd slipped a ring on her finger, peeled off the mask and shown her his true colours when it was far too late to run.

If only she could turn back the clock and change things.

Not wanting thoughts of Salvatore right now, or the possible mess she'd be clearing up once the truth was out, she turned her mind back to Morgan. Loving him had been magical. Losing him, even though it had been her fault, had been soul-destroying. Having him a part of her life again was all she could hope for, and now she prayed that if he was Chiara's father, he would willingly be a part of his little girl's life.

Time would tell.

The squeak of the swing chair halted as she brought it to a standstill, then stood. She should call it a night, and treat tomorrow like the gift it was. So she made her way inside the house. Grabbing a flannelette shirt from a hook near the back door, she tugged it on. It smelt of Morgan and she wanted to fall asleep in it. After popping her cup in the dishwasher, she walked through the darkened hallways, her bare feet padding softly against the timber floors. Pausing briefly at the foot of the stairs, she imagined what it would feel like to be heading up to the master bedroom, to him. The way his touch sent electricity through her body, the way his deep voice made her heart skip a beat, the way they had once been so in love. It made her ache for him, in every way. But she couldn't have him. Not now. Not ever.

CHAPTER 15

Shoving her bedroom window open at first light, Jess propped her elbows against the sill and breathed in the sweet tropical scent of frangipanis, salty air, horses and freshly cut grass. The lorikeets were celebrating the arrival of a new day, their melodic song carrying from the big old gum tree. She smiled to herself as she gazed out over the sprawling countryside that Morgan called home. It was certainly a little piece of paradise. As she watched the sun climb higher and higher into the sky, she felt a sense of peace washing over her. It was as if the world had slowed down just for a moment, giving her the chance to gather her thoughts and reflect.

And that's when her secret hit her hard in her chest. She couldn't keep it hidden for much longer. It was a heavy burden to bear. She knew Morgan deserved to know and she couldn't live with the guilt of that much longer. Soon she'd be back in Florence, with the answers she needed. And then she could deal with it, and not a minute earlier. She closed her eyes tight, wishing she could somehow make the uncertainty vanish until then. She was tired of pretending that everything was fine. That she was fine. Because she wasn't. If she were being honest with herself, her life was far from it. Afraid of what was going to happen when she read the results – because, essentially, it could go either way – she forced a steadying breath, and when that one didn't work, she tried for another. If it turned out that Morgan wasn't Chiara's dad, it would feel like the greatest loss. It would mean she'd never look back, to him, or to here. She wouldn't have a reason to. And she couldn't leave Italy, knowing that Chiara was leaving her biological father behind – not that Salvatore would allow it, either. Cursing her past choices, she turned and stomped towards the bathroom, where she hoped a shower was going to snap her out of her sudden low mood.

But it didn't.

She sank into the swing chair and hugged her knees to her. Resting her chin on top, she looked out and over the land that Morgan had put every drop of his blood, sweat and tears into. Just where he found the time, between flying for the RFDS and tending to his property, she hadn't a damn clue. But he was doing it, and he was hitting goals, left, right and centre. And maybe she and Chiara could have been part of his life if she'd stayed, instead of running away. Or would that have meant she would never have had her baby girl, because Salvatore really was her dad?

Blinking back tears, she tried to shake the overwhelming feeling of regret that had settled inside her. It was as if all the twists and turns her life had taken had led her right back to where she'd started, and yet everything was different now. She had a daughter, a secret she couldn't keep hidden for much longer, and a man she still loved, but who might not forgive her for what she'd gone and done.

She stood and slipped her feet into her shoes at the back door. She needed to do something, anything rather than sitting there dwelling on it all. She had to make things right, but she couldn't do that until after the wedding. And with that understanding, she made her way towards the round yard, where she knew Morgan would be working with Malibu. She could carry this secret for a little longer. She had to.

Leaning on the railings, she watched him put the mare through her paces. After stopping the gorgeous palomino short, he guided her into a sharp turn then, with a tug on the reins, instructed her to back up, which the horse did with smooth, graceful movements. Her heart swelled with admiration at how Morgan's gentle, kind approach had paid off. Just like everything he put his heart and soul into had bloomed, flourished, succeeded. He was going to have an amazing legacy to leave to his children one day, that was for sure. It broke her heart to know they weren't going to be *their* children. But they might already share one, and she hoped, with all her might, that Chiara might have the opportunity to become a part of his life.

Morgan spotted her and she felt her breath catch in her throat. He looked just as handsome as ever with his sun-kissed skin glowing in the morning light. He rode over to the timber railing, stopped next to her and dismounted.

'Hey,' he said, smiling at her with those blue eyes that made her heart skip a beat. 'What brings you out here so early?'

Jess fought to keep herself from melting beneath his gaze. 'I just wanted to watch you working your magic with Malibu.' She tried to keep her voice steady.

Morgan raised an eyebrow, clearly not convinced. 'Is everything okay?'

She hesitated for a moment, her secret dangling on the very tip of her tongue. 'Yup, all good.' Reaching out, she ran her hand over the horse's flank. 'Do you ever miss riding bulls?' It was a total deviation from the conversation, but that's what she wanted.

'Nope, not one little bit.' He shifted his tall strong body from boot to boot. 'Why do you ask?'

'Just curious.' She grinned. 'I was your biggest fan back then, but you know that, right?'

Morgan chuckled. 'I do remember that. You were always cheering me on from the stands.'

She smiled at the memory. 'I still can't believe you gave it all up to become a pilot.'

Morgan shrugged. 'It was time for a change. Besides, flying for the RFDS is a whole different kind of rush.'

'I bet it would be,' she said, looking to the sky he called home when he was at work.

She missed the days when they used to do everything together: daily chores, living life, sharing love. They'd shared a wonderful life, until it had all fallen apart. The days when she'd go to every rodeo with him seemed like a lifetime ago, before everything had unravelled between them. Now they stood at a crossroad, and she wasn't sure what the future held for them. Morgan Savage had seen her at the best, and worst, and everything in between, and his love for her had never faltered. Even now, she knew he loved her still. In his own unique way.

'Want to walk with me?' Morgan snapped her from her thoughts as he gestured over his shoulder. 'I just have to go and grab something from over yonder.'

'Yeah, sure.' She ducked beneath the railings.

They wandered towards the tack room. Morgan ducked inside and reappeared with a bucket of lucerne hay. 'A bit of a treat, for all her hard work.' He held the bucket up, smiling.

'She's going to love you for that,' she said, tucking her hands into the back pockets of her denim shorts.

When what she really wanted to say was, *I love you, Morgan. Noooooooooo!*

She mentally slapped herself for thinking such a thing as Morgan stayed in the round yard, and she slipped back on the other side. She didn't want to be distracted by her feelings for him. But at times it felt as if it was out of her control. As if *she* was out of control. All she could think about right now was the two of them. Naked. In bed. Making up for all the years they'd lost. As she watched him taking the saddle off Malibu's back, she wanted to storm over and grab him by his collared shirt and haul him to her, nice and close, so she could whisper her deepest desires against his neck.

Stop it, Jess, right now, before you do something stupid, again!

Her mind racing, she let go of the breath she was holding. Her heart was pounding so hard she was surprised it hadn't beaten its way out of her chest. She might be feeling insanely reckless, but she wasn't stupid enough to follow through. Heat rushed to her cheeks while she did her best to swallow past the lump in her throat. How did he have this power over her, while standing five metres away? And how was she meant to fight him off, for the remainder of her stay, when the chemistry between them was through the roof? She had no idea how she was going to continue to resist him. It felt like she was playing with fire and, like some pyromaniac, she couldn't help but feel drawn to it. Mentally, emotionally, she knew she had to keep her distance, but her body had other ideas.

Less than an hour later, having driven over to Shanti's and finally told her what her best friend already knew about her feelings for Morgan, Jess stared at her across the coffee table and grimaced. 'Surely I'll meet another bloke who makes me feel like Morgan does, right?'

'There may be plenty of fish in the sea, Jess, but none of them come close to Morgan.' Shanti sighed and tipped her head a little, regarding her with compassion and understanding. 'My advice is, don't walk away from him a second time, Jess, not without really thinking about how your life is going to be without him in it.'

Jess knew she was right. Morgan was one of a kind, and he would make her the happiest woman, for the rest of her days. But with the secret she was keeping, and the miles of ocean between them, as well as the fact that they'd tried once, and failed, she truly felt like the odds were stacked against her, and against them.

She couldn't help the way she felt about him, but she could do her best to make light of it. 'I totally get what you're saying, but I think that ship has already sailed, Shanti.' She nodded at her own words. 'Therefore, you can give up wishing for us to be back together, little miss cupid.'

Shanti shrugged. 'What can I say, I'm a romantic at heart.'

Jess chuckled at her response, but inside, her heart felt immensely heavy. She knew Morgan was the one that got away, the one she let slip through her fingers, and she didn't think their relationship could ever be. Although Shanti was right to say she had been handed a second chance, because of her secret she was going to have to disregard it. For now, at least. And she hated the fact. Her throat clamped with raw emotion and she took a deep breath, trying to calm herself down. Morgan made her feel things she didn't even know existed inside her anymore.

'Jess,' Shanti said, her gentle voice breaking through her thoughts. 'You love him, and he loves you, and that's a fact.'

She looked at Shanti and tried to smile. 'I know what you mean,' she said. 'But sometimes love just isn't enough.'

Shanti cocked her head to the side, studying Jess with a shrewd gaze. 'Is that what you really believe, or are you just scared?'

Jess opened her mouth to protest, but Shanti held up a hand to stop her. 'I'm not judging you. I just want to know what's holding you back.'

Jess sighed and looked away. 'I don't know,' she said softly, feeling terrible for not telling Shanti why she wasn't just scared, but was absolutely terrified. 'It's just ... complicated.'

Shanti nodded understandingly. 'Love is always complicated. But it's worth it, too, if it's with the right person.'

Jess nodded. She knew that her best friend, and soon-to-be sister-in-law, was right, but it didn't make things any easier. Her heart felt heavy, like a weight was pressing down on it, and it made it terribly hard to breathe. Flopping back against the couch, she couldn't help but replay sweet memories in her head. Memories of Morgan's touch, the sound of his deep laughter, the way he looked at her like she was the only person in the world. But those reminiscences were overshadowed by a deep-seated fear and crushing doubt. Not a good combination for trying to revive a long-ago love with another. They'd be doomed from the get-go.

She sat up again, and flashed Shanti a smile. 'Right, I better get a move on if I want to get to the end of my list before the shops close.'

'Are you sure you don't want me to come with you?'

'I'm positive, you go and enjoy some time with my annoyingly handsome brother.'

'Thanks, Jessie.' Shanti waggled her brows and grinned playfully. 'I most certainly will.'

'Oh, yuck.' Jess shot to her feet and covered her ears. 'I don't want to know any more, thank you very much.'

Laughing, Shanti rose and walked her to the door of her mum's cottage. 'Bye for now, I'll see you back here around five-thirty.' She pecked Jess's cheek. 'Love you.'

'Love you, too.' Jess gave her a hug then disappeared out the door. 'And I'll be here on the dot, I promise, with a bottle of bubbly,' she called over her shoulder.

Just shy of four pm, Jess was scrambling to get all her maid of honour duties done. After one too many coffees, she felt like a frog in a sock as she used her caffeine high to her advantage. Her arms heaving with shopping bags, she hurried across the road, towards her mum's VW. She couldn't wait to show Shanti what she'd come up with for the wedding favours.

Backing out of the parking space, she indicated then headed towards home. *Home.* She rolled the word around in her head, letting it give her all the feels. It made her think of her childhood, her brother, her mum and dad, Annie, Morgan, Chiara, Nonno ... all of them, in one way or another, were her quintessential home.

And that made her wonder what the hell she was doing trying to live out her days in a country she loved, but didn't feel at home in. Until arriving back in Silverton Shores, she hadn't missed having a man around. But she did miss having Morgan around. But what if he wasn't Chiara's father? What then? And how would she ever leave her nonno behind if he was? The very thought made her feel trapped. Blinking through sudden tears, she brought the VW to a sliding halt, but she couldn't do the same to her racing heart. Instead, it gallivanted faster. Her hand going to her chest, she gulped in salty sea air. And she stayed there, parked at the curb, overlooking the Pacific Ocean, for a little while longer, until she felt safe to drive home.

* * *

Right on 5.40 pm, the popping of the champagne cork was around the time her emotional day turned into one hell of a night.

Shanti wiggled her hips to a Dolly Parton song as she poured them both a glass. 'You and I are going to have so much fun tonight.'

'Cheers to that, my darling friend.' Clinking glasses, Jess threw her drink back.

Shanti peered over the rim of hers, while taking a sip. 'Whoa, slow down or you'll be bailing on me before we've even left the house.'

'Nah.' Jess waved her hand indifferently. 'This isn't my first rodeo.'

Shaking her head, Shanti laughed. 'It may not be your first night out, but it's certainly your first big one in a long time.'

'Fair point, Miss Shanti, I promise to pace myself.' Jess nodded.

'Just remember, you're meant to be the pragmatic one.' Shanti stabbed a finger at her own chest. 'And I'm meant to be the daydreamer.'

'What do you mean?' Jess scrunched her brows up. 'I'm not daydreaming.'

'Maybe not daydreaming,' A cheeky glint shimmered in Shanti's eyes. 'But you *are* dreaming about a certain someone ripping your clothes off.'

Jess knew exactly who Shanti meant. 'Stop it,' she said, playfully shoving her.

Shanti spiritedly shoved her back. 'Never.'

Jess smacked a kiss to Shanti's cheek. 'I love you.'

Leaning her elbows on the kitchen table, Shanti smiled. 'I love you, too, Jessica Sabatini, bucketloads.' She tipped her glass of bubbly back. 'Now, come on, let's get this crazy show on the road.'

Jess leapt off the stool and to her feet. 'Yes, let's.'

Her voice of reason had saved her from making quite a few really bad decisions in her life, but tonight she wanted to gag it. For once, she wanted to throw caution to the wind and give herself permission to let her hair down and completely enjoy herself.

* * *

Sunset was painting the sky – it would be dark very soon. About the time Morgan liked to kick his boots off and put his feet up, not pull his going-to-town boots on and head in to join the masses of inebriated townsfolk. Dinners were one thing, but a rowdy night at the pub, that was another. He had no idea how Roberto had roped him into coming out tonight, but here he was, pulling into the chock-full car park of the Roundyard Tavern. Unlike Jess, who'd seemed excited about her night ahead when she'd basically flown like a jet out the door, hollering something about running late, he honestly wasn't in the mood to drink or socialise. But he figured he owed Roberto for being a great mate, and that's why he was there. And he also wanted to keep a covert eye on Jess, and make sure she got home safe and sound. It might also be a case of him not wanting some sleazy drunken bloke to lay a finger on her. But he wasn't telling anyone that.

Stepping out of his Troopy, he clicked it locked and shoved the keys into his jeans pocket. As he walked towards the entrance of the tavern, he could hear the sound of music and laughter spilling out and onto the street, just like the drunkards would be later, at closing time. *Here goes*. He took a deep breath and pushed open the door. The warm glow of the interior welcomed him, but the hullaballoo didn't. Even so, he strode in confidently.

'Well, well, look who the cat has gone and dragged in, hey!' The bulky doorman grinned. 'I have to see it to believe it, Savage.' He held out his hand. 'It's been a long time between drinks on a Friday night, bud.'

'Yeah,' Morgan said, giving his old school mate a handshake in greeting. 'Tell me about it.'

'Well, have a good one,' the bloke said before checking the next person's ID.

It was a typical Friday night, and the place was packed with the same people, doing the same thing – standing three deep at the bar as they waited for drinks. Almost every person in here knew him on a surface level and only a handful knew him inside out. He liked to keep it that way. He scanned the room, but Roberto was nowhere in sight. Maybe he'd nipped to the little boys' room. He'd find him soon enough. Until then, he'd hold off grabbing a beer because he wanted to shout Roberto whatever his mate was drinking.

Finding a dark, quiet-ish corner, he rested his back up against the wall and enjoyed his view from the sidelines. Gyrating bodies bopped and swayed to the beat of the country music. Some had rhythm, and, by god, some had two left feet. A disco ball spun overhead, and coloured lights flashed in time with the beat, showering their smiling faces with shards of flittering light. But, other than keeping an eye out for Roberto, he was searching the sea of faces for only one other. Unable to spot her in the huge room, packed with people, he took a deep breath, watching the chaos around him. It was overwhelming, but he was used to it. He'd grown up in this town, after all. He'd been coming to this tavern since he was old enough to drink. But it had been a few years since he'd been an eager participant in the Friday-night festivities. He was snapped out of his thoughts when he heard a familiar voice call out his name. He turned to see Roberto weaving his way through the crowd, two beers in hand.

'Hey, mate, sorry I'm late,' Roberto said, handing over a beer. 'I had to stop by the house and grab my lucky hat, which, thankfully, wasn't ruined when our house flooded.'

'Thanks, buddy.' Morgan chuckled, taking a swig of beer. 'You and that hat,' he said, shaking his head.

Roberto laughed. 'Hey, don't knock the lucky hat. It's gotten me out of some tight spots before.'

Morgan grinned. 'I won't argue with that.'

They clinked their bottles together in a toast and took a sip. And as they stood there, catching up, Morgan's eyes wandered around the room. Still no sign of Jess. He wondered if she'd even arrived yet. Just as he was about to suggest they go have a game of pool, Roberto excused himself to take a phone call. It was then that Morgan heard a laugh that he recognised all too well.

Turning his head in the direction of the sweetest sound, he saw her.

His Jess.

Looking sexy as hell.

Her head tipped back, she was laughing, and the bloke across from her was ogling her like he was about to pounce. Jealousy raised its ugly head and his temper flared when the bloke hooked his arm around her waist and pulled her close. Laughing, she shoved him away. But her admirer wasn't about to give up his discourteous attempts, instead trying again but at the same time spilling his beer down the front of her. Although Morgan and Jess weren't together, to him, protecting her felt as natural as loving her. Over his dead body would he stand back and watch such disrespect happen. Muscling his way through the throng, he called her name when he was a metre from her.

She swung around, and her face split into the biggest of smiles. 'Oh my god, Morgan, what are you doing here?'

'The same thing as you.' He shot the offensive bloke a look of warning.

The young jackaroo looked taken aback but quickly recovered, offering a hand. 'Hey, man, I didn't realise she was taken, sorry 'bout that.'

Morgan took his hand but gave him a firm shake, making sure the bloke knew he meant business. 'Well, now you do.'

Jess sidled up to him, wrapping her arm around his waist. 'Thanks for the save, Savage, but I can handle myself, you know.'

Morgan's gaze softened as he regarded her. 'I know you can, but I stepped in to make sure you don't have to.'

'Well, thank you.' She smiled up at him, and Morgan felt as though his heart was about to burst out of his chest.

'I'd forgotten how fun this place could be,' she called over the thump of the music.

'Yeah.' He couldn't help but chuckle at her high-spirited face. 'It certainly looks like you're enjoying yourself.'

'Hey, Morgan, how goes you?' Shanti appeared and threw her arm around him.

'Hey, Shanti, I go pretty good, how about you?'

'Me.' She prodded herself in the chest. 'I'm fantastic.' She glanced around. 'Where is my husband-to-be?'

Morgan leant into her space. 'He's taking a call outside.'

'Ahh, I'm going to go look for him.' She glanced at Jess. 'I'll be back.' And off she went, jiving from side to side as she did.

Laughing at her best friend, Jess then turned her attention back to him, and took a tentative step closer, her cheeky smile filled with her Sabatini sass. 'Want to go head to head in a game of pool?'

'Sure, why not.'

'Great.' She clapped her hands together. 'Twenty dollars says I'll whip your jean-clad butt.'

Morgan loved her vivaciousness. 'You're on.'

Half an hour later, leaning over the pool table, Jess slid the cue back and forth as she tried to line up the ball. Then, with her bottom lip clamped between her teeth oh so cutely, she took her shot. It fired across the green felt and hit its mark, slaying the second ball sideways and into the netted pocket. Bystanders erupted in cheers. Morgan's pride took a beating.

'You owe me twenty big ones, Savage.'

'Yeah.' He was by no means a sore loser, so he flashed her a gallant smile. 'It looks that way.' He pulled his wallet out of his pocket and handed a twenty-dollar note over. 'There you go, paid in full.'

'Okay, thank you.' She snatched it, and grinned. 'My shout, what are you drinking?'

'Just a mid-strength, thanks, Jess.'

She screwed her face up. 'A mid-strength?'

'Yeah, I'm driving.'

'Oh, cool, okay then, come with me.' And she grabbed his hand, dragging him towards the bar.

After passing Roberto and Shanti, cuddled up in a corner booth – they'd gone missing when the game of pool had begun – they arrived at the bar, and Jess ordered them both a drink. Morgan watched as she leant over the counter, her tight dress revealing a hint of cleavage. He averted his gaze, trying to quell the desire that was rapidly building inside him. Then, drinks in hand, they stood back, chatting about this and that, their conversation light and their laughter easy. After a little while, without a word of warning, Jess took his hand and pulled him towards the dance floor. He'd generally refuse a bout of boogying, but he wasn't about to say no to Jess. The music was loud and upbeat, and the crowd was moving as one, swaying and gyrating to the rhythm. They found a spot near the centre of the floor and began to move together. His heart was racing as his body moved in sync with hers. At times, her beautiful frame was pressed against his, and he could feel the warmth of her skin through the thin material of her dress. Lost in the heat of the moment, he placed his hands on her hips, pulling her closer, and she giggled, the sound like music to his ears. Totally comfortable in each other's company, they moved together to the beat, their bodies in perfect harmony.

As the song came to an end, Jess looked up at him, her eyes brimming with excitement. 'Let's get out of here,' she said, taking his hand and leading him towards the exit.

Morgan was glad for the quick exit as the pounding bass and intermittent lighting was starting to wear thin.

'Hey, Savage, are you heading out?' the bouncer called from across the room.

'Yeah, I think I've had enough for one night,' he replied, not taking his eyes off Jess.

Yanking the door open for Jess, he followed her out, and it was only when he felt his first inhalation of fresh air that he finally felt as if he could breathe again.

She turned to face him with their hands still intertwined. 'I had a good time tonight,' she said, her eyes meeting his. 'Thanks, Morgan.'

'Me too,' he replied. 'But what are you thanking me for?'

'Nothing, and everything,' she said with a tender smile. She let his hand go and clapped hers together. 'Now take me home, before I drink too much and make a fool of myself, again.'

'Righto, sounds like a good plan.' He looked back towards the door. 'Should we go and let Shanti and Roberto know we're heading home?'

She shook her head. 'They've already gone. Shanti texted me when we were on the dance floor, to say bye and that they'd catch us tomorrow.'

'Oh, well then, let's go.'

As they fell into step with one another, she wrapped her arm into his. After settling themselves side-by-side in his Troopy, they made their way home and into their own beds, where Morgan carried the memory of swaying her across the dance floor into his sleep.

CHAPTER 16

After mentally deep-diving into his life, and the secret he was keeping from Jess, for what felt like half the night, Morgan woke up to the sun slanting through his curtains and into his face. Grimacing against it, he sat up and tried to rub the sleepiness from his eyes. Turning his wrist, he read the time on his Fitbit – 8.23 am. Geez. It had been a long while since he'd slept past seven. He needed to get a shift on. There was no rest for the wicked around here. Today he had a chore list a mile long, and after he'd accomplished that he was going to head over to Annie's to try and unburden his heart. And hers, for that matter. He knew he couldn't keep this hidden from Jess forever, but the thought of being the one to have to tell her made him tense. She was the only person he'd ever truly loved, and the idea of losing her because of a secret that had nothing to do with him, although he'd kept it under lock and key, terrified him. It should be on Annie to deliver the news, but if she failed to do so he had no choice but to be the bad guy. He had to tell Jess, and before she went back to her life in Italy. He couldn't keep living with this weight on his shoulders.

After making his bed, then grabbing his clothes for the day, he strolled into his ensuite bathroom and stared at the state of himself in the mirror. His face was rough with stubble, and his hair was a mess. He ran his hands through it and sighed. He needed a shave, a hot shower and some eyedrops for his red eyes. He turned the taps and waited for the water to heat up. No matter how hard he tried, he couldn't shake the image of Jess from the night before. Her body pressed against his on the dance floor, the way her hair swayed with every movement, and the softness of her smile when they'd said goodnight. He'd be a madman to deny the attraction he felt towards her, but he also knew he couldn't act on it. And that, in itself, was a massive feat.

Once the water was hot, he stepped into the shower and let it wash over him. He closed his eyes and let out a deep breath, trying to calm his nerves. Like listening to a sad love song on repeat, he couldn't help but think of his and Jess's past, and the love they once shared. It had been intense, passionate and all-consuming. But then life had gotten in the way, giving them a challenge to rise above, together, but instead they'd gone their separate ways. He'd always wondered what would have been if they had stayed together, but now, with the secret he was keeping, he knew their love might never be rekindled. It was too complicated, too messy. He had to focus on the present and the future, not the past. But to move forward, he needed a clear conscience.

As he lathered up, washed his hair, shaved his scruffy face, dried off and then got dressed for the day, he ran all types of scenarios around in his head. Good outcome: Annie finally agreeing to 'fess up. Worst-case scenario: Annie losing it and telling him to get out of her house. And there were a few in-betweens too. Whatever might happen, he had to face the music and deal with the consequences. As he cleared the staircase two at a time then made his way to the kitchen, the smell of coffee and the familiar melody of Darius Rucker singing 'Wagon Wheel' filled his senses, as did the gorgeous woman swaying her hips in time to the catchy tune. Jess was so caught up in her own little world at the stove, making herself a couple of fried eggs, she didn't even notice him as he strode into the bright, airy room. She was wearing a simple T-shirt and cute little denim shorts with diamantés on the back pockets – and she looked breathtakingly beautiful.

Smiling to himself, he leant against the counter, watching her dance to the music. There was something soothing about the gentle clatter of utensils and the aroma of cooking food. It was like everything was right with the world, even if it was just for a moment. He couldn't help but let out a soft chuckle at her carefree attitude. She'd been through so much in her life, and yet she still managed to find joy in the little things. It was one of the many things he admired about her. There was a lot to be said for optimism, and gratitude. And she made him feel both, in spades.

'Morning,' he said, finally getting her attention.

'Oh crap.' Jess spun, spatula in hand. 'I didn't hear you come in.' She smiled at him. 'Good morning.'

'I gathered.' Morgan grinned back at her. 'You're nice and chirpy, you have a good sleep?' With his galloping heart reaching for her, he fought to keep his voice steady.

'The best one I've had in ages.' She shrugged softly. 'I don't know if it's the fresh country air here, but I feel like I could sleep for days.' Her smile was soft and alluring, and Morgan couldn't help but feel the magnetic pull between them.

'Glad to hear it,' he said.

'Would you like a couple of eggs while I'm at it?' She pointed to the frying pan with her spatula.

'Yeah, nah, but thanks. I might just have a couple of bits of toast.'

Jess leant against the counter, sipping her coffee. 'So, what's on the agenda for today?'

He grabbed two bits of bread and popped both into the toaster. 'Well, I need to mow the two acres around the homestead, fix the windmill, and get a lick of paint on the tack shed.'

Jess raised an eyebrow. 'Sounds like a busy day.'

'Yeah, it is, but it all needs to be done.' He grabbed the butter and Vegemite. 'What are you up to for the day?'

'I haven't got any definite plans.' She popped her eggs on top of sliced avocado, then glanced over her shoulder. 'I'm going to head out for a bit, maybe do some shopping or something like that.'

'Okay, sounds good.' Morgan tried to keep his voice casual as he contemplated what would happen if she called in to Annie's while he was there.

His toast ready to go, he lathered butter and Vegemite in equally thick layers and decided to eat on the run. 'I'm off, so I'll catch up with you later on.'

'Righto.' Sitting at the breakfast bench, Jess smiled as he headed towards the door. 'Enjoy your day doing.'

'I'll try, and you enjoy your day moseying,' he called back.

As he strode towards the front door, his heart felt achingly heavy with what he knew he needed to do. Taking a deep breath, he stepped out and into the sunshine-filled day, grabbed his work boots and welcomed his offsider to join him. Patting Teeny's furry head, he felt comforted by his doggy mate's company. He'd always been in awe of the unwavering loyalty that dogs provided, something he'd found sorely lacking in most of his relationships with people. Even Jess. For a brief moment, as he walked towards the machinery shed, he entertained the idea of confiding in Teeny, imagining he was a wise old sage who could give him advice. But then he laughed at the ridiculous thought, shaking his head and instead focusing on the tasks that lay ahead.

By mid-afternoon, he'd accomplished everything on his to-do list. He was covered in sweat, horsehair, Teeny fur, grease and dirt, but it felt good to get things completed. As he made his way back to the homestead for a quick freshen up and a big drink of icy cold water, he saw Jess's VW was still gone, which filled him with relief. Knowing what he was about to go and do, he'd find it tough to look her in the eyes right now. He wanted to face the music and get this over with as soon as possible. But how would Jess react when she found out? Would she understand he'd been stuck in the middle of it all? Would she forgive him? He couldn't bear the thought of losing her. Completely. Again.

Time would tell if that was going to be the case.

After a quick pit stop at the bakery, he pulled up out the front of Annie's. The encroaching storm clouds had pushed their way across the sky, and now hogged almost every square inch of it. It felt like a fitting move by Mother Nature considering he, too, felt as if a storm was brewing. It sucked to be torn between two women he cared about, but he had to withstand the torture. Once and for all, Jess deserved the truth. And he wasn't leaving here until he made Annie see the sense in that.

On autopilot, he stepped out of the Troopy and made his way up the garden path, towards the tiny duplex. He stood at the front door, mammoth lamingtons and two pieces of macadamia slice in hand, knocked, then waited for it to be answered. Footfalls approached, and then the wooden door swung open.

'Morgan, hey.' Annie glanced past him, as if expecting Jess, too.

'Hey, Annie, is this a good time?'

Her eyes fell to the brown paper bags, stamped with the bakery's logo. 'It's always a good time when you come bearing treats.' She pecked his cheek then stepped aside. 'Come on in and please, mind the mess.'

As he stepped inside he was immediately hit with the strong scent of cigarettes and stale alcohol. His eyes scanning the living room of the studio-style duplex, he was shocked to see it looked like a war zone. Clothes were scattered all over the place, and there were empty pizza boxes and beer bottles littering the coffee table, as well as an ashtray overflowing with cigarette butts. Annie had always been a bit of a wild child, but it seemed like things had gotten out of control. He couldn't help but feel a sense of sadness for her, and guilt for not seeing the signs.

'What's going on, Morgan?' she asked, settling onto the couch and patting the spot next to her. 'And please tell me this visit has nothing to do with me talking to Jess.'

Huffing, he contemplated the demon that had been plaguing him for way too long, while struggling to stay calm and keep his head straight. 'Yeah, it does, Annie.'

'Morgan,' she said, her tone cautionary. 'I thought I told you to drop this.'

'Well, I'm not going to.' He shifted in his seat, stalling for a few moments. 'I'm sorry, Annie, but Jess doesn't deserve to be kept in the dark any longer.'

'Don't you think I know this, Morgan, I mean for god's sake, can you see the state of my place?' She waved her arms around as she shot to her feet. 'You keep going on and on about how it's affecting you, and what I should do, but have you stopped to think about the pressure I'm under right now, between back-to-back shifts and Jess being back here, and how it's affecting me?'

'Yes, I have thought about it, Annie, quite a lot.' Seeing her like that sent his heart careening off its tracks. 'And you've always played it so cool when I've broached the subject.' He cleared the emotion from his throat. 'But now, seeing you, and this place, I can see what it's doing to you.'

Annie's eyes flickered with a hint of sadness. 'It's not your problem, Morgan. I'll deal with it in my own way.'

'But you're not dealing with it, Annie. You're drowning in it.' Morgan's voice rose in frustration as he watched her grab a cigarette and light it. 'I care about you, you know that, but I care about Jess too. And I honestly can't keep this secret any longer.'

Annie took a deep drag on her cigarette and exhaled, the smoke curling around her face. The resounding silence was thick, almost suffocating, as she stared at him with a mixture of guilt and defiance. 'You're really going to do this, aren't you?'

'I have to. I can't keep living with this hanging over my head.' Morgan stood up, feeling both relieved and nervous as the words left his mouth. 'If you haven't told her before she's ready to go back to Florence, I'm going to take it as my indication to tell her everything I know.'

Annie nodded slowly, her expression difficult to read. 'I guess I can't stop you.'

'No, you can't,' Morgan said, his voice firm. 'But I'm not doing this to hurt you, Annie. I'm doing it because it's the right thing to do.'

Annie's eyes flashed with anger. 'And what about me? Do you even care about the consequences of your actions if you go and tell her?'

Morgan's heart sank, but he knew he had to do what was right. 'I understand it will put you in a really awkward place, but it's not fair to keep this from her. She has a right to know.'

'You've always been a man of morals, Morgan, I'll give you that much.' She let out a weighty, impatient sigh, as ashes fell onto the carpet. 'But you do realise you're risking everything, right? Our friendship, Jess's trust, your relationship with her?'

'I know.' He ran a hand through his hair, nerves starting to get the best of him. 'But as I've reiterated, it's the right thing to do. And I'll face the consequences, whatever they may be.'

Annie took another drag on her cigarette before stubbing it out in the overflowing ashtray. Then, with the slightest of smiles, she fastened her steely gaze to his. 'Please, leave, and if you say anything, anything at all, I'll never forgive you.'

He nodded, feeling an odd sense of closure. 'Okay, I'll see myself out. Try and take care of yourself, and even though you may think you hate me right now, I'm here if you need anything, anything at all,' he said as he walked away.

Racing footsteps came up behind him, and as he stepped out the doorway and turned around, the door slammed shut in his face. He stood there for a few moments, considering his next move. Should he walk away, and keep his mouth shut, or should he do what his heart was telling him to? Was it even his place to set a foot into their lives? Damn straight it was. Jess was his world, and he owed her that much.

As he retraced his steps towards his Troopy, the first few drops of rain began to fall. He slid into the driver's seat, took a deep breath and leant back against the seat, his mind spinning with thoughts and emotions. Annie's words echoed heartbreakingly in his head.

If you say anything, anything at all, I'll never forgive you …

Starting the engine, he took one last look towards the duplex and prayed that in time she would.

Three hours later, Morgan walked over to the kitchen window and gazed out at the wide-open pastures now flooded with the rosy hues of sunset. His land was undeniably beautiful, but his heart was way too heavy to relish it. He couldn't shake the feeling of guilt and dread that had settled in his chest since he'd left Annie's place. But he'd made a promise to himself and it was a promise he intended to keep, no matter the cost to himself. The thought of being the one to break Jess's heart as he shattered her world, of having a front-row seat to witness the trust and love she held for him disappearing before his very eyes, made him feel sick to his stomach. Fundamentally, he wanted to protect her, to shield her from the harsh realities of life, to bring her nothing but joy, but the truth was necessary, no matter how painful. Maybe, possibly, by some miracle, Jess might see what he had to tell her as a blessing.

He was just about to head upstairs for a shower when a knock at the front door had him turning in the opposite direction. His strides were determined as the rapping got louder, more insistent. 'I'm coming.' He yanked the door open to see a red-eyed, puffy-faced Annie. 'Hey.' He stepped aside, and she stepped in beside him. 'Are you okay?'

Annie shook her head, and without a word she crumpled into him. Hugging her, he silently consoled her as she sobbed her heart out, as his own heart sank even lower. And he remained quiet until she seemed to regroup a little, just enough to untangle her arms from around him, and step back.

She barely met his gaze. 'Jess isn't here, is she?'

'No, she isn't home yet.' He reached out and placed a hand on her shoulder. 'I'm so sorry, Annie, I didn't mean to upset you like this.'

Nodding, Annie sighed heavily, her tears slowing. 'I know you didn't, Morgan. But you have to understand this is a very delicate situation.'

He nodded, rubbing her back soothingly. 'I know. And I'm sorry for putting you in this position. I just couldn't keep it to myself anymore. It just feels wrong, in every way.'

Annie wiped her eyes with the back of her hands. 'I understand that. And I'm sorry for how I reacted earlier. It's just …' She trailed off, looking down at her feet.

'It's just?' Morgan asked gently.

'It's just that I'm scared, okay?' Annie blurted out. 'I'm scared of what will happen when Jess finds out the truth.'

'I know you are. But keeping something like this from her isn't fair to anyone.' He put a hand on her shoulder, giving it a reassuring squeeze. 'And I'll be here for both of you during this difficult time, you know that, right?'

'Yes, I wouldn't expect any less from you.' Annie looked up at him, tears still glistening in her eyes. 'Thank you, Morgan.' Her gaze softened. 'I appreciate your concern for Jess, because as you know, I love her dearly, too.'

'I know you do.' He briefly squeezed his eyes against rising raw emotions. 'I could only imagine how confronting this is for you. Is there anything I can do to make it easier?'

'No, this is something I have to do myself.' She wrung her hands. 'Although, I do have one request.'

'Yes, anything.' His heart rate quickened as he waited anxiously. 'Annie?' His mind raced with what it could possibly be. Was she about to ask him to distort the truth? To lie to Jess? He braced himself for the worst.

Annie took a deep breath before speaking, her voice barely a whisper. 'Please give me some time to think about this. I need to figure out the best way to approach the situation without hurting anyone more than necessary.'

Morgan nodded, feeling a weight lifted off his shoulders. 'Of course, I totally get that.'

'And I don't want to do anything before the wedding.' She sucked in a shaky breath. 'I don't want anything to cloud Shanti and my brother's big day.'

He gave her a small smile of understanding. 'I completely agree. We can't allow this to ruin their special day. That's the last thing any of us want.'

Annie nodded, looking relieved. 'Thank you for understanding. I'll make sure to talk to you before I do anything else.' She wiped at her eyes one last time, taking a deep breath. 'I should probably head off now, before Jess arrives home. I don't want her to see me like this, because then I'll have to lie about why.' She reached out and hugged him. 'Thank you for being here for me. It means a lot.'

He hugged her tight. 'I'm here for you any time; you're like a sister to me.'

She stepped back and looked at him sadly. 'I really wish you and Jess had gotten married.'

'Me too, Annie, me too.' He couldn't hide the dejection from his voice.

'You're a good man, Morgan Savage, one in a bazillion.' She placed a hand over his heart, which was breaking beneath. 'Talk soon.' She dropped her hand back to her side and turning, headed back to her car.

Morgan watched her drive away as relief flooded him.

Finally, after all these years, the truth was going to set him free.

CHAPTER 17

Dreams of a white picket fence surrounding a quaint farmhouse, with her and Morgan sitting on the verandah, her hand upon her swollen belly as she watched their two children playing in the backyard, came to Jess as she slept. It felt so peaceful, so real, so blissful, she didn't want it to end. But reality wasn't having a bar of her fantasies when the screeching of her alarm clock woke her. Grabbing it from her bedside table before her eyes had time to open, she tossed it across the room. It bounced off the cupboard door and landed back at her feet, still resounding.

'Blasted thing!' She tossed back the covers that she'd tugged over her head. 'Argh.' Scrambling to the foot of the bed, she snatched it up and thumped the top, halting its incessant beeping noise.

Huffing, she plonked it back in its place. Rubbing her eyes, she tried to shake off the lingering images of her dream as she sat up on the edge of the bed. It hurt like hell to know she'd never, ever have such a life with Morgan. And it hurt even more to know another woman would, one day, because he was way too lovable to remain single forever. She could feel her heart breaking down the middle at the thought of Chiara never having a normal life with Morgan if it turned out he was her father, and all because of her stupid decision, all those years ago. Taking deep breaths to try and calm herself, she tried to shake off the feeling of disappointment. She had no right, no right at all, to take ownership over Morgan. But her dream had been so vivid, so real, so spellbinding.

Sighing, she ran her fingers through her tangled bed hair. It was foolish of her to dream of a life that was impossible. In reality, she was a divorced single mother, quite often struggling to make ends meet, with a secret that had her stuck on shaky ground. There was no white picket fence, no farmhouse, no husband, no happy ending. Just her and Chiara, living in a tiny apartment all the way over the other side of the world, far away from those she loved with all her heart and soul.

Reality was really sinking in.

She shook her head, trying to clear the thoughts from her mind. She needed to focus on the present, on what she could do to make a good life for herself and Chiara. That's what she had some control over. As for the results she would learn in a few days' time, when she got back to Florence, well, she would deal with all of that then.

Rising, she walked over to her cupboard, tugged out a T-shirt and a pair of shorts, and began getting dressed for the day. As she tied her hair up in a messy bun, she tried to push aside her thoughts of Morgan and their impossible dream life. She had to focus on the reality of her situation. She had a job to go back to, bills to pay, and a beautiful daughter to take care of. She couldn't afford to get lost in her reveries. Her life wasn't some fairy tale. It was raw and real and quite often tough.

As she opened her bedroom door, the mouth-watering scents of bacon and coffee lured her faster down the staircase, as did the sound of Morgan's voice, all husky and deep, singing along with Waylon Jennings. Passing through the lounge room, and down the hallway, she stopped short of stepping into the kitchen when she was met by the man, literally, of her dreams, wearing nothing but a pair of boxers. She'd seen him without a shirt before, but it was still all she could do not to drool.

Clearing her throat, she stepped into the kitchen, trying her best to ignore the heat that flooded her cheeks. 'Good morning.' Her voice sounded a little too high-pitched as she tried to avert her gaze from his perfectly sculpted body.

Turning, Morgan greeted her with a charismatic dimpled smile. 'Oh, hey, Jess, sleep well?' Something within his gaze hinted at a familiar kind of mischief.

'Apart from a mosquito who thought it'd be grand to invade my room for the night, I sure did.' Caught red-handed, in Morgan Savage's cookie jar, she laughed a little like a hyena. 'How about you?' she added, recovering as fast as she could.

Did he know she'd been standing there, watching him?

'Not guilty, I didn't invade your room.' He lifted a broad shoulder, a cheeky grin quirking his lips as he waited for her to cotton on to his joke, and once she did, a little later than she should have, he rolled his blue eyes and grinned. 'I slept pretty good, thanks.'

Jess grinned back, appreciating the banter. It was good to have a friend like Morgan, someone who knew her well enough to make her laugh. 'Well, the smell of bacon and coffee certainly beats a mosquito any day.' She shimmied past him at the stove. 'Would you like a cuppa?'

'Yeah, why not, thanks, Jess.' He passed her an already used mug. 'Be my second one for the morning.' He leant against the counter, his bare chest on full display. 'I've whipped up a decent breakfast, so I hope you're hungry.'

'Mm-hmm.' Ravenous for more than just food, Jess couldn't help but admire the intricate designs of his tattoos. 'I'm very, very hungry.'

'Good, because I've made enough to feed a small army.' He chuckled and got back to business at the frypan.

Her eyes fell to the thin scattering of hair at the waistband of his boxers right before she busied herself making them both coffees, all the while perving at him whenever she got the chance. Talk about being glued to his bare chest and pecs.

Yum!

'The weatherman is predicting storms for this afternoon,' he said while flipping the sizzling pieces of bacon. 'But by the looks of the bright blue sky out yonder, I reckon he's pulling our legs.'

Smiling as she passed him his cuppa, she raised a brow. 'You do, do you?'

'Hell yeah, I do.'

After taking a sip from her coffee, she pulled up a stool opposite him. 'Say it like it is, Savage.' The aroma of bacon and coffee made her stomach grumble in anticipation.

'I always do,' he replied, smirking. 'You should know me by now, Sabatini.'

She couldn't help but laugh at his cockiness. 'I do, Savage. All too well.'

'Yes, you most certainly do.' He chuckled lightly.

'And FYI, you're the funniest, most hardworking and honest man I reckon I've ever met.'

'Mmm, thanks, Jess.' This time there was a slight undercurrent in his tone, as if sadness had just snuck its unpleasant head into what had been a light-hearted bantering session.

Having just given him what she thought was a compliment, Jess found herself at a loss for words, and for a few moments there was an uncomfortable silence between them as Morgan dished up their bacon and eggs. Even as he passed her plate over and sat beside her, and they ate, he seemed lost in thought, and his playful demeanour was well and truly gone.

Baffled at the sudden change of mood, Jess couldn't help but wonder what was weighing heavily on his mind, so she decided to break the silence. 'Is everything okay, Morgan?'

He looked up at her, his eyes clouded with emotion. 'It's nothing, Jess. Just some stuff I've been dealing with lately. But I think I've got it under control.'

She could tell he wasn't being completely honest with her but decided not to push the issue. Instead, she tried to lighten the mood. 'Well, if you ever need someone to talk to, I'm here for you.'

He smiled, a genuine one this time. 'Thanks. That means a lot to me.'

'I hope whatever it is, that you ...' She was going to say *sort it all out*, but her words halted when he placed his hand over hers.

Warm. Strong. Protective.

'I really want you to know, Jess, that no matter what the future holds, I will always have your best interests at heart, okay?' His regard of her was beseeching.

'Yes, okay.' Suddenly deeply concerned, she tipped her head, holding his gaze. 'Are you sure you've got whatever it is under control?'

'I hope so.' He held her eyes captive, as if silently trying to tell her more.

What was happening here?

Her sudden inability to think straight was all because of him. She was almost too afraid to move, for fear of leaning into him and kissing him. Beneath his heated gaze, for a few precious seconds, she felt powerful, sexy, wanted like she'd never been wanted before. Not even by him. And she wanted more of that feeling. More of him. But at the same time she was acutely aware she was setting herself up for utter failure and complete heartbreak – and inevitably setting him up for the same. She didn't want to do that when he deserved the absolute world. If she allowed herself to have feelings beyond the boundaries, then she'd have to feel *everything*. The pain of the past, and the lack of their future. And that would be like throwing herself into an ocean where there was no hope of survival. She'd drown beneath the emotions. So, to survive, she needed to keep her heart guarded. She needed to be realistic.

Oh, for god's sake, she needed him.

He didn't need the likes of her.

But that lost look in his eyes, oh god help her, it made her want to comfort him with a hug. Yet she knew better than to cross that line. So she pulled her hand away, breaking the spell.

Morgan drew in a breath, then sighed it away. She wanted to say something, anything to break this, whatever it was, coming between them.

Then Mother Nature stepped in as a distant clap of thunder almost made Jess jump out of her skin.

The awkwardness broke as Morgan smiled. 'Well, well, well, looks like the weatherman was right all along.' Standing, he gathered their plates and cups.

'Yes, sounds like it.' She grabbed the salt, pepper and tomato sauce, and busied herself putting each away.

Even though she was relieved that the sudden change in the weather had broken the tension between them, Jess couldn't help but feel a sense of uncertainty growing within her. She knew there was more to Morgan's troubled air than he was letting on. And she couldn't shake the feeling that it had something to do with her. But he very clearly didn't want to talk about it, and she wasn't about to push him to.

By the time they'd finished tidying up the kitchen, black clouds had swallowed up every inch of blue as the storm started to quickly intensify. The sound of raindrops hitting the roof filled the room. She strode over to the window, watching as the rain came down harder and harder, until it was almost deafening. Then, just as it had in the last big storm, lightning flashed and a loud clap of thunder rumbled through the homestead. It was stormy outside, and quite dark, so they had the lights on. The electricity flickered a few times before finally going out, plunging them into shadowy dimness. There wasn't a ray of sunshine to be seen.

'Holy crap, that one was massive.' Shivers ran down her spine and she wrapped her arms around herself.

'Yeah, it was a doozy.' Morgan seemed unfazed, but Teeny was clinging to his side. 'Well, it looks like we're stuck inside for a while.'

'That's okay,' she said with a shrug. 'We can find something else to do.'

His hand resting on Teeny's big mug, he raised an eyebrow as the playful glint in his eyes returned. 'Oh really? And what did you have in mind?'

Jess felt her face flush as she realised what she had implied. 'I—I didn't mean it like that,' she stammered, feeling embarrassed. 'I just meant we could … play a game or something.'

Morgan chuckled at her rare moment of shyness. 'Relax, Jess. I knew what you meant.' He extended his hand to her. 'Come on, let's go and find something to do to pass the time.' He looked to Teeny. 'Come on, buddy, that includes you, too.'

She took his hand, feeling a thrill run through her at the contact as they wandered down the hall and into the lounge room, which was a little brighter than the kitchen. Even so, Morgan lit a couple of candles. In the flicker of candlelight, Jess could see him clearly now, his features accentuated by the shadows. His eyes gleamed mischievously as he took a seat next to her, their arms brushing against each other. Jess tried to ignore the sparks that flew through her as they got themselves settled. Just because the wild weather was perfect for making love all day long, it didn't mean it was about to happen.

No way Jose!

With Teeny sticking close by, they spent the morning playing board games and the afternoon watching movies on Morgan's laptop, in between bouts of munchies where they devoured a packet of Barbecue Shapes and a tub of bacon and onion dip, half a jar of olives, some caramel popcorn and finally a family-sized packet of salt and vinegar chips washed down with a big bottle of coconut water. Loving every second they were spending together holed up in the homestead, Jess begrudgingly accepted that the storm would soon pass. But by sundown the wind still howled, and flashes of lightning sporadically lit up the room, casting eerie shadows on the walls. Every time it did, she could feel her heart racing, both from the darkness and the proximity of Morgan.

Packing the Monopoly board away, Morgan looked to her. 'Should we make ourselves a nice hot chocolate?'

She grinned at the thought. 'Yeah, why not, I'll flick the gas hob on and grab a saucepan to boil the milk.'

Morgan rubbed his hands together. 'Plan, Stan.'

The milk had just started to heat when the lights flickered on again. Jess had been in the process of pulling mugs out of the cupboard, and Morgan was grabbing the Cadbury chocolate powder from the pantry. They both jumped and turned to face each other at the same time, her nervous giggle breaking the silence. Then a sudden, distant rumble of thunder made them both jump again. Morgan teased her about it, and she teased him back. A few minutes later, she poured the hot milk into the waiting mugs and they both headed back to the lounge room and settled onto the couch, thick hot chocolates wrapped in their hands. And as she took satisfying sips of the sweetness, Jess couldn't take her eyes off him. Morgan Savage was truly a work of art. She watched his Adam's apple bob as he sipped his drink, and her eyes fell to a thin line of hair that ran down the centre of his chest, disappearing into the board shorts he'd changed into at some point in the day. For the life of her, she could do nothing but simply stare.

Then, as if out of the blue, the loudest clap of thunder she'd heard all day had her shrieking.

Morgan chuckled at her reaction. He popped his empty mug on the coffee table and pulled her closer, his arm wrapping around her shoulders. 'Don't worry, I've got you,' he murmured, his chocolate-laced breath warm against her ear.

Jess couldn't help the shiver that gave rise to delicious goosebumps. She was worried, but not about the storm. She was worried about the way she felt around him, about the way her body reacted to his touch. She knew that what they had was dangerous, that it could lead to heartbreak and devastation, but in that moment all she wanted was to give in to the passion and hunger that coursed through her veins. She turned her head to look up at him, her eyes meeting his. In the candlelight, his eyes were even more intense, a deeper shade of blue that seemed to hold all the secrets of the world.

'Thank you,' she said softly, unable to tear her gaze away from his.

Morgan leant in closer, his lips hovering just inches from hers. 'For what?' he whispered.

Melting beneath his touch, her body gravitated towards him even as her mind screamed at her to stop. 'For everything,' she replied, her voice barely a whisper.

And then, without warning, his lips were on hers, gentle at first, but gradually growing more urgent as they both melted into each other.

The storm raged on outside, but inside the homestead they were lost in their own world, the flickering candlelight casting shadows on their entwined bodies. And as the passion between them grew, Jess knew that she was in too deep. But in that moment, she didn't care. All she wanted was Morgan, and the safety and security that he promised.

CHAPTER 18

Yet again, what in the hell had he been thinking last night?

Thank god he'd seen sense before they'd torn each other's clothes off. As had Jess. It had been a mutual untwining of bodies, at the exact same moment, seconds after the electricity had returned. Wordlessly, clumsily, they'd slid to opposite ends of the couch and stared at each other in bewildered shock, before bidding each other a quick goodnight, and disappearing into their respective bedrooms.

Standing beneath his second freezing cold shower in less than twelve hours, Morgan tried to rid himself of the longing still burning through him like a wildfire. In the heat of the moment, with Jess's gaze fastened to his and the storm raging outside, he'd craved to both possess and protect her, in equal measures. Now he couldn't seem to shake off the uneasy feeling that had been lingering since seeing sense. He knew he'd gone too far in kissing her. Again. She wasn't sticking around. And he wasn't about to pack up and move to Florence. And he couldn't go down that long, lonely road a second time round. The last time had almost destroyed him. Besides, there were way too many question marks hanging over their heads for them to go anywhere near the boundaries they'd enforced – quite well, up until now. She needed him to be her friend, and that was it. So, come hell or high water, that's exactly what he was going to be for her.

Only a couple more days. You can do this, Savage.

Half an hour later, his hands shoved in his jeans pockets, he stepped closer to the kitchen window and rested back on the heels of his boots.

'Morning, Morgan.' Her voice carried from the doorway, and he turned to catch sight of her softly smiling face. 'You okay?'

He was nowhere near okay, but he nodded anyway. 'Yeah, all good.' A flurry of memories rushed back, of them cuddled up, their all-consuming kisses. 'Sleep well?'

A quick heartbeat passed before she replied. 'Yes, thanks.'

'Good.' He had to stop fantasising about getting her naked before it created a real problem. 'Listen, Jess, about last night …'

'It's okay,' she interrupted him. 'I know it was a mistake. We shouldn't have let our emotions get in the way.'

Emotions. So she really did still care for him. 'I'm sorry, Jess, it won't happen again.' Feeble, but it was all he had right now.

'I'm sorry too.' She nodded. 'Let's get past it then, shall we?'

'Yes, let's.' He cleared his throat and fought for something casual to say. 'Do you remember how much time we used to spend in the saddle?'

'Of course I do.' A sentimental smile lifted the corners of her oh-so-kissable mouth. 'I may be nine years older, but I'm not senile …' she grinned, '. . . yet.'

'Ha, no, you're not …yet,' he replied playfully, thankful for their easy banter. 'I was wondering, would you like to go for a gallivant today?'

Her face lit up. 'Would I ever!'

'Great.' His weary heart cartwheeled. 'I'll go get the horses saddled up, and be back to grab you in say,' he glanced at his watch, 'an hour, give or take.'

'Sounds great, I'll make sure I'm ready to go.'

Morgan headed outside, took a deep breath and then let it out slowly. He was glad Jess was handling what had happened the night before well, but he was still feeling the consequences of his actions. He knew he had to keep his emotions in check for the sake of their friendship, because if everything went belly up, he couldn't imagine his life without her in it.

With Teeny at his side, he gathered both the horses from their paddocks and walked each over to the stables. Humming to himself, he brushed them down, checked their hoofs, and ensured their saddles were secure. Finally, both the horses were saddled up and ready to go. He headed back over to the homestead where Jess was waiting for him, dressed in tight-fitting jeans and a flannel shirt, her hair pulled back in a plait. He couldn't help but feel a pang of regret for what he could never have with her. But he pushed it aside and greeted her with a smile.

'Ready?' he asked, his voice light.

'More than ready,' she replied, her eyes sparkling with excitement.

They walked together back to the stables, where he helped her up and onto her horse. Mounting Cash, he led her out and into the open. They set off at a leisurely pace, and the fresh air and stunning scenery did wonders for his spirits. As they rode side by side, talking and laughing like old times, it was easy to forget the awkwardness of the night before. He couldn't help but feel grateful for moments like these, where he and Jess just enjoyed each other's company.

'Hey, Savage.' She looked to him, a challenging glint in her eyes. 'Race you!'

Before he could react, she shot forward, her laughter carrying. She glanced over her shoulder and he pushed Cash a little harder. After crossing the first of two trickling creeks, they followed a hairpin curve that abruptly turned upwards. Lost in the moment, together, they rode like the wind, neck and neck towards the ridgeline. Earth flew from the horses' hoofs as they neared the top, with Jess suddenly taking the lead. Wanting her to win, Morgan gave her a few seconds' grace. She'd already dismounted by the time he reached her. And it was worth every bit of coming second, when her sassily triumphant grin set his heart on fire.

Dismounting and wandering to her side, he had to tear his eyes away from her for a moment.

Holding her hand up to shade her eyes, she smiled. 'My god, I really do love it up here.'

Following her gaze out and over the land, he tugged the brim of his hat down. 'Yeah, me too.'

'There's just something about not being able to see another living soul.' Her expression faltered, but only for a breath. 'Very unlike Florence, where there's hustle and bustle most of the time.'

'Well, you're welcome, anytime, to come here and breathe, and so is Chiara, of course.' Wrapping his arms around her, he cuddled her in nice and close while at the same time doing his best to convey that this was a friendly hug.

'Thanks, Morgan, I reckon Chiara and I will take you up on that sometime.' She pressed her cheek against him.

Taking comfort in the thought, Morgan also contemplated the fact that it felt as if she was home here, but it wouldn't be for much longer, and the thought of her leaving shattered his buoyant heart into a million pieces. He couldn't bear the idea of not having her by his side, to hold and cherish every moment they had left on this earth. But he knew he couldn't be selfish enough to ask it of her – she had a life to live, dreams to chase, a daughter who needed her, all far away from here. Still, it didn't stop him from wishing she could stay.

'Should we head back?' His gentle voice broke the comfortable silence.

'Yeah, I reckon we should,' she replied softly.

As they made their way back down the ridge, much more slowly than they'd climbed it, he couldn't help but steal glances at her, taking in every detail of her face. Her beautiful eyes, the way her plaited hair fell perfectly over her shoulder, and the curve of her hips that he longed to hold onto. It was almost too much for him to bear. He knew he had to keep his feelings at bay, but with each passing moment it became harder and harder. He wanted her with every fibre of his being, to touch her, kiss her, love her in every way imaginable. But he knew it could never happen, not after what had transpired between them before. They'd had their chance. And it had been blown to smithereens.

He tried to focus on anything other than the woman riding beside him. But it was no use. Every time he caught a glimpse of her from the corner of his eye, his heart skipped a beat. He had to get a grip on himself, or he was going to do something stupid. Again. It didn't help that she looked more beautiful than ever in the dappled sunlight, her hair catching the breeze and her skin glowing with a healthy flush.

He was in trouble.

They reached the stable way too soon for his liking, and he watched as she dismounted her horse and started to unsaddle. Doing the same, he could feel the heat emanating from her, and it made him even more aware of his own desires. He had to focus on something else, anything else, before he lost control.

'Hey, Morgan, are you okay?' Her voice brought him back to reality, and he realised he'd been staring at her.

He cleared his throat. 'Yeah, I'm fine. Just lost in thought.'

She smiled softly. 'Anything you want to talk about?'

He shook his head, trying to push away the thoughts that threatened to consume him. 'No, really, it's nothing.'

She nodded, understanding in her eyes. 'I'm here if you need me.'

You have no idea how much I need you, Jess.

They stood there for another long moment, the tension between them palpable. He wanted to reach out and touch her, to pull her into his embrace and never let go, but he knew he couldn't. Not without risking everything.

Instead, he took a step back and gestured towards the horses. 'I'll put these two away, if you want to head back to the homestead.'

'Okay, as long as you're sure, I mean, I don't mind helping.'

'Nah, I'm all good, thanks, Jess.'

'Righto, well, I'll catch you back there then.'

'Yup, I've got a bit to do after this, and then I'll head over next door and grab the roses from the flower farm.'

'Great, thanks, Morgan.'

'No problemo.' He watched her disappear out the stable door, taking another piece of him with her.

* * *

Cooking always helped to take Jess's mind off things. And right now, after kissing Morgan the night before, even though they'd broached the uncomfortable subject and agreed to move past it, she needed to cook like her life depended upon it. She needed to distract herself from the fact that she still wanted him. Immensely. Even as she tried to push her attraction to him aside, it continued to gnaw at her. She knew it was wrong, that she couldn't act on it, but the desire was still there, smouldering just below the surface. As she diced the vegetables for the beef and Guinness stew, her mind wandered to the endless possibilities of what could've happened if they'd played with the fire burning between them. She dropped the veggies into the preheated pressure cooker, and her cheeks flushed as she recalled his hands on her body, his lips on her skin, and the way he'd looked at her with such intensity. But it was all just a fantasy to believe it could happen again, or go any further than they'd already taken it, and a dangerous fantasy at that. She couldn't afford to lose him as a friend, not after everything they'd been through together. Not after how hard they'd worked at mending their tattered relationship.

As the timer beeped she placed the wooden spoon down and dashed towards the oven. Hot air hit her in the face as she swung the door open, and she reached in, grabbed hold of the tray with the oven mitts and slid it out. Plonking it onto the sink, she smiled. The aroma of freshly baked cinnamon rolls filled the kitchen, and by the looks of their fluffy centres with the perfect gooey, golden crust, she knew that she'd nailed it this time. She couldn't wait for Morgan's verdict when he tucked into one. Closing her eyes, she took a deep breath, letting the delectable scent fill her senses, and then turned the kettle on to make herself a cuppa.

Waiting for the water to boil, she glanced around the room. With cinnamon scrolls, chocolate chip cookies, and her special rum-soaked gingernut log setting in the fridge, along with the stew she was in the middle of prepping for their dinner, her efforts had been well worth it, although the kitchen resembled a disaster zone. So too did her clothes. She could only imagine the state of her hair and face. Licking the beaters after mixing the butter, cinnamon and brown sugar together had been unavoidable, as had taking a few sneaky mouthfuls of biscuit dough as she'd been rolling it.

The sound of footsteps approaching down the hallway caught her attention. Wiping her lips and cheeks, in case of sugary remnants, she turned around to see Morgan standing at the threshold, looking oh so handsome, his arms full of the roses they'd ordered.

'Wowsers.' Lifting his sunglasses to the top of his head, he looked her up and down. 'Who won, you or the kitchen?' He placed the fifty roses onto the dining table.

She grinned, then grimaced. 'I reckon it's a tie.'

'Ha, go you.' He closed the distance between them and sniffed in deep. 'It smells bloody amazing in here.'

Jess chuckled, taking a deep breath in too. 'Thanks, I've been experimenting with some new recipes, and refining a few favourites too.' He was standing so close to her, she couldn't help but admire his rugged good looks, and the way his button-up shirt clung to his muscular frame.

He raised an eyebrow, a smirk playing on his lips. 'Well, I think I need a taste test to confirm how good things really are.'

Jess felt her heart race as she regarded his piercing blue eyes. 'Sure, I'll grab you a plate,' she replied, trying to keep her voice, and knees, steady.

With two plates retrieved from the cupboard, she turned back towards him, not realising that he'd stepped up behind her. They smacked into one another. Morgan reached out to steady her, his hands lingering on her waist for a moment longer than necessary. She felt her heart skip a beat as she looked up at him. His eyes searched hers, and she felt herself getting lost in their blue depths.

Noooooo, Jess, don't!

'Righto, let me get you a cinnamon scroll and a biscuit to start with.' She passed him the goodie-laden plate.

Morgan took a bite of the scroll and let out a moan of pleasure. 'Oh my goodness, Jess, this is incredible,' he said with his mouth full.

She smiled, feeling a sense of satisfaction. 'I'm glad you like it.'

'Like it?' He looked shocked. 'I love it!'

'Yay! Mission accomplished,' she said gratefully. 'I'll just get this stew going, and then we'll get cracking with the roses, hey?'

'Sounds like a plan,' he garbled through his bite of the biscuit. 'Wow, this is yum too!' More pleasure-filled moans followed.

Needing to do something with her hands, other than grab Morgan by the collar and kiss him again, Jess picked up the first rose. She tore the bud from the top, and then sprinkled the velvety petals into the bucket. Then she repeated, and repeated, and repeated, and Morgan joined her, until all fifty roses were plucked naked and the bucket was now overflowing with a mountain of silky red petals. The sweet, floral aroma filled the air, and she smiled as she envisioned Shanti walking down her pretty petal aisle. The task had been tedious, but it was worth it. Resting her hands on her hips, she stretched side to side, trying to ease out her lower back.

Beside her, Morgan rolled his shoulders, then pressed his knuckles into his neck. 'Who would've thought that plucking rose petals would be so demanding?'

'Ha, yeah, tell me about it. I'll be glad when the bucket of petals is safely tucked up in the fridge.' She grimaced, her hands going to the rocks deep within her shoulders. 'I feel like my body has been hit by a truck.'

'I can give your shoulders a rub, if you like,' Morgan said casually.

She turned to face him, her eyes lighting up at the offer. 'That would be amazing, thank you.'

'Okay then, one shoulder massage coming up.' He gestured to the dining chair. 'Pull up a seat and get yourself comfy.'

'Yes, sir,' she said spiritedly, following his orders quick smart.

He came up behind her and placed his hands on her shoulders, applying just the right amount of pressure. She groaned in relief, her muscles slowly loosening beneath his touch. She couldn't help but notice the way his strong hands felt on her skin, how her body responded to his touch, and how a pleasurable warmth was spreading throughout her. She closed her eyes and let out a soft sigh, the tension in her body slowly draining away with each of his skilled strokes.

'Mmm, that feels so good,' she murmured.

'Good, I'm glad I can help.'

Moving fluidly, rhythmically, he progressed his hands downwards, to her upper back, kneading the muscles with what felt like practised expertise. Succumbing to his touch, she couldn't help but lean into his fingers, all the while with her body craving him more and more, and like a match to kindling, her body was set on fire. She bit her lip, imagining his talented hands running all over her.

'Is that better?' Morgan's voice was low and smooth, sending quivers all over her.

'Mmm, much better,' she purred, turning her head to look at him.

Their eyes met, and in that moment the desire between them was palpable.

She needed to stop this.

Now!

'I reckon all the knots are well and truly gone.' Easing out of his reach, she offered a sideways glance as she stood. 'Thank you, Savage.'

Sharp intelligence filled his gaze. 'Good, mission accomplished.' It was clear he knew she was trying to put distance between them.

She broke eye contact with him. How in the hell could he drive her insane, and make her want him, in equal measure? Getting back to dinner preparations, she fought to keep her mind on the job, all the while feeling Morgan watching her.

'I'm really not that enthralling,' she finally said.

'Actually, you are.' His voice wrapped around her, turning her towards him.

'Morgan, we can't keep doing this.'

'Doing what?' He shrugged as if bewildered by her comment.

'You know exactly what.' She took steps, stopping just short of him. 'A lot has changed in nine years, and we don't want to hurt one another by delving into remembrances of our past.'

Morgan remained silent while regarding her with such knowing intensity she almost ran from the kitchen. But she forced herself to stand her ground, to stay controlled, careful, guarded.

'Jess.' His eyes were filled with sympathy, and worry creased his brow. 'What aren't you telling me?'

What a fool she was, to think he couldn't see through the cracks in her armour. This man knew her, sometimes better than she knew herself. The emotion lodged in her throat gripped tighter, making it impossible to reply. But she had to tell him something. Maybe not the whole truth. Maybe half of it would suffice. Enough to make him understand why she couldn't stay, why she couldn't do this with him. Or maybe she should just come out right now and tell him everything? Even though she didn't have a definitive answer yet. For a heartbeat, and then another, they just stared at each other. She wanted to tell him what she was hiding. With all of her heart. But then she blinked, and her voice of reason stormed to the forefront like an infantry soldier ready for battle.

'I can't do this, Morgan.'

'But, Jess, I'm sorry, please don't walk away.'

By some miracle she managed to hold her tears in until she was out of sight. Wrapping her arms around herself, she drew in a shuddering breath as she climbed the stairs. Morgan called out after her, begging her to stop. But she couldn't. Bile burned the back of her throat as she kept striding away. Hurrying towards the bedroom, with her mind in an absolute spin, she closed and locked the door behind her, then began stuffing her things into her suitcase.

'Jess, please open the door.' Morgan's concerned voice carried as he knocked.

'Please, just leave me be.'

'Jess?'

'Morgan, please.'

There was a moment of silence, then she thought she heard him walk away.

And that's when she took a breath and tried to calm down. What in the hell was she doing? She couldn't do her usual trick and run. She'd made a promise to the two people in this world who'd never, ever, let her down, and she was sticking to it. She had to push through, for Roberto and Shanti's sakes. Defeated, annoyed with herself, ashamed of her over-the-top reaction to a question she could have easily answered in another way, a much better way, she sat on the edge of the bed, her hands trembling. She knew she couldn't keep pretending everything was okay. She had to tell Morgan the truth about not knowing who Chiara's father was, him or Salvatore, even if it meant hurting him. But she wasn't about to open that can of worms right before the wedding. It would have to wait.

Taking a deep breath, she stood up and walked over to the door, her heart pounding in her chest. As she opened it, she found Morgan standing on the other side, his eyes filled with concern. 'I heard you packing,' he said, his voice wavering. 'You're leaving, aren't you?'

Jess felt tears welling up in her eyes as she nodded. 'I panicked, but I'm not leaving, not yet anyway,' she said, her voice barely above a whisper. 'I'm sorry, Morgan, but I'm not who you think I am.'

'We're both different people now, Jess.' Morgan stepped forward, his hands reaching out to cup her cheeks. 'But essentially, our cores are still the same.'

Her hands coming to gently cover his, she nodded as she held his gaze. 'Let's just focus on the wedding, and after that we can talk about whatever we feel we need to, okay?'

He nodded. 'Okay.'

Then, pulling her to him, he held her close, and she held him too, like she never, ever wanted to let him go.

CHAPTER 19

It was the day before the wedding, and with so much still to do, along with the roiling emotions she was feeling when it came to her and Morgan, Jess felt overwhelmed. With a wave of dizziness overcoming her, she safely pulled the VW onto the side of the road, killed the engine and rolled down her window. Salty sea air stirred her hair, sweeping tickling locks of it against her cheek. She tucked it behind her ear, sighing. For nine long years she'd missed the sparkling ocean of Silverton Shores. But she hadn't realised just how much. This seaside town had given her so many happy memories, but she'd also suffered her deepest grief here. She'd give almost anything to go back to the days of being a toddler then, in the blink of an eye, a teenager, happily living life, carefree, hopeful and naive, with two parents who loved her dearly. But she couldn't ever go back. She had to find a way to move forward, so she could provide the same sort of secure, loving, happy childhood she'd had to her darling Chiara.

It was bittersweet, being back here. Nothing had changed and yet everything had. It was a paradox if ever she'd felt one. Tears slipped as she remembered the days that she used to spend on the golden shores with Annie, Roberto and their mum and dad. It had been so much fun, playing in the waves and building sandcastles that would eventually be swallowed up by the rising tide. Then, contentedly exhausted, she'd enjoy a bubble bath and some dinner before her father would carry her to bed and tuck her in, reminding her just how loved she was by him and her mum. Her present situation was such a stark contrast to those days. Florence was breathtakingly beautiful, but it wasn't here. It wasn't home. God, how she wished she could bring Chiara back here, so she could raise her in the footsteps of where she'd been. Somehow, some way, she believed it would help heal the last of her anguish and give her the closure she needed over her parents' untimely deaths.

Needing to get a move on, she straightened and swallowed down her yearnings – it would provide no comfort, obsessing over it. She had maid of honour duties to fulfil, and fulfil them she would. With one last lingering look at the ebb and flow of the ocean, she started the engine and turned back towards Morgan's. It was getting harder and harder to act normal around him after she'd had the chance to tell him everything, but couldn't, and now she loathed herself for it. But there was no going back. She'd made her bed – or dug her own grave, depending on how she wanted to look at it – and now she had to sleep in it. In the end, it was probably better for him to only know the outcome of the paternity test – that there had even been one – if he needed to.

A few hours later, after completing her errands in town and now feeling hot and bothered, Jess pulled up beneath the big old gum tree. She sat in her mum's restored car for a moment, gathering her thoughts and her courage. She knew what waited for her inside, and it was a feat, but she had to face it. Taking a deep breath, she stepped out of the car, grabbed the bags from the back seat, and walked towards the front door of the homestead. An hour later, unpacked and rehydrated, she looked at the eighty-five cannoli shells that stared back at her from the kitchen bench. In the interest of her sanity, she pretended to be fine and dandy with the humungous task ahead of her.

Music, I need music …

She turned on the stereo and her phone's Bluetooth, and searched her Spotify list. She decided on some Frank Sinatra … cool, calm, composed, that's what she needed to be. Then, and only then, did the epic piping session begin. After strapping the apron around her waist, she got to work. Carefully, she opened, poured and then stirred the entire jar of pistachio paste she'd brought over from Italy into the mixture of cream and ricotta. And as the smooth voice of Frank Sinatra filled the homestead kitchen, she felt herself relax into it. Baking always had that effect on her. It was therapeutic, allowing her to forget about the stresses of daily life and get lost in the process of creating something delicious. Then, as she piped the creamy mixture into the crispy shells, she contemplated the way food could transport her to a different place and time, and she felt grateful for the escape it provided her.

Totally engrossed in her task, and swaying her hips in time to the music, she jumped when the flyscreen door of the kitchen smacked shut. She spun around, still holding the piping bag, to see Morgan standing in the doorway, his eyes fixed on her.

She could feel her cheeks turning red as she hurriedly wiped her hands on the tea towel beside her.

'Hey,' she said, trying to sound casual.

'Hey,' he replied, his gaze lingering on her. 'What's happening?'

'I'm making the cannoli for the wedding reception,' she said, holding up the piping bag as if to prove it.

Morgan walked over to the bench and peered at the piles of cannoli shells. 'Wow,' he said, sounding impressed. 'There's a lot of them.'

'Sure is,' Jess said, feeling a little flustered.

'Are you feeling okay today?' he asked, way too casually.

'Yeah, I'm good.' She looked away before she could catch a glimpse of sympathy in his eyes. She didn't deserve that. Not in the slightest.

His hand came to rest softly on her back. 'Can I offer a helping hand?'

'No but thank you.' She forced a tiny, quivering smile. 'I've only got another ...' she counted the ones she'd already done, '... fifty-three to go.'

'Righto, but only if you're sure you can handle all those bad boys.'

'I reckon I can,' she said as casually as she could.

She turned away from him, focusing on the task at hand – the cannolis. As she piped the filling into the shells, she tried to push the guilt and shame out of her mind, but she could feel him, standing at the sink, drinking his water and watching her. She couldn't help but feel a wave of discomfort at his attention, as covert as it was. It was hard enough keeping her secret from him but feeling his genuine concern for her made it all the more difficult.

If only he could give her a little space.

Morgan, however, wasn't about to leave and let her be. 'I honestly don't mind calling it a day and helping you instead.'

She stopped piping and turned to face him. 'Like I said, I've got it covered, but thank you.'

'But you don't have to do all of these alone.' Morgan took a step forward, his hand reaching out to touch her arm. 'Let me help you.'

Jess pulled away from him, shaking her head. 'I'm good, thanks.'

Morgan furrowed his brow, concern and hurt etched on his face. 'Okay then, I'll leave you to it.'

'Sure, catch you a bit later on.' She turned back to the cannolis, feeling defeated, horrible and just plain bitchy. But she couldn't be around him right now. It was too hard. She had to protect herself, and him.

Morgan sighed, and tugging his hat back on, headed back outside, leaving her exactly where she needed to be, with her hands busy, her mind focused and her breath going back to some kind of normal.

* * *

The morning of the wedding arrived. Bleary-eyed from her lack of sleep, after a catch-up call with Chiara and her nonno, Jess tried to focus wholly and solely on her duties as a maid of honour. She'd even managed to put a smile on her face for the pre-wedding photos as she, Annie and Shanti had enjoyed their pre-ceremony time together, but in the midst of cheering glasses of bubbly, having her hair and make-up done, and fighting back emotions as she'd helped Shanti into her stunning antique lace gown, her mind kept flittering elsewhere. She couldn't stop thinking about Morgan and the conversation they might need to have, about the devastation it could cause and the heartbreak it would likely bring. She couldn't stop beating herself up for keeping everything from everyone she held dear, and for so long. And she couldn't stop wondering, now the truth was so near, if it was Salvatore and Chiara who deserved to know about it all before Morgan did.

As the ceremony began, Jess moved in time to the music as she walked down the rose petal aisle, the softness of her silk gown brushing against her trembling legs. She could feel Morgan's gaze on her, but she was too afraid to meet his sapphire blues, for fear of breaking down. Sunlight shone through the stained-glass windows of the church, its beams like a kaleidoscope of colour, making the space feel even more magical than it already was. Breathing in deeply, she took her place next to Annie. Trying to hold back happy tears, she watched Shanti take the limelight, her arm in the crook of her mother's, her steps in time to 'I Can't Help Falling in Love with You', sung by none other than the man himself, Elvis Presley.

Jess's heart melted as Roberto and Shanti exchanged their pledges and promises, then exchanged rings. As the priest read a passage about love and loyalty, she couldn't help but think about her own cancelled wedding and the pain she'd caused Morgan because of it. Time and time again she had to hold back emotions, tears of joy and tears of deep-seated heartbreak, knowing the man of her dreams was standing mere metres from her, and yet felt so far out of her reach.

As the newlyweds shared their first kiss as husband and wife, she finally met Morgan's gaze. The intensity of his regard made her heart skip more than a few beats. The love and longing in his eyes were unmistakable, and she felt the familiar pang of culpability in her chest. She wanted to reach out to him and tell him how much she still loved him, but the fear of hurting him, of breaking his heart all over again, held her back. There was something unsaid between them, something that needed to be addressed. And until that happened, her heart and hands were tied.

Cheering along with the guests as Shanti and Roberto made their way down the aisle, her heart momentarily soared knowing that her best friend and brother were finally together. Thank goodness she'd thought to tuck a tissue into her bra, because she needed it to dab the corners of her eyes. It had been a long journey for them, with a lot of ups and downs, but with undivided dedication to each other they'd made it work. Roberto and Shanti were living proof that love could and did prevail. As the ceremony came to a close and the applause died down, even though Annie was right beside her and she was surrounded by people, she felt very alone. Her heart yearned for a love like theirs, a love that could conquer all obstacles. The kind of love that she would've had with Morgan. The kind of love she'd royally stuffed up, in every way possible.

More fool her!

The afternoon smoothly rolled into the evening, and with two hours of wedding photos now behind them, along with the formalities of dinner and speeches, the part Jess had been looking forward to most was here. Watching eagerly from the sidelines, she held up her phone, camera at the ready to capture the first dance as the newlyweds took to the glimmering dance floor. Swaying gently to Etta James' 'At Last', after a few twirls

Roberto tipped his beautiful bride back, and her veil floated as the play of light caught their love-filled expressions. Jess clicked one, two, three times, freezing the perfect moments in time in quick succession as she gushed with all the emotions – she still believed in the power of love, she just didn't know if she was destined to ever be so lucky to have a man love her like Roberto loved Shanti. There was a lot to be said for tying the knot with your childhood sweetheart. It meant you knew each other inside out and back to front, which made for a solid foundation, one that would help each person get through the hard times.

The kind of love she and Morgan had once shared.

At the end of the moving song, Roberto looked over to her and offered a knowing smile. Hugging herself, she returned it. Spinning in Roberto's arms, Shanti followed her new husband's gaze and winked at Jess, her smile as bright as the sunshine she seemed to carry with her everywhere she went. Jess was surprised her bestie didn't leave little sparkles of it with every step, the way her spirit glowed so radiantly. She was blessed to call Shanti her best friend. If only she lived nearer, she'd be able to spend much more time with her, and Chiara would quickly understand why she adored her new Aunty Shanti so very much.

Unable to bring herself to join the guests moving onto the dance floor, she grabbed the chance to step outside for some fresh air. Trying to suppress the tears threatening to spill down her cheeks, she leant against the wall of the building. As she took deep breaths, she couldn't help but think about how mesmerising the day had been and how happy she was to have been there to share it. The love between Roberto and Shanti was profound, and it made her heart ache with a bittersweet combination of joy and sorrow. She'd once been a hopeless romantic, one who believed in finding a soulmate and living happily ever after. And with Morgan, she'd proved it was real. But now she truly believed she was never going to have the love her brother and Shanti shared, nor did she deserve to. But Morgan would, she was almost certain of it. And the woman he would love until his very last breath wasn't going to be her. She closed her eyes, trying to push away the negative thoughts. But as she did, she heard footsteps approaching.

She opened her eyes cautiously, not sure who it could be. But when she spotted who was heading her way, her heart stalled then galloped. 'Morgan.' Embarrassed he'd caught her feeling sorry for herself, she sniffled, straightening.

'Hey, Jess.' His warm hand gently touched her shoulder, and his kind eyes looked at her with heart-touching concern. 'Are you okay?' he asked softly.

'Yeah.' She chuckled, way too forcibly. 'I'm just a big goofy sook, that's all.'

'Yeah, weddings can be emotional, huh.'

'Damn straight they can.' She smiled at his agreeable expression.

They stood there in silence for a moment, the only sound the distant music and laughter from the reception. Jess wanted to say something, anything, to break the tension between them, but the words wouldn't come.

Morgan beat her to it. 'Would you like to come back inside and dance with me?'

She went to say no, then switched it up. 'Yeah, why not.'

'Come on then.' He offered her the crook of his arm. 'Let me lead the way.'

When they got back inside the hall, the lights had been dimmed and the polished floorboards gleamed beneath the spinning disco ball. All around the ceiling, draped fairy lights flickered and glimmered. By Morgan's side, Jess felt the thunderous beating of her heart somehow blocking her sensible thoughts, and she swiftly felt like they were in another world, one where anything was achievable and mistakes were impossible. Where love prevailed and conquered.

Reaching the dance floor then relaxing into him, she felt as if everything around them faded away, leaving them in a ballroom of their very own. She liked how Morgan took the lead as he swayed her. She was wearing three-inch heels, but she still felt tiny next to him. And then, when the music slowed and he drew her that little bit closer, he made her feel ethereal, feminine, protected, wanted. The bits of her he was touching tingled: her hands, the lower arch of her back – her heart. Ignoring the little voice in her head warning her to be careful, she met his gaze, but he wasn't giving much away. She was lost in all that was him, the floor seemed to sway beneath her gliding feet, and she abruptly felt as if she was freefalling. Her body hummed with satisfaction, but her heart was heavy with remorse, dragging her down, down, down. Her legs were suddenly weak and then reality slapped her hard in the chest. She couldn't stay here, playing fantasy with Morgan. She had a life, and a beautiful daughter, back in Italy.

There was no way she'd ever be calling Silverton Shores home again.

No way at all.

But then the entire world hushed and stilled as his finger found the bottom of her chin, and he gently brought her teary gaze to his. Feathering his fingers across her cheek, he tucked some loose hair behind her ear. Her heart raced as she felt his warmth so close to her, his touch sending shivers down her spine.

She wanted to lose herself in his arms, to forget everything else and just be with him. She wanted it so much, she felt herself teetering on the dangerous edge of him.

As if sensing the workings of her heart, he leant in closer, his breath warm on her skin, and whispered in her ear, 'I got you, Jess.'

And in that moment, with those four words, he told her everything. How much he still loved her. How much he wanted to be with her. How much he missed her. She kept her gaze locked to his as his fingers trailed down her back, stopping in the curve. A quiver of need raced through her. She wanted this man. More than she'd ever wanted him before. Time hadn't healed the gaping hole. Instead, it had lain dormant, waiting, hoping, longing for the moment he'd be able to slip back into his place in her heart. With only the slightest bit of hesitation, she rested her head against his chest as his arms came possessively, protectively, around her. Dizzy with longing, she breathed him in. He smelt of leather and spice, all naughty and nice.

She knew what she wanted, and she wanted him.

Morgan Savage had always been her weakness. The one and only man who knew how to make her body sing and her heart swell with love. No matter how hard she fought him off, she innately knew she couldn't resist him. She imagined dragging him to some dark corner of the room and pushing him against the wall. She pictured kissing him with the hunger that had been building up inside her the past few weeks. And she longed for him to respond with equal passion, his hands roaming all over her body, exploring every curve and crevice with an expertise that only he possessed. For he knew her. All of her. He knew her strengths, her weaknesses, her dreams and her fears. If only he knew her secret. Would he embrace the truth? Would he forgive her for it? As she stopped swaying and looked up into his piercing blue eyes, she saw the same desire and longing mirrored back at her, with secrets of his own dancing among the shadows.

* * *

Morgan was sick and tired of being sensible. This woman drove him wild, in every way, and he wanted to be wild with her, now, and hopefully, forever.

'Should we get out of here?' His heart raced as he locked eyes with her and waited.

'Mm-hmm.' She almost purred her reply.

He didn't need any more of an invitation to follow his ravenous need for her. Holding her hand, he led her off the dance floor, through the tables and towards where she'd left her coat and bag. Nerves flickered, but he ignored the warning sensation to bring this to a grinding halt. And as she gathered her things and they made their way outside, where the cool night air hit them, he smiled into it, because nothing and nobody was going to stop him making passionate love to the woman he loved with every inch of his being. Close to his side, he felt her shiver and instinctively wrapped his arm around her, pulling her in closer. She leant into him, taking comfort in his warmth as they strode away from the light and noise. They walked in an intimate silence, the only sound coming from their shoes crunching on the gravel driveway of the reception hall.

With quiet darkness enclosing them, he finally broke the silence. 'My room, or yours?'

She smiled coyly at him, the moonlight reflecting in her eyes. 'Yours,' she said, her voice low and sultry.

Then, together, they trampled any rules either of them had silently placed and snuck like thieves into the dead of night and towards his hotel room. Reaching it, he fumbled with the key card, his fingers shaking with nerves and anticipation. She leant against him, pressing her body close to his. He could feel the heat emanating from her skin, and it only made him more desperate to kiss and hold her. Finally, the lock clicked and he pushed the door open.

Jess followed him in, placed her diamanté-studded purse on the dresser, then provocatively glanced at him over her shoulder. Shedding his jacket, he ripped off his tie, tossing both to the side. He could be a very patient man when he needed, or wanted, to be. Now wasn't one of those times. He didn't want to stop to think things through like every other time they'd come so close. He didn't need to come up with reasons why they shouldn't do this. All he needed was her. Overcome with primal hunger, he wanted to feel and taste and fixate. He wanted Jessica Sabatini to know just how much he craved her, needed her, loved her. Closing the distance, he stopped inches from her and slowly slid the zipper of her soft, silky dress downwards, groaning with longing as it dropped to the floor.

He kissed the side of her delicate neck. 'Are you sure about this, Jess?'

'Yes ...' came her breathless response, urging him on.

As she followed his lead, he felt his control slipping. With every breathless moan, he gave more of himself to her. His hands roamed freely over her body, teasing, caressing, until he felt her begin to quake beneath him. He had to touch every bit of her sweet skin. Grasping the clasp of her lacy bra, he flicked it and it slipped off her. He glided his hands over the rounded fullness of her breasts as she turned to face him. Sliding his hands down the luscious curves of her, he paused at her waist, then her hips. She was exquisite and, for now, she was all his.

Dropping to his knees, he brought his lips to her sacred place, savouring her sweetness with tender licks, sucks and the gentlest of nibbles. She shuddered beneath his dancing tongue as he lingered, bringing her to the brink of euphoria. And he wanted, needed, ached to give her so much more. Before she had time to tumble into ecstasy, he stood, and she wrapped her arms around his neck. She was all he'd ever wanted. He knew she'd always held a piece of him, but now, after spending almost two amazing weeks with her, all of him belonged to her. Once again.

'I need you,' she whispered, as though reading his thoughts.

He needed her too, all of her, now and always.

Gently pressing his lips to the side of her neck, he trailed kisses up to the very place he knew drove her wild. Nibbling and sucking, he paused to whisper just how much he wanted her. A soft moan escaped her, and goosebumps raced over her skin. Then she held his gaze as she began undoing each button of his shirt. He brought his hands up to caress her breasts, slowing his touch as he brushed over her rock-hard nipples. A low growl was his reply to her fingertips trailing down his chest. Her lips parted, and he met her there with a bone-melting kiss. She returned the favour, igniting every nerve in his body as they manoeuvred their way towards the bed.

She tumbled backwards, and wriggled over to make room for him. Undoing his belt, then the zipper of his chinos, he finally bared every inch of himself to her. Her eyes blazed with hunger as she silently beckoned him to her. But he held back. Stayed by the side of the bed. For a breath, and then another, he admired her shapely silhouette lit softly by the leadlight lamp. He was lost to her, completely. More than he'd ever been. Sliding in beside her, he rolled her onto her back and climbed over her. He pressed up on his hands as she cradled him between her thighs. He held nothing back as he explored her every curve, every angle, relishing how she was melting beneath his lingering kisses. He moved, slowly, and she found his rhythm. He took his time, knowing this might be the only chance he got to make love to her like he'd been aching to.

But he prayed that this wouldn't be so.

Crying out his name, she dug her heels into the backs of his thighs, forcing him deeper. He gave her what she asked for. Her fingers dragged through the hair at his nape and she pulled him closer still. Her head fell back as she dug her nails into the skin of his back. He thrust faster, deeper, his laboured breath matching hers. She was close. So close. But he wasn't ready for her to freefall just yet. Lingering and holding her gaze, he paused, waited, and watched her unravel. She bit down on her lip in an attempt to suppress her cries of release. Then, and only then, did he take her wrists into his hands and gently pin them above her head. In this erotic breathless moment, he wondered whether he'd ever get enough of her. Her tight muscles rippled around him. He was close now, too. So very close. She moaned into his mouth as he hit her spot. Arching her back, she grasped his shoulders, every inch of her tightening as she trembled. And he chased her higher, higher, until the brink was both of theirs to savour. Reaching the pinnacle, he tumbled over with her.

Satiated, breathless and deeply in love, he rolled over to the side, bringing her with him and cradling her against his chest. He'd never felt so alive. He knew he'd never be the same again. It was a slow descent from whatever place he'd hovered and soared to with her, but once he'd fully landed he relished the way her body was still pressed against his.

He'd never felt so ... whole.

And he didn't ever want to let her go.

CHAPTER 20

Sleep began to release Jess from its embrace, and as she rose to the surface of reality, she felt lighter, happier, loved. For a few blissful breaths, she savoured the rise and fall of Morgan's burly chest as his heart drummed beneath her cheek, slow and steady. The sheets were wrapped around their tangled legs, and their arms were wrapped around each other. She wanted to stay like this. Forever. Recalling how his touch had teetered between gentle and soothing, to hungry and heated, and the way his gaze had been faultlessly reassuring, she sighed ever so softly. If only she could stay here all day, pretending the outside world didn't exist. Pretending they had a future, a life they could share. Pretending that he knew her secret. Pretending that he had understood why she'd kept such a thing from him, and immediately forgiven her. Pretending she knew the outcome of the test, and that the three of them could become the family they should have been.

Glancing up at his rugged handsomeness, she smiled. Last night, and all through the night, their lovemaking had been magical. And the look in his eyes when he'd leant in and kissed her, knowing they were about to make love … even now, it sent flashes of hungry heat through her. Never had she felt so alive, so satisfied, more herself than ever before. She didn't want to regret this. She wanted to remember his every caress, his every kiss, his every groan, fondly, tenderly, lovingly.

To do that, she needed to get out of here.

Now.

Before anyone discovered her in his room.

Carefully, she shifted to the side of the bed then, one foot after the other, planted herself to the floor. Her clothes were scattered all around the place. Quietly scooping each item up, she slipped everything back on. Morgan stirred and rolled onto his side. Freezing, she held her breath. She didn't want to explain why she was rushing out of there. Then, tiptoeing out of the room, she made her way just as quietly down the hallway to the fire exit, where she quickened her steps until she was out of sight and heading towards the sun-drenched coastline.

Slowing turning her face to the sunshine, she closed her eyes and drew in a deep breath of the fresh sea air drifting through the overhanging trees. Her heels dangling from her fingertips, she followed a little path that would lead her to a private beach where she hoped to goodness nobody was up just yet. Given the lateness of the reception, she guessed most people would still be sleeping their hangovers off. When the untainted view of the ocean met her eyes she brought her hand over her chest to where her heart was still racing from the events of the night before, and she couldn't help but feel a sense of regret slowly creeping up. She didn't regret being with Morgan, she couldn't, but she did regret that she had to leave so abruptly. She knew he'd be hurt when he woke without her there, but there was no way on this earth she was going to spend today explaining what they'd been up to all night long to anyone who discovered them together.

With her mind and heart in a spin, she made her way down to the shoreline, the sparkly white sand soft and warm beneath her feet. The ebb and flow of the crashing waves helped to calm her nerves, but only a little. Sinking down and hugging her knees to her, she closed her eyes, breathing in a lungful of the salty air. And little by little, she began to find her balance and put things into perspective. Finally feeling at peace with what had happened between them, she wanted to stay in this moment forever, to forget about the real world and all its problems, to believe with all of her heart that she and Morgan were going to work things out, that they were somehow, some way, going to end up back together, living as a happy family at Savage Acres with Chiara showered by their love for each other, and her.

The perfect end to what could have been a tragic love story.

But she knew that was impossible. She had responsibilities, people who depended on her. She couldn't stay here forever, no matter how much she wanted to. She opened her eyes, taking in the beauty around her. The ocean stretched out before her, endless and full of wonder. Seagulls soared overhead, their cries echoing in the air. With the water reaching and lapping at her feet, she got lost in her thoughts as she replayed the events of the night before. She wanted to run back to Morgan, to feel his touch and be wrapped in his embrace. She wanted to feel the intimate passion they'd shared for only the second time in their lives, to relive the ecstasy that had consumed her. Over and over again. But she knew it was impossible. Not only did she not want people asking questions she didn't know the answers to, she also couldn't live with herself for succumbing to him again before she'd told him what she should have all those years ago. Then they could have worked it all out together.

Shrill ringing in her handbag made her jump, and she quickly reached in to grab her phone. There was no caller ID. 'Hello?'

'Jess, grazie a dio mi hai ascoltato.' Her nonno's voice was rushed, almost indecipherable.

'Nonno, what's wrong?' Hearing his urgent tone made her insides knot with tension. 'And please slow down and try and speak English.'

'Tesoro, it's Chiara.'

Sudden anxiety roiled her gut as she shot to her feet. 'Oh my god, what's happened to her?'

'No, mi scusi, she's safe, but she's very upset.' He inhaled sharply. 'Salvatore told her he didn't want her coming to stay with him this weekend, because he's too busy.'

'Oh my goodness, poor Chiara.' Blinking back tears, she felt her mum hat slip on, nice and tight. 'I'll be on the first plane I can get a seat on.'

'It's only two more nights before you fly home, we can wait until then to see you.'

'No, Nonno, I'm not leaving her a moment longer than I have to. Not when she's so upset.'

'Okay, I understand, and I'm so sorry, Jess.' Her nonno's voice broke.

'Nonno, it's not your fault.' She fought to hold her composure, feeling a pressing need to be there for him, too, along with Chiara. 'Can I talk with her or is she already asleep?'

'Let me check.' The door creaked as he eased it ajar. 'She's fast sleep,' he whispered. 'And I don't want to wake her.'

'Of course, yes, let her sleep.' She sniffed back emotions. 'Can you please tell her I love her, when she wakes, and that I'll call you when she does.'

'I will, I promise.' He sniffed. 'Let me know if you can change your flight back to us, si?'

'As soon as I know anything, you will.'

'Okay, bella, we love you, ciao.'

'Love you both, Nonno, very much.'

After saying goodbye, she hung up and dropped to the sand, tears welling and streaming down her cheeks. Her heart ached like hell at the news of Salvatore's selfish ways. Not that she should be surprised. Damn it, she was supposed to be the one to protect her baby girl, to keep her safe. Always. And yet here she was, gallivanting over the other side of the world, spending the night with her ex and dreaming of an unrealistic future with him. Hugging her knees to her chest, she let the tears fall. The illusion of the life she'd been living here hit her hard in the chest. As much as she'd loved her time with Morgan, she also wanted to run back to Italy, to her life there, where she didn't have to spend each and every day hiding behind her lies.

* * *

Stirring lazily, Morgan rolled over, ready to smile, but instead he was met with an empty side of the bed. Cold dread swept through him. Had he gone and effed everything up? Surely not. He knew, without a shadow of doubt, that he hadn't imagined the unbridled passion, or the look of love in her eyes. Pain seized his heart as the memories of her leaving him high and dry flooded back. He took a deep breath. He could not, would not, let this, them, become a train wreck once again. He loved her. And he wanted to be able to tell her that. Time and time again. He wanted her to know that he couldn't stand to lose her a second time around. He needed her to know that this time he would fight, until his last breath, for her. For them. If it came to that. What other choice did he have, when she owned every single bit of his heart? He also wanted her to know that if they could make it work, he would love Chiara as if she was his own.

He quickly sat up and rubbed his eyes, hoping this was all a bad dream, but the emptiness of the bed only confirmed that it wasn't. After dragging on a pair of board shorts and a T-shirt, he slipped his feet into his thongs. And as he gathered his wits, and his courage, for what he was about to do, his mind wandered back to the past. He remembered the good times they'd shared, the laughter, the intimacy, the love. But he also remembered the utter agony that her leaving had left him with. He was no saint. He'd sometimes messed up throughout their relationship. Forgotten their anniversary and fallen asleep when he was meant to meet with her, gotten too drunk a few times. He and Jess had both made mistakes, but he was willing to forgive and forget, to start anew.

With new-found determination, he grabbed his keys and headed out the door. His instincts told him to go to the beach first – Jess had always gravitated towards the ocean when her heart was in turmoil. Avoiding the paths that led to the dining room, he honed in on the pathway that led down to the beach. And there, just like he'd thought, he found her sitting by the shoreline, a lone figure with her arms wrapped around herself as if she was afraid she was about to shatter into a million little pieces.

He approached her slowly, silently praying she wouldn't walk away from him. As he drew closer, he noticed that her eyes were red and puffy from crying. His heart sank as he realised just how much pain he'd caused her by following through with his longings, and his love, for her. All he wanted to do was wrap his arms around her and tell her that everything was going to be okay. But he knew it would take more than words to win her back. If anything, he braced himself for losing her a second time.

'Hey,' he said softly, breaking the silence.

She turned to his voice, her eyes widening. 'Morgan, what are you doing here?'

'Looking for you.'

'Why?' Sympathy, or was it pity, wrinkled her brow.

He swallowed past the tight knot in his throat. 'Come on, Jess, please, stop this.'

Her arms folded defensively. 'Stop what, exactly?'

'This.'

Her shoulders lifted. 'I don't know what this is.'

He shook his head, sighing. 'That makes two of us.' He pulled up a piece of beach beside her, sitting close to her side. 'Please, Jess, talk to me.'

'About what?' Turning to him, she rested her cheek on her knee.

Morgan felt beside himself with frustration and hurt. 'Can you honestly sit there and tell me you don't want me?'

'No, Morgan, I can't.' Her words were straight to the point, as was her red-rimmed gaze.

Taken aback by her unhesitating reply, he paused as he caught his breath. 'Okay, good, then how about you do something about it.'

'I can't.' Her tone was impassive.

'Why not?'

An exhaled breath dragged the words from her lips. 'Just in case you've forgotten, I have a daughter, Morgan, and she needs me, like I mean, really needs me.'

'Of course she does, you're her mum.' He shook his head, baffled by her response. 'Every child needs their mother.'

'Yes, they most certainly do.' Nodding as if reminding herself of the fact, she watched the seagulls playing above the gentle sea. 'I really do love this place.'

'Well, why don't you and Chiara move back here?'

Deep sadness etched into her pretty features as she shook her head. 'I can't.'

'Why not?' Morgan asked, feeling desperate.

Jess turned to him, tears brimming in her eyes once more. 'Because I can't keep running away from my problems, Morgan. My life in Florence is complicated, but it's still my life. I can't just up and leave it behind, as if it never meant anything to me. Besides, my nonno is there, and he needs me too, now that Nonna is gone.'

Even though he totally understood her, Morgan felt a wave of frustration wash over him. 'So, what? We're just supposed to give up. Not even try?'

Jess shook her head. 'I'm not saying that. I'm saying that we need to be realistic here. We can't just ignore the obstacles in our way, hoping they'll magically disappear. We have to face them head-on, no matter how difficult it may be.'

Morgan's heart sank. 'And what if we can't? What if it's just too hard?'

Jess took a deep breath, her gaze flickering towards him. 'Then maybe it's just not meant to be, Morgan.'

He felt like he'd been hit by a ton of bricks. He'd been so sure they were meant to be together that he was willing to fight for her. But now, hearing her words, he felt defeated. 'But I love you,' he whispered, his voice cracking with emotion.

Jess turned to him, her eyes softening. 'I know you do, Morgan. And I love you too. But sometimes love just isn't enough.'

He felt like he couldn't breathe. 'What are you saying?'

Jess took his hand, giving it a gentle squeeze. 'I'm saying that maybe it's time we let each other go. For both our sakes.'

Morgan felt like he'd been punched in the gut. Letting go of Jess was the last thing he wanted to do. But as he looked into her eyes, he saw the truth in her words. They were both stuck in difficult situations, and maybe it was time to accept that their love was not enough to overcome it all.

He let out a deep sigh, trying to hold back his tears. 'I don't want to let you go,' he said, his voice barely above a whisper. 'But I don't know what else to do.'

Jess squeezed his hand tighter. 'Maybe we just need to take a step back and focus on ourselves for a while.' Her shoulders lifted ever so slightly. 'Who knows what the future holds?'

He nodded, feeling a sense of resignation wash over him. He knew she was right, but it didn't make it any easier. 'I don't want to lose you,' he said, sadly.

Jess leant in, pressing her forehead against his. 'You'll never lose me completely, Morgan. Even if we're not together, you'll always have a piece of my heart.' She placed her hand over where his was breaking beneath her touch. 'Trust me on that.'

With no words left to say, he pulled her to him, allowing his embrace to anchor her to him one last time. He was out of his depth, and so was she. He had to be the one to stop them drowning. He had to let her go. The hurt was going to happen all over again.

Heaven help him.

* * *

And just like that, the following morning, with his hands shoved deeply into his pockets, he stood on his driveway and watched her leave with Annie, two days early. And just like the last time, a piece of his soul went with her. Loving her the way he did meant having a broken heart. Again. As the car disappeared from view, he let out a deep sigh. He knew this was the right thing to do. He couldn't keep holding on to something that was never meant to be. It was time to move on. To try and forget their love. Just how he was meant to do that, he hadn't a damn clue, but he was going to do his very best, for her sake and for his own. He wondered if Annie was going to tell her the secret they'd been keeping on the way to the airport.

At least now he didn't need to put himself in the middle of it.

Jess's life was her own.

And his was his to deal with.

CHAPTER 21

Oh, how things could change in what felt like the blink of an eye. One minute she and Morgan were making love all night long, and the next they were agreeing to let each other go. And it was all her fault they couldn't find a way forward. Because she was too terrified to tell him the truth, at least not until she knew for certain. Why put him through such a thing, when she might not have to? So she'd given him nothing, when he really deserved everything. She could've handled it all differently and told him the dilemma she was facing. Maybe he might have helped her, been there along the way. But instead she'd done her usual trick. Retreated. Run.

Coward!

One sleeping tablet, washed down with three glasses of wine, had allowed her to sleep most of the way back to Florence. Although she still felt like death warmed up, and then some. With her luggage now safely loaded into the boot of the taxi, she settled herself in the back seat. Making sure her seatbelt was snapped in tight, and her feet were firmly planted to the floor, she readied herself for the typical Italian driving that would have her holding onto anything in arm's reach for dear life until she made it home safely. Squeezing past other cars, down laneways almost too thin for cars, let alone pedestrians too, the driver navigated his way while shouting at any crazy person that got in his way. But even the chaotic driving couldn't distract her from the guilt that gnawed at her insides. Guilt for running away from Morgan when he needed her the most. Guilt for keeping the truth hidden all these years, and guilt for the inevitable pain and heartbreak that would come when the paternity test came back.

On the one hand, she prayed Salvatore was the father.

On the other, she prayed he wasn't.

As the taxi pulled up to her apartment close to ten-thirty at night, she paid the driver and made her way up the three flights of stairs to her door. As she unlocked it and stepped inside, the familiar scent of her home enveloped her. Bleary-eyed, she walked through the empty rooms, her footsteps echoing through the silence. She couldn't wait for Chiara's laughter to fill it when she came home early the next morning. It was so strange to be back here after a few weeks away. She'd never ever left since moving here, so it was like coming back to a home that was no longer hers. Sighing, she made her way into her bedroom, unzipped her suitcase and started to unpack. She wasn't ready for sleep just yet. As she folded her clothes, she couldn't shake the feeling that she'd made a mistake. That she'd let fear guide her actions, instead of facing what could've been a wondrous future, head-on, if she'd found the courage to do so.

It was almost one o'clock when she gave up trying to sleep, and instead decided on walking her frustration and heartbreak out. She stepped out of her apartment block and across the deserted piazza, then turned down one of the cobblestone streets that would lead her across the Arno river, and to the Duomo. For a little while, with most people tucked up in their beds, she walked alone except for her shadow. Just across the bridge, she steeled herself as a lone man came from the opposite direction, his shoulders hunched against the cool wind. And it struck her – what in the hell was she doing walking the Florentine streets on her own at such an ungodly hour? Usually a hive of activity during the day and well into the night, at this hour it was like a ghost town.

But it was the best time to view the magnificent Duomo.

Raising her eyes to the stunning Renaissance dome of the cathedral, she felt the knot in her stomach tighten as the man passed her by. His glance was a little wary, as she imagined hers to be, too. They acknowledged one another with a slight nod. She breathed a sigh of relief as she brought her attention back to the massive structure towering over her, its walls illuminated by the soft glow of the moon. She stood still for a moment, taking in the beauty of the place and letting the silence surround her. It was peaceful, and in some way it made her feel less alone. The complex details of the marble facade, the eye-catching frescoes and the intricate sculptures all came together to create something truly magnificent. Something that had stood the test of time and witnessed the rise and fall of empires. Something that had been there long before she was born and would still be there long after she was gone. It was humbling, breathtaking, inspiring – exactly what she needed.

She walked around the perimeter of the Duomo, her footsteps echoing through the deserted piazza as she traced her fingers along the cool marble, lost in thought. It was times like this when she wished she still had her mother to talk to. Julie Sabatini had always had a way of making things seem less daunting. But she was gone, leaving her to navigate the mess of her life alone. She thought about Morgan and the love they shared. She thought about the mistakes she'd made, and the pain she'd caused both of them. She thought about the future and what it held for her. And then she thought about Salvatore, and the truth she'd been hiding from everyone, including herself. There was a lot she needed to fix, to make right, so she could enjoy some much-needed peace. Fingers crossed the paternity results came in the mail soon, because it was unbearable to wait much longer.

Her steps faster this time, she turned back towards her apartment, the sound of her heels echoing in the empty street. The wind picked up as she crossed the river again, sending chills down her spine. She pulled her coat in tighter and quickened her pace. She felt as if she was ready, now, to close her eyes and allow sleep to take her to whatever places she needed to be.

The following morning, bright and early, Chiara's laughter reached her before she did. Standing in the piazza, Jess turned around and saw her daughter running towards her, her pigtails bouncing with every step. Her own smile was from the heart as she opened her arms to embrace her girl. For a moment she forgot about everything else that was happening in her life and just held her daughter close. This, right here, was all the family she needed.

'I missed you so much, Mum!' Chiara said, hugging her super tight.

Nonno approached, and she flashed him a loving smile. 'I missed you too, baby girl.' She kissed her daughter's forehead, then brought her nonno in for a group hug. Untangling after a few moments, she looked to Chiara, her smile unable to go any wider. She was so grateful Nonno had thought to take Chiara away for two nights to distract her from the fact that Salvatore had deserted her in his designated time, yet again. 'How was your trip to the seaside with Nonno, sweetheart?'

'It was so much fun! I got to build sandcastles and swim in the ocean,' Chiara said excitedly. 'And look what I found!' she exclaimed as she shoved her hand in her pocket then held out a small seashell. 'It's so pretty, just like you.'

'Oh, Chiara, it's absolutely beautiful.' Taking the seashell, she examined it closely. It was a delicate shade of pink, with elaborate patterns etched by Mother Nature into its surface. 'And you're absolutely beautiful, too.' She was touched by her daughter's words, but at the same time, a pang of guilt hit her. She now realised she'd been so caught up in her own problems over the past year that she hadn't been fully present, and whole, for her daughter. But from this moment on she would be, one hundred percent. No matter what was going on around her, or to her.

'Should you, me and Nonno go upstairs and have some breakfast?' She raised her brows. 'I got us all our favourites from the bakery.'

'Oh yummy!' Chiara jiggled on the spot. 'Yes please.'

'Si, bella,' Nonno agreed with a smile. 'That would be lovely.'

As she and Chiara walked hand in hand up the stairs with her nonno close at their side, the weight of guilt settled on her shoulders once again. She might not have all the answers right now, but she would soon enough. In the kitchen, the sweet aroma of freshly baked croissants and coffee filled the air. Jess watched Chiara's face light up at the sight of the chocolate croissant on the plate. Simple pleasures made for a sweet life. She'd missed her daughter so much and was grateful for the little moments like this. Then, like any normal Italian family wanting to appreciate food and each other, they sat around the table, chatting and laughing, enjoying their breakfast together. But even in the midst of their happy morning, Jess couldn't shake off the nagging feeling of uncertainty and guilt that had been plaguing her. She couldn't keep running away from the truth and the consequences of her actions. Soon she may need to face up to Morgan, Salvatore and, most importantly, Chiara. She would take responsibility for her mistakes and find a way to make things right, whatever the outcome might be. That she was sure of.

That night, after a wonderful day together, as Jess tucked Chiara into bed and kissed her goodnight, her mind was consumed with thoughts of Morgan once more. She couldn't shake the feeling that he was the missing piece in their life. The one person who could make everything right again. But she also knew that if what she instinctively felt was correct, telling him the truth would come at a cost. And with her fragile state, and Chiara's need for stability, she was terrified of it unsettling their lives further still. So, for the first time in nine long years, she got down on her knees and prayed to the God she'd lost all faith in after her parents' deaths, but now felt compelled to turn to.

Making the sign of the cross, she ended her prayer with an amen, then pushed up to her feet. Heading back out to the kitchen, she looked to the table, then to her nonno. In front of him sat a large yellow envelope, and she could tell by the absorbing look in his eyes that it was the answer she'd been waiting for. She'd had it addressed to him so it didn't go missing like Chiara's passport had. Her hand went to cover her gaping mouth, and her very first instinct was to run and hide, so she could pretend she didn't need to know. But then her nonno gave her a gentle, encouraging smile, one that gave her the courage to walk towards him, pull out a seat, and sit in silence. The envelope sat between them. She'd lived with the burden of not knowing upon her shoulders for so long, she barely recalled a time when she hadn't felt weighed down by it.

'Bella.' Giuseppe Sabatini peered over the top of his glasses. 'You're going to have to open it at some point.'

'I know, it's just …' Uneasy dread seeped into her veins as she stared at the envelope. 'What if Morgan is her father, and then, what if he isn't?'

Reaching across the little table, he gave her hand a reassuring squeeze. 'Either way, you're going to have to know to be able to deal with it, si?'

Jess nodded, knowing he was right. So, with a sigh of resolution, she reached for what would inevitably be her future. It felt like a lead weight as she lifted it from the table. Her heart in her throat, she slipped a finger beneath the seal, and once it was open, peered inside. Running her eyes over the wording, her stomach twisted with another rush of dread, but then her eyes snagged on one sentence towards the bottom. All kinds of emotions stirred, and she blinked in disbelief. Although she hadn't had anything of Morgan's to send along with Chiara's hair, she did have a sample from an old brush of Salvatore's to test his paternity.

'Jess.' Nonno peered at her through his thick-framed glasses. 'Is it good news?'

'Yes.' She was both crying *and* smiling now. 'Nonno, I was right, Salvatore is not her father, which means that Morgan is.'

'Oh, bella.' He stood way faster than he should've been able to and came to her side. 'This is wonderful news.'

'Yes, it is.' Clutching him, she allowed her roiling emotions to somewhat settle before pulling back a little and looking into his kind eyes. 'Oh, Nonno, I'm relieved with the result, but how am I going to tell Chiara that Salvatore isn't her dad?'

'Honestly, I think she'll be shocked at first, but once that subsides I believe she'll be keen to meet the man who'll finally love her like she's meant to be loved.' He cupped Jess's cheeks, regarding her with fatherly love. 'And the same goes for you, my beautiful granddaughter.'

Jess took a deep breath and wiped away her tears. She knew telling Salvatore would be tough. She knew it would change everything. But she also knew it was the right thing to do. She owed it to him, to Morgan, to Chiara, and to herself to be honest. So, with her nonno's encouragement, she picked up her phone and dialled Salvatore's number. Her heart raced as she waited for him to answer.

'Jess? Why the hell are you calling me at this hour?' he asked snappishly.

She glanced at the clock, noting it was only nine-thirty. 'I'm sorry, but I need to talk to you. Can we meet in the morning?' Her voice was barely above a whisper.

'Christ, Jess, I've got meetings first thing, can't it wait?'

She locked glances with her nonno and found her Sabatini sass. 'No, Salvatore, I'm afraid it can't.'

A woman's voice sounded but was swiftly hushed. 'Is it really that important?'

Salvatore hadn't even thought to ask if Chiara was okay. The bastard. 'Yes, take my word for it, Salvatore, you're going to want to know what I have to say.'

He huffed impatiently. 'All right, okay, where do you want to meet?'

They agreed to meet at a small café near Jess's apartment. And bright and early the following morning, with Nonno at her apartment looking after Chiara, she made her way there. Her mind was consumed with thoughts of what she was going to say. How was she going to tell him that he wasn't Chiara's father without him exploding?

When she arrived, Salvatore was already there, drumming his fingers on a table outside. She took a deep breath, steeling herself for what was to come, and sat down across from him. He looked at her expectantly, and she knew there was no turning back. She fidgeted in her seat, unsure of how to begin. The words were stuck in her throat and she couldn't budge them. The silence between them was deafening, and she could feel the weight of his gaze on her.

Come on, Jess, you can do this!

'Salvatore, there's something I need to tell you.' She cleared her throat and looked down at her clasped hands. 'It's about Chiara.'

'What about her?' he asked, his brow furrowed in worry and confusion.

Shit, come on, Jess, spit it out!

He leant forward, his dark eyes searching hers. 'Jess?'

'She's not your daughter,' she said, way too quickly.

Salvatore stared at her, his eyes widening in shock. 'What are you talking about?'

'I had a paternity test done, and it turns out you're not her father,' she said, her heart racing. 'I was with Morgan two weeks before you and I met that night, and I wasn't certain, when I found out I was pregnant, who the father was, and I was scared you'd leave me if I told you I was unsure.'

'Damn straight I would have left you.' His hands slamming down upon the table, Salvatore shot up to stand, glaring at her. 'How could you do this to me?' he growled, his voice spiked with hatred and anger.

Jess flinched at his reaction, but she knew she had to stay strong. 'I'm sorry, Salvatore, but I had to know the truth.'

'And what, you just decided to spring this on me out of nowhere?' he said, his eyes blazing with fury.

Yeah, like you telling me we were over because you'd met someone else …

Jess took a breath. 'I know this is a lot to take in, but I'm not the only one affected by this. Morgan has a right to know that he's a father, and Chiara has a right to know who her biological father is,' she said firmly.

Salvatore shook his head, his expression darkening. 'You're right, this is a lot to take in.'

'I know, and I'm sorry. I needed to be certain before I spoke with you,' Jess said, her voice softening.

He cursed at her, running his fingers through his hair. 'You know what, I'm actually glad for this.' He nodded, smirking. 'Because it means I don't have to pay you another single bit in child support.' Then just like that, he sniffed, straightened his tie, and became poker faced. 'Chiara's been a total brat, and I've had enough of her upsetting Mariana, so take this as my exit out of her life, for good.'

'Please, Salvatore, don't take this out on Chiara.' Jess's heart stung. 'She's still the same little girl you've always loved. Nothing's changed in that regard.'

'She *is not* my little girl, never has been, and never will be.' He slapped ten euros on the table. 'For the coffee, so I know I don't owe you a goddamn thing.' He paused, his eyes narrowing as he pulled something from his pocket and slammed it down, too. 'Here's her passport back, I took it for safekeeping, but I won't be needing it now.'

Jess couldn't hide her shock, or her contempt. 'You stole it from my apartment?'

'I didn't steal it, I just borrowed it.' He shook his head, smirking at her. 'Don't ever contact me again, you or Chiara, you hear me.'

With that he stormed off, leaving Jess sitting there in a flood of tears. Her instincts had been right; he had stolen the passport to stop her from taking Chiara to Australia, and not because he wanted time with Chiara but because he wanted to make his ex-wife suffer. It just showed how callous and calculating he truly was. And as for the mention of money and calling Chiara a brat when her little girl was far from one, it was as if he'd been waiting for a reason to bow out of Chiara's life. In the long run, sad as it was, Chiara would be better off without him. Turning her gaze away from him thundering away, she caught eyes with the people at the nearest table. They couldn't stop staring at her. Utterly ashamed, she was desperate to get out of there. But, worried her shaking legs wouldn't carry her, she sat for a little longer, trying to compose herself. Wiping away her gathering tears, she took a deep breath, knowing she had to be strong for Chiara's sake. The next little while was going to be tough, and her darling girl needed her. She was going to do everything in her power to bring only good into their lives from this moment forth. Pushing her seat back, she put the passport into her handbag and stood, squared her shoulders, shot the still-staring and now whispering couple a scowl, then strode away.

Opening the door to her apartment, she found Chiara sitting on the couch, cuddled up to Nonno and watching her favourite cartoon. Her mind raced with thoughts of how she was going to break the news without shattering her beautiful little heart.

Jess offered her nonno an appreciative glance and he offered her a kind-hearted one back. 'Hey, sweetie,' she said to Chiara, choking up.

'What's wrong, Mum?' Chiara asked, her brows furrowing in concern.

'We need to talk.' Jess sunk down next to her.

Chiara's eyes widened in alarm. 'Did I do something bad?'

'No, sweetie, you didn't do anything wrong,' she said, putting her arm around her. Nonno's hand touched hers on the back of the couch, silently supporting her. She took a deep breath, gathering her thoughts, and her courage. 'There's something I need to tell you, and it's going to be hard to hear.'

Chiara's eyes widened even further, and her bottom lip began to quiver. 'What is it?'

'I did a special test, and it turns out that Salvatore isn't your real father,' she said as calmly as she could.

'What do you mean?' Chiara asked, her voice trembling.

'I was with another man, before Salvatore, and …' Jess's heart broke at the look of confusion on Chiara's face. 'His name is Morgan,' she added softly.

'The Morgan you were staying with in Australia?' Chiara's eyes welled up with tears. 'But I don't even know him.'

'I know, sweetie, and I'm sorry. But he's a good man, and I bet, when I tell him the wonderful news, that he'll want to get to know you,' she said, trying to keep her own tears at bay.

Chiara shook her head, her tears spilling over. 'Now I understand why Salvatore has always treated me like he has, because I wasn't his little girl.'

Mortified at seeing Chiara so torn, Jess cupped her cheeks. 'Oh, sweetheart, he didn't know, I've only just told him about it.' She sniffed and wiped Chiara's tears. 'Salvatore is not a very nice man, and that's not your fault.'

Chiara nodded, her tears starting to subside. 'What happens now?'

'I don't know yet, sweetie. But I promise you, we'll figure it out together,' Jess said, pulling her daughter in nice and close.

Nonno joined the circle of love by wrapping his arms around the pair of them. 'Vi amo entrambi, così tanto.'

'Oh, Nonno.' Jess smiled through her tears at the man who'd shown her and Chiara nothing but unconditional love. 'We both love you very much, too.'

For a few long moments, the three of them sat there in silence, wrapped in each other's arms. Jess knew this was just the beginning of a long and difficult road, but she was determined to do whatever it took to help Chiara get through it. Together, they would face this truth, and whatever else came their way. She just needed to put the final piece of the puzzle together. Morgan needed to know. He *deserved* to know. And she hoped, prayed, wished upon every single star in the sky, that once she explained everything, he would find it within his big beautiful heart to understand and, hopefully, to forgive her. What happened between them afterwards was in his hands – and fate's. All she cared about right now was her darling Chiara getting to know him.

As the three of them untangled, she looked to her nonno with tears in her eyes, overwhelmed by the emotions that were coursing through her. 'Thank you, Nonno, for everything you do for us,' she said, her voice thick with emotion. 'I don't know what we'd do without you.'

'I'll always be here for you both.' He smiled kindly at her and his eyes crinkled at the corners. 'I know this hasn't been easy for you, but I'm proud of you for facing it.'

Jess nodded, unable to speak anymore. She knew that there were still challenges ahead, but for now she was content with the knowledge that Morgan Savage was her darling daughter's dad.

CHAPTER 22

Morgan knew he was laying his heart on the line. But Jessica Sabatini was worth the risk. A burst of adrenaline and fear raced through his veins as he punched his credit-card details into the keyboard of his laptop. The processing wheel spun in circles, then twenty seconds later, his very last hope for a future with Jess stared back at him. He pressed print, and the airline ticket was in his hand. He couldn't believe he was doing this. He was flying all the way to Italy to tell Jess he wasn't letting her go. That he was going to fight until his very last breath for her. Because he loved her, and he believed their kind of love was enough to conquer all obstacles in their way.

It was a crazy move, but he had to take the chance. He had to try. This time she wasn't getting away from him that easily. This time he'd step up to the plate, walk the line, whatever he had to do to be the man he truly was, and chase her all the way to the other side of the world. Hell, he'd have swum if he'd had to.

Two hours later, his text tone chimed.

I'm out the front, bro.

Thank goodness for Roberto and Shanti offering to stay there and take care of Teeny and the farm, or he wouldn't be able to pull this off.

Coming now, he texted back.

Grabbing his Akubra from the desk, he tugged it on, grabbed his duffle bag from the floor, gave Teeny a loving goodbye head ruffle, then strode out of the homestead. In a little under thirty-four hours, he'd be staring into the eyes of the one and only woman he'd ever loved with every single piece of his heart. He just prayed Shanti was right, that it was all going to be worth it and they'd work things out.

In what felt like the blink of an eye, he was on the plane, waiting for take-off. Tapping his pocket, he made sure the letter Annie had given him to give to Jess was there. He couldn't help but feel a sense of anxiety wash over him, knowing he was leaving everything behind in Silverton Shores on a wing and a prayer. He'd never been one for impulsive decisions that involved other people, but when it came to Jess he was willing to take the risk. His heart raced as the plane taxied then, wheels up, reached for the sky with the roar of the engines echoing in his ears. Looking out the window, he watched as Cairns fell away beneath him.

When the plane reached cruising altitude, he took a deep breath and tried to calm himself. It was too late to turn back now; not that he wanted to. Although he couldn't shake the feeling that he might be making a mistake, might be chasing after something that had already slipped through his fingers. God, he hoped not. As the hours passed, he drifted in and out of sleep, his mind filled with thoughts of Jess and the future they could have. He tried to imagine what she was doing, where she was, but it was like trying to grasp smoke.

With a changeover in Singapore to a bigger plane, finally, after what felt like an eternity, the aircraft slowly began its descent towards the Florence airport. Leaning against his window, he could just make out the Italian coastline, and he couldn't help but feel a sense of wonder at the beauty of it all. It was now early morning, and despite his jet lag he was feeling exhilarated about seeing Jess in a matter of hours. After passing through passport control, he raced to the baggage claim, found his duffle bag, and made his way through customs and out into the arrivals hall. He took a deep breath and, with his heart racing, he strode out of the airport and into the bright sunshine. Grabbing his phone from his back pocket, he tried to turn it on, but it was completely flat. He must have forgotten to turn it off when he'd left Australia.

Damn it!

Rifling through his bag, he found Jess's handwritten address. Thank goodness he'd followed old school ways, instead of only saving it in his phone. He hailed a taxi, buckled himself in and endured the crazy ride that Jess had told him about, and by god, she hadn't been wrong. His driver was manoeuvring the streets like he was on a racetrack. Out the window, the Renaissance city was jaw-droppingly stunning – the architecture, the narrow thoroughfares, the colourful buildings. His focus was held for a little longer, but as the driver veered through the roads that seemed almost too thin to even walk down, his nerves began getting the better of him. He breathed against the rush of adrenaline.

He could do this.

He *was* doing this.

Finally, and mercifully in one piece, they pulled to a skidding stop outside Jess's apartment block. He stepped out of the taxi and paid the driver, who spoke as fast as he drove, and with his duffle bag now over his shoulder, scanned the surroundings. He took a moment to take it all in before he centred himself and walked up the steps to the entrance of the building. He strode inside and climbed the stairs, his footsteps echoing. Arriving at her door, he breathed in nice and deep, and then knocked. And waited. And knocked again. There was no noise, no Jess, nothing. In his flurry, he hadn't even considered the fact that she might not be home.

Deciding he'd have to come back a bit later, he retraced his steps, disappointment weighing heavily on his chest. He'd travelled thousands of miles to see her, and she wasn't even there. Go bloody well figure! Back out in the glorious sunshine, he hailed another taxi and gave the driver the address of the hotel he'd prebooked – he hadn't arrived under the assumption that he'd be making himself at home with Jess. That wouldn't be very gentlemanly of him, not in the slightest. As he was driven across the Arno river and back through the city, he couldn't help but feel defeated. He'd come all this way, but what if it was all for nothing? What if she didn't want to see him? What if she'd just ignored his knocking?

Stop it, Savage, stop it right now!

After arriving at the hotel, he checked in and headed up to his room. He dropped his bag to the floor and collapsed onto his bed, suddenly feeling drained and exhausted. Closing his eyes, he tried to shake off the defeated feeling, but it lingered like a heavy weight on his chest. He needed to do something other than lying here torturing himself. Grabbing his phone and travel adapter, he got his charger and plugged it in. A minute later, it came back to life. Hallelujah! He scrolled through his contacts until he found Jess's Italian number. Hesitating for a brief moment, he stabbed the call button. The phone rang for what felt like an eternity before it went to voicemail. Deflated, he took a deep breath and left a message.

'Hey, Jess, it's me, Morgan. I'm in Florence!' He tried to steady his voice. 'I just landed and I'm at my hotel. I stopped by your place, but you weren't there. I really hope you're okay and that we can talk. Please call me back when you get this message. I miss you.' He went to hang up, but then added, 'A lot.'

As he hung up he sighed, feeling a mix of disappointment and fear. With a heavy heart, he decided to explore a bit of the historic centre of Florence to try and take his mind off things. So, one foot in front of the other, he wandered aimlessly, becoming totally enthralled by the majestic beauty of what Jess had described perfectly. The cathedrals, the bridges and the piazzas were all stunning. Walking down the little laneways and cobblestone streets that seemed to go on forever, he breathed in the vibrant atmosphere. After a couple of hours, he stumbled upon a welcoming café and decided to take a break. The space was quaint, with wooden tables and chairs, potted plants and a warm, inviting atmosphere accentuated by some jazz music. He ordered an espresso and sat down to savour the rich aroma. As he sipped the most divine coffee he'd ever tasted, he watched the people bustling by on the street outside. There were couples walking hand in hand, tourists taking pictures, and locals going about their daily business. He couldn't help but feel a little envious of their carefree lives. He wished he could be like them, living in the moment, not worrying about the past or the future.

But he couldn't shake off the feeling of longing he had for Jess. She was the one thing missing from his life, the one thing he needed to be truly happy. He took out his phone and checked for any missed calls or messages. There was nothing. He tried to push the thought of her to the back of his mind, for now, just until she rang him back, but it was impossible. After finishing his coffee, he paid the bill and stepped back out and onto the bustling street, feeling a sense of loneliness wash over him. But he told himself he wasn't going to sit around and wait for her call. He was going to head back to the woman who owned every inch of his beating heart and hope to god she was there this time.

* * *

Cycling over cobblestones, past the galleries, leather shops and clothing stores, was a feat in itself, let alone avoiding the crazy traffic flying down laneways only big enough for one car. Jess kept her eyes peeled in every direction, where the many restaurants were overflowing with people enjoying their front-row seats at the outside tables. Reaching her destination – a small café tucked away in a quiet backstreet – she leant her bike against the wall and stepped inside, the smell of fresh coffee and pastries making her mouth water. The sound of smooth jazz filled the room, creating a calming atmosphere. The café was small, and almost all the tables were occupied by people talking and enjoying their drinks. Which was how she liked it.

Weaving through tables and potted plants, she approached the counter and ordered a cappuccino and a chocolate croissant. While she waited for her order, she took a seat at a nearby table and pulled out her notebook and pen. She'd come here, away from the distractions of her busy life, to sit and write what she was going to say to Morgan when she called him. Here, she always found the peace and quiet she needed to breathe and think logically. As soon as her order arrived, she put her pen down, took a sip of her cappuccino and let out a contented sigh. The frothy milk and espresso were the perfect balance of bitter and sweet, and the chocolate croissant was flaky and buttery, melting in her mouth. She closed her eyes and savoured the moment, feeling like she could stay in this café forever.

If only. She had so much to do, and tonight she would be calling Morgan.

Speaking of the devil…

She leant forward, staring through the windows.

The man across the road looked a hell of a lot like him. Could it be? She held her breath and blinked into the slant of sunshine. But then, just like that, the man was gone. She sat back and sighed. Her mind was playing cruel tricks on her, and she couldn't blame it in the slightest. They'd left so much unsaid, so much unresolved. And she had so much to tell him now that she knew for certain. A sense of homesickness washed over her as she took tentative sips from her coffee. Tears stung behind her eyes, but she blinked faster, warding them off. She wasn't about to cry, not again. Just a few streets away, Piazza Santa Maria Novella would now be packed with people enjoying their day as the city stirred to life. She, on the other hand, was trying to regather after a long sleepless night spent missing Morgan, and Silverton Shores. But she needed to pull herself together, because this afternoon was all about preparing for Chiara's birthday.

An hour later, after breaking three eggs into the bowl, she went to grab the melted chocolate from the microwave when a knock had her turning in the opposite direction. She hesitated for a moment, wondering who it could be. Walking towards the door, she quickly wiped her hands on a tea towel, leaving smudges of chocolate on the fabric.

'Nonno!' She smiled warmly. 'You're early.'

'Always,' he said, with his usual warm smile.

Chiara raced in beside her, reaching for her beloved great-nonno.

Nonno took Chiara into his arms, his wrinkled face breaking into a smile. 'I couldn't wait to see my favourite girl,' he said, his Italian accent thick. 'And smell what's cooking in the kitchen, of course.'

Chiara giggled, burying her face in Nonno's neck. Then, grabbing his hand as he placed her back to the floor, Chiara led him over to the kitchen counter, where the bowl of eggs sat beside a pot of melted chocolate. 'Me and Mum are making some brownies,' she said, beaming up at him. 'Want to help me mix everything together?'

Nonno's eyes twinkled with delight. 'Of course, bambina.'

As Nonno took over the mixing, Jess leant against the counter, watching him and Chiara work together in harmony. She had always loved spending time with him, hearing stories about his life and learning new recipes from him, and now Chiara was doing the same. Ever since she was a little girl, he'd always been a big part of her life, even from afar, and she couldn't imagine living without him.

Nonno spooned the mixture into a baking dish and placed it in the oven. 'There we are,' he said, wiping his hands on his apron. 'What shall we do while we wait for the brownies to bake?'

'Watch some cartoons?' Chiara asked eagerly.

'Yes, let's do that.' He took her hand in his and they wandered over to the couch.

As Jess got back to preparing the main course of ragu sauce to go with the locally bought pasta, Chiara's favourite, her body swayed to the beat of the Italian music playing in the background.

Ten minutes in, Nonno reappeared, a finger to his lips. 'She's fallen asleep.'

'Oh bless, she must be exhausted.'

'As you would be, too.' Nonno placed his hand on her arm. 'The only regrets you'll have in your life, bella, will be the things you didn't do, trust me on this.'

Biting her bottom lip to stop from crying, she nodded. 'Thank you, Nonno, I appreciate you so much.'

He kissed her forehead. 'I know you do.'

Another knock at the door had her looking to Nonno with confusion, then racing from the kitchen to see who it was. The face she was met with almost brought her to her knees, but she grabbed hold of the door just in time to stop herself. There was a moment of hesitation as they just stood there, staring at each other.

'Morgan.' His name rushed out of her trembling lips.

'Jess.'

'What are you doing here?' With her mind whirling, she didn't know what else to say.

'Visiting you.' He smiled but it was a little hesitant. 'Can I come in?'

'Yes, of course.' She stepped aside. 'Come in, please.'

Footfalls came up behind her, and she turned to see Nonno, staring at her, his eyes wider than she'd ever seen them. 'Nonno, this is Morgan.'

Giuseppe's face spread into a huge smile. 'Ah, Morgan, finally we meet, benvenuto.' And before Morgan had a chance to work out what the word meant, Nonno did just that, and welcomed him into his arms with a firm, manly hug that was genially returned by Morgan.

'Nice to meet you, too,' Morgan said with a smile, as the two stepped back from each other.

A few seconds ticked by. Clearing her throat, Jess looked to her nonno.

'I'll go and check the cooking,' he quickly said, by way of excusing himself.

Now on their own, Jess looked at Morgan, really looked at him, for way too long. Was he really here? Did he know about Chiara already? But how? She wanted to welcome him into the lounge room, but Chiara was asleep in there, and until she told him about her, she didn't want to put either of them in an awkward position.

'Sorry to be a bit lost for words, it's just, I can't believe you're actually here,' she said, finally finding her voice. 'In my apartment, all the way over the other side of the world,' she added, trembling to pieces on the inside.

'It is a bit of a surprise, so I get it, Jess.'

'A bit?' she said with a strangled-sounding chuckle. 'More like a lot.'

'Yeah, about that.' He grimaced. 'Sorry for not pre-warning you, but I wanted a chance to tell you in person, that …' He reached out and took her hand in his as his blue eyes searched the depths of hers. 'I love you, and I can't bear the thought of not being able to love you every day for the rest of our lives.'

'Oh, Morgan, I love you, too, so very much.' Jess couldn't stop the sudden tears now falling. 'But there's something very important I have to tell you, before we talk any more about us, and how we feel about one another.'

Morgan's expression immediately fell into one of concern. 'What is it, Jess?'

She fought to find the right words for something as big as this.

With her abrupt inability to speak, he stepped closer to her, his expression softening. 'I know we've had our ups and downs, but I love you more than anything. And I know I want to spend the rest of my life with you, and with Chiara, if she'll allow me to, that is.'

This man was the most wonderful human being she'd ever met, and he loved her, deeply. Would he still feel the same when she told him? Her breath caught in her throat. She knew this conversation had been coming, but she hadn't expected it to be face to face.

Footsteps quickly approached, halting her words, and Chiara appeared, rubbing her sleepy eyes. 'Mum, who's this?' She padded towards them.

Chiara's eyes darted to Morgan, and Jess could see the wheels turning in her head. Her heart stalled then raced. 'Oh, darling, hi, you're awake.' She held out her trembling hand and Chiara took it.

'Mum, you're shaking.' Stopping short of Morgan, Chiara looked from her, to him, then back to her. 'Is this the Morgan man you told me about?'

'Yes, my love, it is.' She was terrified of how Chiara was going to react, before she'd even had time to speak to him privately. Maybe she'd done this all backwards, but it was too late to change that now. 'He thought it would be nice to surprise us with a visit.'

'Wow, yes, that is a big surprise.' Chiara nodded.

Feeling the walls pressing in on her, Jess pointed to the kitchen. 'Why don't you go and see how Nonno is doing, and we'll be in soon.'

'No way.' Chiara shook her head. 'I want to get to know my …'

With no other option, Jess clamped a hand over Chiara's mouth. 'Sweetie, Mum needs to talk to Morgan first, okay?'

'Jess? What's going on?' Morgan's eyes stayed glued to Chiara's.

'Oh, oops.' Chiara looked up at Jess, her gaze sweetly innocent. 'Haven't you told him about me yet, Mum?'

CHAPTER 23

Jess didn't answer either of them. She just stood there, her face turning as white as a ghost. Morgan dragged his glance of shock from her and back to Chiara's wide blue eyes. Her little bare feet twisting anxiously, she looked at her mum and then smiled at him, and in that pivotal, mind-blowing moment, where the world seemed to screech to a grinding halt, everything slipped into place. Returning Chiara's smile, he then brought his questioning gaze back to Jess's. Just as she was clearly struggling, he found it impossible to string a sentence together, but he didn't need to try, because her silence told him everything he was dying to know.

'She's mine …' he finally said, 'isn't she?' Even now, he itched to reach out and ease the lined concern from Jess's brow.

Her gaze falling to the floor, she took a beat, and then another, before she brought her tear-filled eyes back to his. 'Yes, Morgan, she is.'

Even though he felt as if the wind had just been knocked out of him, Morgan had no choice but to treat this as good news, for Chiara's sake. There was no way in hell he was going to let his little girl see him flinch. 'Well, hello there, Chiara, can I give you a hug?'

She nodded, shyly. 'Yes.'

He crouched down and gently embraced his daughter. Throwing her arms around his neck, Chiara clung to him tightly. 'It's so lovely to meet you, sweetheart,' he said, choking past raw sentiment.

'It's really nice to meet you too, Morgan,' she said, her head buried into his shoulder.

An overwhelming flood of emotions rushed through him – joy, protectiveness, awe, excitement, happiness – as if she'd just been born into the world, and into his life, and he couldn't believe he was holding his daughter. He'd never imagined this moment. With the way time was passing him by, and his inability to move on from Jess, he'd never believed he'd be lucky enough to have a child. But here she was, in his arms. Tears built, and fell, and he didn't bother wiping them away. As much as he wanted Jess to join in their embrace, he knew this was a moment that belonged solely to him and Chiara. They deserved that much, after being kept away from each other for so long.

Chiara was the first to let go, and she offered him a cute smile. 'I'm going to go and help Nonno now.'

'Okay, see you soon.' Standing, Morgan watched her go, and then turned to Jess, who was standing there with tears flowing down her face.

Feelings of anger and betrayal filled him. But as he stared into her eyes, all he saw was pain and regret, and knowing Jess the way that he did, he knew there had to be a reason. A valid explanation that he needed to find out. 'Why didn't you tell me?' His voice was rough with emotion.

Jess sucked in a breath. 'I wanted to, Morgan, I really did.' She stepped closer to him, her voice trembling. 'I wanted to tell you sooner, but I wasn't certain until I got the paternity test back yesterday. I was going to call you tonight, to tell you, once Chiara was in bed.' Her hands went to her heart. 'I promise that's the absolute truth.'

Although he was deeply hurt, Morgan's heart softened as he watched the woman he loved tangle herself up in guilt and remorse. He knew what it was like to keep a secret, and his was just as big, in a different kind of way. 'So, just clarifying, you didn't know for sure, when you were in Australia?'

'No, I didn't.' The fear and uncertainty were clear in her gaze.

She was waiting for his reaction, and even though he was hurting, he didn't want to add to her pain. They had to find a way to get through this, together. 'Now I get why you were so distant, after our night together.' He reached out and took her hands. 'You were torn.'

'Yes, I was, and I'm so sorry I didn't open up then. I truly am.' Sobs broke, and she shook like a leaf. 'I was a broken girl when I found out I was pregnant, and I made a very bad choice to not find out who the father was back then.'

'I believe you, Jess, I do.' He held her tear-filled gaze with his. 'I just need some time to process this, to honestly say I can forgive you, but for now I can at least try and understand it all.'

'Thank you, Morgan, I couldn't expect anything more.'

With nothing left to say for now, he pulled Jess into a tight embrace, their tears mingling together. For the first time in a long time, even though he'd been blindsided and shellshocked, he felt complete. He had a daughter, and if they could find a way through all of this, he also had the woman he loved with all his heart. And nothing else mattered in that moment.

Because where there was hope …

'We'll figure it out,' Morgan whispered, pressing his forehead against Jess's. 'I want to be a part of Chiara's life, and I want to be with you.'

'I really want that too.' Jess nodded, a small smile tugging at the corners of her lips. 'With all of my heart and soul.'

'I know you do. I can see it in your eyes.' He smiled and gently kissed her.

And as Jess kissed him back, so tenderly, so softly, he felt like he'd finally found his place in the world. He knew there was still much to be resolved between them, but right now it didn't matter. All that mattered was the overwhelming love he felt for his new-found daughter and the woman who'd brought her into his life. This was just the beginning of their new journey together.

The room was quiet, save for their deep breaths. It was a shared moment of peace, of healing for them both. But as much as he wanted to stay in that moment forever, the reality of their situation weighed heavily on his mind. They had a lot to talk about, a lot to figure out. And she needed to know what he'd been keeping from her, too.

He pulled away, taking her face in his hands. 'I've got something I need to tell you about too, Jess.'

'Okay.' She placed her hands over his, and smiled softly. 'I'm sure it can't be anywhere near as shocking as what I just told you.'

'Hmm, I'm not sure about that.'

'Morgan, you're worrying me.' She reached out and grabbed his hand. 'What is it?'

He heaved in an almighty breath. 'Annie gave me this letter to give to you. It will explain everything you need to know.'

* * *

Jess's eyes widened as Morgan handed her the letter. She recognised Annie's handwriting on the front of the envelope immediately. Her heart beat faster as she tore it open, her mind already racing with questions. What could Annie have to tell her? What could Morgan have been keeping from her? Her hands shook as she read, and she fought to keep the piece of paper steady.

My dear Jess,

Let me start by telling you how much you mean to me, and how much I love you. And no matter what comes of this letter, I will always feel that way, and be here for you. I just hope, in time, after reading what I'm about to tell you, and the reason why I've done what I have, that you can find it within your beautiful heart to forgive me.

Growing up, you certainly learnt how devoted to the church Julie and Enzo were. I did what they asked of me because of this. Even though I can be compassionate to why they felt this way, now I look back on my decision, I regret it, immensely. I've missed out on so much. You've missed out on so much. And time isn't waiting for any of us. Morgan, bless his big beautiful heart, is the one that eventually made me see sense, and also helped me to understand how it would be best for me to tell you the truth. We have so much to catch up on, together.

Okay, here goes, I know this is going to come as a shock to you, but my sweet Jess, I'm your biological mum. Now I know right now you'll be shaking your head, and not wanting to believe me, but it's the truth. And I really want to make all the years we've lost up to you, somehow, some way, if you'll allow me to.

I won't say much more, because I know you'll need time to absorb what I've told you. For now, please know I love you with every bit of my heart.

Annie (Mum) xx

As her world tumbled out beneath her, the letter fell from her fingers and fluttered to the floor. Morgan stepped towards her, but she held her hands up to stop him. She sucked in a breath, and then another, trying to make sense of the life she thought had been so normal, up until the point her parents – or should she now say grandparents – had died. She didn't know what she was meant to say, to Annie or to Morgan. To anyone for that matter. Her mind was reeling, and she felt angry, hurt, betrayed and confused, all at once. Just like Morgan would've felt only moments ago. And yet he still wanted to be here for her, to comfort her. God how she loved him so.

She looked up at him, trying to find some clarity in his eyes. 'You knew about this?'

'Yes, I did.'

'Why didn't you tell me sooner?' she asked, her voice choked with emotion.

'Because Julie and Enzo made her promise to never tell you, but then when they passed, and I asked her to rethink this, she told me she was never going to break the promise she'd made to them.' He sighed and shook his head. 'When I knew you were coming back to Australia, I started pushing Annie again to tell you, and long story short, here we are.'

She tried to let it all sink in. 'Does anyone else know?'

'No.' He shook his head. 'Nobody does.'

She glanced towards the door of the kitchen. 'Not even Nonno?'

He shook his head again. 'I don't think so.'

'Wow.' She wrapped her arms around herself. 'This is crazy.'

Morgan took her hands and squeezed them gently. 'I know it's a lot to take in. But I'm here for you, Jess. Whatever you need, whatever you want to do, I'll support you.'

Jess felt tears stinging as she looked lovingly at the man beside her. The man who'd come all the way to Italy to fight for her. The man who'd embraced his daughter, their daughter, with tears of absolute joy in his eyes. The man who was willing to stand by her no matter what.

'Thank you, Morgan,' she whispered. 'I love you, more than I can put into words.'

'And I, my beautiful Jess, love you.' Morgan put his big strong arms around her.

Drawing in a shaky breath, she melted into him as she struggled to accept the fact that the woman who'd raised her wasn't her biological mother, but her grandmother. It was both devastating and heartening to know that if she could move past this hurt, she and Annie had an entire life to catch up on, and live, together, just like Morgan and Chiara did.

Tipping her gaze up to him, she offered a tender smile. 'So, Savage, what do we do now?'

Morgan continued holding her tightly. 'I'm not sure right now,' he said softly. 'But I do know that we'll figure it out together.'

Jess nodded, feeling a sense of comfort in his embrace. She knew there would be a lot of questions and emotions to navigate in the days, weeks and months to come, but she also knew he would always be there for her, and she for him, no matter what.

CHAPTER 24

A year later

One decision had almost altered their lives forever, but then fate had stepped in and offered a helping hand. And man oh man, Jess was so pleased she'd accepted the olive branch, as had Morgan. It had been a tough road, navigating all the potholes left by unearthed secrets, but the three of them had stuck close and the unconditional love she, Morgan and Chiara had for one another had carried them through. Now it felt as if all the pieces of their lives had been put back together, and she felt whole, happy, blessed. She and Morgan had found the end of the rainbow, and it was a magical place, filled with all she'd ever imagined their love, and their life together, could be. Their names were tattooed on each other's hearts. Engrained for eternity. They were now, and forever, one.

Life had changed so much since the day she received Annie's letter. She'd spent weeks reeling and coming to terms with the revelation that her whole life had been built on a lie. But with the love and support of Morgan and Annie, she'd finally found the strength to move on and build a new life back in Australia, one that was both honest and fulfilling, with Roberto and Shanti always nearby, for anything, anytime.

Family was absolutely everything, to all of them.

She was relaxing on the swing chair when a soft whine came from behind her, and then a cold wet nose nudged her dangling hand. Laughing, Jess turned to the furry bundle that was Teeny Junior, or TJ for short. 'Okay, little one, I'm coming,' she said, patting the puppy's little head before standing up.

Over on the top step of the homestead's verandah, Morgan threw a frisbee for TJ to fetch, and Jess couldn't help but smile at the sight of the little pocket rocket that was TJ, chasing after it alongside his daddy Teeny. It was a beautiful day, the sun was shining and the birds were singing. She felt content, happy to be here in this moment, surrounded by so much love. Padding over to where Morgan was now sitting with Teeny panting beside him – TJ was still chasing after the now tumbling frisbee, his little tail wagging with excitement – she sat down beside the man of her dreams and leant into him, feeling the warmth of his body against hers. Smiling, Morgan wrapped his arm around her, and she nestled closer, feeling safe and loved.

Life was good.

Actually, life was perfect.

As she looked out at the sweeping hills and green paddocks that surrounded their home, and then to the cottage that had been put to very good use, she couldn't help but feel a sense of satisfaction. It was hard to believe that a year had passed since Annie's letter had turned her world upside down. In that time, she'd come to learn so much about herself, about love, and about the power of family. Life really was unpredictable – sometimes the most unexpected things could lead to the most beautiful outcomes. That was certainly the case for her, Morgan and Chiara. She'd always known she loved him, that he was the one person in the world who could make her feel whole. But it wasn't until she'd faced the darkest parts of herself that she truly appreciated just how much he meant to her. He'd been her rock during the hardest times and had never once wavered in his support. He'd held her whenever she'd cried, listened when she'd needed to talk, and never judged her for her past mistakes. With him by her side, she felt like she could conquer anything that came their way. And she hoped he felt that she did the same for him. Their love was one that had withstood the test of time, and she knew it would only continue to grow stronger with each passing day.

'Mum, come out and play with me!' Chiara squealed from the back lawn.

'Okay, I'm coming, sweetheart.'

Jess smiled and stood up, feeling Morgan's arm fall away from her. She stretched her arms and legs before making her way down the steps and towards their daughter. She was going to offer to play catch, but then she thought better of it. Grinning, she grabbed the hose and, fingers poised over the spout, aimed it at Chiara. Racing left to right, Chiara squealed with delight, sometimes missing the spray, other times running straight into it. As she watched her joy, Jess's heart swelled with love and gratitude. Morgan had proven himself to be every bit the man she'd hoped he would be and more. He was a devoted father to Chiara and a loving partner to her. Through obstacles and adversity, they'd built a beautiful life together, full of laughter and love, and she couldn't imagine ever wanting anything else.

Feeling a pang in her back, Jess turned the hose off and smiled. 'Mum needs to sit for a little bit, love, is that okay?'

'Yes, of course it is,' Chiara called back, her attention now grabbed by an incoming missile called TJ.

Heading back up the stairs, Jess pondered all the pain, the heartbreak and the struggles that had led to this perfect life with her little family. And she knew that no matter what the future held, they would face it together, with love, laughter and unbreakable bonds. As she settled into the swing chair once again, Morgan sat beside her, his arm draped over her shoulders. They sat in comfortable silence, watching their daughter and puppy play in the yard while Teeny settled himself at their feet. It was moments like these that made Jess realise just how lucky she was.

Ten minutes later, with an ice block in her mouth, Chiara bounced across the verandah towards her great-nonno, who was living his best life by relaxing on the day bed in the shade, his smile as wide as the sunset-filled horizons he so loved to watch every single day. Then after they'd all had some dinner, he'd head back to his cottage to watch the Western movies he loved so much.

'Nonno, Nonno!' Chiara hollered, jumping onto the day bed. 'Tell me the story about when you were a handsome young man, and you stole my great-nonna's heart.'

Nonno chuckled, his eyes twinkling with joy. 'Ah, bambina, you want to hear that story again?'

'Yes, yes, tell me please!' Chiara bounced up and down, eagerly waiting for the story to begin.

Jess watched the exchange, feeling grateful for the strong family ties that surrounded them. It was easy to get caught up in the hustle and bustle of everyday life, but moments like this reminded her of the importance of family and the love that held them all together. And as Nonno began his story, Jess leant into Morgan's side, feeling his arm wrap around her once more. She looked up, catching his gaze, and he smiled down at her, his eyes filled with the same love and appreciation that she felt.

'You're amazing,' he whispered in her ear, his breath warm against her neck. 'I love you so very much, my sweet Jess.'

Jess melted into him, feeling her heart race with excitement and desire. With him loving her, she felt alive, like nothing was impossible. 'I love you too.' She couldn't resist running her fingers through his shaggy hair. 'More than words can say.'

Morgan's eyes sparkled with mischief. 'Prove it,' he said, before capturing her lips in a passionate kiss.

Jess felt a surge of desire shoot through her as she pressed against him, feeling his hard muscles against her soft curves. She felt so safe and protected, but also wild and uninhibited. Then he pulled back a little, with a mischievous smile that promised precisely what he'd do when he got her behind their closed bedroom door later, leaving her wanting more.

A sound caught their attention, and she turned to see Chiara running towards them, her laughter echoing through the air. Morgan smiled as she threw herself into his arms, hugging him tightly.

'Daddy, Daddy! Look what Nonno gave me!' she exclaimed, holding up an old horseshoe.

Morgan took it from her, admiring it. 'This is beautiful, princess.'

'I want to keep it forever.' She hugged it to her chest.

'Then we'll keep it forever,' he said. 'We'll hang it above your bedroom door, for good luck.'

Chiara beamed up at him, and Jess couldn't help but feel overwhelmed with love. As the three of them settled into the chair, legs and arms tangled around each other's, she let out a deep sigh of contentment. The sun was setting, casting an orange glow across Savage Acres, illuminating the landscape. Everything they'd ever wanted was right here, at this very moment.

'I can't imagine my life without you and Chiara,' Morgan said softly, squeezing her hand.

'I feel the same way,' Jess said, turning to look at him. 'I never thought I could be this happy.' Morgan leant in and placed a gentle kiss on her lips. 'I love you,' he whispered.

'I love you too,' Jess replied, resting her head back on his shoulder.

'Eww, girls and boys kissing each other is waaay gross,' Chiara said, giggling then leaping off the chair.

Both amused, they watched as Chiara descended the stairs then disappeared around the corner of the homestead, giggling and chasing after Teeny and his bounding offspring.

'I can't believe how lucky we are,' Morgan said, grinning.

I know, right?' Jess sighed contentedly. 'I thought I'd lost everything, but now I have everything I've ever wanted.'

They sat there for a little while longer, enjoying the warmth of the setting sun on their skin and the sound of the gentle breeze playing with the wind chimes. Life had certainly thrown them curveballs, but they'd faced them together and come out stronger than ever.

'Jess, I have something for you.' Morgan stood, reached into his pocket and pulled out a small velvet box. 'I've been meaning to give it to you for a while, but I wanted to wait for the right moment, and seeing as it's exactly a year since we started this wonderful journey together, I thought what better time than right now.'

Jess's heart skipped a beat as he opened the box to reveal a delicate gold ring, with a single diamond twinkling in the last of the sunlight.

'Oh my gosh, Morgan, it's beautiful,' she whispered, tears pricking.

Morgan took the ring out of the box and held it between his fingers, then, dropping to his knee, he looked up at Jess and took her hand in his.

'Jessica Sabatini, I love you more than anything in this world. I've loved you since the day I met you, and I will continue to love you for the rest of my life. Will you make me the happiest man in the world and marry me?' he asked, his voice brimming with passion.

Jess's heart felt like it was about to burst as she looked deep into his eyes. It was as if the whole world had faded away, leaving just the two of them in their own little bubble of happiness. 'Yes, Morgan Savage. Yes, I will marry you!'

With the broadest, most charming of smiles, Morgan slid the ring onto her finger, and it fit perfectly. Then he straightened and, to the ecstatic cheers of Nonno and Chiara, they held each other tightly. And as they embraced, Jess remembered all the moments they'd shared together, all the wild adventures and the passionate nights, all the love and the hurt and the healing. Morgan had always been the man of her dreams, and now he was finally hers, and she was his. Forever. They'd always known they were meant to be together, but this moment made everything feel more real than ever before, like they were truly destined to spend the rest of their lives together.

As she glanced up at him, Morgan wiped a tear from her cheek and smiled. 'I can't wait to spend the rest of my life with you, soon-to-be Mrs Savage.'

'Me too, my wonderful, sexy, amazing man.' Jess smiled back at him. 'Jessica Savage, hey, I love the sound of that.'

Although their lives had taken very different paths, they'd inevitably been led back to one another, as if it had always been written in the stars that she and Morgan encouraged Chiara to wish upon. And she often did, with unbridled excitement.

Morgan Savage had been her first love.

Her only love.

And she was going to love him through this lifetime, and into the next.

ACKNOWLEDGEMENTS

A colossal, wholehearted thank you to the amazing bunch of talented peeps at HarperCollins Australia, you're all so incredibly talented and supportive. I count my lucky stars I'm published by such a delightfully nurturing publishing house. To my awesome publisher, Rachael Donovan, thank you for guiding me every step of the way along this often exciting, and sometimes challenging publishing road – my writing journey is made all the more enjoyable by having you sitting shotgun for the ride. My meticulous editors, Laurie and Kate, I cannot thank you both enough for making the editing part of my manuscripts painless, and dare I even say it – enjoyable! There are so many wonderful folks who work behind the scenes at the HarperCollins headquarters to help bring my stories to radiant life … I wish I could hug each and every one of you.

To YOU, my cherished reader, thank you for grabbing my stories from the shelf, be it hardcopy or ebook, and diving into the pages. Some of you may be newbies, so a very warm welcome to the Mandy Magro family, and for those of you who've been with me since way back yonder, I'm sincerely humbled by your hunger for my hunky heroes and feisty heroines, and all the crazy animal characters too. Believe me, an author's voyage is one filled with a heady combination of choppy waters and calm seas, ups and downs, weary-eyed deadline chasing and middle-of-the-night epiphanies – and although at times it's exhausting, the delight of happy dancing when the postman arrives then hugging my book in tight, or hearing from a reader who has thoroughly enjoyed my written world, makes every single second of the sometimes gruelling adventure worth it.

Until my next book has you absconding from what can sometimes be a wildly chaotic world, nestled under a blanket with a cuppa in hand, or a lovely glass of vino, or with the aircon set to sub-zero as you ward off the Aussie heat, remember to love with all your heart, to laugh out loud, to boot scoot or rock-and-roll dance around the house if your heart desires, to look up at our beautiful sun-drenched or starry night sky often, and most importantly of all, keep smiling and dreaming.

Mandy xx